THE DOVE

Book II

The Prophecy Trilogy

By

DINAH MCCALL

Dedication

The cover of this book and the cover I had redone for the WINDWALKER, which was book one of the Prophecy Series, is the culmination of a twenty-three-year dream I've had to have Native American models on the cover of my many Native American romances.

It is no accident that I had to publish the books myself to make it happen, but I sincerely hope it triggers an awakening within the publishing world that the models are there and their stunning faces portray the beauty of their race.

I have Kim Killion to thank for helping me make this dream come true.

I have Rick Mora, actor/model, to thank for a positive response to the request.

And, I have my own granddaughter, Logan Sala, to thank for helping make her grandmother's dream a reality.

These beautiful cover models represent the Yaqui/Apache and Muscogee Nations and I am forever grateful to both of them for putting the proper faces on this trilogy and making my dream come true.

To the dream-makers, this book is for you.

Chapter One

They came when the sky had no moon, moving through the jungle toward Naaki Chava like the night crawlers they were, on a mission to steal the girl called Tyhen.

The torches the warriors carried cast demonic shadows in the red paint on their faces, and the long, black feathers in their hair bounced like the tails of the paradise birds as they ran.

Both the thunder of their footsteps and the fire they carried sent natural predators into hiding, leaving their path undeterred into the great city where Chief Cayetano ruled.

A jaguar crouching on a tree limb above them hissed when it saw them coming, then hunkered motionless, watching with yellow eyes as the warriors passed below.

The young man leading them was a zealot—a dark priest named Coyopa. But for a small wrap worn around his hips, he was naked to the world. His body was hairless, an affliction that he had turned to his advantage, claiming he was this way so that nothing stood between him and the Gods, but his soul was as black as the night in which they ran.

He had seen the girl they were after in a vision and was both awed and envious of what she was. Although she was still young, her untapped powers would increase as she grew up. He wanted her and that power for himself.

The plan was to put a spell on the guards and sweep through the palace, killing all who stood between him and the girl. It was easier to turn captives to his ways when they knew there was nothing to go back to.

****

The faint scent of smoke from the palace in Naaki Chava came from torches at the end of the maze of hallways where palace guards stood watch at every entrance. On this night, while danger came at them in the dark, Cayetano and his family slept unaware.

Yuma and his adopted brothers, Adam and Evan, shared a room in the palace at one end of a long hallway. The chief and his wife, Singing Bird, slept at the other end, while their fifteen-year-old daughter, Tyhen, and her servant, Acat, slept in the room between.

In the years since Singing Bird had returned from the future with what was left of the Native race, Naaki Chava had not only grown, but thrived. But it was the baby she brought in her belly, and Yuma, the eight-year-old boy whose life she saved who had become pivotal to the future of their race.

Even at the tender age of eight, Yuma had known without being told that the baby she carried would one day belong to him, that he would protect her with his life, and she would love him forever.

What he hadn't known was that the night he made his first kill, he would not only be saving the life of Singing Bird and her unborn child, but that it would break a thousand-year-old curse and set their race of people on a path to changing and saving the future of the human race.

As Yuma grew older, his feelings for Tyhen deepened. She was no longer a child who shadowed his every step. She was a beautiful young woman who'd grown taller than everyone in the palace except for him and the twins.

Adam and Evan had also come from the future with secrets and psychic powers few knew they possessed. They had grown into men more knowledgeable and powerful than the lone shaman who dwelled in the temple, and they had long ago pledged their loyalty and lives to Cayetano and his family.

And so they all slept, peaceful and unaware of the impending danger.

****

Tyhen slept on her back with one arm flung over her head, the other lying across her flat belly. Her once reed-thin body had filled out into willowy curves and her legs had grown so long during the past year her bed was now too short. Sometime during the night, she'd pushed her hair away from her neck, and now it spilled out onto the sleeping mat pillowed beneath her head. Even in repose, her features were stunning, but how could they be any less? She was the daughter of a god and a woman who was a red feather warrior.

She knew her truth, that the man who put her in her mother's belly had been a Windwalker, an ancient and powerful spirit. She had known her destiny before she'd drawn her first breath, just like she knew that Yuma was her soul mate and that she would love him above all men.

Like everyone else in Naaki Chava this night, she'd gone to sleep without concern until she began to dream. As the dream progressed, she began to toss and turn, rolling from her back to her belly, and then back again.

Acat, her servant, heard her distress and got up to make sure she was not ill. Once she was satisfied Tyhen's skin was warm only from the lack of moving air and not a fever, she crawled back onto her sleeping mat and drifted off to sleep.

Unaware of her nurse's concern, Tyhen continued to dream until a sudden vision of fire and feathers and the men who carried them brought her to her feet. Her first thought to warn the others, and then she heard the twins' voices in her head.

We saw them, too. Tell Cayetano. Yuma is already alerting the guards.

Her heart was pounding as she ran out of her room and then down the darkened hallway, calling Cayetano's name.

****

As deeply asleep as he was, the second he heard Tyhen's voice he was awake and shaking Singing Bird, who was still asleep in his arms.

"Singing Bird, something is wrong!" he cried and leaped to his feet.

Singing Bird heard her daughter's voice before she opened her eyes. Her heart pounded as she grabbed a wrap and ran out of the room behind him.

They entered the hall just as Tyhen came out of the shadows, her long, dark hair flying out behind her.

In that moment, Singing Bird didn't see her child; she saw Niyol, her Windwalker, running toward her in the canyon. All the emotions of loving and losing him swept through her so fast it left her momentarily speechless, leaving Cayetano to take control.

"What's wrong?" he cried as Tyhen leapt into his arms.

Tyhen was trembling, her arms locked so tight around Cayetano's neck he could not see her face, but he could feel her heartbeat and her fear. He also knew she had the gift of sight and guessed it was more than a bad dream that brought her running.

"What is it, my little whirlwind? What do you see?" he asked.

Tyhen's voice was trembling. "There are warriors in the jungle running with fire. They come for me!"

Before he could comment, he heard the clank of spears and shields and the sounds of running feet. It was Yuma and the twins followed by a large number of the palace guards carrying torches.

Cayetano's eyes narrowed angrily. "No one will hurt my daughter."

But Tyhen was still locked into the vision of the men in the jungle and desperate that they understand the urgency.

"Yes, yes, they will. A bad man leads them to the swinging bridge. You have to stop them there or it will be too late."

"Heed her words and give her to me," Singing Bird said and took her daughter's hand.

The twins' gift of sight had given them instant access into her dream, and now they shared her vision. They not only saw the warriors, but the face of the priest who led them, and even though they were familiar with the world of the occult, they suddenly shuddered.

"The priest's name is Coyopa. He prays to the dark ones," Adam said.

"She's right," Evan added. "Stop them at the swinging bridge or not at all."

Cayetano turned to his guards. "Gather my warriors. We will fight them."

They rushed off to do his bidding while Adam continued to argue his brother's advice.

"You cannot fight his magic. Wait until they're on the bridge then cut it. Gravity is stronger than his evil," Adam said.

Yuma was silent, though seeing Tyhen shaking with fear filled him with rage. All he could think about was keeping her safe, and when he heard the twins warning, it gave him the answer.

"I'll do it," he said, then turned and ran to get his machete.

"Wait, Yuma, wait!" Cayetano yelled, but he was already gone. "We go!" Cayetano said.

Yuma was the beginning and end of Tyhen's world, and what she'd said had sent him headlong into danger. She was on the verge of new tears when her mother took her by the hand.

"Come with me," Singing Bird said and then motioned for the twins and Acat to follow as they returned to Singing Bird's quarters. As they did, a dozen palace guards immediately stationed themselves outside the door.

Singing Bird settled Tyhen on her bed and the others around them, then sat cross-legged in their midst and began demanding answers. She turned first to the twins. Over the years they had grown tremendously in body and stature. Their pretty faces had matured into handsome ones, framed by black, wavy hair that hung past their shoulders. After all this time, she still couldn't tell them apart.

"Adam, Evan, tell me what you see."

The brothers closed their eyes.

"Forty warriors with red paint on their faces and black feathers in their hair," Adam said.

"Led by a priest who calls on dark spirits," Evan added.

Singing Bird's hands curled into fists as she stifled a new wave of fear. This felt like before when she was still on earth, trying to bring their people back in time. Only then, the magic and the spirit were on her side; this time it was not.

"How do you fight against such a man?" she asked.

Tyhen sat cross-legged on the mat beside her mother, rocking back and forth with her eyes nearly closed. She, too, was watching, but it was Yuma she saw, moving swiftly through the jungle with a torch in one hand, a machete in the other.

"Fight evil with good," she mumbled, still locked into the heartbeat of the man who loved her.

****

Yuma ran without caution, desperate to get to the swinging bridge first. Being in the jungle at night was dangerous, but knowing they were coming for Tyhen scared him more. He knew Cayetano and his warriors trailed him, but he didn't know how far behind him they were and couldn't let it matter.

He wished for a moon and someone who had his back. His pulse leaped when he heard the squall of a jaguar on the hunt, but it quickly settled, knowing the fire in his torch would keep the big cat at bay. The deeper he got into the jungle, the quieter it became. This made him anxious. Animals knew when men were about. Was he too late? Had the war party already crossed the swinging bridge?

His body was bathed in sweat and the constant impact of foot to ground was a continuous reminder to go faster.

Tyhen's safety came first.

He lengthened his stride.

****

Coyopa was running on a drug-induced high, locked into the vision of the girl he'd seen in his dreams. He was following the pull of her heartbeat, and the closer they got, the stronger it became.

He was so focused on the prize he forgot to watch where they were going. When they emerged into what he thought was a clearing, it was soon apparent they had come to the edge of a cliff.

Coyopa stopped abruptly. He had not seen this! Why had he not seen this?

"Look there! A bridge!" one of his warriors cried, and his shock receded. That was why he hadn't known because it was not an issue after all.

"We go!" he yelled and was the first man to start across.

The moment he stepped on it, it began to swing. His gut knotted. In the dark, they could not tell how far it was to the other side. It also occurred to him that it might not be strong enough to hold them all, but it was too late to stop, and the warriors were right behind him. By the time the last warrior hit the bridge, it was swaying precariously.

Coyopa held the torch up over his head and looked down, but couldn't see the bottom. He stopped and turned around, shouting for them to slow down. But the void over which they stood swallowed his voice, and the men kept coming without heeding his warning.

****

Yuma heard voices and what sounded like echoes. He knew that when he left the cover of the trees, they would see his torch.

Then he heard Tyhen's voice in his ear and almost stumbled.

Put it out. Put it out and hurry. They are on the bridge.

He didn't hesitate as he jammed it into the damp undergrowth and leaped forward. Within moments, he began seeing flickers of light. She was right. They were already on the bridge and he was there on the other side, watching them in the dark.

He could barely see their bodies from the fire they carried, but they were many and there was no time to waste. Without hesitation, he swung the machete, chopping at the massive braids of vines that formed the bridge hacking at first one side and then the other. All he had to do was weaken them enough to give way.

****

Coyopa sensed their danger, even though he could not see what lay ahead or below, but his warriors were in a panic and wouldn't listen as the bridge continued to sway.

Furious, he thrust his torch above his head and screamed. The sound was so loud that all forty of his men froze, which exacerbated the creaking of the bridge within the silence. But it was the steady *chop, chop, chop* they were hearing that shocked them most.

Coyopa keyed in on the sound and closed his eyes. In his mind, he saw the warrior at the end of the bridge hacking at the ropes. He wondered how they'd known he was coming, but didn't have time to pursue the answer. He had two options. He could stop and chant a spell and hope it wasn't already too late, or they could run.

Chop, chop, chop.

His heartbeat pounded in rhythm to the sound.

Chop, chop, chop.

He thrust his torch high into the air and screamed. "Run!"

****

Yuma wouldn't look up. He couldn't get caught up in the fear of what was in front of him because there wasn't any time. One strand of the massive braid that formed the bridge's handrails was already cut through on both sides, and he was working on the second when he heard the scream.

He began to swing harder, and when the second strand broke, he gritted his teeth and shifted his stance.

Chop, chop, chop.

The bridge was swinging violently. They were so close now that the glow from their torches was bright enough he could see their faces.

Chop, chop, chop.

Another strand gave way.

He felt, rather than saw, when the bridge began to sag. The only thing holding it up was a single strand of braided vine and even as he swung the machete, it gave way.

It made a snapping sound when it broke, and when the right side of the bridge suddenly dipped, he heard screams and looked up. Men were dropping head over heels into the gorge, still holding the burning torches to light their way to the rocks below.

Less than fifty yards away and still holding the handrail, the priest pointed a finger at Yuma as the last side broke.

Yuma felt the rage as he watched the bald head and painted face disappear from sight as the bridge fell out from under him.

Yuma dropped to his knees as their death screams faded away, the muscles in his shoulders jerking from exhaustion.

You saved me.

Yuma closed his eyes as his chest began to tighten.

"You belong to me. I will protect you with my life, and you will love me forever," he whispered.

Forever.

He was still kneeling when Cayetano and his warriors came out of the jungle.

At first, Cayetano feared Yuma had been wounded. But then the young warrior slowly stood and turned around.

"It is done," Yuma said softly.

Cayetano came forward, holding his torch above his head. The look in Yuma's eyes was haunting.

"What happened? Did you see him?"

"Yes, and he saw me."

"What do you mean?" Cayetano asked.

"He was pointing at me and shouting as he fell." The invisible grip around Yuma's heart grew tighter. "I have been cursed."

Cayetano's heartbeat skipped. "No. You cannot know that."

Yuma put a hand on his chest and shuddered.

"But I do," he said.

His eyes rolled back in his head as he fell.

****

Back in the palace, Tyhen suddenly threw her head back and screamed.

Singing Bird's heart nearly stopped as she grabbed at her daughter.

"What's wrong? What happened? What did you see?"

Adam and Evan knew. They saw Yuma on the ground. They could feel the life leaving their brother's body as surely as if it was their own.

Acat didn't know what was happening, but it was all too much. She began to cry, which only added to the chaos.

Tyhen jumped to her feet and began issuing orders.

"Yuma is dying. Adam, Evan, pick two guards and come with me. We don't have much time."

Singing Bird reached for her daughter, but Tyhen slipped out of her grasp.

"No, Mother, no! This is not for you. This is for me. If I don't go, he'll die."

Singing Bird was scared. "But this is dark magic. What if—?"

Tyhen gave her mother a strange look. "Mother, did you forget? Windwalkers cannot die."

Singing Bird reeled. Not once had it ever occurred to her that Tyhen could have inherited any part of that.

When she saw Niyol's expression on her daughter's face, she said no more.

Tyhen ran out of the room with the twins at her heels. They stopped long enough to pick two guards to go with them, but she ran on without them. They caught up with her at the jungle's edge.

Adam grabbed her by the arm. "Stop, Tyhen. Let one of the guards go first with a torch. You can't see where you're going!"

Tyhen could feel the life draining out of Yuma's body and reacted in anger as she pulled away.

"You're wrong. I see everything! You are the ones who need light. Run fast or I'll leave you all behind."

Chapter Two

Cayetano was frantic. He had no power against curses, and his priests and the twins were too far away to help. He could feel Yuma's heartbeat but it was too slow. Yuma was the son he would never have and the thought of losing him was frightening. If Yuma had only waited, this wouldn't have happened.

But the moment that went through his head, he let it go. If Yuma had waited, they would have been too late. The dark priest and his warriors would have already crossed the bridge and all would have been lost. Yuma had been willing to sacrifice himself to save her, and now they had to try and save him.

Cayetano leaped up, pointing at his warriors.

"Pick him up! We go back to Naaki Chava now!"

The men gathered up their fallen friend, moving as quickly in the darkness as they could safely go.

****

Yuma felt like he was floating. Even though the pressure on his heart was excruciating, the weight of his body seemed to have lessened. He tried desperately to focus. He needed to get a message to Tyhen. She had to know he would never leave her, not even if he walked in the spirit world, but he couldn't focus so much as a thought.

I am coming, Yuma. Wait for me! Promise you will wait for me!

His soul quickened. Tyhen! He should have realized she would know. He wanted to assure her that he'd heard, but he couldn't promise what she asked. He couldn't bear for his last promise to be a lie. All he could do was let go, saving whatever strength he had left for the journey ahead.

****

Tyhen's legs were long, but it was fear that lent speed to her stride. Despite her warning that she didn't need light, one of the guards had run ahead of her anyway with a torch held high above his head, and when it was necessary, he cleared their path with his machete.

Adam and Evan ran behind her. In many ways this felt like the night they'd made their escape from Bazat, the man who'd held them prisoner in the next city over when they were children.

They also knew Yuma was dying. They had already keyed in on the curse that felled him, but they were not healers. They could not save Yuma's life no matter how fast they ran. It was the worst night of their lives.

Tyhen was running without thought, moving as fast as she could without heed for the sharp leaves slicing at her face or the blood-sucking insects sticking to her skin. None of it mattered as long as she got to Yuma in time.

While she was not old enough to begin the journey for which she'd been born, she understood the way of a man with his woman. She knew the emotion of physical pleasures from her dreams, and that she would never be whole without him. It was what kept her running. She had no idea how long they'd been in the jungle when all of a sudden his life force became so faint she could no longer feel it. The panic that swept through her was blinding.

No, Yuma, no. Don't go! Wait for me! Do you hear me? I can save you. Windwalkers do not die!

The muscles in her legs shook and her lungs burned, but the silence horrified her.

"Please, my ancestors... help me," she whispered, and then put down her head and lengthened her stride.

She ran past the guard with the torch, then she outran the light, moving blindly through the jungle toward the man who held her heart. When she began hearing drums and then singing, she knew the Old Ones had heard her cry. Now all she had to do was follow the sounds.

****

Cayetano's only focus was getting Yuma back to Naaki Chava, and the last thing he expected to see was Tyhen coming out of the darkness, screaming Yuma's name.

He caught her on the run.

"Daughter! Have you lost your mind? Why have you come?"

She pushed out of his arms. "Where is he?"

"Here! He is here!" the warriors cried as they lay Yuma down.

She grabbed the knife from Cayetano's belt, ran to Yuma, then dropped to her knees. There was no time to explain anything to anybody.

"Bring the light!" she cried and was instantly surrounded by the men carrying torches.

She ran the knife across her wrist so fast that they didn't see what she had done until the blood began to run.

Cayetano dropped to his knees beside her and grabbed her arm to stop the flow, thinking she was trying to take her own life.

"No! Don't!" she screamed and yanked her hand away. She parted Yuma's lips and let her blood flow into his mouth.

Cayetano was shocked by what she'd done, and at the same time in awe. This night was a turning point. No matter what happened to Yuma, it was evident the girl he claimed as his daughter was a child no more.

Tyhen leaned down until her mouth was only inches away from his ear, then she began to whisper.

Yuma heard the voice before he understood the words. He could feel her breath against his cheek. It was Tyhen! Was he dreaming? Was he already dead? Swallow? Did she tell him to swallow? He wanted to ask, but the words were not there.

Tyhen didn't know she was crying or that the blood from the cuts and scratches on her skin were dripping onto his face. All of her focus was on his throat, watching for a sign that he had heard her and was swallowing the only thing that would save his life.

She grabbed him by the shoulders and shook him.

"Please, Yuma, please. Swallow what is in your mouth. You are my heart. You are my life. I cannot do what I have to do without you in it."

But when he didn't move, she fell forward on his chest, sobbing. If he died, she would die with him and fate could do what it wanted with her people. She would have no part of this battle of good and evil without him.

****

When Yuma finally felt the liquid in his mouth, he automatically swallowed. The taste was slightly salty, metallic. He swallowed again and again until his mouth was empty, then waited to die, but it didn't happen.

Something was changing. The fist around his heart began to ease. He was no longer floating, and the weight of his body felt almost crushing. It took him a few more moments to realize something was on his chest, something he needed to move.

When Yuma suddenly raised his arm, Cayetano let out a war cry that made Tyhen jump. She looked up just as Yuma's fingers ran through her hair, and when he opened his eyes, she took a breath. If he wasn't going to die, then neither was she.

Yuma saw the bloody scratches on her face and her tear-swollen eyes and thought she had never been more beautiful.

"Are you real?" he whispered.

Her lips were trembling, but her voice was strong. "Yes, I am real, and you are going to live."

"How did you save me? I was cursed to die."

She leaned close to his ear again so that the warriors would not hear. "Windwalkers do not die."

He felt the moisture on his lips and touched it, then frowned when he saw the blood. Then he saw her wrist and his nostrils flared.

"What did you do?"

"You shed blood to save my life before I was born. I shed blood to save you," she whispered, but she was beginning to shake.

Between the distance she'd run and the blood she was losing, she felt faint.

Yuma looked beyond her shoulder to Adam and Evan, who were standing behind her. "My brothers, bandage her wound."

Evan tore a strip from the garment he wore wrapped around his waist, then knelt beside her and used it to bind her wrist.

As the men stood watching, they heard the snarl of a big cat, then the death cry of its prey.

Cayetano frowned. This was not a safe place to be.

"We go now!" he said.

Tyhen stood abruptly, and then swayed on her feet.

Cayetano grabbed her before she fell. "Rest easy, my daughter. I will carry you home."

"No, I cannot go," Tyhen cried.

Cayetano frowned. "What now?"

"Take Yuma home, but I have to go to the bridge."

"There is no need. They are all dead."

"There is a need. Please, my father. The body died, but the spirit did not."

The skin suddenly crawled on the back of Cayetano's neck as he contemplated dealing with a demon spirit instead of the man possessed by one.

"We will take her," Adam said abruptly. "She's going to need us. Leave some guards here. We won't be long."

Cayetano did not like it. He did not hide from his enemy, but he'd seen what it had done to Yuma and feared that kind of power.

"Then I'll wait here until you return. Both of you should carry her to the bridge. She's too weak to walk," he said.

"No," Tyhen said and strode off into the darkness

with Adam and Evan behind her, carrying torches to light the way.

Not a word passed between them as they returned to the gorge. Even before they reached the rim, they felt the evil. The sight of torches still burning among the dead bodies below was eerie, but it was nothing to the spirit hovering above the chasm. It was a ball of fire, pulsing like a beating heart and growing larger by the second.

"Can you block him?" she asked.

They nodded.

"Then do it," she muttered.

The twins joined hands and focused as Tyhen lifted her arms to the moonless, star-studded sky.

The spirit suddenly screamed and shot fireballs into space in an effort to dissipate itself so it could not be contained—but not in time. Adam and Evan put a mental wall around it, giving Tyhen the time she needed.

She'd never done anything like this before, but it seemed her soul knew how. She took a deep breath and closed her eyes. Words came to her, then through her, as she began to chant. The drums she'd heard earlier rode with the wind that came sweeping down the gorge, fanning the burning torches below. Then it rose around Tyhen in a high-pitched whine, whipping her hair against her face and tugging on her clothing. She stood within it, chanting louder and faster.

When it began to spin out into the space above the gorge, the twins were the only ones to bear witness to what happened next.

One second the angry spirit was there, and then it was not. It had been sucked up into the maelstrom she had created and sent back to the dark where it belonged.

When the drums stopped, so did Tyhen. She knew before she opened her eyes that it was gone.

"It is done."

The twins remained silent. There was little to say about what they'd seen, but it was obvious what it had taken out of her to do it. Her body trembled from exhaustion. When she turned to walk away, Adam slipped a hand beneath her elbow as Evan took the other. It was time to go home.

****

By the time they reached Naaki Chava, it was nearly sunrise and Tyhen was asleep in Cayetano's arms. He'd waited anxiously for them to return, and when he'd seen her staggering into the clearing, he swept her off her feet and carried her close to his heart all the way home. He loved her so much; it had never mattered that she was not his own.

"There comes Singing Bird," Adam said.

"She's crying," Evan added.

"Thank you for everything you did," Cayetano said. "Go rest. I will deal with this."

They nodded and spoke soothingly to Singing Bird as they passed her.

From the frantic look on her face, Cayetano guessed Yuma and the others had already told her what had happened.

"She's all right," he said quickly. "She's just asleep."

Singing Bird was crying as she ran her hands all

over her daughter's body. "I was so afraid. I let her go. I let her go."

He didn't often see Singing Bird's tears, but when he did, they hurt his heart. "You did the right thing. We'll talk later. Help me get her to her room."

"Yuma said Tyhen cut her arm so I called for our healer to come. She's there waiting."

Cayetano didn't know how to explain exactly what he'd seen. "She saved Yuma's life with her blood. I don't know what's happening with her, but she's changing."

Singing Bird stared at her daughter in disbelief, then shook off the shock and led the way to Tyhen's room. Yuma was standing by the door.

"You are supposed to be resting," she said sternly.

"Where is she?" Yuma asked.

"Cayetano comes," she said, pointing to the doorway.

Moments later he appeared with Tyhen in his arms. Before she could explain that Tyhen was only asleep, Yuma staggered backward in shock.

"What happened?"

"She's just asleep," Cayetano said.

Yuma wiped shaky hands across his face, and when he spoke it was a statement, not a question. "I will sit with her."

Singing Bird touched his arm. "You are still weak. You need to—"

"I will sit with her," he said again and walked into the room behind Cayetano.

Cayetano looked at Singing Bird and then shrugged. "It is beginning. Let him. If we don't, when she wakes up, she'll go find him."

Singing Bird took a deep breath. She'd known

since the night Yuma saved her from Bazat that this day would come. Tyhen was without experience, but she trusted Yuma would not cross a line until the time was right. She turned around and led the way into her daughter's room.

The healer, Little Mouse, stood up the moment they walked in, and when Cayetano lay Tyhen on her bed, the healer went to work, cleaning the cut on Tyhen's wrist, then smearing the wound with an ointment she'd brought. She placed two medicine leaves on it and then bound it with a strip of clean cloth.

Singing Bird touched the tiny woman's shoulder as she spoke. "Thank you, Little Mouse."

"Do I stay?" she asked.

"No, but do not go down to your home in the dark. You will sleep here in the palace until morning."

Little Mouse nodded. She knew where the location of the servants' quarters because she'd slept there before and scampered out of the room.

Yuma got his sleeping mat and put it at the foot of Tyhen's bed, then sat down and crossed his arms as if daring someone to make him move.

Singing Bird sighed. "Call me if you need me."

Yuma nodded.

Cayetano glanced back as they walked out. Acat, the woman who had been Tyhen's caretaker since birth, was settling down on her sleeping mat and Yuma was on guard. It should be enough.

****

Tyhen slept all the way to sundown. She woke up as

Little Mouse was dabbing medicine on the cut in her wrist, then sat up and grabbed her hand.

"Yuma?"

Little Mouse pointed at the man asleep on the floor at the foot of Tyhen's bed.

Tears welled, blurring Tyhen's vision.

"He is well?"

Little Mouse smiled. "He is well."

Tyhen sighed, then leaned back and let her resume her task.

"Will this mark me?" she asked.

"Not on your face. You are already healing. Maybe here," she said, pointing to the cut on her wrist.

Tyhen felt the tears rolling down her cheeks as she closed her eyes.

Windwalkers do not die.

There was so much knowledge she'd been born with, but this was the first time that fact had been tested. Obviously Windwalkers healed fast, too.

Little Mouse smiled as she left, passing Acat who was on the way in.

"Is it too late for food?" she asked.

Acat was happy her sweet child was hungry. It was a sign she was well.

"I will find food and drink," Acat said and scurried out of the room.

Tyhen nodded, her gaze still locked on Yuma.

Wake up, she thought and exhaled softly when his eyes suddenly opened.

"I am awake," he said slowly. He sat up then looked around the room. "Where is Acat?"

"Bringing food and drink."

He looked at the raw wound on her wrist until his vision blurred. "You saved my life."

She nodded. "And I would do it again and again and—"

He felt the passion in her voice. "You are still young," he said softly.

She sighed. "I am grown in every way that counts."

He eyed her soft curves. "And I gladly wait, regardless. You belong to me." *And I will love you forever.*

She smiled shyly. Even though he hadn't spoken aloud, she heard it anyway. She scooted down to the end of the bed then leaned over and stroked the side of his face.

"I know you will protect me," she said. "But you did at the near-cost of your life, which should not happen again."

He saw a flush of color on her cheeks and thought there was none more beautiful than her face.

Moments later, Acat came back carrying a tray laden with food and drink.

Tyhen motioned to Yuma. "Come eat with me."

He got up and moved closer. Acat handed him some fruit and bread, and a cup with a drink made of chocolate. He drank until the cup was empty and then began peeling the banana as Tyhen chose a piece of fruit and piece of the bread made from the corn and maize they grew in the fields.

She ate like she was starving, ever-conscious of Yuma's steady gaze. As she took a bite of the fruit, a drop of juice ran down her chin. Yuma reached out, caught the drop with his finger, then licked it off.

Suddenly frightened of the feeling that ran through her, Tyhen shuddered then looked away. He was right. She was still too young.

Yuma saw the uncertainty in her eyes and sighed. He'd waited over fifteen years. Soon it would be sixteen, and for her, he would wait a lifetime more. Some things were just meant to be.

****

It didn't take long for word to spread throughout the city about what happened at the gorge, and that the swinging bridge was gone.

Singing Bird had expected a reaction and thought she had prepared her daughter for the worst, but the next morning as they walked down to the school where Singing Bird taught, she was shocked. People looked at Tyhen with new eyes and then looked away, suddenly afraid of the chief's daughter.

Tyhen didn't care. She'd done what she had to do to save Yuma and she would do it again. She walked with her shoulders back and her chin up. She'd always known she was different. Now they knew it, too.

Singing Bird gave her daughter a quick look and then relaxed. She didn't know what had happened at the gorge and didn't ask, but Cayetano was right. Tyhen was changing. She thought she'd been ready for the inevitability of this day. She'd always known it would be Tyhen who would finish what she started, but the time when that would happen was suddenly upon them and she wasn't ready.

Still the children awaited her at the school, and once she began the day, she pushed her worries aside. Tyhen was no longer a student and worked with her, teaching younger children the math and the language of the New Ones, teaching them how to count, and the letters that made the words, and then how to read and write them. Of all the things the New Ones had brought with them, knowing the strangers' languages and how they did business would be the one thing that would put them on an equal footing with the people who would come to take their lands.

Two days a week volunteers from the New Ones came in and taught the students other languages as well. The older students were already fluent in French, Spanish, and English, and Singing Bird had been working on creating an alphabet that would be universal for all Native languages, and in return, teaching it to the New Ones so that the traditional languages of their tribes would not be lost.

Adam and Evan had created a process to make a kind of paper from the pulp of several jungle plants, and the paper had been bound together to form books.

There were books with the alphabet and books with stories. There were books with history as far back as anyone in Naaki Chava could recall and books of stories from the future. There were how-to books that had pictures and directions on everything from metal working to ceiling fans and dug wells. There were books about the precious metals that the strangers would be seeking, and the lands they would covet.

If the New Ones knew how to do it, they wrote about it, even to the point of explaining electricity and all kinds of inventions from the future. The books weren't large, but they were many according to subjects and were made over and over in duplicate so that wherever people parted ways, they took a bundle of these books with them to teach others. It was Singing Bird's dream that within five or ten years, every tribe on what she'd known as North and South America would know these stories and the languages, and know the urgency of teaching them to the ensuing generations.

****

Two months later:

It was the rainy season. Even when it wasn't raining, water dripped from every leaf, every tree, every roof, and onto the ground. The jungle growth was so thick the sun rarely made it through the canopy and walking on the leaf-littered ground beneath it was often slippery.

The first time Singing Bird mentioned that walking on the ground was as slick as walking on ice, everyone but Yuma and the twins looked at her in confusion.

Cayetano laid down the food he was eating and stared.

"What is ice?"

Singing bird looked up, a little startled she'd used a phrase from the past. That past belonged to Layla Birdsong, the woman she'd been in the time of Firewalker, and she rarely thought like that anymore.

"Uh... ice. Ice is, well, it's when..."

"Frozen water," Adam said, then realized he'd only added to the confusion.

Now Tyhen was frowning. "What word is frozen? What does it mean?"

Singing Bird shifted into her teacher voice. "Okay, you know how I teach the young ones about other parts of the world and what happens in our future?"

Tyhen nodded.

"So some places are very dry and have no rain. Some places have different kinds of weather and some are only cold. We know cold. It's how we feel when we get sick with a fever. Remember how you shake and want to be covered? So frozen is colder than cold. When we say it's going to freeze, that means the weather is going to get so cold it turns the water into ice. When the water is ice, it's very hard like a rock and will not pour out of a jug. That's when we use the word frozen. The water is frozen. When it is like that, it hurts to hold a piece of ice on your tongue, and if the ground is icy, it's so slippery that you cannot stand up and you fall down. If you get too cold in this kind of weather, your body loses feeling and sometimes people die from being too cold."

"I do not like slick as ice," Cayetano stated.

"I do not like frozen," Tyhen added.

Singing Bird sighed. "And yet you, my daughter, will see all of this and more before your work is done."

Tyhen's eyes widened, and then she glanced at Yuma to see his reaction. He was smiling. She didn't know whether to be insulted that he was laughing at her or relieved he wasn't afraid.

"I will not be afraid of frozen," she muttered.

Yuma laughed.

She glared.

Singing Bird rolled her eyes.

"I miss ice cream," Evan muttered.

"What is ice cream?" Cayetano asked.

Singing Bird sighed. "It's something cold and sweet and good to eat. I miss it, too," she said. "But I do not miss Firewalker and that is enough talk about what is gone."

When she got up from the table and walked out of the room, Cayetano looked at Yuma and frowned.

"Why is she sad?"

Yuma shrugged. "Probably for the same reason all of us are from time to time. We are grateful to be alive and feel honored that what we did by coming here will make a difference to all the generations to come, but we had a different way of life and now it's gone. And so are the people we loved. I go back there in my dreams to visit my father, then I wake and I am here."

He looked down for a moment and then back up. When he did, Tyhen thought she saw tears in his eyes. Then he looked at her and smiled.

"But here is good. Different, but very good."

Cayetano didn't like Yuma's answer. He didn't like to think about the past because in Singing Bird's past, she was Layla Birdsong, and he was not a part of that world.

He got up from the table and walked out. He needed to make sure she wasn't crying. It hurt his heart when he saw her cry.

Tyhen glanced at the twins. "Are you sad, too?"

Adam shook his head.

"No," Evan added. "We were not happy in the past. Now we are."

She nodded, but wouldn't look at Yuma. She didn't want to see tears in his eyes. She didn't want this place to be lacking because that meant she wasn't enough.

She took a piece of bread as she got up from the table and then walked out of the room. She knew Yuma was behind her. Still, she said nothing as she paused just inside the doorway to look out.

The rain had stopped, but the birds were still

sheltering up in the trees beneath the leaves. She stepped outside onto the stone walkway and began tearing off pieces of the bread and tossing them out onto the ground.

Within moments, birds began coming down from the trees, pecking hungrily at the unexpected treats.

Yuma watched her, wondering what she was thinking. He knew she was upset and he knew he shouldn't have laughed at her. Like Cayetano, it hurt his heart when she was sad.

"I'm sorry I laughed at you," he said.

She kept tossing bits of bread.

He walked up behind her and then stopped just short of touching her.

"I'm truly sorry," he said softly.

Tyhen could feel the warmth of his breath against the back of her ear and there was a knot in her belly. She needed to say something but words wouldn't come. All she managed to do was just shrug.

Cayetano put his hands on her shoulders, then let them slide down the length of her arms all the way to her elbows.

"Do you forgive me?" he whispered.

She spun around to face him. "You laughed at me."

He could hear the hurt in her voice. He wanted to wrap his arms around her and hold her close, but settled for a touch of her cheek instead.

"One day I will take you to a land where you will see such things as ice and animals very different from what you know here. You will see people like us but different. Some will be more like the New Ones who came from the time of Firewalker. And the message you bring to them, and to all the others in that land, is what's going to change everything we were. By the time that happens, you will be a woman of great power and magic. The twins have seen it. It will be so. And then you can laugh at me in all my ignorance."

Her eyes widened. Even as he was speaking of it, she was seeing it—vast flat lands and mountains so far away they looked blue. As the vision continued, she saw the flat land give way to mountains and deep rivers and large herds of strange animals.

"You will be with me?"

"I will be with you."

She shuddered, and then the vision disappeared and another truth became reality. "When we leave here, I will never see this place again."

"I will be with you," he repeated.

Her eyes filled with tears. "I will not see my mother or my father again."

He cupped her chin. "I will be with you."

Tears rolled down the curve of her cheeks. "And I will be with you," she said, then laid her cheek against his chest and closed her eyes, willing the tears away.

Chapter Three

Three months later: Festival of the Corn

Cayetano was taking his best hunters into the jungle again. There would be much feasting during festival week, and while there were many good hunters in Naaki Chava, the chief took it as a point of pride that the palace provided a large portion of the meat. This was their third hunt in as many days, and if they had good hunting again today, it would be the last needed for the week-long event. He was on the way out of the palace when Adam came running up to stop him.

"Cayetano! I have been looking for you!"

Cayetano frowned. "Is something wrong?"

"Could we talk where others don't hear?" Adam asked.

Now he knew something was wrong. He led Adam out a side entrance and walked a short distance away from the building before they stopped.

"This is far enough?" Cayetano said. "Tell me."

"Evan and I have been having the same dream for three nights and we believe it is a warning. Something is going to happen during the time of the festival that could be a threat to Tyhen."

Cayetano frowned. "What kind of danger?"

"Many shamans are coming to see her, maybe even challenge her. They know about what happened to the dark priest, that Yuma was cursed, and what Tyhen did to save him. No one but Evan and I were there when she went back to the swinging bridge, and we did not speak of it, but the shamans saw it in their visions. Now they want to see her for themselves. If they don't like her, they will brand her as a witch, which will cause people to fear her and her powers. But if they see her and feel no threats, they may look upon her as a quiet, but kind, young woman who uses her power for the good of her people."

He frowned. "I do not like that they come here to judge her. Their opinions matter not to me."

Adam kept trying to explain. "But they will matter to Tyhen. If she does not have the people's trust, she will not be able to do what she was born to do."

"But she does good things now," he argued.

Adam touched Cayetano's shoulder in a calm, almost comforting manner.

"Word of the woman who rides the wind will spread beyond Naaki Chava, even beyond the mountains into the lands far to the north, and when it does, she will follow."

Cayetano's eyes widened and his heart began to pound. Singing Bird had told him Tyhen's path was to help change the future, but he did not like to think that she would be leaving here to do it.

"But why must she go so far?" he asked.

"You already know this. She must unite all the tribes everywhere so when the first strangers from across the big water come to this great continent... and they will come, they will not be able to control your people or take away their lands."

His shoulders slumped. "So that in the future Firewalker will not come."

"Yes. She has to succeed in uniting the tribes or the strangers who come to this land will drive us away all over again."

Cayetano's eyes narrowed angrily at the thought. "When do these priests come?"

"They will come into the city on the first day of the festival as the old shaman, Ah Kin, is blessing the harvest."

"She is still a young girl, not a thing to put on display," Cayetano said.

"Her soul is ancient and you have no choice," Adam said.

Cayetano shrugged off Adam's touch and tightened his grip on his hunting spear. "I go to the hunt now," he said sharply and walked away.

Adam sighed. He knew Cayetano would think about what he'd been told, and by the time he returned, would be in a better frame of mind to discuss it.

Then he heard footsteps coming up behind him and turned around. It was Evan.

"I just told Singing Bird," Evan said. "She's upset but accepting. How did Cayetano take it?"

Adam rolled his eyes. "He heard me out, then argued and went hunting."

Evan shrugged. "He will be better when he returns. He always has to think on a problem before he can act."

"Where's Yuma?" Adam asked.

"Looking for Tyhen. She's the one this is going to impact most."

"I'm glad I'm not him," Adam said.

Evan nodded. "Me too. Did you tell Cayetano about the old shaman?"

"No, but he is behind this confrontation," Adam said.

"I know. What should we do?" Evan asked.

Adam's eyes narrowed angrily. "Nothing, unless we have to. We wait and see how Tyhen handles them. I think she will be fine. If she can dispatch a dark spirit like the one at the swinging bridge, then a bunch of old men who have visions should not bother her. If they are as powerful as they claim to be, then they will soon know her true worth and get behind her. If they choose to challenge her, then we can be certain they are charlatans, and there are ways to deal with people like them."

Evan eyed his brother, admiring the wide set to his shoulders and the beauty of his face. It never occurred to him that he looked exactly the same, because he never felt as capable as Adam.

"I like living here in Naaki Chava," Evan said.

Adam looked at his brother curiously. "You are worried about leaving here one day."

Evan shrugged. "Here is happy and safe. We never had that before."

"We didn't die when Firewalker came for a reason, Evan, and this is it. Is it not our destiny to help Tyhen complete her quest?"

Evan sighed. "Yes."

Adam put his arm around his brother's shoulders. "Then that is enough discussion about something that has yet to happen. Let's go see what the women are cooking. I have not eaten today."

They walked away, confidant that for the time being, all the warnings had been delivered, when in actuality, one had not.

Yuma was still looking for Tyhen, and when he realized Acat and some palace guards were missing, he guessed they'd gone down into the city to the market. Still troubled by what he had to tell her, he armed himself and left the palace.

****

Since the arrival of the New Ones, the open market in Naaki Chava was thriving. They had their own style of handmade pots and hand-woven baskets as well as colorful lengths of cloth much different than the weavers of Naaki Chava. Once the women of the New Ones had found a source for raw wool from a trader on the other side of the mountain, they built looms and began teaching the younger ones the craft.

The initial shelters that had been provided for the New Ones had begun as little more than one-room dwellings, but they were that way no longer. The dwellings of the New Ones were now the envy of others. They had wooden floors made of bamboo instead of floors of clay, and instead of going up to add more rooms, they built out, having more than one room on the ground floor. They built what they called porches on the outside, and added shutters for the windows. They built beds to sleep on rather than the sleeping mats on the floor, and their metal and blacksmith skills were far beyond what had been known. They added water wheels at the river to move water to different locations in the fields, and used bamboo for pipe, plumbing water inside their houses. Everything they touched was an improvement to the way of living, and most notably, the schools. The leap in evolution was already happening.

When they were not busy in the fields, they shared their talents and skills by teaching the others and tried not to dwell on what they'd lost. But sometimes they would reminisce about what the world had been like, and talk about the things they missed most.

Those were the times Tyhen treasured, sitting quietly at her mother's side as she visited with her friends, the Nantays, and trying to imagine a world with such magic. As she'd grown older, Tyhen had searched them out on her own, and today, while Acat was haggling with a vendor, she noticed Johnston Nantay had his table set up in the marketplace and wanted to see what he had to trade.

The guards followed her as she walked away from Acat, but she paid them no mind. As the daughter of a chief, they were always there.

Johnston saw her and lifted a hand in greeting. When he realized she was coming to his table, he smiled.

"Little Tyhen, even though your name means whirlwind in the language of your mother's people, you are no longer little! You have grown even taller since I saw you last!"

Tyhen smiled. The New Ones were so much easier to talk to than the others. They had witnessed her mother's feats and did not feel threatened by what others viewed as magic.

"My mother says I am too tall."

Johnston shook his head. "You are a woman of power. It is only fitting that your appearance should match it."

She chose to ignore the mention of power and looked at the things on his table instead.

"You have smoked jerky. No one makes it as good as you do," she said.

Johnston's smile grew wider as he picked up a piece of the dried meat and handed it to her. "Do you remember how I taught you to make it?" he asked.

She nodded. "Yes. I will do this one day for myself."

Johnston eyed her curiously, but didn't comment as he watched her tear off a small bite of the dried meat with her teeth.

"Good," she said and was about to ask him about the handmade knife she picked up when she heard a woman scream.

In her mind she saw a large bird swooping down from the sky. She dropped the knife and started running. Her guards were behind her, trying to keep up, while Acat, realizing she'd let the chief's daughter wander off, was even farther behind, crying and calling her back. She ignored them all, and the farther she ran, the clearer her vision became.

A condor had been circling the sky for a meal, and a small child was playing at the edge of a field where her mother was working. The enormous bird was only seconds from snatching it up, and the mother was running toward the baby. In Tyhen's mind, she could see others following close behind, but they were all going to be too late.

Just as she cleared the marketplace, she saw the

massive wingspan of the condor diving toward earth. Without conscious thought, she screamed and swung her arms up into the air.

A blast of wind came out of nowhere, hitting the condor head on and forcing it upward, pushing it higher and higher until it soared out of sight.

Seconds later the mother reached her baby, scooped her up into her arms and then dropped to her knees, too shaken to stand.

Tyhen's arms were still over her head when she felt the guards moving closer. Suddenly a hand snaked around her waist and she heard Yuma's voice near her ear. The urgency in his voice was impossible to miss.

"Come with me."

Her heart skipped a beat. "What's wrong?"

"They saw what you did."

She frowned. "So? Should I let the baby die?"

"No, my love, and at the same time, I cannot let you die. I see fear on their faces."

"I will not run away."

She pushed out of his arms and turned toward the crowd behind her. When she started toward them, they jumped aside to let her pass as if they were afraid of what she might do to them. She passed through with Yuma on one side and her guards on the other, making sure she walked unharmed.

She ignored the whispers, her head held high. When she reached Nantay's table back at the marketplace, she picked up her jerky and took another bite as if nothing had happened. She knew the crowd followed her, but refused to acknowledge their fear.

Johnston watched her without speaking, thinking of Layla Birdsong's grandfather, George Begay, and how proud he would have been of this child. She had her grandfather's visions and her mother's magic. He hoped he lived long enough to see what she did with it, and if it would make enough difference in their world to keep it from dying all over again.

"How did you make this blade?" Tyhen asked as she picked up a long knife near the edge of the table. Its shape was unlike the kind the warriors of Naaki Chava carried. It was wider at the hasp and came to a long point at the end.

"I traded for some pieces of metal a few months ago."

"Is this something from your time?" she asked.

"In our time the metal would have been harder and sharper. It was called steel, but this is good enough."

She felt of the edge of the blade again, then set it aside.

"It is a fine knife," she said softly. "If it is agreeable, I would trade three pots of honey for it."

"I would be honored," he said.

"I will send it to you before sundown today."

"I will bring the honey," Yuma offered.

Johnston nodded, picked up a leather scabbard, slipped the knife inside, and handed it to Tyhen.

Satisfied with her trade, she had the weapon in one hand and her jerky in the other.

"Now can we go?" Yuma whispered.

She turned to the crowd and held up her jerky. "This is good," she said, bit off another bite, and walked away with Acat and the guards behind them.

Yuma was still worrying about how to tell her about the upcoming confrontation with the priests when Tyhen tore off a piece of the jerky and gave it to him without speaking.

He popped it in his mouth. As he began to chew, it reminded him of the jerky he and his father used to make with their first deer of the season. He was still thinking about his father when Tyhen's steps began to slow.

"I know about the shamans," she said. "I saw them coming in my sleep last night."

He relaxed. Again, he should have known.

"How does it make you feel?" he asked, then saw her dark eyes flash.

"It makes me angry. They come to challenge me, to test me. They expect me to perform tricks like one of the monkeys in the marketplace. I am no monkey and I do not do tricks."

"So what are you going to do?" he asked.

"Show them what Firewalker did."

He stumbled and then quickly caught himself. "But how? You weren't there."

"But I was. I was in my mother's belly when she ran back to save you. I saw the world on fire."

The hair rose on the back of Yuma's neck. "I had no idea."

"No one does, but now you know, and soon they will, too."

"Can you do that?"

She nodded. "All I have to do is think it and then put it in their heads."

Yuma felt like he should drop and kneel. Such power was beyond his comprehension, and the moment he thought it, she glanced up at him.

"Don't ever do that," she said.

He frowned. "Do what?"

Her voice was shaking. "You do not kneel to me. I am no god, and one day I will be your woman."

They were near the palace when Yuma motioned for the guards to stand back. Then took her by the hand and walked a short distance away.

"We have yet to make love, but you are already mine."

Her heart skipped a beat as she saw his face and then quickly looked away. Passion was still unsettling. She didn't know how to reconcile her feelings with the blood rushing through her body. The power of what she felt for him was frightening, and she wondered if when they finally made love, she would burn up in the heat.

He slipped a hand beneath her hair and pulled her to him.

"Fear not, my little whirlwind. Nothing happens until you're ready."

She laid her cheek against his bare chest and closed her eyes. She knew his scent as well as she knew her own name.

"I'm not afraid," she said.

"I am," he said, stroking the length of her hair.

She leaned back. "What do you fear?"

"I am only a man. You are a Windwalker's daughter."

She made herself look up at him then, even if the feeling scared her.

"You will be enough."

He sighed. Once again, she'd read his heart. "Then I fear nothing," he said.

She slipped her hand into his and resumed their trek to the palace with Acat and the guards still at their heels. She was going to have to tell her Mother what had happened down in the city and listen to Cayetano's concerns for what was coming, but what would be, would be.

****

By nightfall, the parents of the child she'd saved were praising Tyhen's name to all who would listen. Most of the fear had dissipated, leaving behind a tale told and retold until her single act of mercy reached heroic proportions.

But there was one person in Naaki Chava who did not appreciate the growing power of Tyhen's presence. It was the old shaman, Ah Kin.

Ah Kin was the last of the shamans who'd been here when Singing Bird brought the New Ones through the portal. The others had died off one by one without being replaced, which did not bode well for him. Now Cayetano relied solely on the pretty young men who wore the same face. He felt worthless and alone. If it was the last thing he did, he wanted to make the chief sorry.

****

The first day of the festival began with the sunrise ceremony.

Cayetano and Singing Bird stood side by side on the upper steps of the temple, dressed in their ceremonial clothes. The loincloth around Cayetano's waist was white as the sun on a cloudless day and hung just above his knees. The gold thread woven into a geometric design at the hem was as thick and heavy as the jade stones around his neck, but it was the cape of red feathers signifying his status of chief that gave him a most regal presence.

Although Singing Bird had come back to Naaki

Chava with the New Ones, she still had enough of Layla Birdsong left in her to be uncomfortable in the bare-breasted style of the local women, and from the start had worn shifts or sarong-style wraps to cover her nudity.

The blue and gold design woven around the hem of her white shift was striking, as was the bib necklace that lay flat against her chest. The tiny circlets of hammered silver and gold were fastened together in an intricate design, and there was the one long, red feather tied in her hair, signifying her unusual status of warrior.

Tyhen stood slightly behind them. Her shift was without any decoration and had been made with two slits up the front to reveal her legs as she walked. Her long, dark hair was unadorned. Her only nod to the ceremony was an ornate necklace of rare, large turquoise stones worn in honor of her mother's people.

Yuma was beside her, wearing an unadorned loincloth, which was the traditional clothing of a warrior, while the twins', who stood on the other side, wore clothing similar to his, but made from the skins of jaguars. They were all three striking young men, but it was Yuma who held her gaze.

Instead of tying his long hair up in a loop at the back of his neck like the other warriors, he honored his heritage and wore it down, framing a wide forehead, high cheekbones and a strong chin hinting at a stubborn streak. His face was shining from the heat, highlighting the warm tone of his skin. He stood braced as if for combat, his feet slightly apart and on guard against anything or anyone who would harm Tyhen.

She knew the shamans who would come to judge

her were not far away, and she knew what was at stake.

The old shaman, Ah Kin, was standing at the topmost tier of the temple in a ceremonial robe the same color as the purple orchids that grew wild in the jungle. He was waiting to welcome the first rays of the new sun. A phalanx of warriors encircled the temple, forming a barrier between the people and the chief.

For Ah Kin, the playa below was but a sea of faces, and the moment the first rays of the new sun broke the horizon, he lifted his arms to the sky and began the long ritual that ended with giving thanks to the Sun God and the Rain God for providing them with such a good harvest. The last thing Ah Kin did was bless the day. At that point, his job was done.

He then stood in all his glory, watching as the people began coming forward to leave their offerings at the temple's base, standing witness to the gifts while remembering the old days and how revered the shamans had been. Now no one even bothered to look up or seek his attention for a special blessing.

The slight fueled his anger to the point that when he finally saw the purple robes of the visiting shamans who were walking into the playa, it was all he could do not to cheer.

He moved hastily down the temple steps to greet them.

"Cayetano, the shamans are here," Evan whispered.

Ah Kin was halfway down the steps when Cayetano stepped forward and raised his hand. The sound of his voice carried, silencing the crowd.

"What strangers come to Naaki Chava?"

Ah Kin frowned. It was obvious by the color of their robes that they were shamans. It should have been his right to greet them. Once again he'd been shuffled off to the side.

The twelve shamans were accompanied by twice as many warriors. When Cayetano spoke, they stopped short of the temple steps. Rarely were they ever challenged and they didn't like it. A single shaman stepped forward to speak for the rest.

"I am Votan, shaman of Matzlan. I and my fellow shamans come from below Naaki Chava, and from above. We come from the other side of the mountain, and from the valley between. We have heard about a woman with great power who lives in your palace, and we want to see her and judge her for ourselves."

"She is my daughter, and she does not perform tricks for your entertainment," Cayetano snapped.

Votan frowned. He wasn't used to being denied.

"Why are you hiding her? Does she practice bad magic? Maybe she communicates with the dark ones. Maybe you—"

"Stop! Stop now!" Tyhen cried and came striding down the steps in long, angry strides.

Cayetano was furious with the shamans, and when he would have called her back, Singing Bird stopped him with a look.

Yuma was right behind her, and when Tyhen stopped on the steps far below Cayetano, he grabbed her hips with both hands, making sure she went no farther.

She reached back as she leaned against him, laying her hand along the side of his face to reassure him she was fine, and then gazed down at the shamans and their guards.

"I am called Tyhen. I am the woman you accused of dark magic. The last shaman who came after me lies dead in the gorge below swinging bridge. Do you wish to join him?"

They couldn't believe their eyes. She was very tall, taller than their biggest warrior, and she commanded attention when she spoke. The fact, that she had just threatened them was not what they'd expected of one so young. They moved closer to each other as their guards brandished their spears and shields.

"Are you threatening us?" Votan shouted.

Tyhen pointed back at them, and as she did, the air around her stirred, lifting her hair away from her face and neck, even though the day was still.

"You came into my city. You threatened me."

Her voice carried across the playa and beyond, and the crowd around the shamans was becoming restless. They might be a little fearful of their chief's daughter, but they did not like strangers coming into their city and threatening her. Scary or not, she belonged to them.

They began to shout out at the shamans and make gestures of dismissal as they moved closer to the men in the purple robes.

Ah Kin's gut knotted. The people of Naaki Chava already stood behind her. This was worse than he expected. He started to take charge of the confrontation when the twins were suddenly in his face. They said nothing, but he read the warning in their eyes and dropped his gaze.

Votan could feel anger building in the crowd behind him and knew they were in danger. He held up his hands.

"It was not a threat! You mistook my—"

Tyhen raised her voice. "You did threaten me and now you lie about it."

Votan glared. He didn't like her, but he feared what could happen.

"Then I am sorry," he said.

Yuma's hand was on her hip. Tyhen could feel his anger as his grip grew tighter. She threaded her fingers through his hand and stood her ground.

"What was said cannot be unsaid. The damage has been done. Still, you came into my city wanting to know me, so heed my words. If you claim to know about me and my powers, then you also know about the New Ones who now live among us. Is this so?"

Votan nodded, but his voice held a hint of derision. "We heard the stories, but we do not believe these people came from the future."

Tyhen waved her arm across the playa. "Make way for the New Ones. Let the shamans look upon their faces so that they may also call them liars, and then look at all of the people of Naaki Chava who witnessed their arrival through the portal, and call them liars, too."

Then she turned and pointed at Ah Kin, well aware he'd been a part of this.

"Ask our own shaman, Ah Kin. He was at the portal gate with the Old Ones when they arrived. He saw their burns. He saw their strange clothing. He knows the truth. Ask him!"

Ah Kin's mouth opened, but no sounds came out. He had not expected this. He had not seen any of this happening. The twins must have blocked it, which meant they must have known all along that the shamans were coming. This might just be the worst mistake of his life.

Votan glared at Ah Kin and then looked away, trying not to panic as the crowd of people shifted before them. He glanced at the people moving toward him. He focused on their appearance and was shocked into silence. They had light skin and dark skin and every shade of brown skin, and they were taller, like Tyhen. Some of them had blue eyes. Some had eyes the color of new grass, while others had eyes as dark as night. They spoke among themselves in a language he did not understand. He frowned.

"They are not people like us. They are not pure," he said.

Tyhen's voice rose in anger. "Pure? What is pure? As long as a drop of our blood is in their veins, they are a part of the whole and it was not given to you to judge. These are the New Ones. They are all that is left of what we would be."

Votan looked at the other shamans. They were staring at the people in disbelief.

"What do you mean, of what we would be?"

"In your visions, do you see strangers coming in great ships?"

Some of the shamans nodded.

"In your visions, do you see these strangers killing our people, leaving their babies in our mothers' bellies, and stealing our land?"

More were nodding.

Tyhen moved closer to the edge of the tier on which she was standing, and as she did, Yuma moved with her. She lifted her hands, as if beseeching the Old Ones for a favor, and as she did, the air became lighter, carrying her words all the way across the city and the people below.

"Your visions are true. The strangers will come in

great numbers and take what is ours. Although we fight them, we cannot defeat them because we were also fighting among ourselves. Generation after generation, our tribes have been killing people from other tribes or turning captives into slaves. Then we let the strangers into our lives, and because we were not one, we became weak and could not fight them anymore. Firewalker became angry with us and destroyed earth and everything on it. These people are all that's left. They lived to come back to us when it would have been easier to die. They came to help us change. Singing Bird went back to that time and led them here. I was born to help change our fate, too. This is what my power is for. For you! For them! For all the people everywhere, so that in the long time to come, better choices will be made, and Firewalker's anger will never burn, and people of all nations and colors will not die."

"This Firewalker. Is this a spirit?" Votan asked.

"No, it was a solid mass, alive and burning as it fell from the sky."

They frowned and began whispering to each other.

"We have never seen such a thing and do not believe this is possible," Votan said. "If you have this great power, then show us what Firewalker is like."

"You want to see Firewalker and his wrath?" Tyhen asked.

"Yes, yes, we want to see," Votan said. "It is why we came."

Tyhen walked all the way down the temple steps until she was standing on the playa in front of them.

"Then look into my eyes."

Chapter Four

The shamans moved closer.

Tyhen didn't retreat and, without hesitation, took herself back onto the Navajo Reservation; to the Canyon de Chelly and Layla Birdsong's race to save her people. And when she went, she took them with her.

Although no one else could see what they were seeing, it was immediately obvious the shamans were shaken by their first glimpses of the future. They drew closer together, holding onto each other in fear of what was before them and seeing things for which they had no name. They saw a massive gathering of people and the cars they came in, the motorcycles on which they sat, the strange clothing and burned faces and bleeding lips, the land without trees or water.

In their frame of reference, they were seeing thousands of people in great distress, walking among large shiny demons that made growling noises as they rolled, and sometimes spewed smoke and swallowed people, only to spit them out as they chose, still alive and in one piece and uneaten.

They saw the fireball in the sky and death all around as the people moved through the barren canyons. They saw babies crying, people dying, and animals attacking people and the same animals attacking each other.

When they saw Layla Birdsong leading the way on the motorcycle Niyol left behind, the strange clothing that she wore, and the vast numbers of people behind her, they were in awe that it was a woman who led them.

The farther Tyhen took them, the hotter it became until sweat ran down their faces and their eyes were squinting against the great Firewalker's glare. Their breathing was becoming labored, as if they, too, were on the march.

When their lips dried, cracked, and then began to bleed, Votan moaned. He wanted it to stop but he couldn't look away. The shaman beside him suddenly grabbed his chest and dropped down to his knees, his face contorted with pain.

"Make it stop. Make it stop."

Tyhen didn't hear them. In her head she was safe within Layla's belly, but still with the people.

One shaman suddenly looked up, then screamed and covered his face, but it was too late. Firewalker had taken his sight.

When the shamans' skin began to blister, their guards stepped back in fear and turned away, afraid that what was happening to the shamans they'd been sent to guard would happen to them as well.

The shamans were trembling, their muscles jerking with spasms. In their heads, they were running now, running with the woman who led them, running through a land of canyons devoid of everything but rocks and sand and they knew they were going to die. Their bodies burned as with terrible fevers, and the smell of cooking flesh was in the air. The fireball in the sky was coming closer and growing hotter. People who had been running began to falter and fall. One shaman began to weep. Another prayed for a quick death and still they watched because she wouldn't let go.

Just when they believed they could not take another step, they saw the portal begin to open, and the people ran toward it with the renewed hope that they would not die after all.

The shamans felt as if they were running with them and understood the portal meant salvation. It wasn't until they saw who held it open that they realized the Old Ones had come to save them. And so they ran for their lives while the world behind them exploded and burned.

The moment they were through the portal, Tyhen blinked. Released from her vision, the shamans dropped, crying and moaning from the pain.

She saw the shamans prostrate on the ground before her. All of them had suffered burns in varying degrees. Some were openly weeping, stunned by the devastation they had seen. The one who had been struck blind was dying, and the one who'd grabbed his chest was already dead.

Tyhen had not known that would happen to them, but the moment that thought went through her head, she heard Adam's voice.

You only did what they asked.

She turned around and looked up at the twins. They were watching her and they were right. She had only done what they asked.

Votan lifted his hand. "You are a woman of great power. We saw Firewalker and we saw the New Ones. We saw them suffer and we saw them dying. Forgive our doubts. Forgive our hurtful words. Forgive me."

"I'm sorry for your pain, but I only did as you asked. I don't need your apologies. I need all of you to go back to your people and tell them what you saw. Send your visions to other shamans. Send them as far as they will go and keep them moving. Fighting among ourselves made us weak. We lost our way and Firewalker destroyed the world. In the days to come, New Ones will come into your cities to share their knowledge. They know where we went wrong. We have to be smarter and stronger so when the strangers come, we meet them united—many tribes but one people.

Votan moaned. "Yes, I will. We will."

Women began coming out of the crowd and offering water to the shamans while others came to tend to their wounds and carry away the dead. A short time later, they were seen staggering out of the city far less confrontational than when they'd come in.

Cayetano hated what had happened. It brought a dark cloud on what should have been a week of celebration and he blamed Ah Kin.

He turned and pointed at his shaman. "We will talk."

Ah Kin was picking nervously at a scab on his arm, oblivious that it had begun to bleed, and when he saw the look on Cayetano's face, he turned and scurried back up the temple steps.

"End the ceremony, my love," Singing Bird said softly.

Cayetano lifted his arms and smiled at the mass of people before him.

"The discord is behind us. The festival has begun. It is time to celebrate the good harvest. Eat. Feast. Thank the gods for what they have given us."

The cheer that rose from the crowd was so loud that all the birds from the nearby jungle took flight. There were so many colors in the sky at once that it looked as if a rainbow had just shattered into a million pieces.

Yuma was in awe of how Tyhen had handled the incident and whispered in her ear.

"It is good. They see you now as the peacemaker... the dove, but you do not fly in fear like your feathered friends."

She was exhausted, but at peace. The thing she had dreaded was behind her. She leaned against him, grateful for his presence.

"I have no fear with you at my side," she said softly.

Yuma's heart swelled. Today he had seen the woman she would become.

"What can I do for you?"

"I wish to separate myself from this festival, at least for a while until people have some time to forget about what happened."

Yuma slid a hand beneath her hair, cupping the back of her neck. He could feel the tension in her body and could only guess what it had cost her to show the shamans that vision.

"I'll take you back. It appears Cayetano has business with Ah Kin, and your mother is already making her guards nervous as she walks away with old friends."

Tyhen saw her mother leaving with Shirley Nantay and an assortment of young children, most of whom were her students. The family had long since grown used to Singing Bird's dual allegiance. They knew she loved her family more than her own life, but a part of her heart would always be with the New Ones.

Tyhen was still watching the animation on her mother's face when her attention suddenly shifted to Adam and Evan. They came running, both talking at once.

"Ah Kin is in trouble," Evan said.

"And Cayetano is furious," Adam added.

"As he should be," Yuma said. "I'm taking Tyhen back to the palace to rest."

"We're coming, too," Adam said.

Evan grinned. "The young women are flirting. It makes Adam nervous."

Adam shrugged. "We have no interest in women. It is wasted on us and the easiest way to end it is to remove ourselves. So, let's go. The day is getting hot."

They started back to the palace, making their way through the festival-happy crowd. Tyhen was happy just walking at Yuma's side and listening to the chatter when all the voices began to fade.

She was looking down, but she didn't see the stark white limestone pathways on which she was walking or the sandals on her feet. Instead, some kind of thick fur had been wrapped and tied around her feet all the way up to her knees. Her clothing was heavy and strange, and the cloak covering her entire body was made of some kind of animal skin. She could see the animal from which it had come, but did not have a name for it, and she didn't know where she was.

As she walked, something white was falling from the sky. The air hurt her face, and when it went up her nose it burned. She was sad—so sad, but she didn't know why.

By the time they reached the palace, the tears were so thick in her throat she was afraid to open her mouth for fear she'd scream. This would be her last festival and she would be gone from everyone she loved, gone from Naaki Chava, never to return.

She stumbled. When she would have fallen, Yuma steadied her stride and his presence was an affirmation of what was promised to her in the midst of her pain. She would not be gone from Yuma. He would be always at her side and it would be enough.

****

Ah Kin had run up the temple steps into the door at the top, then down the inner stairs to his chambers. He stopped just inside the room, eyeing the place that had long been his home, remembering how he had come here as a novice.

Back then, he'd only had the gift of sight and had been taught the other tricks and deceptions practiced by the older shamans. Now he knew how to create illusion, and how to incite people with mythology and fear. He'd known everything there was to know about staying in power, and it had been enough until Singing Bird returned with the New Ones. After that, it began to go fade.

Chak, their oldest shaman, had betrayed Cayetano and died with the chief's spear in his back. Another shaman died a year later from snake bite. One by one, the shamans died from natural causes, leaving Ah Kin as the last, and this pitiful existence was all he had left.

A torch burned from a stand near the table where

he took his meals, highlighting the thin layer of dust that covered everything in the room. It was a shock, seeing it with new eyes, even more proof of how he'd been deluding himself.

He had no place to hide. He'd gambled on the visiting shamans being able to turn the people against Cayetano and his daughter, but he'd lost. He could try and sneak out while the festival was in full swing, but he was an old man and there was no way he could trek through the jungle to another city safely, nor did he have any hope of finding a place for himself there if he tried. He closed his eyes and concentrated, looking for a vision that would tell him what to do, but he got nothing.

When he began to hear voices, he panicked. Cayetano was coming. He hadn't expected him this soon. So did he stay and face the great chief's wrath, or end this his way now? The answer was a given as he ran into an anteroom, then to a large, lidded jar on the floor next to a prayer altar.

His hands were shaking as he removed the lid, then took a deep breath and thrust his arm into the jar, waiting for the strike. When the snake's long, saber-like fangs pierced the flesh in his wrist and the fire began crawling up the inside of his arm, he wet himself.

The Fer de Lance venom was deadly and already coursing through his body as the thick-bodied snake came out of the jar. Ah Kin stood up and staggered backward, hit a wall and slid down onto his backside as the snake slithered to the doorway and out of sight.

Seconds later, Ah Kin's eyes rolled back in his head as the muscles in his body began to seize. The venom was destroying tissue with every heartbeat. Soon everything inside him began to bleed. The first tiny droplets of blood came out as tears. Then he began to bleed from his ears and from his nose, then from the corners of his mouth. The voices he'd heard earlier were closer now, but they would be too late. He would escape Cayetano after all.

****

Cayetano found Ah Kin lying in a pool of blood, then saw the empty jar and the lid lying on the floor. When he saw the bite mark on his wrist, he knew what Ah Kin had done, and why.

"The Fer de Lance is loose. Find it and kill it."

A half-dozen of his guards raised their torches and left to search the temple while the others stayed at his side, awaiting his orders. He had no empathy for the dead man at his feet and wanted him gone. He turned away in disgust as he picked out four of the guards.

"Take him away."

The four guards saw the fury in his eyes and the jerk of muscles along his jaw and were almost afraid to ask.

"And what should we do with his body?"

He tossed his head as if the answer was obvious. "He betrayed me and he is a disgrace to our ancestors. Burn it." He then strode out of the temple with the rest of the guards at his heels.

****

It was a relief to get back to the palace and out of the

growing heat of the day. Acat was at the festival, as were most of the servants, so it was Yuma who was left to tend to Tyhen. Her behavior was strange and it was beginning to concern him.

The twins went to the kitchen in search of food, leaving them alone. When they got to her room, he took off her sandals and the heavy turquoise collar she'd been wearing, then dipped a cloth in the basin of water and began wiping her face and neck, trying to cool her skin. She was shaking, and he thought it was from the heat and exhaustion. He had no way of knowing she was still locked into a vision and getting her first taste of what it was like to be cold.

He poured some water into a cup and then lifted her head, urging her to drink.

"Just take a sip, Tyhen. It will cool you."

But she couldn't hear him. She was no longer in the land of cold and white, but in the jungle watching a mountain breaking apart and wondering if they were going to die. Smoke and rocks were shooting into the air while a river of fire flowed down the side, sweeping everything away in its path. In her head she was screaming the word "run," but she couldn't tell who was with her, only that she wasn't alone.

Unaware of what was happening to her, Yuma poured a tiny bit of water into her mouth.

The moment it hit Tyhen's tongue she choked and coughed. And just like that, the vision was gone. She was in her room, and Yuma was kneeling at her side.

"I had a vision."

Yuma saw the tears in her eyes, laid the wet cloth aside, and pulled her into his lap. He smiled as she settled easily into the familiarity of his embrace.

"Tell me," he said.

"This is my last festival."

His heart skipped a beat. "No. You aren't old enough to—"

"What is old enough? I have a purpose and it has been shown to me. There is nothing more to be said."

He bowed his head and closed his eyes, trying not to think of the dangers within the impossible tasks lying ahead of them. But he'd pledged his love and life to her the day she'd been born. Now it was time to make good on that promise.

"So when does this happen?" he asked.

"I'm not sure, but soon in the days to come. There are many things I need to learn first and I will learn them from the New Ones."

"What can I do to help you?" he asked.

She laid a hand on his chest. "Just help me stay strong, as strong as your heart."

He swallowed past the lump in his throat. "It will be done," he said softly. "But not today, not during the festival."

She leaned closer.

"We will do it after the festival?"

"Yes. We will do it after."

****

After the discovery of Ah Kin's body, Cayetano went to find Singing Bird. He had no stomach for celebrating today, yet he would not leave her down in the city without him. But when the people saw their chief and his guards coming through the streets, they ran out with food and drink, wanting to share their bounty.

Cayetano and his guards accepted graciously and his disposition improved as the food settled in his belly. They ate as they walked, following the drum sounds all the way to the sector where the New Ones lived.

He didn't come down into the city often, but every time he did, he could see the changes in the people's lifestyle and the influences the New Ones had brought to their world.

The streets in Naaki Chava were made of limestone-type bricks like the playa surrounding the temple, but the small bamboo huts and thatched roofs the people had always lived in were slowly being replaced with what Singing Bird called houses, like smaller versions of the palace.

They had found different uses for the edible plants growing wild in the jungle that they'd taken back into the city and cultivated into their fields.

They trapped young tapirs in the jungle then carried them back to their homes, put them in pens and fed them out for killing as needed, instead of having to always go hunt. A few years back, some traders from the mountains had come in with birds they called chickens that laid an egg every day and raw wool, which the women turned into blankets. The cotton grown in the Naaki Chava fields, they turned into their style of clothing. Now, after some bargaining, the traders came at least twice, sometimes three times a year, keeping the New Ones in chickens and wool. In return for the shelter the New Ones had been given, they had brought a new way of life to Naaki Chava.

As Cayetano neared the houses where the Nantay brothers lived, the drumming was so loud he could feel the beat inside his chest, and the singing that accompanied it made the hair rise on the back of his neck. He didn't understand the words. Singing Bird said it was in the Navajo language, but he liked how the rise and fall of the voices matched the rhythm of the drumbeat.

He quickened his step, anxious to see the dancers in their ceremonial dress. It was unlike anything the people in Naaki Chava wore, but beautiful just the same.

He was greeted warmly as he walked toward their dwelling, but his gaze was on the crowd around the drummers. Singing Bird would be somewhere nearby. And then he saw her still wearing her ceremonial dress, but with more feathers in her hair in the tradition of Layla Birdsong's Muscogee tribe.

It was always hard to watch, knowing there was a part of her heart and memories that he would never be able to share, but it was part of his penance for helping create the discord that had led to Firewalker's wrath.

Within seconds of his arrival, it was obvious Singing Bird had sensed his presence. She suddenly turned, scanning the crowd until she saw him, then lifted her arm into the air and waved.

And just like that, the spark of Cayetano's jealousy was gone and he felt nothing but gratitude that she was alive and well and still his woman.

He moved toward her, threading his way through the crowd, and as soon as the people saw who it was, they gave way. She slipped a hand beneath his arm and gave him a questioning look, knowing he'd gone to confront the old shaman. He shrugged as if to say it was over, then turned his attention to the dancers and the drums and let the beat flow through him.

Chapter Five

In the ensuing days, Tyhen threw herself into the festivities and only Yuma knew why. She was making memories, and in a way, also saying good-bye to a way of life she would leave behind. While his heart hurt for her, there was a part of him that was ready to leave. He wanted to go home, even though he accepted that what was there would be unrecognizable to what he'd known. But he wanted to breathe the air and walk the land, and he believed he would feel the connection in his soul. He ached for the chance to help his people, the Cherokee, escape Firewalker's wrath.

The third day of the festival was the day of games, and teams had been practicing for weeks. The traditional stick ball games were for the men and always a popular one to watch, but it was the thing the New Ones played that Tyhen liked best. They called it called baseball and she'd grown up playing it with the children her mother taught. Although she was a child no more, it didn't matter. The game was played by people of all ages. They hit a ball with a stick, then ran around designated places on the ground they called bases. It was easy to hit the ball. The hard part was running around all four bases before someone threw the ball back. She had long legs and she could run. She wanted to play ball again, to run with the wind in her hair and the sun on her face and know the only thing to worry about was beating the throw that would put her out.

She was digging through the trunk that held her clothing, looking for one particular shift. It was comfortable and old and easy to run in, but she hadn't had it on it in many months.

As soon as she found it, she stripped out of her other clothing and pulled it over her head. It was a little tighter across the chest, but that was because her breasts had grown. Even more disconcerting was the fact it was now at least a hand's width above her knees. She pulled a little, trying to stretch it and then shrugged. It didn't matter. She was only going to play. She was wearing sandals to walk down to the city, but she would play ball in her bare feet, and was so excited to be going that she was almost bouncing as she left her room.

Acat caught up with her in the hall and made noises about the less-than-ceremonial style of her clothing, but Tyhen just laughed and waved her away.

"I go to play ball," she said.

"You do not go alone," Acat said.

Tyhen frowned. "I have before."

"But this is festival and there are many strangers in the city. It might not be safe."

Tyhen sighed. She hadn't thought of that. Already, the glow had been taken off the day. She was still standing in the hall, trying to figure out what to do next when Yuma came around a corner. The moment he saw her he lengthened his stride.

Tyhen's heart skipped a beat. Just watching him walk made her belly ache. His face was pleasing to her eyes. She'd seen him without clothing plenty of times, but all of a sudden the thought of standing before him without her clothes seemed daring, even shocking. Heat rose within her, flushing her face.

Before she had time to gather her thoughts, he was talking and she had to concentrate to catch up on the conversation.

"... are you going?"

"What? What did you say?" she asked.

He smiled. "I asked, where are you going?"

"I wanted to go play ball with the New Ones, but Acat says I cannot go alone."

He glanced at Acat. "I will take her and stay with her until the game is done."

Acat nodded, confident she'd done her part to keep Tyhen safe. She was still uneasy that she'd let Tyhen get away from her in the market the day the big bird tried to take the baby, and didn't want a repeat of that incident or something worse.

"Can we go now?" Tyhen asked.

"Yes. I just need to deliver a message to Singing Bird on the way out."

She followed him to the kitchen, then out through the back door. "How do you know where she is?"

"The twins told me."

"Is anything wrong?" she asked.

"No. Nothing is wrong. They wanted to let her know that some of the New Ones who had moved away a few years ago have come back for the festival."

He stopped to pull a strand of hair out of her eyelashes then smoothed it down into place. It wasn't anything he hadn't done before, but to Tyhen, it felt different. He was so close she could see the bead of sweat rolling out of his hairline. The urge to touch him was so strong she physically shuddered and looked away.

Unaware of her thoughts, Yuma held her hand as they walked through the garden, satisfied just to be with her.

"There she is," Tyhen said, pointing toward the clearing where they grew squash and corn.

Singing Bird heard them, looked up, and waved, then picked up the basket of vegetables she'd just gathered and started back to the palace. Yuma ran to meet her, relieving her of her burden as they walked back together to Tyhen.

Singing Bird took one look at her daughter's clothing and frowned.

"That is not suitable for the festival."

"I go to play ball," Tyhen said.

"You are the daughter of the chief. You should not—"

Tyhen lifted her head; her eyes suddenly blurred with unshed tears.

"No, Mother, I am the Windwalker's daughter and this will be my last festival. Allow me to pretend one more time that my life is still my own."

Singing Bird reeled as if she'd been slapped. Her chin quivered as she struggled not to cry, then she gave up and threw her arms around her daughter, too stunned to let go.

Tyhen was shaking from the sudden burst of emotion as she wrapped her arms around her mother's neck and rested her chin on the top of Singing Bird's head. It was strange to be a child so tall with a mother so small.

Singing Bird felt Tyhen's sorrow and looked up, then frowned and wiped the tears from her daughter's cheeks.

"I am sorry. I did not plan this, or ever dream your life would be this way."

Tyhen sighed. "It's not your fault. It is my destiny. I'm sorry I acted so childishly."

Singing Bird shook her head and then gave Tyhen a gentle push. "Go and play. Run with the wind."

Tyhen smiled. "Yes, I can do that."

Yuma's heart was sad for both mother and daughter, but like Tyhen, his path had been chosen for him as well. He'd just had a longer time to get used to it, and he remembered he still hadn't delivered his message to Singing Bird.

"Adam and Evan sent me to tell you that Betty Tiger is at the festival. You will find her at her parents' home."

Singing Bird's heart was breaking. She had not expected Tyhen's journey to begin so soon, but she would not let her know how she felt. Having the excuse of old friends to see was perfect timing.

"This is wonderful news, but I have dirt on my clothing and have to change." She took the basket from Yuma's hands. "Go enjoy your time, daughter. I will see you later." Then she hurried away.

"She's sad," Yuma said.

Tyhen shrugged. "So am I."

Yuma frowned. "What can I do to make this better?"

"Take me down to the city."

****

Whack!

The impact of the handmade baseball against the bat was music to Tyhen's ears. It was the pitch she had been waiting for and the ball sailed over the pitcher's head in a perfect arc. She was already running past first and heading to second when the ball began to descend. She was on her way to third base when the boy in the field dropped the ball.

At that point, her legs were stretched out in a long, rapid stride. Her hair was flying out behind her, her arms churning against her side as her bare feet kicked up dust with every step.

"Run, whirlwind, run!" Yuma yelled, laughing and cheering with the rest of her team as she rounded third and headed for home.

The fielder was scrambling to get a grip on the ball. His throw was strong, but Tyhen's legs were long. She was almost home before the ball left his hand.

She caught sight of the ball from the corner of her eye as it sailed past the pitcher. She threw herself into a slide. The shift she was wearing rode up her legs as she slid into home in a cloud of dust.

"Safe!" the umpire called.

Tyhen was grinning as she got up dusting off her backside. She looked around for Yuma and saw him laughing and cheering just before her teammates came rushing to congratulate her. Her home run had won the game.

"Tyhen! Tyhen!" they shouted while laughing and clapping her on the back.

The sun was in her eyes and she could taste blood where she'd bitten her lip as she slid home, but this was a feeling she would never forget. Someone thrust a cup of juice in her hand. She drank it thirstily then handed it back for another.

The players began gathering up their belongings, making way for yet another pair of teams to compete. They could have stayed to watch, but Tyhen was hungry and Yuma was waiting.

One of her teammates patted her on the back, still smiling from the victory. "You are so fast! You have to promise be on our team every festival," she said.

And just like that, the joy was over. Tyhen managed to keep the smile on her face as she nodded in agreement, but that was never going to happen. When Yuma came up behind her and slipped a hand around her waist, she leaned against him.

"I'll bet you're tired and I know you're hungry," he said. "Let's go find something to eat."

Even though she felt hollow inside, she kept a smile on her face as she nodded in agreement.

"That hit was amazing!" Yuma said.

"It made a loud noise," she said.

"Sounded like a gunshot," Yuma said, then caught himself. She might not remember what that meant, but when she didn't comment, he realized where her thoughts had gone and knew there was nothing he could say to make it better.

****

Singing Bird visited with the friends she'd invited to the palace and ate the food she served them without giving herself away. She hid her sorrow as they left and continued to keep it within her all through the evening, until the sun was gone.

She was standing at the window, staring up at the moon, when emotion finally overwhelmed her. She dropped to her knees and began to sob. It was a full-circle moment. She'd lost Niyol in the Arizona canyons, and now she was losing his daughter as well. This wasn't right. It wasn't fair. She'd sacrificed herself to change Cayetano's fate and fallen in love with the spirit he became. Now she was losing the child she'd made with the Windwalker, and it was like losing him all over again. How many times could a heart break before it quit beating?

Cayetano heard her crying before he opened the door, and the sound lent speed to his steps. He raced into their quarters, slamming the door behind him as he scooped her up in his arms.

"My love! My heart! What has happened to make you so sad?"

She just shook her head and covered her face as he carried her to their bed. His voice was gruff, betraying his building anger and concern.

"Has someone harmed you? Did they insult you? I will find them and break their neck."

"No, no, nothing like that," she said and began wiping her face, trying to get her emotions under control. The last thing they needed was for Cayetano to go on a rampage. "Tyhen told me this will be her last festival. She will be gone from Naaki Chava within the year and we will never see her again."

Cayetano closed his eyes against the pain. This was his fault, his penance, his price to pay. The woman he loved more than life had not only sacrificed herself to save his soul and their people, but now she was sacrificing her only child to the quest as well.

"I am sorry."

Singing Bird heard the devastation in his voice, quickly wiped away her tears, and put her arms around his neck.

"No, it is not your doing any more than mine. It is what it is, and that is all. I'm just sad, but this happens to many parents. Children pick their partner and walk away to a new life. It is how life is meant to be lived. I have you, my love, I have you, and it will always be enough."

Her sorrow had shredded his soul. He loved her so much it hurt to draw breath. "You are my heart. If you cry, it does not beat."

She stood up, unwrapped her shift, letting it fall to the floor at her feet.

Cayetano dropped his own clothing and laid her down on their bed. He was already erect and aching as he slid into the warmth between her legs. No matter how many times he made love to his woman, it always felt like their first time, back when they were young and their blood was hot, back when it was magic.

****

Tyhen was dreaming. She knew it was a dream because although the wind was blowing, she could not feel it on her face. Her throat hurt and there was blood all over her fingers, but she couldn't remember why. She heard people crying and screaming and before she could figure out what had happened, Acat was leaning over her and shaking her shoulder and Yuma was running into the room.

He dropped to his knees beside her bed and laid his hand on her forehead, feeling for a fever.

Tyhen pushed his hand away and frowned at Acat. "What's the matter with you two?"

"You screamed," Acat said.

"Like you were being murdered," Yuma added.

At that point, Cayetano came running with two of his guards behind him. "What happened?" he yelled.

Tyhen sighed. "I am sorry. I am sorry. It was a dream."

Singing Bird slipped into the room and quickly sent the guards away and sent Acat to the kitchen for a sleeping potion for Tyhen. Once they were alone, she closed the door and turned to face her daughter.

"It has begun," she said.

Tyhen frowned. "What has begun?"

"You are not dreaming. You are having visions of what will be," Singing Bird said.

Tyhen sat up. Her voice was shaking, her eyes wide with shock. "The other night I dreamed a mountain exploded and fire ran like water from its mouth. That cannot be."

"A volcano," Yuma said.

Singing Bird nodded.

Tyhen covered her face. "You mean that thing is real?"

"I have seen such a thing," Cayetano said as he smoothed the hair from her face. "But it was a long time ago when I was a child, before we came here to Naaki Chava. Many people died."

Tyhen shuddered.

"What did you see tonight?" Yuma asked.

"My throat was hurting and there was blood all over my hands. People were standing all around me. Some were crying and some were praying."

Singing Bird frowned. "Were you hurt?"

She shook her head. "I don't know. I woke up."

Singing Bird frowned at Yuma.

"I will never be far away," he said softly.

Singing Bird's shoulders sagged. At that moment she felt helpless and old. When Acat came back with the sleeping drink, instead of giving it to Tyhen, Singing Bird drank it herself, then excused herself and left.

Tyhen felt broken, helpless to recreate the safety of home.

Yuma saw the pain and fear on her face and couldn't walk away.

"I will stay with you," he said.

Acat lay down on her sleeping mat and turned her face to the wall.

"Lie down, little whirlwind," he said softly.

"I won't sleep," Tyhen said as she crawled back onto her bed and rolled over on her side.

"Then neither will I," he said and got into the bed behind her, put his arm over her body, and pulled her close.

Shocked by the intimacy, Tyhen was trembling so hard she could barely breathe, but when he didn't move again, she began to relax. She never felt the skip her heart took as it shifted into the rhythm of Yuma's pulse. All she felt was the wash of comfort roll through her as she closed her eyes.

Chapter Six

The last day of the festival was bittersweet for Singing Bird. All of her old friends who'd made the trek to Naaki Chava were packing up to go home, making farewells difficult to face.

Singing Bird sent several packets of new books she'd made down to them and had already said her good-byes. She was putting up a brave front, but her heart was breaking. All too soon she would be waving good-bye to Yuma and Tyhen, too. She didn't know if the twins were going to go with them, but if all four of her children left at once, she would be lost.

Cayetano was in the throne room settling a dispute that had arisen between three families during the festival. It was too soon for Singing Bird to resume her classes, so she started toward the kitchen. Even though she was the chief's woman, everyone worked and today she needed to stay busy.

The door to Tyhen's room was open as she passed. Thinking she might be inside, she stopped and went back, but it was empty. Then she remembered she'd seen her leaving with Yuma and the twins. She started to leave, then stopped and gave the layout of the room a second look.

Tyhen slept in a bed that was not on the floor like the beds the New Ones slept in, while Acat preferred the woven sleeping mats from the old ways. But it was the sight of Acat's bed that had Singing Bird thinking. Originally she had stayed as a nursemaid and a servant, but Tyhen didn't need that any longer. Truthfully, the only person Tyhen needed now was Yuma.

Singing Bird knew and accepted sex as a natural way of life, and since she was looking for a job to keep her busy, she decided this was it. It was time to give Tyhen a room of her own.

The first thing she did was roll up Acat's sleeping mat and then left with it under her arm. She and Acat came back a few minutes later with more bedding and another small shelf and table. After moving the bed from one side of the room to the other, she stood back to look.

"Acat! Bring new candles and torches and send one of the girls with a pitcher of fresh water, and two cups for the table."

Acat giggled. "You make a place for Tyhen and Yuma."

Singing Bird shrugged. "It is time."

"He is very handsome and very tall," Acat said.

Singing Bird nodded. "His people were from a tribe called the Cherokee. Many of them came here."

Acat stopped, eyeing Singing Bird carefully, remembering when she'd first come with the New Ones that she'd been different, too.

"Was that your tribe?" she asked.

Singing Bird stopped, letting memories wash over her. Her eyes were filled with tears when she looked up.

"My father was Muscogee. My grandfather was Navajo."

"But they did not come," Acat said.

Singing Bird's voice was shaking. "My father died when I was younger. My grandfather died on the walk to Naaki Chava."

Acat heard the sorrow in Singing Bird's voice. "Then that is good. They did not have to face Firewalker," she said.

Singing Bird turned around and looked at Acat in amazement. "You are right, and I never thought of it like that before. Thank you, Acat. Thank you for that. It has given me a different way to look at their absence in my life."

Acat beamed. "I will get torches and candles now."

"Don't forget the water and cups."

"I will not forget," Acat said and hurried away.

Singing Bird moved from bed, to table, to shelf, touching this and moving that, continuing all around the room until she was back at the bed again. If Tyhen and Yuma had not already been together, it would happen soon. She wanted her daughter to be happy and feared those days would be few and far between.

****

Adam and Evan were the obvious choices to take over the duties of the temple until or if Cayetano decided to replace the shamans. However, they had already announced they would not live in it. It was too reminiscent of where they *had* lived before Firewalker.

Landon Prince, the man responsible for the experiment resulting in their births, had accumulated a massive collection of mystic and magic items, and the temple was a dark reminder of that time. The good part about Firewalker was that it had killed Landon Prince before he killed them. And now that they were here in Naaki Chava, they didn't need illusion and tricks to be the eyes and ears for Cayetano. What they knew was real.

By the time they reached the temple, a large number of people were waiting. The men in the group would do the heavy lifting and the women would clean. But as everyone started inside, Tyhen hung back.

Yuma saw the dark frown on her face and picked up on her reluctance. "Is everything okay?"

"No."

Adam looked back. "Are you coming?"

She repeated her answer. "No. I am not welcome there."

Evan frowned. "What do you mean?"

"The spirits do not want me."

Adam frowned. "We will perform a cleansing ceremony after we finish, and clear the air of any angry spirits."

"I want no part of it," she said, still remembering what she'd dealt with at the gorge.

"We will see you later," Yuma said and led her away.

She was quiet as they walked.

Yuma had his spear, so instead of walking back through the city, the fact that he was armed made him comfortable enough to take the trail through the jungle that led back to the palace. It would be a change of scenery and hopefully take her mind off of dark things.

Little did Yuma know, but Tyhen's mind was not on dark things, but on the rise and fall of Yuma's chest, and the way his hair moved against his neck with the rhythm of his stride. Everything about him was pleasing to her eyes. She thought about the journey to come in the days ahead, and what it would be like to take it with him. She already trusted him, and she had love *for* him, but she had yet to share that love *with* him.

"What are you thinking?" Yuma asked.

Tyhen was taken aback that he'd asked her that question when the answer would have been "thinking of you." Instead, she gave him a less specific response.

"The uncertainty of our future."

He took her hand as he set his spear against a tree. "We may not know the details of what we'll find or the dangers we'll face, but we know what we're supposed to do. That is a given, as are the feelings I have for you. There is nothing uncertain about that, and I have never denied them or hidden them from you."

"I know, but—"

He put a thumb over her mouth. "The word 'but' does not exist between us."

He took her hand and pressed it over his heart, then put the flat of his hand on her breasts. Her face flushed, but she stood her ground.

"Feel that?" he asked.

"I feel your heartbeat."

"No. Close your eyes," he said softly, and then when she did, he asked again. "Do you feel it now?"

For a few moments she didn't move, and then all of a sudden her eyes flew open, her lips parting in amazement.

"They beat in rhythm! Our hearts beat at the same time, at the same pace!"

He pulled her close, so close he could feel the warmth of her breath against his face.

"Apart, we are a man and a woman. Together, we are one."

Tyhen shivered. The ache to know him was strong.

Yuma could see the want in her eyes. This day had been a long time coming. "Only you, little whirlwind, can tell me when to stop."

He cupped her cheeks, slid his mouth across her lips, centering on the warmth and settling into the kiss like they had done it a thousand times before.

When the world began to spin, Tyhen put her arms around his neck. It was better than she could have ever imagined and then it was not enough. Her heart was pounding and there was a knot in the pit of her stomach.

Yuma didn't dare take his hands from her face for fear of where he'd put them next. He'd known forever that the kiss would never be enough, and then she moaned.

He tore his mouth from her lips.

She staggered then opened her eyes. "I didn't say to stop."

"But I heard—"

She grabbed his shoulders in frustration.

"What you heard is my pain. I ache for you, Yuma, only you. I belong to you. I want to be with you."

Yuma leaned forward until their foreheads were touching, and this time he was the one who groaned.

"I have waited a long time to hear these words, but here is not the place. I cannot put you in danger, and laying you down in the middle of the jungle is that and more."

He felt her frustration as she hid her face against his chest. "Walk with me," he said and took her hand.

When she acquiesced without a sound, he picked up his spear and turned around.

"Where are we going?" she asked.

"Back to the palace."

Her heart sank. It was an impossible place to be when all she wanted was to be alone with him.

"When we get there, I will find a place where we can be alone, and I will ask you again if you are sure."

Tyhen's heart soared. She turned, her eyes flashing. "I said yes here, and I will say yes there, but I will not walk with you."

"But why—?"

"You'll have to catch me." She flashed him a grin and turned around. Leaping forward, she began running back the way they'd come.

Yuma didn't hesitate as he gave chase. He could hear her laughing ahead of him and grinned. Making love to this "woman on the verge" was suddenly out of his control.

****

Tyhen heard Yuma thrashing through the undergrowth behind her and ran like there were wings on her feet. She wanted to be caught, but not too soon. When she burst out of the jungle behind the temple, she was running at full speed and laughing.

Adam saw her first and had a moment of panic. She'd gone in with Yuma, but was coming out alone. And then he saw the joy on her face and heard the laughter and knew it was a game. Seconds later, Yuma ran into view, giving chase.

"Run, Yuma, Run!" Adam shouted.

Evan turned to see the race in progress and added his encouragement, but he was cheering for Tyhen. "Run, little whirlwind! Don't let him catch you!" Evan shouted.

Tyhen's head was down and her legs were flying as she dashed across the playa toward the street leading through the market. It didn't take long for the people there to realize a race was in progress. They quickly joined in the excitement, cheering the chief's daughter as she ran.

Yuma was running hard and slowly gaining, but it wasn't easy. He had watched her play baseball plenty of times, but never realized how fast she really was. If he hadn't needed the breath to run, he would have laughed. She needed this moment of joy as much as he needed her.

Tyhen heard the shouts and laughter, but the faces were a blur. She was all the way through the market and starting up the slope toward the palace when Yuma's shadow suddenly loomed in front of her. Her heart skipped a beat. He was closer than she thought!

Just the thought of being taken down from behind made her lengthen her stride, putting everything she had left into the effort. But her best was not enough as the shadow grew bigger, coming closer and closer. Now she could hear the thump of Yuma's footsteps and the short, rhythmic sound of his breathing.

Her capture was imminent and the joy that shot through her was physical. She looked up at the palace. When she saw it was too far away and she was never going to make it, she started laughing.

Yuma grinned. She knew she was caught and still she wouldn't stop. He dropped his spear and lunged forward, grabbing her left arm and bringing her to a sudden halt.

She spun around so fast he nearly fell on her, and then she launched herself at him, throwing her arms around his neck.

"You caught me!" she cried.

"Yes I did," he said, laughing. He swung her off her feet and threw her over his shoulder, then pointed at a young boy who was standing nearby. "Boy! Hand me my spear!"

The boy bolted out from behind the table where he'd been standing and grabbed the spear, then ran all the way back to Yuma, excited to be touching the weapon of such a mighty warrior.

Yuma nodded his approval, then winked as the boy laughed and ran off. Yuma shifted his load to a more comfortable position and started toward the palace with Tyhen hanging upside down, laughing hysterically.

****

After making the changes to Tyhen's room, Singing Bird tried to focus on something else, but to no avail. She took a piece of fruit out to her bench near the entrance overlooking the city below. It was one of her favorite places to rest. She began peeling back the skin with her fingers and took a small bite, but the taste didn't tempt her and began feeding it to the tiny monkeys who came down from the trees. Usually, they made her laugh, but not today. Instead, she took a deep, shuddering breath, swallowing past the knot in her throat as she gazed down into the city, then realized she couldn't see for the tears.

"Why, Niyol, why? Why didn't you warn me this would happen? Wasn't what we lost to Firewalker enough? You were a greedy messenger of death, taking my only child, too. I hate you! I will hate you with every breath in my body for the rest of my life."

Cayetano walked up behind her in time to hear her angry vow and quickly sat down beside her. The monkeys scampered back up into the trees as he took her in his arms.

"No, Singing Bird, no. Listen to what you say. It was hate that began all of this, remember?"

She covered her face and began to sob. Her voice was trembling, her shoulders shaking with every breath. "I don't know how to give her up."

Every sob was like a knife in Cayetano's heart, and a reminder that all of this turmoil fell back on him and what he'd done so long ago. He pulled her into his arms and held her tight, then tighter still.

"I'm sorry. I'm so sorry, my little bird. Forgive me. Please forgive me."

It was the utter sorrow in his voice that pulled Singing Bird back from the edge. She began wiping away her tears as she turned to face him.

"There is nothing to forgive and it is long since over. It was just a moment of weakness and I let it in. I beg your forgiveness. This is not how the wife of the chief of Naaki Chava should behave."

He took her hands and kissed them both and then placed them on his chest. "What can I do to make you happy?" he asked.

In the moment of silence before she spoke, they suddenly realized there was more than the usual amount of noise coming from the heart of the city. They stood up and looked down the road toward the marketplace.

"What is happening down there?" she asked.

Cayetano pointed. "There! Someone is running!"

Singing Bird gasped. "It's Tyhen! Something must be wrong!"

Cayetano panicked. Where were the guards? Where was Yuma? And the moment he thought the name, he saw the man running behind her.

"Yuma is behind her," Cayetano said. "See! It's only Yuma."

Singing Bird's anxiety subsided. Whatever was happening, he wasn't far behind.

Then the closer they came, the more certain Cayetano became that nothing was wrong. When she started up the slope toward the palace, he could see she was laughing.

"They are racing!" Cayetano said. "See! See! She's laughing."

Singing Bird went weak with relief and grabbed Cayetano's arm.

"And he just caught her," Singing Bird said.

When Tyhen turned and threw herself into Yuma's arms, Singing Bird felt a moment of surprise, and when Yuma threw her over his shoulder, Singing Bird looked up at her husband and then looked away. Maybe it was because she was a woman and saw beneath the obvious, but there was more to that race than speed.

She didn't want to be a witness to what was happening between the boy she'd saved, and the girl she'd born. They didn't need her anymore. Her job now was to come to terms with it.

"I want to go inside now," she said.

He was confused, thinking she would be curious as to what started the race. "But don't you want to—?"

"No, I don't think they need us. Come with me, my love, and leave the celebration to the runners."

"Celebration? What do-?" And then it hit him. "You mean they are—?"

"She has recently faced two frightening adversaries and come out a victor both times. She is a child no longer. We will leave her to what comes next."

When she took Cayetano's hand and led him away, it was a silent nod of permission for Tyhen to step into her own.

****

Yuma carried her all the way up the slope to the palace entrance before he put her down.

Tyhen was weak from laughing and when he put her down, she dropped to her knees, folding her arms across her belly.

"I laughed so hard my stomach hurts."

He grinned. "That is what you get for thinking you can run away from me."

She looked up. "I wanted to be caught." She saw the look on his face and forgot what she was going to say next.

Yuma pulled her to her feet, and without saying a word, led her into the palace. Tyhen's heart began to pound. She couldn't think. All she wanted to do was feel.

The hallways were dim and quiet. They could hear laughter and talking in another part of the palace, but they were moving away from the sounds, rather than closer.

The blood was rushing through Yuma's body at such a pace it made him feel lightheaded. This wasn't just about sex. This was a fulfillment of part of his journey. She was his to protect, even die for, but she was also his to love.

When they reached the hallway leading to the family quarters, Tyhen gripped Yuma's hand. They passed the room where Cayetano and her mother slept. She knew his room was at the far end of the hall, but it also belonged to the twins, too.

"In here," she said softly as she pushed the door to her room open, and then stopped, stunned by the sight of the new, rearranged room.

"What happened in here?" Yuma asked.

She turned to face him. "You happened," she said, then pulled the shift over her head and dropped it at her feet.

He closed the door and shed his clothing where he stood.

They stared at each other without touching while the room and the air began to spin around them.

"What makes this?" he whispered.

"We make it and I am the Windwalker's daughter. Only you can make this stop."

He picked her up in his arms and carried her to the bed while the wind blew her hair in his face. He was surrounded by a scent he could not identify until he laid down beside her and realized it was the scent of her body still sweaty from the run with just a hint of musk. Then he heard the faint sound of drumming as she parted her legs and pulled him to her.

"Make love to me, Yuma, before we both blow away."

He slid between her legs and stopped just before the pain.

She wrapped her fists in his hair and locked her legs around his waist.

"Do it!" she cried and felt the momentary jolt and tearing as he pushed past the barrier.

"I am so sorry," he whispered, but at the moment of joining, all motion inside the room had stopped.

It was as she'd said. Only he could make it stop. He was the anchor that kept the storm at bay.

He began kissing her face and then her lips, then gently licked the tip of each breast, reveling at the softness of her skin and the heat in her eyes.

Tyhen had known *how* to do this, but she could never have imagined the feelings that would result. When he began to move, rocking slowly between her legs, she closed her eyes. The pain was gone and all she wanted was to ride the building heat.

Yuma watched the changing expressions on her face while trying to maintain a steady pace. But she was so tight and hot that it was difficult not to give in and let go.

He was watching for the flush on her cheeks and the flare of her nostrils. He would know when she was ready and he wanted this to be right. But he had not counted on the passion of an untried girl.

"More, Yuma, more," she whispered, digging her fingers into his forearms.

He deepened the stroke, moving faster and harder,

and all of a sudden, her eyes flew open and the stunned expression of ecstasy on her face was something he would never forget. When her lips parted and her eyes rolled back in her head, he felt the muscles inside her body contracting around him. He was no longer in control.

The climax came in mind-numbing waves, one after the other rolling through him and leaving him weak and speechless.

Tyhen hadn't turned loose of Yuma since the first contraction hit her, and now that the climax had passed, she was still holding on. When she felt his shudder, then heard him finally moan, the joy that went through her was palpable. She'd done that! She'd given him that pleasure and she'd made him that weak. Now she understood the depths to which a man would go for the woman he loved.

"Yuma?"

He shifted slightly, rising up on his elbows to look down at her face.

"Is it always like this?" she asked.

"When love is there, yes."

"It was the best thing I ever felt," she said.

He grinned. "It will get better."

She gasped. "No! If it gets better, I might die."

"You won't die, and it does get better."

Her eyes narrowed as the muscles across her belly began to tighten once more. "Show me," she said.

So he did.

****

When Adam and Evan came back from the temple late

that evening and found all of Yuma's things gone from their room, they looked at each other and grinned.

"Finally," Evan said.

Adam shrugged. "It should be no surprise to anyone," he added.

"Except maybe Cayetano?" Evan said.

"No. Singing Bird will smooth the way. She always does."

Evan looked down at his clothing and frowned. "I'm filthy."

"That's because we have about two hundred years of accumulated grime on us. I'm going to the bathing pool. Are you coming?"

Evan nodded. "As soon as I get something clean to wear back."

"Good idea," Adam said as he grabbed a clean wrap and headed out the door behind his brother.

As they left the palace through the back entrance, trouble came in the front.

****

Johnston Nantay came running up the palace steps carrying a large, bulky object wrapped in an animal skin.

"I need to speak with Singing Bird. Tell her it's Nantay and ask her to hurry!"

One of the guards headed inside to get her as Johnston began to pace. When Singing Bird came running out, he heard the panic in her voice.

"Johnston! What's happened? Is someone hurt?"

"No. It's this. You have to see this."

He thrust the parcel in her arms, then waited as

she pulled back the wrapping. When she gasped, his heart sank. He was right. It did mean what he'd thought.

"Where did you get this?"

"A trader brought it, thinking because there were New Ones here that we might know what it was, that we might want it."

Singing Bird was trying not to panic, but the implications were huge.

"Is he still here?" Singing Bird asked.

Johnston nodded, then looked apprehensive when Cayetano came striding out of the doorway.

"What is happening? What is that you are holding, Singing Bird?"

Singing Bird pulled the covering back further to show him.

"It's a piece of stone with runes on it."

He frowned. "What are runes?"

"A race of people called Vikings used them as written language."

"Can you read it?" Johnston asked.

Singing Bird shook her head. "No, but it doesn't matter what it says, so much as where it came from." Her frustration was evident. "This is maddening, not knowing what time in history we are already living, or what damage may have been done to the tribes north and south of us."

"What about the tribes?" Cayetano asked.

Singing Bird sighed. Trying to blend the past with the present was difficult and Cayetano was lost.

Cayetano didn't realize the markings meant, but Johnston knew. Like Singing Bird, he was sick. He didn't want to believe that their Last Walk might have been in vain.

"Do you want to talk to the trader? I will go get him if you do," Johnston said.

"Yes. Bring him here," Singing Bird said.

Johnston turned and ran. It wouldn't be long before it got dark and he didn't want to have to find his way back through the city without a torch.

"Why does this matter?" Cayetano asked, as he walked back inside with Singing Bird.

"It means strangers from across the big water have already been in our world. They have come and gone, which means others will come after them."

Cayetano's eyes widened as realization dawned.

"Then it has already begun?

"Yes, and the people most vulnerable are unaware of what's happening. Find the twins and bring Tyhen and Yuma, too. I want them to see this."

Cayetano didn't bother to send a servant. He went after them himself.

Chapter Seven

The twins washed up quickly, anxious to return to the palace before sunset, and walked inside the back entrance only moments before Cayetano found them.

"Singing Bird needs you now. Go to the throne room."

They dropped their dirty clothing inside the kitchen entrance and grabbed a torch, lighting it from the one burning on the wall as they went.

Cayetano knew where he would find Yuma and Tyhen. Singing Bird had prepared him for the shift in living quarters and had already come to terms with it. Still, when he got to her room, he stopped and pounded on her door rather than rush inside to something he was unprepared to see.

****

Yuma was stretched out on the bed beside Tyhen when the pounding began. He rolled out of bed naked and ran to the door. When he saw Cayetano, he could tell by the look on his face there was trouble.

"What's wrong?" he asked.

Cayetano didn't waste words. "Singing Bird needs both of you to come to the throne room now."

"Tyhen is asleep. I will wake her and—"

"I'm awake," she said as she threw her legs over the side of the bed.

Unashamed of her nudity, she pulled a shift down over her head before she stood up.

"Get your sandals," Yuma cautioned as he fastened his loincloth. "No walking barefoot in the dark, even if it is inside."

She quickly tied them on, and together, they followed Cayetano, who lit the way.

She glanced once at Yuma, but couldn't read what he was thinking, and then it didn't matter. It was as he'd said. Apart, they were just a man and a woman, but together they were one, and stronger for it.

Their hasty footsteps reflected the urgency, while the flickering torch cast ominous shadows on the walls, adding drama and, for Tyhen, the addition of fear. She didn't know what had happened, but she knew it had to do with her and that was enough.

As they approached the throne room, light spilled out of it onto the tiled flooring in the hall, highlighting the armed guards who stood on either side of the doorway, while the thick walls muted the voices within.

Yuma could feel Tyhen's gaze on him more than once, but he couldn't look at her without showing fear, fear for her. Yet when they entered the throne room, he reached for her hand.

****

Singing Bird saw them coming and quickly waved them over. The twins were sitting side by side on the bench next to the table, studying the tablet.

Tyhen walked up to her mother, saw the stone with

the marks and frowned. "Mother, what is happening?"

"This. Do you see the marks on it?"

"Yes. What do they mean?"

Yuma knew by the excited way in which the twins were talking that it was big. The fact they'd lapsed back into the twin speak from their childhood was telling. They only did that when they didn't want anyone else to know what they were saying and knew it couldn't be good. He put a hand on her shoulder as if bracing her for the answer.

Singing Bird glanced at the twins and frowned. "Stop that. Say what you have to say aloud to all of us."

"Oh, sorry," Adam said. "We didn't mean to hide anything. It's just a habit from our childhood. Evan agrees with me on this, by the way."

"So are those markings really runes?" Singing Bird asked.

"Unmistakably, but we don't think they are very old. The carvings are still sharp. There's no erosion whatsoever on the individual marks, so this tablet is not old," Evan said.

Tyhen frowned. Nothing they said made sense. "What does this have to do with me, and don't say it doesn't because that's *all* I know."

Yuma's gut was in a knot. He knew the implications. "Does this mean the Vikings have already come?"

Tyhen frowned. "What are Vikings?"

Singing Bird clutched her fists against her belly as she began to pace. "They were explorers, men who sailed from their homeland to our land. Men who built homes on the land that did not belong to them and thought nothing of what they'd done. There were many others who came after, but in the time of New Ones, it was believed they were probably some of the first."

Tyhen lifted her chin and at the same time, unconsciously straightened her shoulders. "Then it has already begun."

Adam took her hand. "Touch it, Tyhen."

She laid her hand on the stone and closed her eyes. A face slid through her mind so fast that she gasped and jumped backward.

"What! What did you see?" Yuma asked.

Tyhen was shaken. She had visions, but never from the single touch of an object. She glanced at Yuma and then back at the twins.

"He's dead, isn't he?" she asked.

Adam smiled and elbowed his brother. "I told you she would know."

Cayetano had had enough. He pushed past all of them, grabbed the leather wrapping, and threw it over the stone in disgust, then turned on his family and thumped his chest with his fist as his voice rose in anger.

"I am chief of Naaki Chava. I want people to stop talking and ignoring the people who do not understand what is being said."

"I'm sorry," Singing Bird said. "It was such a shock I didn't take time to explain. I'm going to let the twins tell you because they know more than I do."

Adam stood abruptly, properly honoring Cayetano's presence.

"This stone has Viking marks on it that mean words in their language. This stone tells the name of a man who died, and this was laid on top of his grave as a marker. And since Vikings always put their dead to sea in a small boat then light it on fire, I'd say this man died a long way from water or they wouldn't have buried him."

Evan picked up the story. "It also means that these Vikings have already come to your land, and when they leave, they will go back and tell *their* people what a wonderful, rich land it is, and that will bring men from different lands who ride the great water, too."

"Which means, my time in Naaki Chava is coming to an end even faster than I believed," Tyhen said. "There is no time to waste. It will take a long time to walk from this place to all the other tribes. It will take even longer to spread the word of what happened and ask them to accept the New Ones who will stay and help them change."

Cayetano listened without outward emotion, but his heart was breaking and Singing Bird was crying. It was not a good night.

Moments later, Nantay and the trader were escorted into the room and Singing Bird wiped her face and turned to face them. She would show weakness to no one but her inner circle.

"Singing Bird, this is the trader who brought the stone. His name is Izel," Nantay said.

The trader was a short, squat man with wide shoulders and bowed legs, and it was obvious from the look on his face he was afraid for his life.

"Izel! Come forward," Cayetano ordered.

Izel shuffled up to the chief and then dropped to his knees, shaking and moaning.

Cayetano frowned. "Your life is not in danger. Stand up and answer Singing Bird's questions."

Izel leaped up, nodding rapidly.

Singing Bird frowned and pointed at the bench. "Sit, Izel, before you fall."

He plopped down onto the end of the bench, glancing nervously at the stone tablet beneath the leather cover and then staring at the twins. They were obviously from a different race, and their identical faces added to the mystery of who they were and where they'd come from.

Singing Bird shifted into her teacher voice. "Izel, look at me."

He quickly shifted focus.

"That's better. Now tell me, where did you find this stone?"

"I found it on my trading journey. It was in the jungle and lying on the ground. When I took it to the next village, an old man told me that when he was a boy, men in a canoe came to their shore. The canoe was very long and there were many men rowing it. They came ashore wanting food and water. It was given to them, but they didn't leave. One of their men was sick, and after he died, they wouldn't take his body with them. Instead, they dug a hole and buried him. Then they laid the stone on top to mark the place."

Singing Bird frowned. This wasn't Viking tradition, but Adam and Evan had already locked into the story.

"They didn't want to touch him because he had a disease they didn't want to catch," Evan said.

Tyhen moved to where the little man was sitting, then laid a hand on his shoulder, just to see if her new gift still worked. The moment she touched him, she got more than she bargained for.

"The old man told you to put the stone back, didn't he?" she asked.

Izel's eyes widened and then his chin began to quiver. Once again, he feared for his life. "Yes."

"Why didn't you?" she asked.

Izel was shaking. "I couldn't find the grave again, and I thought it would be better to keep it than to mark the wrong place."

"Do not lie. You thought you could get something in trade for it, didn't you?" Tyhen said.

Izel put his hands over his head, slid off the bench, and dropped to his knees again. "You have magic! I did not know you had magic!"

"It doesn't matter," Singing Bird snapped. "You lied to Cayetano. You lied to me, and you have lied to my daughter."

Cayetano pointed at the two guards who'd escorted the man into the room. "Take him to the steps of the temple and guard him until sunrise. Once the sun is up, make sure he leaves Naaki Chava."

Johnston Nantay looked at Singing Bird, and then at Cayetano. "Great Chief, unless you have need of me, I will walk with them through the city. It is not a good place to walk alone after dark."

"You may go, and we thank you," Cayetano said.

Nantay nodded, but instead of leaving immediately, he turned to Tyhen. "You will not make your walk alone. We all knew this day would come. The New Ones have talked and many of us will make the walk with you, just like we made the Last Walk with your mother."

Singing Bird's eyes welled both with gratitude and added sadness. Once again, she would be losing people she loved, but it was good. The more people accompanying Tyhen, the safer she would be.

Tyhen nodded. "I knew. I have already seen you walking with Yuma in my dreams, and I thank you for the sacrifice you will make to leave your homes."

Johnston's smile was gentle, but he shook his head in denial of her words. "We all know that nothing will be the same, but we look at it as going home, not leaving one. When you can, come to my house. I will show you things we have made to prepare for the journey."

"I will come tomorrow," she said.

Cayetano glanced at Singing Bird in sudden fear. Would she want to go back, as well?

Singing Bird saw the look on his face and immediately took his hand. "We will miss you, but we understand."

Cayetano's panic ended. "This is so," he said and then shifted focus. "Take the trader to the temple and give Nantay a torch to light his way."

Moments later they were gone.

Cayetano eyed the people who'd become his family and then his gaze moved to the twins. "Do you go, too?" he asked.

Adam and Evan wouldn't look at Yuma and Tyhen.

"No, Cayetano. We stay with you until you no longer need us."

Singing Bird was startled, but relieved.

Cayetano nodded, obviously pleased with their answer.

Yuma was shocked. All they'd ever talked about growing up was protecting Tyhen, and now they were backing out?

"Go to bed! All of you," Singing Bird said. "There is still time to discuss details in the days to come."

Tyhen dropped her gaze and stared at the floor all the way out of the room. By the time they reached the hall, tears were running down her face.

Yuma took her hand, but they kept walking.

The twins were right behind them and soon caught up. "There's something you don't know," they said quickly. "We will stay with Singing Bird for a while, but not forever. We will be joining you at a later time."

"You two can't find your way through the jungle without someone leading you, and you know it," Yuma snapped.

Evan's voice sounded as sad as he looked. "We have a way, and we will find you. Just know that we will never abandon you, Tyhen. Never."

She couldn't talk without sobbing aloud, and didn't want her mother to hear her, so she said nothing.

When they got to her room, she walked inside, leaving Yuma in the hall with the twins.

"What's going on?" Yuma asked.

Adam put a finger to his lips to indicate quiet. "We'll tell you everything we know tomorrow, when we can talk beyond these walls."

He had to be satisfied with that and went in after Tyhen, leaving the twins in the hall.

"This is harder than I thought," Evan whispered.

"But we have no choice. We owe our lives to Singing Bird. We have to see them to safety first," Adam said.

"Agreed," Evan added. "So let's go to bed. I'm exhausted."

Adam sighed. "I miss the days when we could watch television in bed."

"And the cookies and ice cream," Evan added.

Then they shrugged in unison.

"But there's no more Landon Prince, so it's a fair trade," Evan said.

"A very fair trade," Adam added.

Although they were satisfied with their lot in life, Tyhen was still trying to come to terms with hers. She turned to Yuma as he closed the door behind him, shutting the torchlight out and leaving the room bathed in moon glow.

Even in the shadows, he saw tears glistening on her cheeks, but when she spoke, her voice was firm, almost commanding.

"Tomorrow I will go to Nantay's to see what the New Ones have made."

"We will go," he said, correcting her.

She nodded, then dropped her shift on the floor and crawled back in her bed, turned her face to the wall and closed her eyes.

Yuma unwound his loincloth and crawled into the bed beside her and then slipped his arm around her body and pulled her close. He could feel the tension in her muscles and thought she was still crying, but he didn't try to comfort away the tears. Now was time to cry because in the months to come, tears would be a waste of time.

****

It was just after sunup and the twins were in the kitchen, ignoring the giggling servants as they rummaged for food when Yuma came striding into the room.

"We talk now," he said shortly and led the way out into the early morning.

It had rained during the night and the sound of dripping water was constant. The air was already steaming and insects abounded, feeding off the rotting fruit the monkeys had dropped from the trees above.

They walked in silence all the way past the north end of the palace and out into a clearing before Yuma stopped and turned to face them.

"Is Tyhen all right?" Adam asked.

"Is she mad at us?" Evan added.

Yuma waved away their questions. "What do you know that we don't? Why are you staying behind? What did you mean when you said, 'until you don't need us anymore?' Are Cayetano and Singing Bird going to die?"

Adam stared intently into Yuma's eyes without immediately answering.

Yuma glared. It had happened plenty of times before, but he was in no mood for it today and shoved him backward.

"Stop it! I know when you're reading me. Answer my question."

"You don't tell this to Tyhen," Adam said.

Yuma threw up his hands in frustration. "She touched the trader and knew he'd lied. I keep nothing from her, ever. Whatever it is, she has to know. Her journey is too important to withhold secrets."

Adam's shoulders slumped.

Evan put a hand on his brother's arm in comfort and picked up the conversation. "The mountain that faces the temple is a volcano. It has been asleep for nearly five hundred years, but it is going to wake, and when it does it will spill burning rocks and fire down into Naaki Chava. Many will die, but most will escape because we will be here to give warning. We have to stay or Cayetano and Singing Bird *will* die, along with everyone else."

Yuma spun toward the mountain, imagining the horror. When he turned around, his jaw was set.

"How long before this happens?" he asked.

"We can't be sure, but it will be after Tyhen leaves the city."

"You can't wait until the last minute to tell people. They will need time to pack belongings and find a new place to live. They can't just go running off through the jungle and trade one death for another."

Evan frowned. "We know this. We are staying behind to handle this in the proper way. Cayetano will know. Singing Bird will know. They will tell the people. But you and a lot of the New Ones will already be gone."

There was a knot in Yuma's belly. The knowledge of this was yet another burden to carry. "How will you ever find us?"

"Do you remember how we escaped Firewalker?" Adam asked.

Yuma's eyes widened. "The spinning cube! It opened a portal!"

"We will find you. That is all you need to know," Evan said.

Yuma blinked away tears. "You are my brothers. I did not want to lose you."

"You are our brother, too," Evan said softly.

"And we won't lose you," Adam added.

"Tyhen is looking for you," Evan said.

Yuma glanced over his shoulder, half-expecting to see her coming toward him.

"I'm telling her what you said."

"Don't tell anyone else," Adam said. "We have to tell Cayetano and Singing Bird first and now is not the time."

Yuma nodded and headed back to the palace at a lope.

****

Tyhen knew Yuma was talking to the twins. She could have gone, but she didn't want to. If it was bad, she didn't want to look weak by crying again.

There was a part of her that was already walling off emotion. It had to happen or she would never be able to make the journey. As she moved about the room, washing the sleep from her face and choosing clothing for the day, she thought of Yuma. The magic of being with a man was new and amazing and even better than her dreams. But crossing that line from childhood into maturity had done more than give her pleasure. She'd felt the shift the moment she'd touched the trader last night and knew it for what it was. The Windwalker had given her more than life and a quest. He'd given her many special gifts to help make it happen, and when she crossed the bridge from child to woman, even more had been activated.

Instead of waiting for Yuma to come back, she went in search of food and was eating a piece of fresh bread and thinking about eating another piece of coconut when Yuma entered the kitchen through the back entrance. She tried to read the expression on his face but couldn't. And then he smiled and her heart skipped a beat.

"Have you eaten?" she asked.

He shook his head as he wrapped his arms around her. When she offered him a piece of her bread, he opened his mouth like a little bird waiting to be fed.

"Ummm, good, but not as good as you," he said and then grabbed a handful of nuts and a banana. "I'm ready to go whenever you are."

"Did you talk to the twins?" she asked.

He nodded. "I will tell you once we're outside."

Her eyes widened. "You don't want others to hear."

As usual, her perception was on target. "You are right. I don't want others to hear."

"I need a drink," she said, but Yuma was way ahead of her. He dipped a cup into a jug of water and handed it to her.

Her hands were shaking as she took the cup, but her gaze was steady. "Thank you."

He cupped her cheek then brushed a crumb of coconut from the edge of her lower lip. "You're welcome," he said softly.

He waited as she drank, then took her by the hand and walked her through the palace and out into the sunshine.

The streets in the city below were laid out in straight lines that intersected in perfect squares like white ribbons of icing, and the buildings in which the people lived were like the tiers on the birthday cakes from Yuma's past.

Early sunlight glittered on the river that wound through the valley, and if Yuma squinted just right and let his imagination run free, he could pretend the shining river was the lights from the candles, counting off his years. He'd only had eight years of that life before it had all come to an end. He'd lived here almost twice as long, but the memory kept in his heart was of the home from his past.

This morning, the beauty of the sight before him was gut-wrenching, knowing that it would disappear beneath the fire of burning lava. He looked past the city to the mountain beyond and then pointed.

"When you look at the mountain, what do you see?"

She frowned. "I don't understand."

He took her by the hand and the moment they touched, she saw the top blow off the mountain, sending huge chunks of rock in all directions as a great cloud of ash began spreading across the sky. Below the cloud, a river of fire spilled out from the rim of the new crater, eating its way down the mountain toward Naaki Chava.

She yanked away from his grasp as if she'd been physically burned, then fell to her knees and covered her face. But the image was still there, seared into her mind. Even worse, it was the same vision she'd had, only she had not known it was Naaki Chava.

Yuma knelt beside her. "This is why the twins stay behind. They can't save the city, but they can help save the people including Cayetano and Singing Bird."

"What will happen to everyone? Where will they go?" Tyhen whispered.

"I think that is not for us to worry. We go one way before it happens. They will go another way in time to survive. Once everyone is safe, Adam said they will join us."

She shook her head. "That's impossible. They will never, never be able to find where we are."

"He says they can. Remember they were not on the

Last Walk with your mother, but they found her anyway. They'll find us the same way they got here. What you need to know is all of this is not our concern. It can't be. Do you understand?"

She lifted her head and stared down into the city, staying silent for so long Yuma didn't know what to think, and then she turned to face him. When he saw that fierce expression on her face, he knew she would be okay.

"I am ready to go to Nantay's."

He pulled her to her feet, but when she started down the street alone, he let her go. She needed to pull herself together so he followed a couple of steps behind.

Chapter Eight

Tyhen was numb. She knew Yuma was behind her. She could hear his footsteps, but she wouldn't look back, couldn't look back and see the sympathy on his face. Even though she wasn't leaving today, the cord had been cut from all she'd known. Pain would come, but not now. Not when everything for which she'd been born was at stake.

She looked out across the valley at the river and the houses to the jungle beyond, then up at the mountain behind it.

It was the enemy and it would prevail.

A bright green bird with a red breast and a long flowing tail flew across her line of sight. She could hear the shrill shriek of a child's laughter and ached at the thought of what was to come. She wondered if the guards had escorted the trader, Izel, away from the city. She hoped he was gone. She didn't want to look upon his face again.

About halfway down the hill, she began hearing drums. At first she thought it was a message from the Old Ones and then realized they were real. Their rhythm was her heartbeat, marking the stride of her steps, and when the drums beat faster, she lengthened her stride. When she began hearing the chanting, she knew they were singing her to them. The louder they sang, the faster she walked until finally she was running.

Yuma had been focusing on the dark fall of her hair and the gentle sway of her hips, so when the drumbeat began, it didn't actually register until she began to run. Then it was like a slap in the face as the sound ripped through his senses, sending a cold chill up his spine.

He knew this! He'd heard this same drumming and the same chant when he was eight years old and waiting on the Navajo reservation for Layla Birdsong to come out of the desert. She came riding that dusty black motorcycle into their midst like a bat out of hell. They had drummed Layla to them, and now they were calling Tyhen. He didn't know what was going to happen, but whatever it was, she wouldn't face it alone.

He started running to catch up.

****

Singing Bird hadn't slept well. She got up before sunrise and went down into Naaki Chava without her guards, and then out into the fields in the valley beyond, pulling weeds and thinning the overgrowth with the other women. It wasn't something a chief's wife would normally do, but there was too much of Layla Birdsong left in her to sit idly by while others toiled.

She was on her knees with sweat running down the middle of her back when she heard the first drumbeat. She stopped what she was doing and stood and then looked at the other women who were doing the same. It wasn't a festival day and there was no more warring for the people of Naaki Chava. She wondered if someone was sick or dying. Was there a crisis of which she was unaware?

She wiped her hands on the sides of her shift and pushed the hair from her eyes as the drumming grew louder. She was debating with herself as to what she should do when she realized what she was hearing, and as she did, a cold chill ran up her spine. She'd heard that same drumbeat and the same chanting when she'd ridden Windwalker's motorcycle up out of the canyons. She took a step forward, and then another when it hit her. They weren't calling her. They were calling Tyhen!

Her mother's heart wanted to run to her child, but there was nothing more she could give her daughter that would take her where she needed to go. There was only one thing she could do for Tyhen. She dropped to her knees and began to pray.

****

The drum held the rhythm; the singers' words held the power, and the closer she got, the louder they sang. When she came around the corner of Johnston Nantay's house and the people gathered there saw her, the drumbeat stopped so quickly she felt her heart stop with it. What followed as they erupted into one loud continuous war cry tore away the last vestiges of who she'd been.

She raised her arms into the air in a gesture of celebration as she strode toward the ceremonial fire, moving toward the elders with her head up and her shoulders back. In a way, they *were* going into war, but it would not be a battle with weapons. It would be a battle between the old ways and the new.

An old man who'd been seated around the fire stood up as she approached, and suddenly, Yuma's voice was near her ear.

"That's Wesley Two Bears. He's Cherokee and one of the oldest to survive Firewalker."

Tyhen nodded once to indicate she heard as she stopped before him. The old man was barefoot, wearing a loin cloth and a small silver ring on a strip of leather hanging around his neck. His skin was burned dark from the sun and his long, gray hair was in braids. His face was wreathed in lines born of pain and sorrow, and she felt like kneeling at his feet. He carried a pair of high-topped, lace-up moccasins in his hands as he approached her.

"We see you, Tyhen. We honor you. These moccasins were on the Last Walk. They ran from Firewalker. They will carry you on your journey as well."

Tyhen was moved by the gesture, and as she touched them, she received a flash of the woman who'd been wearing them and knew it had been his wife who had died here in Naaki Chava.

"I am honored by your gift," she said as he laid them in her arms.

He stepped back into the circle as she turned to speak to the gathered crowd. "You called me and I am here. You know what I have to do. Johnston Nantay says there are those among you who wish to leave with me. Is this so?"

The war cry that followed made the hair stand up on the backs of her arms. The passion of their intent was unmistakable, but she had to make sure they understood how deeply they were getting involved.

"It is very far and very dangerous. I cannot promise all of you will reach the final destination."

Wesley Two Bears lifted his hand, and when her gaze shifted in his direction, he began to speak.

"We are the last of the people from before, and it is our fault Firewalker came. We did not provide properly for our young. We did not teach enough of them to be proud of their heritage and they lost their way. Even before Firewalker, many had already died from an unseen current in the river of their lives. If we die to make right what was wrong, it is a good way to die."

Tyhen nodded. "Then it is good. Are there many of you?"

"These and more," Two Bears said, waving his hand toward the gathering.

She blinked. This was well over half of what was left of the New Ones and it was turning into something she had not envisioned. She was trying to figure out how it would work when, once again, she heard Yuma's voice.

"They have been preparing for years. It will be what it will be."

She turned and saw the trust and faith in his steady gaze.

"What it will be," she echoed softly and clasped his hand.

Johnston Nantay came out of the crowd. "We know what to do. Singing Bird has prepared us, just as she prepared you. We have weapons. We have clothing for different weather, for the cold and the rain and the snow. We have small tents in which to sleep along the way. We have maps we have been making that tell us where to walk all the way through this land. Once we cross into the land that was once known as North America, we will use what landmarks we can recognize to guide our steps, and if everything is strange and new, then we will still find our way. Our only wish is to follow you."

Tyhen was shocked. All these years they'd lived here and she believed that they'd settled in, when in truth, like Yuma, they had been preparing to go home.

Another elder stood. "I ask you this, Tyhen. How will we find the tribes? They will be scattered to the four winds."

"That is my task, and nothing for you to worry. All you need to know is that they will find us."

Wesley Two Bears nodded. "This is good. We have talked among our people, and when we see the new tribes, each time some of us will stay behind with them, while the rest continue on with you. It is the only way to make this work."

Tyhen glanced at Johnston. "Do they know about the stone tablet and what it means?"

"Yes."

"Then you all know the urgency has increased?"

"Name the day and we will be ready," Johnston said.

She was thinking of the mountain that would catch fire. The ones who chose not to go should be made aware of what they would be facing, but she had to talk to Cayetano first. It was his right to set the time for the people's exit, just as it was for her to set the time for hers.

"It will be soon," she said. "I don't know what lies

ahead, but Yuma and I are grateful to have you with us."

Johnston Nantay raised his fist into the air and spoke loudly. "Today we will continue to sing to the Old Ones to guide our steps and protect us on the journey. Tomorrow we begin packing the things we will carry. When the Dove is ready, we will be ready, as well."

"The Dove? Why do you call me this?" she asked.

"Because your quest is to make peace, and in our time, a dove was the symbol for peace."

The name pleased her. "Then I accept the name. Will you show me what you've made?"

"Yes. Follow me."

The drumbeat resumed. As they were walking away, Yuma looked back and saw the dancers. They would make powerful medicine on this night, and as much as he would have liked to be with them, his place was with Tyhen.

She walked without speaking, the moccasins clutched against her chest. When they passed the field where the baseball games were held, she looked away. Childhood was over.

Yuma had been walking and talking to Johnston, but he caught the look on her face as they passed the ball field and slowed down to walk with her, leaving Johnston to lead the way alone.

"What are you thinking?" he asked.

Tyhen looked up. "You want the truth?"

He nodded.

"I'm trying not to. The journey seems impossible and the weight of my responsibility is heavy."

"But you won't be alone."

"It's not the number of people who walk with me

that will influence the tribes we meet. It's me they will judge. If this fails, it's me who will bear the guilt."

"You won't fail."

"But how do you know?"

He rubbed his thumb along the scar on her wrist where she'd cut herself to save his life. "You have already worked magic. When the time comes, you will do what is needed to make the people believe."

She was silent for a little while longer and then finally nodded. "I will dream tonight. Maybe the way will seem clearer."

"We are here," Johnston said as he stopped at the door to a long two-story building.

Tyhen eyed the building curiously as Johnston began opening the shutters on one side of the building.

"For light," he said and led the way in.

Yuma had never been inside, and even though he knew most of what they'd been accumulating, he was surprised by the quantity.

Two rows of deep shelves lined the walls above cabinets. Some of the cabinets had doors, some were just open compartments, and every surface was covered and stacked two deep with a wide variety of goods and clothing.

"This is one of ten buildings we have built. These are tools to build better structures for the tribes to live in. We can show them how homes that do not move give them a stronger claim to the land."

Tyhen frowned. "What do you mean?"

"The people of the plains lived in tepees made of long poles and animal skins. They could put them up and take them down at a moment's notice for ease in traveling, but they followed their food source, rather than create one of their own. In the end, it left them vulnerable. Some people in the dryer parts of the land lived in small, round houses made of mud and grass and abandoned them when necessary. Others lived in caves carved into the side of mountains."

Tyhen thought of the comfort of the palace and the dwellings in the city and shuddered. She hadn't thought about a more primitive style of housing, which made her realize she hadn't given much thought to anything except what *she* had to do.

"These are some of the stronger metal weapons we have been making," Johnston said. "There are better axes and hatchets than what was here, saws to cut down trees for building, knives and spears to protect and feed ourselves. We have bows and arrows with metal arrowheads like the kind your mother brought from the past. Here are cooking vessels and this table has clothing for different kinds of weather."

He unfolded one and showed her how it worked.

"It's made from jaguar skins," she said, as she slipped her arms into the sleeves then frowned and quickly took it off again.

Yuma grinned. "What's wrong?"

"It makes me sweat," she said, wrinkling her nose.

"You won't be sweating when it becomes necessary to wear it," Johnston said.

Tyhen eyed the grin on Yuma's face and remembered the fight they'd had months earlier. "Is this for cold and frozen?"

He nodded.

She sighed and handed it back to Johnston, then followed the men around the room, then up to the second floor, amazed at what they'd thought of and wondering how they would carry it all, when he answered the question before she asked.

"We made packs to carry on our backs with basic equipment for each person, plus some packs we can drag, and look at these," he said, pulling out some rolls of tanned animal skins.

Johnston handed one to Yuma. "Unroll that," he said.

Yuma moved a stack of packs aside and carefully unrolled the supple skin, then looked in disbelief.

"It's a map! Are all of those maps?" he asked, pointing to the other rolls Johnston was holding.

"Yes, but they aren't maps to a specific destination. They are maps of specific landmarks and mountain ranges, things that would not necessarily change shape all that much over a thousand or so years."

"This is amazing and very important," Yuma said.

Johnston beamed. "The tribal elders thought of this."

They were talking of things of which she had no knowledge, but this time it didn't matter. As long as they understood, she was satisfied. She was watching Yuma's face and thinking how much she loved him when she heard Adam's voice in her head.

"Go to the temple now."

I do not go into that place.

"You can now. It has been cleansed. But you must hurry. A visitor is coming just for you, and you must go inside alone."

Who?

"I think it is your father."

But Cayetano is-

"Cayetano is not your father."

She gasped.

"I have to go," she said abruptly.

Yuma frowned. "What's wrong?"

She just shook her head.

"Go," Johnston said. "I'll close up. You know where we are if you need us."

Still carrying her moccasins, she took the steps down from the second floor as quickly as possible with Yuma right behind her.

As soon as they got outside, Yuma asked. "What happened?"

"Adam told me to go to the temple."

"But he knows you don't want to go in there. Did he say why?"

"They did a cleansing of the temple. He said it will be okay."

"But why—?"

She grabbed his hand. "Walk faster."

He lengthened his stride. "Tyhen, what is going on?"

"I am supposed to meet a visitor there."

"Then I'm going with you."

"I have to do this by myself, Yuma."

"That is not going to happen," Yuma said. "We cannot trust—"

"He said it was my father."

Yuma frowned. "Why would Cayetano want to speak to you at the temple?"

"He is not my father," she said and then started running.

Yuma's heart began to race as he hurried to catch up.

When they reached the temple, Tyhen stopped at

the doorway. The day was hot, but she could feel a breeze and knew it had nothing to do with the weather. She turned around, then handed him her moccasins to hold.

"You cannot go any farther," she said and hugged him. "I am sorry. It is not my decision to make."

He nodded to reassure her he understood. "I will stand guard here and wait for you to come out."

She turned and then hesitated before going inside.

"Are you afraid?" he asked.

"How would you feel?"

He sighed. "I cannot begin to imagine."

Her eyes narrowed as she walked inside. The passageway was low and she was tall. If she raised her arm, she could easily touch the ceiling. It made her feel like she was walking into a trap. At the least, she would need light. She lifted a torch from the wall before making her way through the maze of tunnels.

It was a relief to know the angry spirits she'd felt before were absent, but there was a stronger, more urgent reason guiding her steps. She'd never imagined this day would happen, but now that it was, she was curious, excited, and more than a little anxious.

The farther she walked, the darker it became, until all she could see was the space immediately in front of her. Despite the distance she'd gone, there was still a wind at her back, a warning that her visitor's arrival was imminent.

A few moments later, a faint light appeared out of the darkness and she took heart and hurried toward it. She soon found herself inside a large, open chamber. Sunlight had painted a wide swatch of light on the floor in the center of the room. She looked up to find the source coming in through a small opening from up above.

The air began to shift around her as she waited, her heart pounding. Then it moved faster, shifting dust until the beam of sunlight was teeming with it, and still she waited, motionless. When the air began to spin around her, it blew her hair first one way and then another, spinning so fast it was hard to breathe.

She was gasping for breath when suddenly he was before her, his long, black hair floating in the air around his face like the feathered headdress of a Naaki Chava warrior. He was beautiful, and at the same time so fearsome she wanted to run away.

"Are you my father?" she asked.

He nodded once, still silent under her stare.

Moved by the fact that she was actually standing with him, face-to-face, her voice began to shake.

"I thought you did not exist anymore. I thought when the curse was broken, you were gone."

Yet I am here.

Even though he didn't speak, she heard his words.

"What is wrong? Why are you here?"

I came for your mother when it was time, and now I come for you. You have powers, but you will have need of more.

"Then how do I get them? What do I need to do?"

Do nothing. Close your eyes.

She did as he asked, waiting to see what happened next. At first she heard nothing, felt nothing, and then his hand was on the back of her neck, pulling her forward into his arms.

She could still smell the dust stirred by his arrival and the scent of heat from the sun on his skin. She was so anxious about what was going to happen that she had yet to connect with the fact she was in her father's arms. Then his cheek was against her forehead, and when the first of his tears touched her face, she moaned, then staggered. Had he not been holding her, she would have gone to her knees. They held the memory of everything he'd suffered to leave her mother behind and it broke her heart. Then she heard his voice again, rolling through her like water.

You are Windwalker's daughter. You and you alone will complete the change for our people. I have given your story to the nations. The shamans and the medicine men know of you and your quest. The sign of your coming will be marked when they see a white dove, then they will begin a march, leading their people to you. It is your story they will hear. It is your power they will see. End the warring. Build the nations. Make them stronger than the strangers who have already set foot upon our shores. In seven sleeps you must be gone. Now you have heard, and so it is done. I have given you my power. Now I give you my heart.

Heat shot through her, burning so hot and so fast that she thought she would die, and then she did not. When he began pulling away, she wanted to open her eyes, but was helpless to move.

"Wait! Don't go! Will I ever see you again?"

As you see yourself, so you will see me.

The air inside the chamber swirled softly, shifted against her body as if reaching for a final grasp, and died.

The hold he'd had on her will was gone. Tyhen opened her eyes as the sadness swept through her. She took her torch from the wall and began retracing her steps. When she came out, Yuma was still standing in front of the doorway with her moccasins, but the sun was already moving past the top of the sky. She'd been inside for hours and it felt like only minutes.

"I'm ready," she said as she touched Yuma's shoulder.

He turned around, started to speak and then stared. "Tyhen?"

"Yes it's me. Who else would I be?"

"You look... you look different."

She shrugged.

"Was it the Windwalker? Did you see him?" he asked.

"I saw him," she said softly, and slipped her hand in his. "I want to leave now."

Yuma gave her the moccasins, then took a deep breath and stifled every question on his lips.

They began the walk back through the playa, then through the marketplace toward the hill that led to the palace. Twice Tyhen stopped to talk to people trading their goods, once accepting a piece of sugar cane to chew on, and another time to ask about a new baby.

Yuma felt her sadness, but there was also a maturity that had come out of nowhere. When she handed him a piece of sugar cane, he took it with a smile and thanked the trader, promising to bring something from the palace as compensation. But the trader refused, happy to have been the one chosen to give the chief's daughter a treat as they walked away.

They walked in silence for a few minutes more as they chewed on the chunk of cane, and then Tyhen suddenly tossed hers aside and took Yuma's hand without looking at him.

"He told me to leave in seven sleeps."

His heart leaped. This was a shock! Only seven days.

"He told me the shamans will know of me and will be looking for the sign to tell them I am coming."

Yuma tossed his sugar cane away. "What is the sign?"

"A dove. He said they will see a white dove."

A chill ran up his spine. "The same name Johnston Nantay gave you."

She nodded. The rest of what Windwalker said was hers to know. They would see her powers when the need arose, and they had no need to know that he'd died for her, giving her all that was left of him.

It was a sacrifice she would not waste or ever forget.

Chapter Nine

The palace was in an uproar when they arrived. Singing Bird was trying to calm Cayetano, but it wasn't doing much good.

Tyhen and Yuma could hear him shouting all the way down the hall toward the throne room.

"It sounds as if the news Adam gave Cayetano has upset him," Yuma said.

Tyhen tossed her head, impatient with the fact that Cayetano always rejected change. A mountain on fire was out of his control and that's what had set him off.

"And what I have to say is not going to make him happier," she added.

Even the guards looked nervous as they passed them in the hall, which wasn't surprising. They weren't deaf. They could easily hear what Cayetano was saying.

Yuma glanced at them warily then lowered his voice. "It does not appear there will be a need to announce the need to leave Naaki Chava. Word is going to be all over the city before nightfall."

She glanced at a guard as they entered. He looked ready to run and knew she needed end this. "This has to stop," she said.

"Look! There's Tyhen now!" Adam said, pointing toward the doorway.

"Where have you been!" Cayetano yelled, then spun

and pointed at Adam. "This one talks of death and fire and burning rocks and you are gone without a word to anyone. We have important things to discuss before the people can be warned."

"You are not going to have to warn anyone," Tyhen said sharply. "You have frightened everyone within hearing distance. I am sure the servants are already spreading the word down in Naaki Chava. You need to speak to the people immediately before a panic begins."

Cayetano blinked. Tyhen had never spoken to him in such a tone, and as his temper cooled, his perception heightened. Something was different about her. She looked older, but it wasn't her face that had changed. He looked closer, then stifled a gasp. It was her eyes! The child he'd known was not in there anymore. Shocked by the realization, he sat down on the bench with a thump.

Singing Bird was so focused on Cayetano that she missed the exchange between them.

"See. It is as I told you. Your anger goes before reason and the people will be afraid."

"They already are," Yuma said. "I saw it on the guards' faces in the hall."

Cayetano's world was crashing down around him. He had nothing more to say.

Adam was pacing, but Evan was standing quietly aside, cowed by raised voices and anger.

Adam focused on Tyhen, and even though he didn't speak aloud, she heard his voice.

"*Did you see him?*"

Tyhen glanced up at him. *Yes, but say nothing.*

"*I didn't tell anyone.*"

There is no need. It will only make things worse with Cayetano.

Adam's focus shifted to Yuma, surprised by the calm, almost fatalistic expression on his face. There was something more they weren't telling, but what was it?

Tyhen took her mother's hand and then squeezed it gently, remembering all the times Singing Bird had wiped her tears or put medicine on a scrape. All the nights her mother had held her when she cried from dreams she didn't understand.

Singing Bird saw her daughter's face, and like Cayetano, immediately saw the change. But unlike Cayetano, she recognized something he did not, and jerked her hand away. She wasn't seeing her daughter. She saw Niyol. What had happened? Why was this so?

Tyhen knew things were going to get worse once she told them her news, but this was the time to do it.

"I will leave Naaki Chava in seven days. Many of the New Ones will be leaving with me. It is their choice and not mine."

Singing Bird's heart stopped. The pain was so deep it felt fatal, but she said nothing, just as her grandfather had said nothing when she rode away on the back of Niyol's motorcycle another lifetime ago.

Cayetano was still reeling from the news that Naaki Chava would be destroyed, and losing Tyhen so quickly was another shock.

"You have not prepared," he argued.

"The New Ones made preparations for us. They said Singing Bird told them what to do, and it was done," Tyhen said.

Singing Bird couldn't breathe. The fact that she'd actually participated in aiding her own daughter's departure was horrifyingly real. Blinking away tears, she walked over to Cayetano and sat down in his lap. Instinctively, his arms went around her. Welcoming his strength, she leaned into his embrace and began issuing orders.

"Yuma, prepare the guards and tell them to ready the warriors to go with us. Adam, blow the Conch shell. The people will gather at the temple when they hear it, and I expect all four of you to be there standing behind your chief when he speaks. Leave us now, all of you."

Singing Bird put her arms around Cayetano's neck as her children walked away.

As soon as they got into the hallway, they began talking among themselves.

"Singing Bird is very sad," Evan said.

"We are all sad," Yuma said. "Everything is changing and that is always a hard thing to accept."

Despite all the turmoil, Tyhen thought of one change in her life she would never regret, and that was taking the final step to becoming Yuma's woman.

"I have to summon the people to the temple, but I have never done it. I've only seen it done," Adam said.

"It has not happened since I was born," Tyhen said. "How do you make it happen?"

"The shaman blew into a giant shell from the big water. It makes a very loud sound that echoes from one side of the valley to the other and was only used in times of trouble."

"This definitely qualifies as trouble," Yuma said. "Where is it?"

"It used to be in the temple, but we brought it back here after we cleaned the place out. It's in our room. I'll get it," Evan said.

"Do not go until I get back. I will walk with you to

the temple," Yuma said and ran to notify the guards and warriors to assemble and accompany Cayetano to the temple.

Moments later, Evan returned with the shell and Yuma was on his heels.

"It is done," Yuma said. "We have to hurry. The shell must be blown so the people can assemble before Cayetano reaches the temple. We can take a shortcut through the jungle."

"Let's do it," Adam said and followed Yuma and Tyhen down the hall and then out of the palace.

Once they began the trek, they quit talking. The reality of sharing their terrible truth was that some people would not believe it and reject it outright. Some would rebel and refuse to leave. Some would panic and slip away in the night to other villages that, in the long run, might not be any safer than Naaki Chava, but the majority would follow Cayetano and Singing Bird anywhere they led them.

"I think we should walk faster," Tyhen said.

Yuma stepped out of the group and began to run at a lope with the others on his heels. A few minutes later they came out on the backside of the temple and quickly ran inside. Yuma grabbed a burning torch from the wall and led the way to the inner staircase that took them up to the top of the temple. They caught a glimpse of something small and furry darting into the shadows as they started up the stairs, but didn't look back.

As soon as they reached the top, Adam stepped outside a few steps, lifted the shell to his lips, and blew as hard as he could.

Nothing happened. Not a squeak. Not a sound. He

tried once more without success then started to hand it to Evan when Yuma pointed toward the palace.

"Look! They are already coming."

"Give it to me," Tyhen said and lifted the shell to her lips.

The loud, mournful swell of sound ripped through the city, stopping everyone in their tracks. People ran out of their homes, while others came running from the fields and out of the jungle.

Tyhen took a second breath and blew again and the people saw her standing on the upper-most tier of the temple. When they began hearing the thunder of footsteps and realized it was Cayetano and Singing Bird marching down into Naaki Chava, surrounded by their guards and warriors, they began moving toward the temple in waves, anxious to hear why they'd been summoned.

Tyhen smiled shyly as she handed the shell to Adam. "A Windwalker's daughter has much air," she said.

Yuma grinned.

Adam and Evan looked embarrassed. "We will practice."

Tyhen nodded, then turned around and looked out across the city, letting the magnificence of the scene below her unfold. She wanted to remember the sunlight on the playa and the large blue parrots perched on the houses across the way, the shiny black feathers bobbing on the warriors' headdresses, and the blood-red feathers fluttering on Cayetano's cape.

At first she couldn't see her mother, and then when she did was struck by her expression and looked away, not wanting to remember it was fear that she had seen.

The people were gathering in swarms, at first struck silent by the unusual aspect of the gathering, and then the sound of their voices rose as they began murmuring to each other.

Minutes later, Cayetano reached the playa. The people parted to let them pass, and as Cayetano and Singing Bird began climbing up the outer steps of the temple, Singing Bird's children came down to meet them.

Tyhen stopped only feet from where Cayetano stood and looked at her mother. Singing Bird said nothing, but the look that passed between them was telling. Her mother was afraid the people would riot. She could hear her thoughts now, and they were startling. Singing Bird feared they might blame the fire in the mountain on Ah Kin's recent demise. Everyone knew the old shaman had died of snakebite but they didn't know it was self-inflicted. They also knew Cayetano had ordered the body to be burned. Some were going to blame the fall of Naaki Chava on the bad medicine. Some were going to suggest sacrificing Cayetano to appease the gods.

Now Tyhen was afraid. She hadn't known of the undercurrent of dissatisfaction. She'd been so wrapped up in her own life and quest that she'd missed this.

She glanced at the twins.

Did you know the people were upset about Ah Kin's death?

They nodded.

Did you tell Cayetano?

"He said he didn't care what they thought."

She sighed. That sounded just like him.

Yuma could tell they were worried about something. "What's wrong?" he whispered.

"Some are going to blame the fire in the mountain on the way Cayetano dealt with Ah Kin's body. They do not know he killed himself. They think the snake bite was an accident and that he was not treated with respect due a shaman."

"Will they riot?" Yuma asked.

"No, but there will be discord."

Yuma moved closer and lowered his voice even more. "So what if Cayetano takes away their reasoning by suggesting outright that the mountain's anger was because Ah Kin betrayed Cayetano?"

"Then they will want to sacrifice someone to appease the mountain," Adam said.

Yuma frowned. As long as he'd been here, he was still taken aback by the superstitions and brutality of how they thought life should be lived. No wonder Firewalker came.

And then it was too late to consider more options because Cayetano raised both arms to signal silence, and in a rare gesture, Singing Bird slipped her hand in the crook of his elbow as he took a step forward. It was as public a display of unity they'd ever made. And then he began to speak.

"My people! There are two things Singing Bird and I must tell you, and both are heavy on our hearts. The time has come for our daughter, Tyhen, to leave us. In seven sleeps she and a large number of the New Ones will leave Naaki Chava to continue the journey that Singing Bird began. As much as we regret this happening, we are also proud of the sacrifices they make to save our people and the future of our people."

A universal groan of dismay rose from the crowd as they looked upon the young woman, wanting to see her expression, wondering if there would be tears. Instead, she let out a war cry as she thrust her fist in the air.

The war cry the New Ones sent back to her echoed from one side of the valley to the other.

Yuma's heart swelled with pride, but also with a sudden sense of despair. He had grown to know and love these people, and they were giving up a far gentler way of life for uncertainty and danger, all for a chance to go home.

Cayetano held his hand up again for silence and the crowd hushed. "I said there were two things. The other is that we have been given a vision." He swung his arm toward the mountain. "In the vision, that mountain that has sheltered us will come apart, throwing burning rocks and thick, choking, smoke high up in the sky. It will bleed fire into Naaki Chava and our homes will be no more."

Shocked silence lasted for only a few moments and then just as Singing Bird had feared, someone in the crowd cried out.

"Ah Kin's spirit is angry. He was not honored as he should have been."

Cayetano frowned. He didn't like to be thwarted and had not expected this. "Ah Kin has nothing to do with—"

"Sacrifice to the gods and they will save us," another yelled, then a large part of the crowd began to chant, "Sacrifice! Sacrifice!"

This took Cayetano aback. He glanced down at Singing Bird. Her chin was up, her eyes flashing. The small scar at the corner of her mouth was white from clenching her jaw. He looked back up at the crowd and began to shout, trying to be heard over the roar of disapproval.

"We no longer sacrifice!" he yelled.

Someone from the crowd off to Cayetano's right threw a large piece of rock directly at him.

Yuma saw the motion as the man lifted his arm. Without thinking, he leapt in front of Cayetano and pushed him away just in time to take the brunt of the blow. The rock hit him on the side of the shoulder and cut a gash that immediately began to bleed.

Warriors began running up the steps to protect Cayetano, while others in the crowd grabbed the man who'd thrown the rock and put him on the ground.

Tyhen saw the blood on Yuma's shoulder, which triggered the rage that rushed through her. She flew down the steps, past Yuma and the twins, past Cayetano and her mother, running all the way down to the bottom tier where she threw her head back and screamed.

A great wind came out of nowhere, knocking people to the ground. The sound that came with it struck them mute. She unloaded her rage, shouting at the top of her voice.

"Cowards! Stupid, ungrateful children! That is what you are! For every year I have been living, you have been told again and again why Firewalker came. You saw with your own eyes how the New Ones suffered. You counted their numbers and knew that, because they had been given a warning, they had survived. Now Cayetano gave you a warning. It was just like the warning the New Ones received that saved their lives. Now you know that danger comes. You have been given time to pack up and get away. He is saving your lives and all you can think to do is kill someone? You think shedding blood and ending someone's life will stop a mountain from bleeding fire? So who among you wants to die first to feed a mountain? Speak up! I can't hear you."

Not only were they silent, but they were ashamed and looking away, unable to face the truth of her words.

"Then what do we do?" someone asked.

Tyhen pointed at Cayetano. "Ask your chief! He was trying to tell you when you let fear guide your words and behavior. And just so you know, if anyone ever shows such disregard for my father like that again, no matter where I am or how far away I might be, I will know and you will be sorry."

They were shaking where they stood, afraid that she would strike them all dead.

She turned around and ran right into Yuma, completely unaware that he'd been behind her. She glanced at the blood running down his shoulder, then up at his face. She couldn't read his expression, but she knew his heart. He'd put himself in harm's way for Cayetano and he would do it again without thinking, just like he took care of her. She touched his shoulder.

"It is nothing," he said softly.

She looked past him and straight into Cayetano's eyes. The emotion of what he was feeling was there for her alone to see. She'd called him father, an honor he had long ago earned.

Cayetano shifted his gaze from Tyhen to the people below. He was angry and it showed, but it was his silence that frightened them most. They waited for him to speak, and then waited longer, but still he said nothing.

A woman dropped to her knees and began to wail,

begging the gods and Cayetano for forgiveness, and then she threw herself forward, falling facedown on the playa. Others began doing the same until the entire group of dissidents was face down and praying for mercy.

When he finally spoke, there wasn't a sound to be heard but his voice.

"Send the man who threw the rock out of the city. He does not wish to live here anymore. As for the rest of you, know that I have sent runners to the North and to the South. I have sent them to the East and to the West. When they return, I will consider their findings and we will pick a new place to call home. If you are afraid to leave or do not want to go with us, go where you wish or stay and die. It is your choice."

He glanced up at the twins and nodded, then took Singing Bird's hand and began leading her down the steps. When they reached the level where Tyhen and Yuma stood, he paused.

"You have honored me, my little whirlwind. It is enough," he said softly.

"It will never be enough. I can never do enough to show my love and respect. You are my hero."

Cayetano's heart soared. He touched her head, and when she bowed it, he smiled. "You are my daughter forever, forever in my heart," he said softly, then briefly gripped Yuma's shoulder, acknowledging the sacrifice Yuma had made by putting his body in harm's way for him. He walked away with his head up and Singing Bird at his side, surrounded by the guards and warriors who'd pledged him their lives.

Tyhen and Yuma left the temple with the twins and went back the same way they'd come, moving quickly through the jungle and into the palace the back way.

The moment they walked in, they felt the absence of life. It was but a portent of what Naaki Chava would be like when everyone was gone.

"Everyone is gone!" Adam said.

"Will they come back?" Yuma asked.

Evan nodded. "Yes. They were just afraid and went down into the city to be with the others. But they heard their chief. They know no other life but to serve him. They will return."

"Twins, I need you to come with me," Tyhen said and led the way into her room.

The first thing she did was clean the wound on Yuma's arm. The bleeding had almost stopped. She went to a shelf near the window and dug through an assortment of small, covered bowls prepared by their healer, Little Mouse. She found what she was looking for and carried it back to Yuma.

"This will make it heal faster," she said.

He wrinkled his nose. "All of Little Mouse's medicines have a strange smell."

"But they work," Evan said. "Remember when we were still kids and I fell into those bushes with the red flowers and my skin broke out all over?"

"I remember," Adam said. "You begged me to scratch all the places you could not reach."

Their laughter was a momentary relief to the tension of what had just happened and a reminder of how intertwined their lives had been. Breaking up this foursome was going to be hard for all of them.

"Wait. Do not leave yet," Tyhen said and went straight to the trunk where she kept her clothing. Yuma followed.

"What are you looking for?" he asked.

"My little bird necklace. The one my mother wore when she was running from Firewalker."

Yuma remembered all too well the tiny silver bird that had been hanging around Singing Bird's neck the night Bazat tried to kill her. He was the one who found it later, and with Singing Bird's blessing, gave it to Tyhen the night she was born. He was curious as to why she needed it now. She never wore it.

"What will you do with it?"

"Give it to Adam because that is how he and Evan will find us after we are gone."

Adam was surprised by the ingenuity of her intent. "What made you think of that?"

She rocked back on her heels. "There are many things I have to think of before we leave, and this was only one of them," she said and continued her search.

"Can't you find it?" Yuma asked.

"No, and I can't remember... Oh. I know where it is." She dug through the clothing and pulled out a tiny cup from her childhood. When she turned it upside down, the necklace fell into her hands.

She stood up and handed it to Adam. "Will this be connection enough for you to find us?"

"Yes."

She nodded. "Take care of it. I want it back," she said and began putting the clothes back in the trunk.

Adam kept watching her, fascinated by the changes, all of which had happened after she'd met with the Windwalker.

"You're very different, you know."

"So people say," Tyhen said as she shut the lid and stood up.

Yuma frowned and then slid an arm around her waist.

"She is not different. She is just more."

Tyhen was surprised by his perception.

"I am enough," she added, then changed the subject. "So, where will the people go when they leave here?"

Adam glanced at his brother who was unusually quiet. He was afraid of the unknown and not nearly as brave. When Adam gave his brother a mental nudge to draw him back into the conversation, Evan immediately spoke up.

"Even though Cayetano has sent the runners, we have also been spirit walking at night, trying to find a new place, too, but it would take years to carve another Naaki Chava out of this jungle."

"Our best guess has always been that Naaki Chava is somewhere in what used to be called Middle America, right?" Yuma asked.

The twins nodded.

"So take them South and when you reach the coast of what used to be South America, tell them to start building. They have to regroup somewhere and the strangers will come from those seas. Give them a welcome party they won't soon forget. The New Ones have been making maps for years. We can ask Johnston if any of the New Ones have ventured far enough to map coast line on the big land," Yuma said.

Tyhen frowned. "You call this Middle America? Is it big? Will we become lost trying to find your land?"

Yuma shook his head. "No. This land is actually very narrow compared to the lands it connects. As long as we walk north, we will find our way, but after that, tribes will be scattered all over the big land above it."

She shuddered. . "If I think about it like that, the

journey seems impossible. We must take it one day at a time."

"Agreed," Yuma said, and slid a hand across her shoulders. He felt the tension in her body and gave her a quick look. But when she smiled at him, he let the worry go for when they were alone.

Suddenly, there was a knock at the door. Yuma opened it. There were two guards in the hall. "Singing Bird says for you to come to her room now."

"We are ready," she said and then led the way out.

Chapter Ten

When they walked out, they were shocked by the number of guards moving through the halls.

"What's going on?" Yuma asked.

"Singing Bird takes no chances on the possibility of a riot," Adam said.

"They will do nothing," Tyhen said. "If there are still people who are angry, they will simply slip away in the night like the cowards they are."

Yuma was of the same opinion, but said nothing because they'd reached their destination. Since they had been summoned, they entered their mother's private quarters without knocking.

Singing Bird turned to them the moment the door opened and went straight to Yuma. They could still see the anger in her eyes as she cupped his cheek then began checking the wound on his shoulder.

"It will heal," she said softly.

"It is nothing, Singing Bird."

She shook her head. "No. It is something! You put yourself in harm's way for your chief. Ever the warrior, even when you were small, you are both a fierce and faithful man, and a fitting partner for my daughter."

Yuma glanced quickly at Tyhen, who was smiling. This was more than thanking him for protecting Cayetano. It was Singing Bird's public acceptance of their union and he was grateful.

"I will protect her with my life," he said softly.

"And she will love you forever," Singing Bird said, echoing the vow Yuma made the day Tyhen was born.

There was a sound at the door and then Cayetano entered. Like Singing Bird, he walked straight to Yuma.

"That could have been a spear," he said.

Yuma lifted his head. "It would have made no difference, my chief."

Cayetano was struggling with emotions he rarely acknowledged. Before the New Ones, he'd been a man alone, wanting back the life he'd loved and lost. And it had been given to him and more. Thinking about losing two of his children seemed unthinkable. Yuma was another man's son, and Tyhen was a Windwalker's daughter, but they were his in every way that counted. There was much pain on his face as he drew a shaky breath.

"Yuma! Tyhen! You are the children of my heart and I do not know how to give you up."

Tyhen put her hand on his chest. "We will always be here, my father, and I will see you in my dreams."

Cayetano hugged her first and then turned and in a rare gesture hugged Yuma as well.

"Enough," Singing Bird said. "They aren't gone yet and there is much to discuss. Twins, do we have need to worry about a riot?"

"No, Singing Bird. They are all too afraid of Tyhen."

Tyhen stood beneath her mother's gaze without speaking. Finally, Singing Bird spoke.

"Will you tell us, my daughter, how it is that you have gained such power in such a short time?"

Tyhen wouldn't speak of Windwalker in front of Cayetano.

"It was given to me, Mother, just as my others were. I cannot explain any more than that."

Singing Bird knew her daughter wasn't telling everything, but accepted that as her right. "Will your powers keep you safe on the journey?" she asked.

Tyhen nodded.

"Then that is all I can ask," Singing Bird said. "Today is for Cayetano. We must make decisions for our trip as well."

"Take them South," Yuma said. "Remember in the world before Firewalker... remember South America?

Her eyes widened. "Yes! There were many seaports along the coasts. This is a good place to rebuild a city. We will not be a compliant and guileless people again."

"Where is this place? How far is it from here?" Cayetano asked.

"It's more of a question of where we are," Adam said. "This place is in what used to be called Middle America. Yuma said the New Ones have maps. They may know."

Cayetano was lost again. "Maps?"

"A drawing that leads us from one place to another without getting lost," Singing Bird said.

Cayetano frowned. "There are such things?"

"Yes. I will speak with Johnston Nantay tomorrow," Singing Bird said and pointed at Tyhen. "You will come with me.

Then Singing Bird turned to the twins. "We know the sacrifice you make to stay with us and we love and honor you for it."

"You saved our lives," Adam said.

"We stay to save yours," Evan added.

Singing Bird's eyes were full of tears, but she quickly wiped them away.

"Enough has been said for today. You go now. Do what you will. Make your peace with people. Tell friends good-bye."

They left under escort and began the walk back to their respective rooms in silence. When they reached Tyhen's room, they parted company with little more than a look.

Yuma opened the door for Tyhen to go inside, and once they were finally alone, Tyhen let down her guard.

"That hurt my heart," she said, her eyes welling with unshed tears.

Yuma took her hand and led her to the bed, then sat down beside her, still holding her hand. "I want to tell you something. I've never told this to anybody, not even Singing Bird."

Tyhen threaded her fingers through his and then watched his face intently, sensing this was something meant to help her sadness.

"When I was a little boy, I lived in a part of Oklahoma called Tahlequah. It was green like this place, but different. There were lots of trees and mountains nearby, and the weather changed with every season. It was beautiful to me. I don't remember much about my mother. She died when I was very young, but my father was everything to me. He made me proud to be Cherokee and he taught me what it meant to be a man. Even though I was just a child, I understood duty. I understood responsibility. We had a happy life and then one day everything changed. My father was watching television one morning when he saw something that frightened him. I saw the look on his face and then I was frightened, too."

"What is television?" Tyhen asked.

Yuma blinked, then realized what he'd said. "Oh, sorry. It was a way we received messages. Anyway, what he saw was Layla Birdsong fighting for her life and then the Windwalker coming and saving her and taking her away."

Tyhen gasped. "You *saw* that?"

"Yes. It was part of the message we received. That day was the end of joy. That day the elders of the tribe called a meeting and everyone came. Those who did not know about the prophecy were told, and others who knew were reminded and sadly, began making plans to leave. There were some who would not believe that it meant the end of time, and they stayed behind. That day, my father sat me down and told me we were going on a journey. He said the journey would be hard, and there would be times when I would be afraid, and there would be times when we would both be afraid, but we had to be strong because it was a very important thing we were about to do."

Tyhen was mesmerized. Her earliest memories of Yuma were always associated with her and Naaki Chava. There was a part of her that felt left out, that she would never know or understand him as he'd been born. But she listened.

"So we packed our things and the journey began. I did not know it would end the way it did. I only knew that my father said it was a thing to be done, and so I followed because I trusted him. Along the way, he began to get sick. Looking back, I think it was his heart, but I will never know for sure. By the time we got to the reservation where everyone was gathering, he was very weak. We made camp. We waited for Layla Birdsong for two days, then I lost track of time. One morning I woke up and he did not. Some people helped me bury him beside our truck. There was no other place to be. The ground was hard and drying up because Firewalker was coming so close. It was hard to dig a hole big enough to bury him. I slept on top of his grave the last night and heard his spirit in my sleep telling me to be brave, reminding me that I already knew how to be a man, and to follow Layla Birdsong until I breathed no more."

Tyhen was in tears. All these years and he'd held this story inside him.

He touched her face. "And then she came and we began the journey. We called it the Last Walk. Some people helped me along the way. They shared their water with me until there was no more to share, and when they died, I kept walking because I was afraid to stop. When we neared the end of the walk and the people began to run, I ran with them. But I was small and weak, and one by one they all passed me. It would have been easier to just stop and close my eyes. I would have been dead in minutes. But I'd seen death and I didn't want it, so I kept running, even when I no longer felt my feet and everyone had run out of my sight. I was alone in a world on fire, but I didn't quit."

Tears were streaming down Tyhen's face. The pain in her chest was immense, like something inside her was breaking. She was holding on to his hand so tight her fingers had gone numb, afraid to let him go.

Yuma paused and closed his eyes, remembering the last sight he'd had of earth before it died.

"By the time I came into a large canyon and saw the portal, the ground was shaking. Mountains were breaking apart and falling down around me, and dust was so thick I could barely see. But the portal was a white, burning light piercing the cloud of dust. I stumbled, then got up and took only a few more steps before everything began to come apart. The last thing I saw was a young woman with long black hair running toward me. Her skin was burned and her lips were cracked and bleeding, but I knew it was Layla Birdsong, and I knew she'd come for me. She'd promised she would leave no one behind, and she kept her promise."

Tyhen burst into sobs and laid her head on Yuma's knee, clinging to his legs as he dug his fingers through her hair.

"I was there with my mother and I did not see you then. I should have known."

"It would have made no difference. Maybe you didn't see that because it was already the end and you belonged to the beginning. I tell you this, my love, so you will understand that I know how hard it is to leave people you love. And I know how impossible the task you have been given must seem. But our people have already sacrificed much just for the opportunity to go with you on your journey. They want the cycle of violence and hate to end. Whatever sadness you have, know that I cry with you. Whatever loneliness you feel, all you have to do is look at me, and I will share your pain. You are Windwalker's daughter, but you are also the other half of my soul, and I will protect you with my life."

Tyhen sat up, wiping away hot, angry tears from the injustice of what they'd been dealt. When she stood, she was the same fierce young woman who'd challenged the mob at the temple. As she began yanking at her clothing, the air in the room began to shift.

Yuma took a quick breath, instantly aroused by the sight of her smooth skin and soft curves. He stood long enough to remove his clothing, but she was already naked and the air was spinning so fast it was hard to breathe.

The moment he took her in his arms, the wind threw them backward onto the bed. He rolled her beneath him, parted her legs and joined her, and the moment they were one, the wind was gone and the room was still. A flower that had been floating in water only moments earlier dropped down from the ceiling and landed on the bed near her head.

"You are my heart," he whispered, then brushed a kiss across her lips and began to move.

Tyhen wrapped her legs around his waist, pulling him deeper, chasing that blood rush with every move she made. One minute passed into another and another until Tyhen was on the verge of a climax. It was the headiest feeling she'd ever had in her life, and in this bed, their powers were equal. He gave her so much pleasure that she wanted him to feel it, too, so she did.

Yuma was focused on waiting for the signs that would tell him she was there and ready when all thought was wiped from his mind. Breathing ceased as the climax rocked through him, one wave after another going on and on until he thought he was dying, and when it finally began to fade, he collapsed. He came to his senses on top of Tyhen and drew his first shaky breath, wondering if this was how breathing felt to a baby just born.

Tyhen sighed with lustful satisfaction as the tremors of her climax began to ebb. She began combing her fingers through his hair and gently kneading the back of his neck while being cautious of the new wound on his shoulder. She loved the feel of his skin beneath her palms and the hard play of muscles beneath.

"You are perfect," she said softly. "A perfect man, my perfect man."

"Am I still alive?" he mumbled.

She smiled. "Did I give you pleasure?"

He groaned. "Are you responsible for that?"

"I guess. I just shared what I felt so you could feel it, too."

"I make you feel like that?"

She nodded.

He managed a wry smile. "I am better than I thought."

She laughed and threw her arms around his neck. "You make me so happy."

He kissed her. Then he kissed her again and again until he'd kissed the smile from her face and put the lust back in her eyes because that was what made him happy.

****

The family met at sundown to share a meal. They had just begun to eat when they heard drums.

Cayetano recognized them as coming from the New Ones and quickly looked to Singing Bird.

"What is happening? What are they doing this?"

Singing Bird hesitated, and as she did, Yuma

quickly explained. "It is a thing our people do. It's like praying or talking to the Old Ones, asking for guidance and strength. Sometimes it is part of the stories the dancers are telling, like when your people pray to the gods for favors, our people are sending messages to Old Ones, asking for strength and power for the task ahead. This may go on until we leave. Do you want them to stop?"

Cayetano shook his head. "They can do whatever they need to do to prepare for the journey ahead."

Tyhen listened absently to her family's conversation, but her focus was on the drums. She could feel the spirits of the Old Ones all around them, but more importantly, she felt the urgency.

Yuma handed her a bowl with some squash and beans. She thanked him with a smile. She should have been starving because they'd made love most of the afternoon, but her appetite was small.

Adam glanced at her and when she caught him staring, he wiggled his eyebrows and grinned, like he knew what they'd been doing.

She arched an eyebrow and stared back.

You wouldn't make fun if you knew what you were missing.

The smirk died on his face.

We are different. It doesn't interest us.

So... then you can't tease if you are unfamiliar with the subject.

Evan caught the last part of their silent conversation and frowned at his brother.

Adam. Mind your manners.

Adam heard his brother, but ignored him. They always teased each other about everything. It was their one vice.

Then it occurred to him that this meal they were sharing was one of the last times they'd be together like this and, in a rare moment of emotion, felt a swelling pain behind his heart. He grimaced as he rubbed his chest, wondering if that was what it felt like to be sad.

Yuma had grown up with the twins and even though they were grown men, they were often childish in their behavior. They would have never made good warriors, but they were born to be shamans. He hated to leave them, but felt better knowing their particular skills would be part of what kept the people of Naaki Chava safe.

Singing Bird was smiling and talking, but the food that she swallowed sat in her belly like rocks. Despite all of their pretenses, it was not a happy gathering, and the drums were an ugly reminder of what was to come.

Long after the meal was over and they'd all gone to their rooms and then to bed, Singing Bird could not sleep and she wished the drums would stop. She felt safe in Cayetano's arms, but it was a false emotion. They would never be safe again.

****

The drumming stopped at sunrise. Even though many had yet to sleep, there was work to be done.

Shirley Nantay had been to the river early to wash clothing and was draping the wet garments over a makeshift clothes line Johnston had made for her years ago when she heard voices and the footsteps of people approaching. She walked out from behind her house and saw Singing Bird and her daughter approaching, accompanied by a handful of guards. She could tell by the expression on Singing Bird's face that it was not a social call and went to meet them.

"Good morning," Shirley said. "You're out early. Welcome to my house."

"Thank you, Shirley. I apologize for this unannounced visit. Is Johnston here? Tyhen and I would like to speak with him."

"Yes, he's here. Come inside."

Tyhen never tired of seeing the inside of the New Ones' dwellings. They looked nothing like the layout of the palace. When they walked inside, Johnston was at a table peeling fruit. He looked up, expecting his wife, then realized they had visitors and quickly wiped his hands before greeting them.

"Come in, come in! Have you eaten? We have plenty to share."

"We have eaten and thank you. I'm sorry to bother, but we need to talk."

"Please sit," he said, pointing to some benches near their table.

Singing Bird took a seat on the bench, but Tyhen walked to the window instead and looked out toward the fields where the people were already working, then up at the mountain that had become their enemy. She could hear her mother explaining what they needed and where they planned to relocate the people. When she turned around, Johnston was hurrying out the door.

"Where's he going?" she asked.

"Good news," Singing Bird said. "They have a map he thinks will help us. He went next door to send his brother to one of the storage buildings to get it."

Tyhen sat down beside her mother. She had her own news to impart, but one thing at a time.

A few moments later Johnston came back.

"Montford and his two boys have gone after the

maps. They know the one you'll need to see, but it may take some time to find it. They have not been cataloged in any order. If you don't have time to wait, I will gladly bring it to you."

Singing Bird glanced at Tyhen, and then stood up. "I will go back now, but Tyhen will talk to you. She can bring it."

Johnston walked Singing Bird to the door, but when he turned around, Tyhen was standing. Her eyes were fixed on his face as if readying herself to deliver a hard message. He took a slow breath, bracing himself for what she had to say.

"I leave Naaki Chava in six days."

Johnston reeled. "That soon?"

"So I was told."

Shirley ran to Johnston, clinging to him within the shelter of his embrace. She was crying, but Johnston's gaze never wavered.

"We will be ready," he said. "And just so you know, we have packs made especially for you and Yuma. We'll have them ready for you when we gather."

"I thank you," she said and then crossed the room to where they were standing and put a hand on Shirley's shoulder and felt her panic. "Shirley Nantay, I share your fears. I wish this was not so, but it is what I was born to do."

Wiping her eyes, Shirley turned to face Tyhen. "We know. We've known since the first day here that this would not be the end of our journey. We learned the hard way that nothing is forever, and how to be happy with what we had here. It's just that we are older now, and it will be more difficult. Like you, we do what we must."

"You need to know that visions have been given to

all the tribes. They now know what has happened and why we are coming."

"This is good," Johnston said.

"You told me before that not all of the New Ones had planned to come with us. So what do they say now that they know about the mountain and the fire?"

"They will walk with Singing Bird. She led them to safety once. They believe she will do it again."

Tyhen smiled. "My mother will be pleased to hear this. I will make sure to let her know."

Shirley interrupted. "I just remembered I was hanging my laundry. I should go finish the task. Excuse me."

She hurried out of the house, leaving Johnston and Tyhen alone, and the moment she left, Johnston did not hesitate to ask what was on his mind.

"Yesterday... at the temple... we did not know you possessed such powers and want to assure you that none of the New Ones had any part in that rebellion."

"I already knew that."

He looked at her closer. "I have known you since the day you were born. I've watched you grow into a woman. But the woman who stands before me now is not the same woman who was with me yesterday. Something happened to you."

She met his gaze in silence.

"I wasn't asking you to tell me what happened. I am telling you that I know, and it is an acknowledgement of our belief in your ability to make this journey successful."

Tyhen was touched by his faith in her. "I will do what has to be done."

Chapter Eleven

Two guards had been left behind to accompany Tyhen back to the palace. As she walked past the temple and through the marketplace, for the first time in her life, she felt the need for their presence.

The city was filled with dark energy. She couldn't tell if it came from the knowledge that the mountain was going to die and take the city with it or from the dissatisfaction of Cayetano's rule, but it was not a good place to be.

Even the people who would have normally waved at her or greeted her with smiles and offers of treats were now looking away or staring at her in fear. Yesterday she'd frightened them even more by her powers, reminding them she was not one of them. Being different was always the great divider.

As she got closer to the palace, she looked up at the dwelling rising from a sea of green. Once it had been her world, and now it was just a building. The realization startled her.

And so it goes. In my heart, I am already gone.

****

One day ran into the next and the next, complicated by the tragedies of good-byes and fear of the unknown until this day and the oncoming night would be the last she would know in the city of her birth.

It was also the day Tyhen said her good-byes to Acat, the little servant who had been her nursemaid, friend, and confidante.

Acat sat on the floor in Tyhen's room, weeping inconsolably. She was devastated by the news that Naaki Chava would be destroyed, but also because she would never see Tyhen again.

Tyhen finally sat down and cried with her. Oddly, it was Tyhen's tears that pulled Acat from her desolation.

"Don't cry, little whirlwind. I'm sorry. I'm sorry."

Tyhen threw her arms around the tiny woman and held her close. "I'm sorry, too," Tyhen said. "None of this is happy news, but it is the way with life, is it not? I believe it was you who taught me that all living things must die."

Acat swiped the tears from her face as she thought back, and then suddenly smiled. "Yes, yes, I did. It was when we found that little monkey dead outside your window."

"I'd never seen death before," Tyhen said.

Acat patted her knee. "You carried it to the pool of healing water, certain that it would come back to life."

Tyhen wiped her tears and smiled. "And I was wrong, so we buried a very clean, but very dead monkey."

Acat giggled.

Tyhen smiled.

And just like that, the crucial moment of good-bye ended with joy.

"I will miss you and say a prayer to the gods every day for your safety," Acat said.

"Thank you," Tyhen said and was still sitting in the floor when Acat scurried away. She looked around at all she was leaving behind, then hardened her heart and left the room.

She moved quietly through the palace halls on bare feet like the ghost she already was, setting certain things to memory because it was the only way she could take them with her.

The guards standing along the hallways maintained their posts as she passed, but she knew they were looking at her, wondering what would happen to her and where she would go.

It was nearing sundown. The long shadows were already showing on the floor beneath her feet. There was a place she wanted to visit, a secret place from her childhood and she had a need to see it one last time.

Finally, she came to the end of a dark, dusty hall. Once a woman who had been a weaver in the palace had called the room her home, but after she died, it became a place of storage.

Tyhen stepped inside the doorway and was struck by the sight of so much stuff: old benches, bent serving bowls, broken spears, damaged shields, things that should have been repaired but had been put in here and forgotten.

Then she remembered why she'd come and began counting off the tiles from the doorway until she came to the one that was loose. She dropped to her knees and, just as she'd done many times before, lifted it and set it aside.

Even though the light was dim in the room, Tyhen could see her little treasures. A braided piece of leather that Yuma had one day taken from his hair and tied in her hair instead, a tiny piece of hammered silver that had broken off of his shield, a small chunk of turquoise he'd given her after she'd fallen and scraped her knees. There were tears in her eyes as she went through the stash, remembering how dear they'd been to her then, and how small and insignificant they looked to her now. She put each item back as reverently as she'd taken them out, replaced the tile, and then pushed it down with the flat of her hand. It was cool to the touch and she wondered if, when the mountain died, the river of fire would come this far. Finally, she stood up and walked out. Those were pieces of the child she'd been, and since she was leaving that life behind, it was best they stayed with it.

Her steps were swift, her stride long as she moved through the palace. Guards were beginning to carry lit torches to their stations, lighting the halls as she made her way back to her room where Yuma would be waiting. The thought of him made her heart leap and she lengthened her stride.

****

Yuma had said his good-byes to the twins over an hour ago, then stopped by Singing Bird's room but she wasn't there. Instead of going to look for her, he went into their room to wait for Tyhen.

He'd spent a good part of the day down in the city with the New Ones, making sure everything and everyone was ready to leave tomorrow, then saying good-bye to the old ones among them who had chosen to stay with Singing Bird.

He stepped out of his sandals and took off his

loincloth, then went to a large bowl of water and began to wash. Once he was finished, he tossed the water out of the window and laughed when it sent a trio of monkeys scattering in three different directions. They were still screeching and scolding him when he walked away.

He picked up a banana from a bowl of fresh fruit, then changed his mind and put it back. The bed looked far more inviting.

He lay back with his hands behind his head, staring up at the ceiling. This time tomorrow night they would be sleeping under the stars and the thought made his pulse skip.

He stretched, and when he did, his long legs went off the end of the bed. Without traditional measurements, he had no idea how tall he was, but his father had been a big man, and Yuma guessed his final height was over six feet, a perfect match for the Windwalker's daughter.

He was thinking about the pond behind his father's house and the big mouth bass he used to catch there when he closed his eyes, and he was still thinking about home when he fell asleep.

****

Singing Bird had spent the day in isolation, strengthening her resolve for tomorrow. She would not shame her daughter or herself by weeping at their parting. Some things were beyond mortal control and this was one of them.

Cayetano had been noticeably absent all day, and while she wondered what he was doing, she didn't feel the need to find him to satisfy curiosity.

She had walked down to the healing pool during the heat of the day and shed her clothing on the rocks before immersing herself in the clear, bubbling water. This was where they'd brought her to heal from Firewalker's wrath, and this was where she first laid eyes on Cayetano. His presence had been just as imposing then as it was today and she was proud of him, both as a man and as their chief.

She lay back in the water, floating freely as she closed her eyes and prayed to give up her fear and heartbreak to the gods who'd set them on this path. She lost all track of time until she heard someone coming up the path. Quickly, she shifted from floating to a standing position, wishing she hadn't come here alone.

Moments later, her anxiety ended as Cayetano emerged from the jungle.

"I have been looking all over for you," he said gruffly as he shed his clothing, stepped into the water, and then took her into his arms.

She sighed as he pulled her close. He always made her feel safe. "I came to the healing pool for solace," she said softly, then gasped softly as his hands slid beneath her backside and lifted her before easing her down onto his erection.

"I have need of solace, too. We will heal each other," Cayetano said, and let nature have its way with the both of them.

Their stolen moments alone were as healing as the love they made together, and by the time they were on their way back to the palace, the sun was going down.

"This is their last night with us," Singing Bird said.

Cayetano's fingers curled a little tighter around her hand. "As long as I have you, I can bear anything."

Singing Bird glanced up, eyeing the profile of the man beside her. His nose had a slight hook to it; making her think of an eagle's beak. His forehead was wide, his cheekbones sharp and angled toward a strong chin. His long hair was tied into a loop at the back of his neck in the style of the people of Naaki Chava. In a brief moment of connection with her past, she remembered a college history class and seeing a similar profile that had been carved on the stone walls of an ancient Mayan temple. She smiled. Never in a million years would she have ever believed that a man like that would belong to her.

Cayetano sensed her stare and turned.

"Why do you smile?" he asked.

"Because, my chief, you make me happy."

"Your smile lights my life, but we need to hurry. It is getting dark and not even your smile will be enough to light the way back."

She thought of the jaguars that hunted at night and lengthened her stride.

****

Yuma was dreaming, and in the dream, he was watching his father driving in from the pasture with a truckload of hay just ahead of an oncoming thunderstorm. The first drops of rain were beginning to fall as he drove across the cattle guard and headed toward the barn.

Yuma leapt off the porch and was running to meet him as the wind began to rise. He looked up into the underside of rolling clouds turning darker by the minute and started to run, but the harder he ran, the farther he got from the barn. He could hear his father yelling, but the wind had risen to a high-pitched whine, stealing the words coming from his mouth. At that point, Yuma was just about to panic when he heard a voice that had no place in that dream. He opened his eyes.

Tyhen was standing beside the bed taking off her clothes and the wind that he'd felt in the dream had been real after all. But it wasn't caused by a storm. It was the emotional tie between them with a good helping of lust. She crawled into the bed and straddled his body without speaking a word, then lowered herself onto his erection, and just like that, the wind was gone and there was nothing in that moment that mattered more than the storm they made with their love.

****

It was a moonless night. The palace halls were dark, lit only by the smoking torches along the walls.

After Singing Bird fell asleep, Cayetano got up and went out into the halls, talking quietly to each guard as he passed, thanking them for their loyalty and loss of sleep, and promising to take care of them, no matter what.

Unknown to Cayetano, Yuma was on a similar mission. He'd served with these warriors and felt a kinship to them as well. He moved quietly from post to post, saying one last good-bye to the tribe of men who had accepted him without question, asking them to take good care of Cayetano and Singing Bird when he was gone.

When he turned a corner and saw Cayetano

coming down the same hall toward him, his heart thumped. Even though he'd outgrown the mighty chief in height, Cayetano's stature as a man and as a chief was without question.

"So, my son, it seems you do not sleep, either," Cayetano said as he approached.

"It is hard to say good-bye," Yuma said.

Cayetano grasped Yuma's arm briefly. "Walk with me."

Yuma fell into step beside his foster father, still coming to terms with the fact that he would never see him again.

"You have been a good son to me, and you are a strong warrior. Remember all I have taught you. You will need that knowledge and more in the coming years."

"I remember," Yuma said.

"Even though it is promised that you will be well-received on your travels, there will always be those who do not want to give up their power. Be aware of them."

Yuma nodded. "Do not worry. I will see into their hearts."

"People will die along the way. You know this," Cayetano said.

Yuma's gut knotted, remembering how the people died as they ran from Firewalker. This time it would be different, but he knew that death still came to unsuspecting souls.

"Yes, I know," Yuma said and nodded at a guard as they passed his post.

Cayetano was still talking. "Rarely can it be prevented. Do not take the blame onto yourself. Remember that they chose this walk with you."

"I will remember," Yuma promised.

When they reached the war room where most of their weapons were kept, Cayetano took a torch from the wall and carried it inside, then handed it to Yuma.

"Hold this for me. There is something I want to give you," he said and went straight to the place where his personal weapons were stored, then sorted through an assortment of knives before he found what he was looking for. "My father gave this to me. It has a name. It is called Warrior's Heart. Even though we do not share blood, in my heart, you are my son. One day you will pass it to another and that will make me happy."

When Yuma pulled the knife out of the leather scabbard, his vision blurred to the point he could barely make out the deadly curve to the blade or the chunk of jade mounted at the end of the hasp.

"I am honored, my chief. It will be good to take a piece of you with me."

Cayetano was equally moved, but managed a brief nod of satisfaction as they headed out the door. "We should go back to our beds before our women wake up and set the guards in search of us."

They walked in silence all the way back to the chief's quarters, and the look that passed between them was solemn, then Cayetano paused and gripped Yuma's arm.

"Walk strong on your great adventure, my son, and I will walk with you in my dreams."

In a rare gesture of affection, Yuma gave him a hug. "Thank you for saving me. Thank you for being the father I had lost."

Cayetano nodded once, but his eyes were glistening with unshed tears as he went inside and closed the door.

Yuma walked the distance back to Tyhen alone. He entered, quietly closing the door behind him. He slipped the knife into his pack, crawled back into bed with Tyhen, and closed his eyes and fell asleep.

Tyhen had known the moment he left their bed, and even though she wasn't physically with him, she'd seen every step he took, just like she'd seen him running through the jungle on the night he'd nearly died. The moment she felt his weight against her back, she let go of the vision and slept, and in her sleep, walked back through her childhood in Naaki Chava, all the way up to seeing the Windwalker in the temple. In the dream she could feel his arms around her and then the moment of his death, when he gave her his power. Just as she was waking up, she heard her mother's voice, but it was faint and Tyhen could tell that she was crying.

"How do I say good-bye to the child of my heart?"

Don't cry, Mother. When you need me, speak my name and you will hear me.

"Tyhen?"

Yes, Mother?

"This is you?"

Yes, Mother. I heard your cry. I am the Windwalker's daughter. I will always hear your voice.

When she woke again, it was to the sound of rain. It would seem the people were not the only ones who would be crying when they left Naaki Chava. Even the heavens wept the loss.

****

After all the build-up, and all the planning and talking,

the ensuing downpour made their exit from the city anti-climatic.

Adam and Evan had said their last good-byes to Yuma and Tyhen at the palace with a reminder that they *would* see them again, and then the twins had raced down to the temple to blow the Conch shell and gather the people. This time Adam did a decent job of sounding the signal, but considering the blinding flood of the rainfall, few came to see them off.

****

Tyhen's focus was on the journey, not the rain. The day was dark and gray from the overcast sky as she and Yuma arrived at the playa where the New Ones waited. If the sun had come up, they could not see it. When Johnston Nantay approached with her pack, she slipped into it without comment, thanking him with a quick nod and then climbed up a step at the temple so that the people could see her.

Yuma stood at the foot of the temple, only a few yards away from his woman, and all he could do was marvel at what she had become. The rain plastered her shift to her body like skin, showing every sinew and muscle. Her long hair was flat against her head and neck, her feet slightly apart as she braced herself against the pounding rain, but she did not look defeated. She looked ready for war.

The moment the thought went through his mind, she thrust her fist into the air, threw back her head and let out a war cry that even the rain could not mute. It was the perfect salute to their exit, because this journey was, in truth, a battle to save the human race.

As if the downpour wasn't reason enough to take shelter, the answering cry sent everything and everyone within hearing distance into hiding and put the people of Naaki Chava on their knees.

Tyhen's heart soared as the sound reverberated through her body. "We go!" she shouted, then came down off the temple in a leap that sent water splashing into the air and flashed Yuma a grin.

He answered with a laugh, then took her by the hand and headed out, walking behind the New Ones who had been chosen to take the lead, heading due North, straight past the dying mountain and into the future.

****

Rather than add to the confusion with all that the guards and ceremony their presence demanded, Cayetano and Singing Bird had said their good-byes at the palace and watched the procession's exit from their vantage point on the hill above the city.

Singing Bird stood in the rain without moving until the last person had walked out of sight, and then she went back to her room and collapsed, prostrate with grief.

Cayetano stayed beside her, afraid if he left her, that she would die from a broken heart.

Chapter Twelve

The jungle through which they walked was rife with overgrowth, much of which had to be cut down to get past. Thin vines with rough stems tugged and pulled at their clothing, as if unwilling to let them walk away. The rain made the path slick, and the terrain often caused moments of panic as sure feet suddenly slipped off narrow paths.

The New Ones had been wet before, and although it was an uncomfortable start to their journey, it did not faze them. Few spoke, saving their breath for walking the terrain, up hills and down into valleys heavy with the wet jungle growth.

When the rain finally stopped and the sun came out, it didn't take long for their clothing to dry and the insects to descend. Sensing the large quantities of fresh blood, they came in swarms, lighting on the plethora of bare flesh with vicious intent.

Tyhen had been walking without thought, just hoping to get through the first day without incident when the bloodsuckers enveloped them. Like everyone else, she began swatting them as they landed.

"Where on earth did all these bugs come from?" Yuma asked, then spit when one flew into his mouth.

She frowned, then turned around and looked down the long row of people behind her. As far as she could see, people were swatting and fanning at the insects, trying to keep them from their eyes and mouths. Because it had been raining when they left, no one had thought to rub their bodies with the medicine leaves. They'd passed the bushes in the jungle earlier, but obviously no one, including her, had thought to gather some for later.

"I think rain was better," she said.

Yuma wasn't going to disagree. "We need some of Little Mouse's stinky medicine rubbed on our bodies."

"I have a better way," she said.

Without missing a step, she raised her arms and swirled them over her head like she was stirring a stew. Within seconds a wind came, blowing down the line of marchers from the first to the last and blew the insects away. It continued as a breeze against their skin until they were completely out of the thick growth and entering a clearing that consisted of cleared fields and growing crops. In the distance, they could just see the rooftops of the villagers little huts.

The marchers immediately shifted course to keep from trampling the crops, and within minutes, people began coming out of the jungle on both sides of them, carrying fruit and offering drinks as if they'd known that they were coming.

When they spotted the young woman with long legs who walked among them, some dropped to their knees while others began chanting her name.

Tyhen waved, and when she did, they began shouting and pointing in delight that they had seen her for themselves.

Yuma was elated that their first meeting with another tribe had been a positive one, but he was under no misapprehension that it would always be this way. This tribe was still close to home. The truth of her journey would have been well-known to them. When she glanced at him and smiled, he smiled back. No need letting his concern shade the joy on her face.

The sun was directly overhead when they made their first stop beside a river. Some of the older ones dropped where they stood, too exhausted to even fill their water jugs, but the younger ones quickly picked up the slack. When they began to take food from their packs, they chose perishable food first.

Tyhen was tired, too, but she could tell morale was low. She stood silently, looking across the sea of stoic faces. They had endured so much already. She couldn't imagine what they must be thinking, but she knew they were grieving the loss of friends and family they'd left behind because she was, too.

Yuma walked up behind her, sliding his hand around her waist just to let her know he was here. He felt the tension in her muscles and then the release as she cupped his hand and leaned against his strength.

"Are you okay? Do you need to relieve yourself? If you do, I'll watch for you," Yuma said.

She nodded once, then turned and followed him a short distance into the jungle. She wasn't the only woman looking for a little privacy, but paid no attention to the others as she found a clump of bushes and did what she needed to do. She was on her way back when she heard someone crying.

She stopped and then followed the sound to a young woman who was down on her knees, her hands covering her face in a futile effort to muffle the sounds of her sobs.

Tyhen recognized her as she knelt and put a hand on her shoulder. "Are you hurting, Nona?"

The young woman looked up. "No, I'm not hurt. I'm sorry," she mumbled and began wiping away the tears from her face with shaky hands.

Tyhen knew what was wrong the moment she touched her. Nona's mother had become a cripple after her run from Firewalker, she had stayed behind.

"I left my mother behind, too," Tyhen said.

Nona's face crumpled as the tears began all over again. "We'll never see them again, will we?"

A muscle jerked near Tyhen's eye, but she didn't give in to her own emotions. "No."

Nona took a deep breath, and then slammed her hands against the ground. "I hate this!"

"Then why did you come? Why didn't you stay with your mother?" Tyhen asked.

Nona's shoulders slumped. "Because I love my husband, too, and he said it was our duty. Both of his grandparents died during the Last Walk. He is determined that their deaths not be in vain."

"So, do you love your mother more than your man?"

Nona's eyes widened. "No, but—"

"Grieve the loss, but do not regret it. You have to want to be here, Nona. This is hard enough without hard feelings, too. It's not too late. You can go back if you want, but remember, you will not stay in Naaki Chava either, because it will die."

Nona shuddered, then swallowed back a sob and wiped her face.

"I don't want to go back. I'm sorry, Tyhen. Thank you for talking to me."

"You're welcome, and don't ever be sorry to admit how you feel. Just remember, we all hurt, every one of us."

Nona nodded as she got to her feet.

Tyhen stood, brushed the dirt from her knees and then held out her hand. "Walk with me?"

Nona clutched Tyhen's hand like it was a lifeline and even managed a smile as they walked out.

When Yuma saw Tyhen coming out with another woman, he caught her eye, then followed them back to the others without intruding. It wasn't until they parted company that he caught up with Tyhen.

"Everything okay?"

She nodded. "Just a moment of grief. Something I'm sure we're all feeling."

Yuma cupped her face, and the moment they touched, she felt his love flow through her. She watched his dark eyes narrow as a small frown appeared between his brows.

"Remember, when you need, I will cry with you," he said softly.

She sighed. "I love you with all that I am."

He grinned to alleviate the seriousness of the moment. "And you *will* love me forever."

She smiled and then doubled up her fist and punched him lightly on the shoulder. "You should not boast."

He laughed, and then took her hand. "Come walk with me. The people need to see your smile."

Wisely, he was right. Instead of resting, she ate while she visited with the marchers, sharing their aches, and empathizing with the scope of what they were doing. But as she walked among them, something happened that she had not expected. Their outlook gave her spirit a boost. It was a reminder of how they had accepted their burden to see this through.

Finally, she walked down to the edge of the river to refill her water jug and wash her hands and face. She was on her knees, about to lean over and scoop water up to her face when she heard Yuma shout her name.

She looked up just as the snout of a crocodile surfaced only feet from where she was kneeling. She caught a brief flash of Yuma's dark hair and long legs and then he was in the water, locked into the croc's death roll. With one last splash of its tail, the crocodile took them under.

She screamed his name once as she leaped to her feet, then headed for the water with her knife in her hand. All of a sudden there were hands at her waist and then someone was dragging her back and she was screaming.

"Let me go! Let me go! He's going to die!"

"Stop, Tyhen, stop! You can't help. Look behind you! This is your responsibility! Yuma knew that when he went into the water. Let it be!"

When she heard Montford Nantay's words, she knew he was right. The knowledge that she was also a sacrifice for a greater cause was overwhelming. Heart breaking, she slid her knife back in the scabbard and backed away from the river's edge. At that point, time stopped. She saw nothing and heard nothing but the churning water. Although many people came running from all directions to see what was happening, they were of no use.

Tyhen was helpless. Every power she had was worthless if it could not save Yuma's life. She could not part the water. She could not stop the crocodile's heart, and she could not save her man. He was going to have to save himself.

She watched in mute horror as the water churned while the seconds felt like hours. Then suddenly the water turned to blood! When it began spreading across the surface, Tyhen would have fainted but for Montford, who steadied her on her feet.

The blood continued to spread and the water was no longer churning. It was the longest ten seconds in Tyhen's life before Yuma's head suddenly broke the surface of the river, and when he took a huge gulp of fresh air, everyone on the shore took a breath with him. The moment he began trying to swim back to shore, Tyhen pulled away from Montford's grasp and ran into the water after him, followed by a half-dozen men who helped her pull him out.

****

Yuma believed he would die and it didn't matter. When he'd seen the croc so close to Tyhen's head, he reacted without thought. Warrior's Heart, the knife Cayetano had given him, was in his hand before his feet left the ground, and when he hit the water, he landed belly down on the croc's back. His only thought was to stay away from the crocodile's mouth and teeth, and immediately wrapped both arms around the body while trying to get a grip strong enough to use his knife.

The moment the croc felt the threat, it went into survival mode, thrashing and rolling while trying to unload the enemy on its back.

Yuma's first stab with the knife was futile. The

hide was like armor, and once the croc pulled him under, he was fighting blind. Their fight had muddied the water to the point that he could not see where to strike. He just knew he could not let go. The first time the blade hit the soft flesh of the underbelly, he heard Adam's voice.

Again. Do it again.

So he did, stabbing and slashing, over and over, until he realized the crocodile was sinking and taking him with it.

Let go and swim up. Do it now!

Yuma didn't know what was up and what was down, so when he pushed off and began to swim, he could only hope it was in the right direction because he was out of air.

When he broke the surface and took a first desperate breath, he was only seconds from passing out. He kept gasping and blinking, trying to clear his vision and get enough oxygen in his lungs to move. Everything was a blur until he turned toward shore. He recognized Tyhen by her height and dark hair, and the fact that she was running into the water after him. He didn't remember swimming, only that he felt her hands pulling him toward shore.

When they finally pulled him to dry land, he was belly down, but the moment they turned him loose, Tyhen rolled him over onto his back.

"Breathe, Yuma, breathe!" she kept saying.

He was doing his best, still gasping for air, too exhausted to speak. His eyes were closed and he didn't know until she took it from him that he was still gripping the knife he'd used for the kill.

The moment Tyhen saw the deep, bloody scratch down the middle of his chest, she groaned.

"He's been hurt," she said and looked over her shoulder at the gathering crowd. "Someone bring medicine."

A healer quickly came forward, holding a small bag with medicines.

"Let me, little Dove," the man said and began cleaning the wound. When he was satisfied he'd removed all the debris, he spread an ointment down the length of the cut.

Tyhen was on her knees at his side, unaware she was crying. She was angry with herself, for the carelessness that had nearly gotten him killed. She might be Windwalker's daughter, but living in the palace under guard had left her naïve to the jungle's dangers.

As soon as the people realized Yuma was going to be all right, they began to disperse.

Montford touched Tyhen's shoulder.

She looked up.

"Do you have more need of me?" he asked.

"Not now," she said.

He nodded and started to walk away when she called him back. "Montford?"

He turned.

"Thank you," she said.

He smiled and nodded.

They had weathered their first danger on the first day of the journey and everyone was still breathing. Today she would ask for nothing more.

Then she felt Yuma's hand on her arm and her focus shifted. His eyes were open and he was looking at her.

"You saved my life," Tyhen said softly.

He wiped a shaky hand across his face. "When I saw that crocodile surface only feet away from your head, you took a year off of mine."

She laid a hand on his chest, taking heart that she could still feel the blood coursing through his body.

"I am not wise in the ways I should be. I have been too sheltered."

"This trip will make you tough and wise. If I live long enough," he added and managed a weak grin.

She rocked back on her heels. "You are making a joke? I was afraid that you would die because of me and you are making a joke?"

He heard the anger in her voice. "Is this then one of those times when you want me to cry with you?"

She frowned. "No, but—"

"Then will you laugh with me, instead?" he countered.

She stood, towering over him with her hands on her hips, her dark eyes glaring. "You make me crazy."

Yuma slid his knife back into the scabbard then held out his hand. "Help me up."

"I should let you lie where I dropped you," she muttered.

"But you won't because you love me and because it would appear to those around us that you do not appreciate your life enough to thank me for saving it."

Stunned into momentary silence, she sighed then thrust out her hand. When he clasped it, she pulled him up.

Now that he was standing before her with the blood still seeping from the wound upon his chest, she turned her back to the people around them and closed her eyes.

Yuma saw the tears seeping out from beneath her dark lashes and said nothing, but when she reached blindly for his hand, he took it and lifted it to his lips.

Tyhen felt the kiss, and at the same time felt the rapid race of his heartbeat. She'd scared him, too.

"I am so sorry," she said softly.

"Don't cry," he whispered. "You know how that hurts my heart."

She looked up at him through tears and then quickly wiped them away. "Come sit with me. We will rest a little more before we leave this place."

He let her lead him through the crowd, accepting their praise without anything more than a nod or a smile. He hadn't done it for praise. He'd done it for her.

Brother. Are you okay?

Hearing Adam's voice was almost as good as having the twins with them.

Yes. Thanks to you, I am okay.

I only said what you needed to hear. I did not fight that beast. That was you. You are the hero, the Eagle who protects the Dove.

****

Naaki Chava was so silent it already felt dead. Ever since Tyhen and the New Ones' departure that morning, the people stayed close to their homes. The marketplace had not opened and the few people who'd come out moved through the streets as if they were doing something wrong.

Singing Bird heard the servants talking, but she paid them no mind. There were things that had to be done. There was food ready to harvest that needed to be gathered. There was maize stored for grinding, and corn drying as well. Both had to be ground for flour, and many tasks to ready for their own exit from the city. She set people at those tasks and then began sorting through the things in the palace kitchen. They didn't need gold or silver to serve their food and began packing only the necessary things to cook with, leaving everything ornate and ceremonial behind.

She saw the twins only a short time after their midday meal and asked one question. "Are they well?"

They nodded, purposefully omitting the fact her daughter had come close to being croc bait the first day.

"Good. When you dream of the mountain again, you will tell me."

That was no question; it was an order, and they quickly nodded again. After that she was gone.

Cayetano was on his own quest to getting ready. He had copies of the maps the New Ones had given him relating to where they were now, and how far they would travel to reach what had been labeled on the map as South America. He didn't know the words or what they meant, only that it was a destination they needed to reach.

He ordered the cart makers to make new carts so the people would have a way to take what they needed with them and had his warriors repairing any of the weapons that needed care. They were leaving familiar territory, and even though the word had spread that tribes were not to war with each other or take prisoners and turn them into slaves, there was no way to assume that would be honored.

The New Ones who'd stayed behind were making

sure to leave room in their carts for needed building tools as well as the books Singing Bird had made. Some of the people were busy building little cages to take their chickens the traders had introduced in the city. No one wanted to leave them behind. While the sun was still new, they began killing the tapirs they were raising, which moved to the arduous task of smoking all the meat so it would not spoil on their long trek to a new location. It was serious business quitting home, even if the mountain above them was an enemy they could not defeat.

By the time the sun was setting and the torches were being lit, they'd put a good dent into the big job that lay ahead.

Cayetano walked into their room just after sunset and found Singing Bird sitting on a bench beneath one of the burning lights. Tiny winged insects were flying around the fire, drawn to the light in spite of the flame.

She was doing something with leather that he'd never seen her do before and slid onto the bench beside her to watch.

"What is this you do?" he asked.

"I am making moccasins. They will protect our feet far better than the sandals."

"In the jungle, we have no need of this," Cayetano said.

"That is here. Do we know what the land is like where we go? Do we know if there are thorns growing on the ground? Do we know if the rocks are so sharp they'll cut our feet?"

"No."

"Then I am preparing for the unknown," she said softly and knelt at his feet to test the size of the ones she was making against the size of his foot. "Good. It will fit."

"How do you know to do this?" he asked.

"Layla Birdsong's grandmother taught her."

He thought about frowning at the mention of the past and then changed his mind and touched the supple feel of the tanned skin instead.

"This is soft," he said.

"But strong, very strong," she added.

He smiled then pulled her up from the floor and into his lap. "Do we have food to eat here?"

She pointed to the table.

"Do you want to eat now or after we make love?"

She stood up, untied the shift she was wearing and let it fall around her feet.

Cayetano grunted, and then picked her up and carried her to their bed.

****

Adam and Evan were at a loss. They felt the absence of Yuma and Tyhen as physically as if they'd been punched.

"Brother, do you hurt in your chest?" Evan asked.

"Yes," Adam said and rubbed it with the flat of his hand as he looked away.

All of their lives, the only bond they had was to each other, and neither of them had ever lost someone they cared for until now, so feeling emotion was as uncomfortable as a sharp pebble beneath their feet.

Evan was uneasy. "What do you think is wrong? Do you think we are becoming ill? Do you think that we might die?"

Adam sighed. "Nothing is wrong. I think we are sad."

Evan's eyes widened. "We don't do sad."

Adam glanced at him and then picked up a banana. "Maybe we never had anyone to feel sad about before."

"I don't like sad," Evan said.

Adam sighed. "I don't either, but I think Yuma and Tyhen feel the same way, so we should not complain."

Evan took the banana from his brother's hand, peeled it, broke it in half, and gave one piece to Adam. Contemplating sad made him hungry.

Chapter Thirteen

Yuma had no idea how far they'd walked their first day, but by the time they reached a place safe enough for such a large group to gather and bed down, people were so tired they weren't talking. When their little shelters went up, the place looked like a miniature city. Some built fires to cook flat bread on hot rocks while others chose to eat from the food that they'd packed. The New Ones had already organized a guarding system into shifts, and while the majority of the people finally crawled into their tents to sleep, others stood guard around the perimeter. Whether it was a hungry jaguar, or an outlaw tribe out looking for trouble, they would be ready.

Tyhen watched several people putting up their tents and then pulled theirs out of the pack and set it up by herself. Soon, she had a fire going, too. It wasn't cold, but the fire kept insects and predators at bay, not to mention the dark. The moon was new, barely a sliver in the sky and shedding next to no light on the world below.

Hearing jungle sounds around Naaki Chava at night had been common, but they'd always had the protection of the city and their numbers for safety. Now the screams of big cats on the hunt and the death squeals of their prey were unnerving. The only things they still had going for them were their vast numbers and the guards.

Tyhen stood at the edge of their fire and looked out across the area. She had wondered why the New Ones had purposefully moved her and Yuma to the middle of the encampment, but now she could see why. They had all put themselves at risk to keep her safe. Protect her at all cost or this journey was for nothing.

She caught movement from the corner of her eye and saw Yuma heading straight toward her. She couldn't imagine how he had found her when everything looked alike, but she was glad he was back. She didn't know he'd only been a few tents away and had eyes on her the entire time.

Upon arrival, he eyed the tent, the fire, and then her.

She stood a little straighter as if waiting for judgment.

He smiled at her and she started talking too fast because she was afraid it was all wrong, but hoping she'd done a good job.

"Yes, I did all this by myself. I'm ignorant of the jungle, but I'm not helpless. Come sit with me by the fire or the mosquitoes will bite."

"Shirley Nantay sent you fresh bread," he said and handed her a piece.

She took a quick bite, grateful for the warm food as she eyed the cut down the middle of his chest.

"Does that hurt?" she asked.

"Not much."

Her hands were shaking as she handed him a piece of jerky and a banana, then took another bite of the bread.

"How about you?" he asked. "How do you feel after a day like today?"

When she looked up him over the fire, the blaze reflected in her eyes, and for a few seconds he thought of Firewalker and how far he'd come from Tahlequah, Oklahoma.

"How do I feel? Thankful you are alive and grateful for the hot bread and Johnston Nantay's jerky," she said.

He nodded. Tonight was a night for being grateful for many things, not the least of which was that Tyhen's head was still on her shoulders.

He finished his food and began banking the fire as Tyhen packed up what was left and crawled into the little tent.

Inside, it was barely big enough for two adults to sleep in, but it was animal hide and waterproof, and there was a large sleeping mat that fit perfectly inside the structure so that they would not be lying on the ground.

He crawled in behind her, using the glow from the embers of their fire to see his way. She was already curled up on her side, watching him.

"Lay down so that your wound is away from my body," she said softly. "I will lay behind you."

He didn't argue. There was no way he'd be able to sleep with any friction against his chest at least for a couple of days.

He did as she asked, and then sighed with satisfaction as she aligned herself with the curve of his body and slid her arm around his waist. He found her hand and clutched it close against his belly.

"Sleep well, my love. Tomorrow is a new day," he said.

Her fingers curled around his wrist. "Yuma?"

"What?"

"I will never put you in danger again."

"You can't make that promise. We don't know what lies ahead of us. All we can do is the best that we know how and that will be enough."

She didn't answer and he didn't push for one. Exhausted by the events of the day, they fell asleep, wrapped in each other's arms.

****

It was the third day since their exit from Naaki Chava and there was a distinct attitude shift in everyone with regard to acceptance of their lot, even an eagerness to see what lay ahead. They'd been climbing in altitude since early that morning, anxious to get over this latest mountain that stood in their path, and it was the sudden absence of sound that first alerted Yuma something was wrong. He started to mention it to Tyhen, then saw her motionless by a tree just a few feet ahead of him. Her head was cocked slightly to one side, and he could tell she was listening.

"What's happening?" he asked.

Her expression was just short of horror.

"Earthquake, Yuma. There's going to be an earthquake. We need to get everyone off this mountain."

Before she could sound the alarm, a loud *boom* rocked the jungle so loud that all the birds took to the air, so many it momentarily blotted out the sun. At the same time, Tyhen felt the first earthly shudder beneath her feet.

Yuma grabbed her hand as people all around them began scrambling.

"What do we do?" she cried.

"We should be out in the open, but that's not going to happen. Grab a tree and hold on."

The roar that followed the boom sounded like an avalanche as the ground began to shake. People were screaming; some were crying, but they'd all had the presence of mind to grab for the trees to stabilize their footing.

Tyhen had a death grip on a tree and Yuma had his arms around her, but when a large limb broke off above them and came crashing down beside them, she lost her hold and was tossed to the ground. Before she could panic, Yuma yanked her up and pinned her up against the tree.

"Hold on to me!" he said, yelling to be heard above the noise as he reached around her and grabbed hold of the trunk.

Heart pounding, she locked her hands around his waist as he dug his fingernails into the bark.

Unable to hold onto its perch, a monkey dropped from the canopy above, falling to its death only a few feet from where they were. Shocked, she quickly looked away, but when they began dropping with sickening regularity, they became another part of the nightmare.

It wasn't until wild animals began racing past them that they realized there was even more at stake. The animals weren't running downhill to get away or running amok in every direction. They were all running west. That made Yuma nervous. They'd been climbing in elevation for almost half a day, and it suddenly occurred to him that something else besides the ensuing earthquake must be imminent.

After watching yet another monkey fall to its death at her feet, Tyhen closed her eyes, and the moment she did, there flashed a vision of earth giving way above them. She staggered as she pushed out of Yuma's grasp and began to shout.

"There will be a landslide. The mountain is going to give way above us."

Before he could speak, Tyhen took a deep breath, and when she spoke, her words were amplified a thousand fold, spilling out into the jungle for everyone to hear.

"Landslide! Landslide! Run to the West! Follow me! Do it now!"

Even though the earth still quaked, Tyhen began to run, leading the way through the jungle with Yuma at her side and the New Ones at their heels. There was no trail to follow, no machete to cut the growth and ease the way, just people running blindly, slipping, falling, and getting up again with a heart-pounding leap, pushing past bushes and yanking away vines with no way of knowing what waited on the other side.

When the shaking finally stopped, they were still running at full speed, and for good reason. There was a new sound now, a rolling groan that came up from the depths of the mountain as the face of the slope above them came apart, shredding earth, rocks, and trees as it went. Torn from ancient roots, the slope came down, gaining momentum every second.

Tyhen ran with her pack bouncing against her back and her heart in her throat. She wouldn't look back. Her powers were no match for a landslide, and she didn't want to witness the inevitable. Some would not survive this.

Yuma ran with his eye on Tyhen in constant fear they would not get far enough away to keep from being caught in the slide they could not see. All they heard was a heart-stopping roar that pushed them farther, faster.

As they ran, there were moments when he would lose sight of her, and each time a piece of him died until she popped back into view. He'd heard her say that Windwalkers did not die, but he didn't see how anyone—even a Windwalker's daughter—could survive a falling mountain.

Behind them, the New Ones were in a panic. Older people were lagging behind, and others were getting their packs caught in the undergrowth and losing precious time tearing free.

Montford Nantay was running right beside Johnston and Shirley, just as they'd run from Firewalker. Either they'd all live together or they'd die together.

Nona, the young woman Tyhen had found crying in the woods, had a large bloody gash across her nose, but it hadn't slowed her down. She didn't want to die.

Her husband was running a few feet ahead, trying to clear a path through the heavy growth impeding their escape. And despite everyone's fear, the race for their lives was eerily silent. There was no breath for screaming.

When the first boulder finally reached the runners, it hit the ground, bounced over one man's head and landed forty feet away, taking out an entire family. They never saw it coming. One second they were breathing and then they were not. The landslide had arrived, greedily collecting bodies as it went.

The horror of still being alive when the person running behind you had disappeared in mid-step would not be real to the survivors until the panic was over. After defeating Firewalker, it was a hell of a way to die.

****

Despite their frantic need to keep running, it all ended with an abrupt stop at a river's edge. Even the riverbed had been cracked by the earthquake, and they watched from the shore at the massive whirlpool forming. The water was still flowing downhill from its source up the mountain, but the huge crack in the riverbed had formed a vortex and was sucking the water back into the earth from whence it came.

Tyhen turned around and looked up, half-expecting to see the mountain coming down upon them, but to her relief, it was still there. They could hear the rumble of the massive slide, but it was far below them now. When she realized they were actually far enough away to be safe, she threw herself into Yuma's arms.

"We did it! We're still alive!" she cried and kissed him hard and fast.

Yuma's heart was hammering to the point he could barely breathe, but like Tyhen, momentary elation took them past the reality of what had happened.

All those who had escaped were on the ground, too exhausted to move. Tyhen and Yuma began going from one group to another, looking for the wounded, moving them all to one area so they could be treated together while watching for the last of the stragglers as they came out of the jungle. Healers came forward without being asked and began administering medicine to stop the bleeding or helped in setting broken bones.

Yuma worked right beside Tyhen, unwilling to leave her own her own. The area was too unsettled, and the aftershocks were constant.

The landslide had literally cut the face from the highest point on the mountain, revealing the iron-rich earth beneath as a red, seeping wound. Many hundreds of years of tree growth, and the thousands of years it had taken to create the mountain had been destroyed in seconds. A river had been rerouted to nowhere, and precious lives had been lost.

Once the survivors had regrouped, they began trying to figure out how many they'd lost. But they had not started out with a head count or a list of names, and Tyhen quickly realized there was no way to determine the size of the loss. The deaths would go unrecorded save for the friends and family who knew they were gone.

The Nantay brothers were the closest tie Tyhen had left to her mother, and she had been looking for them for almost an hour when Yuma suddenly grabbed her arm and pointed.

"There they are!"

When she saw Shirley and the brothers alive and breathing, she clenched her teeth to keep from bursting into tears.

Johnston saw her first and stopped what he was doing and headed toward her. Without speaking first, he just picked her up and held her, her feet dangling off the ground. Then he began to praise her.

"We heard your voice! We heard the warning! You saved us, Tyhen. You saved us all."

She shook her head, still choking back tears.

"Not all of you."

"We knew when we left that we would not all make it. Nature is not always kind."

Montford and Shirley were right behind him, and they hugged her as well while repeating what Johnston already said. It wasn't an easy thing to live with, but Tyhen was beginning to accept that there would be things she could not prevent.

A Windwalker's daughter was not a god.

Johnston grasped Yuma's arm in a gesture of greeting, then pointed to the river.

"The earthquake did this, I think."

Yuma swiped at a streak of blood that kept running down his belly from a deep scratch beneath his chin.

"I agree, and it's not safe to cross here," he said. "Maybe farther downstream where the water is no more, but not here. The force of this whirlpool would pull anyone down into the belly of the earth."

"Is it safe to stay here until morning?" Montford asked.

Tyhen could still feel an occasional shudder from the earth beneath their feet. When she closed her eyes, she saw a broad expanse of land at the foothills of a mountain, and knew that's where they needed to be.

"No. We need to get off the mountain, and the fastest way to do that is to walk downhill along this river until we find a safe place to cross."

Yuma quickly agreed. "There could be an aftershock that might bring down more of the mountain. As soon as we get the injured ones bandaged, we'll figure out a way to bring them with us."

"We can make a travois, like in the old days," Montford said. "I will get some men started on them." He hurried away.

"What is a travois?" Tyhen asked.

Johnston began to explain., "Two long poles with a blanket or an animal skin tied between them to form a bed. Our ancestors moved belongings, as well as the sick and injured with them in the old days. The travois was pulled behind a horse, but we do not have horses here, so people will pull them and it will work. Yuma, you and Tyhen get your packs and come back to us. Shirley has medicine for your cuts."

"They are nothing," Yuma said.

"No, in the jungle they are something," Tyhen reminded him as she tugged on his hand. "Let's hurry. I want to get moving as quickly as possible. This place doesn't feel right. I don't think it's over."

Yuma nodded and broke into a jog with Tyhen right behind him.

****

Naaki Chava: same day

One of the vendors in the marketplace was setting out flat cakes baked fresh that morning. The vendor on the opposite side of the street had trays of fruits and vegetables set up for trade. Several women were walking toward the fields with baskets on their heads to gather food ready to harvest.

Wesley Two Bears was sitting outside, watching the woman next door making new fire to cook a morning meal. He looked down at his hands, joints knotted with arthritis and wrinkled with age. He was tired of this life, but he was still here. His wife was gone and every other member of his family had gone on the long walk with Tyhen.

He glanced up at the mountain and then stood, stretching his bare legs before grabbing a fishing pole and heading to the river. He was tired of fruit and vegetables. He wanted fresh fish.

Little Mouse was already anxious about leaving Naaki Chava and all that was familiar. She had gone into the jungle early that morning to gather healing plants and roots to take in her pack and had no other thought in her head but her daily routine.

Adam and Evan, accompanied by a couple of guards, were coming back from one last trip to the temple to make sure nothing valuable would be left behind. The only things they'd taken were a couple of small statues, and the Conch shell they'd left there the day Tyhen and Yuma left the city. Although the twins were uneasy, it appeared to be business as usual, just on a much smaller scale. Their sleep had been restless the night before with flashes of people running and crying, but that had not seen any volcanic eruption, and nothing else specific enough to pinpoint.

Still, they were certain enough of impending trouble to mention it to Singing Bird, but she'd only nodded absently and walked away. In her world, everything was wrong, so their warning was no big deal.

"Do you feel it?" Evan asked as they passed a vendor sleeping in the sun.

Adam held up his arm. "All the hair is standing up on my arm."

They'd taken only a couple more steps before they heard the guards whispering behind them.

Adam stopped and turned around. "What's wrong?"

"Listen," the guard said.

The twins listened. "We don't hear anything," they said.

"And that is wrong," the guard added. "No birds, no monkeys, no sound at all from the jungle."

Within seconds all the birds took to the sky. The moment that happened, Adam grabbed Evan's arm.

"Earthquake!"

And to punctuate the prediction, a boom so loud that it popped the twins ears echoed within the city like a cannon shot, followed by tremors so strong it knocked them off their feet.

Down in the city, people began screaming and crying, throwing up their hands and praying to the gods not to let them die. Some fell to their knees, while others ran back inside their homes only to have the walls collapse. Some houses fell in around the people, while others came apart, falling onto the cooking fires outside.

Adam and Evan had dropped to their hands and knees, and when the guards got up and started to run for shelter, they stopped them with a shout.

"Stay outside! It's safer."

The guards stopped and dropped to their knees, but they were not convinced it was safe anywhere and knelt clutching their spears and shields as if they would do battle to defeat this madness.

The twins grabbed each other for support, and the moment they touched, flashed on the day that

Firewalker had finally come to Landan Prince's island. Everything was shaking then, like it was now. The only difference between then and now was Firewalker and the heat. The twins looked toward the mountain, which was an earthly form of Firewalker, and when they did, knew this was their warning. When this earthquake was over, they had to get out of Naaki Chava. There would be another earthquake sometime within the next three days, and they had to be a long way gone when it happened.

****

The palace was in the same sort of chaos. Guards ran into the halls looking to Cayetano for orders. Servants were screaming and praying to their gods to save them.

Singing Bird was in her quarters when the shaking began. She knew the safest place during an earthquake was to get out of a building, but instead of jumping out her window to safety, she ran out into the hall shouting Cayetano's name only seconds before things began falling in behind her.

****

Cayetano was in the throne room with the map the New Ones had given him laid out on a table. He had studied them until the drawings were firmly fixed in his mind. He knew the shape of the mountain to watch for, and then to follow the coast until they came to a large, sheltered bay. That was where ships would come in, they said. That was where they needed to build a new city, they said, a place to show their unity as a people with power to stand firm against the strangers' promises and demands, they said.

As chief, it was hard for him to follow other people's directions, but this was an event out of his experience, and he couldn't make a mistake about relocating an entire city of people.

He was rolling up the map when he heard a noise so loud it made the walls shake, and when the floor beneath him began to move, he looked down in horror. What was this magic that made rocks dance beneath his feet?

And while he was looking down, a chunk of the ceiling came loose a short distance from where he was standing, splintering the tile floor behind him into pieces.

At that point, guards came running.

"Cayetano! Cayetano! The ground shakes. The gods are angry! What do we do?"

Before he could answer, he heard Singing Bird calling his name. He pushed them aside and ran out into the hall just as she appeared at the far end of the corridor.

"Get out! We have to get everyone out!" she yelled and began waving at the servants and guards within sight.

Cayetano caught her on the run and headed to the nearest doorway as bits of the palace rained down upon their heads.

Once they ran out into the sunlight, horror struck as they saw what was happening down in the city. Roofs on houses were falling in, walls were no longer standing, and because of thatched roofs and wooden walls, fires were spreading from house to house. People weren't trying to put them out. They were just grabbing what belongings they could and running in every direction.

Cayetano groaned. "We have to stop them. How can we stop them?"

All of a sudden, a long, mournful bellow rang out across the valley. They looked down the road leading to the city and saw the twins. One of them was blowing the Conch shell and the other one was waving to get the people's attention. They kept blowing and waving, and blowing and waving, until the sound superseded the earthquake's roar, and when it did, people stopped running amok and ran toward the sound.

"They did it!" Singing Bird cried. "They stopped the panic. Now we must get down there. They need to see your face."

****

Tyhen had been helping Susie doctor the gash under Yuma's throat and had just turned around to wash the blood from her hands when the sight before her disappeared and she was back in Naaki Chava with her mother, watching it burn.

She moaned and then swayed on her feet, and when she did, Yuma grabbed her.

"What? What's happening? What's wrong?"

She could hear him, but now she was standing in front of the palace watching her mother and Cayetano running down the hill.

"It's on fire. Naaki Chava is on fire."

"Why?" Yuma asked.

"The earthquake. It happened there, too," Tyhen said.

Shirley gasped. "The cooking fires. The wooden walls and thatched roofs probably fell into the cooking fires. I hope the people got out."

"Run, run," Tyhen whispered, watching the people fleeing the chaos.

Yuma pulled her into his arms and pressed her face against his chest. "Don't look! You can't stop it!"

The moment he touched her, the image was gone. She slid out of his arms and into the dirt at his feet and hid her head on her knees.

Shirley squatted down beside her. "Sad things happen and eventually, everybody dies."

Tyhen sat without moving or talking for so long Yuma began to worry. The sun was halfway toward sunset and they had yet to start walking downhill to find a crossing. He looked around for Montford or Johnston to ask if they were ready to move, and when he turned around, Tyhen was on her feet.

He reached toward her, then stopped and let his hand fall back to his side. She had that look in her eye again, the one where she stirred up a wind to do battle, but her face and voice were devoid of emotion.

"The twins are fine. Mother and Cayetano are okay. They are leaving the city and we need to leave, too."

He nodded. "I'll find Montford and tell him."

"I'll get our packs," she said.

He turned around and grabbed her by the shoulders, his dark eyes as serious as the tone in his voice. "Don't move until I get back."

She blinked as her sight began to refocus and laid her hand over his heart. "Ever my protector, the eagle in the sky watching over the little dove. Go find Nantay. I will wait."

Yuma grabbed her hand and kissed it, then ran off through the crowd. She shouldered her pack, checked to make sure her water jug was refilled, and then checked his pack as well before laying it beside her. And then she waited.

Every so often they could feel a tiny aftershock beneath their feet. It reminded Tyhen of the lingering tremors running through her body after she and Yuma made love. But these tremors were warnings, where hers had been reminders of earlier joy.

She glanced over at the river. The whirlpool was massive now, reaching from one side of the river to the other, leaving the riverbed below visible to the naked eye.

If they walked far enough, they should be able to find safe crossing. She just wanted the people off this mountain and out of this country while they were still in one piece.

A few moments later, she heard Yuma calling her name. She looked back and saw him coming toward her and felt a brief moment of lust. He was so beautiful in her eyes.

When Yuma reached her, he took her arm like a child does playing a game when they run home to touch base.

"They are ready," he said. "They'll bring the injured ones last, so it won't slow down the walk. Are you ready to go?"

"I go where you go," Tyhen said, and in that moment, a memory emerged from Yuma's life before Firewalker.

It was one of the few memories he had of his mother. She was in his father's arms and crying because they were going to have to move. He had seen the sadness on his father's face because it was his job that had caused this. His mother had also seen the sadness, and it made her stop and wipe her eyes. Just as his father began to apologize, she put a hand over his mouth and said, *Whither thou goest.*

He knew what it meant now, and in a world so far away from that one, in so many words, he'd just heard it again. It was a vivid reminder of how strong a woman could be, and how all-encompassing her heart was to the people she loved.

Tyhen was motionless, waiting for him to speak. She could tell something she'd said or done had triggered a memory because he had that faraway look in his eyes. She never liked to see that look because it meant he was in a place she'd never seen. So instead of waiting for him to speak, she slipped her hand into his.

"We go," she said softly.

He curled his fingers around her hand in a won't-let-go grip and then kissed her knuckles and nodded.

When they started walking, the others followed. Soon, all of the survivors were walking downhill, following the bed of the dying river and silently grieving the dead they left behind.

Chapter Fourteen

Everyone from the palace went down to meet the people running up from Naaki Chava. The earthquake had done something that nothing else could have ever done. It had put them all on equal footing. The people from below had the clothes on their backs and what belongings they had rescued from the fires, and when Singing Bird and the servants rescued what they could from the wreckage of the palace, they would be no better off.

There was much crying and screaming until, at Cayetano's bidding, Adam blew the Conch shell one last time. When he did, the crowd went silent, waiting to hear what came next.

Before Cayetano spoke, Adam quickly whispered in his ear.

"We have to leave. This mountain will die within the next three days. This earthquake was a warning."

Cayetano's eyes momentarily widened, but it was the only sign he gave of the shock. He glanced down into the city that was afire behind them and then began to speak, shouting loudly to be heard.

"As soon as we recover what we can from inside the palace, we will leave. The gods have shown us mercy. Shaking the earth was our warning to leave. Sometime during the next three sleeps, the mountain will die."

There was a long moment of silence as the people tried to come to terms with the concept of an earthquake and a fire being a merciful stroke of fate. The city *was* in flames behind them, but the mountain was *still* silent. They decided the chief was right, took a collective breath, and waited for what came next.

"What do you want me to do?" Singing Bird asked.

Cayetano hated to let her out of his sight, but he knew she would be insulted if he didn't let her go.

"Take the servants, find our packs, and bring them outside of the palace. If they have been destroyed, just take what you can find and hurry."

Singing Bird spun on her heel and waved to the servants.

"Come with me," she said and started running back up the hill. They followed without hesitation, anxious to get away from such devastation.

When they reached the palace, seeing the destruction was shocking, but in a way made leaving less painful. What had been was gone. What would be was yet to come.

She could see the servants were hesitant to go inside, fearful something might still fall down upon them.

"We have to hurry," she said. "Grab what you can of your belongings and come back out here to wait."

She led the way through the fallen blocks of stone and the broken tiles, and when the others scattered to their own places to find what they could, she started down the hall toward the chief's quarters.

Making her way through all of the debris was not only slow going, but dangerous. Once she slipped and fell, cutting her knee deep enough that it bled, but she kept on going. When she finally reached what had been the entrance to their rooms, the doorway was but a pile of rock. She had to go around through a connecting room, and then in through a broken wall to get into the space.

Once inside, she began moving through rubble, trying to remember where she'd left everything. There had been a large pack apiece for her and Cayetano, and a small one that she'd meant to carry in her arms. It had medicines and healing herbs and things she could not leave behind. Aware that they would be waiting on her, she began digging through the rubble in haste.

****

Because it was a shorter distance to their room, Adam and Evan entered the palace from the back entrance, only to find that the palace had not suffered as much damage as the front. But once they reached their room, the interior was a different story. It was in shambles.

"Where did you leave our stuff?" Adam asked as he set the Conch shell down on small table that had survived.

Evan frowned. "I'm not sure. I think it was at the foot of our beds, or maybe beside that table by the door."

"There is no longer a table by the door, and I do not see our beds," Adam muttered as they began to search through the debris.

Once they located their packs, they began checking to make sure everything they intended to take was inside. Adam opened his up and put the Conch shell into a space he'd made for it just this morning. He was trying to remember what he'd taken out in an effort so that the Conch shell would fit, when all of a sudden, it hit him.

"Oh no, no, no! The portal cube! The bird necklace. They're gone! I have to find it! It's the only way we have to find Tyhen and Yuma again, and it's not in my pack. Help me look! She told me to take care of it," Adam cried. "She said she wanted it back. She will kill me if I've lost it."

"No she won't. She can't kill us if we never see her again," Evan said.

Adam stared at him. "Did you hear what you just said?"

Evan shrugged. "I stated a truth."

Adam rolled his eyes. "Shut up and help me find the necklace."

"I already know where it is," Evan said as he dug through his pack and pulled out the box with the portal cube. "If it's in with the cube, then it is here. I saw it this morning and put it in my pack."

Adam wiped a shaky hand across his face and held out his hand.

Evan handed it over with ceremony. "You're most welcome," he said.

Adam rolled his eyes as he checked to make sure they were both there. And they were.

"Thank you. Now let's check on Singing Bird and see if she needs help."

They shouldered their packs and didn't look back, leaving the room that had been their home for the past fifteen years as easily as they'd left Landan Prince to die on Bimini Island without them.

****

Singing Bird had finally located the last of their things, but there was no way she could get all of it out in one trip. She was just about to go look for help when she heard voices. Someone was calling her name.

"Singing Bird! Where are you?"

"I am in here," she yelled back.

To her relief, it was the twins. They came in the same way she had through the hole in the wall.

"What do you want us to carry?" they asked.

She pointed to the large pack she'd made for Cayetano.

"That belongs to your chief. You can take it to him."

Adam grabbed it with one hand while Evan picked up the other.

"That one is mine. I can carry that," she said.

"After you get outside," Evan said and pointed to her knee. "You are already bleeding. Cayetano is not going to be happy."

She didn't argue because she knew they were right and took the small one, instead. He tended to lose rational thought where she was concerned and she was grateful for the unexpected help.

"Thank you, my sons."

They nodded and then glanced at each other.

She knew that look. They were keeping something from her, and the moment she thought that, she knew it had to do with the others—with Tyhen and Yuma and the people who'd gone with them.

"What happened?"

"First you need to know that Tyhen and Yuma are okay," Adam said.

Singing Bird's stomach knotted. "Which means others are not. Tell me what you know."

"The earthquake caught them as well. They were halfway up a mountain when it struck."

Evan picked up the story. "They were holding onto the trees to keep from falling down when Tyhen sensed a more serious danger. The quake caused a large landslide above them. She sounded the warning as they began trying to outrun it. Most of them made it, but some of them did not and she is very sad."

She moaned. "They lived through Firewalker and then died like that? It isn't right. It isn't right."

Adam shrugged. "Life isn't fair. Why then should death be any different?"

His words struck her as cold, but when she looked at them, she remembered what the existence of their life had been like before, and realized they were right. Nothing was fair. People are born. People die. It's what they do and how they do it in between those times that matters.

"You are right. I'm sorry. It was just a shock. But you are sure Tyhen and Yuma are safe?"

"Yes, we are certain," Evan said.

"Good. Then we go."

Once they exited the rubble, they began counting off the names of the servants who'd gone inside, making sure everyone was present.

As predicted, Cayetano immediately saw the blood on Singing Bird's leg and stopped everything to make sure she wasn't seriously injured.

"I am fine," Singing Bird said and smiled as she stroked the side of his face.

He knew he should not have let her go inside on her own, but after a look at the cut, took her at her word.

"Is this my pack?" he asked as Adam handed it over.

Singing Bird nodded.

He slipped his arms through the straps, shifted it one way and then another until it felt comfortable on his back and then turned to the vast number of people awaiting his word.

They were scattered around the grounds of the palace and all the way down the hill, carrying only what they'd been able to rescue from the fire. His warriors had retrieved plenty of weapons, but it was not the way he'd planned their exit.

He turned to the twins.

"Is there more to know?"

"There will be more shaking, but nothing like before."

He looked down into the city and tried not to think of what was gone. They'd lost so much already, but nothing could matter but people. Everything else could be rebuilt.

A few more people emerged from the jungle. They'd been there when the earthquake began. There were more wails and more cries of disbelief when they realized what was lost but were soon calmed by the realization that they were lucky to still be breathing.

"Adam, send the signal. We leave now."

Adam pulled the Conch shell out of his pack one last time then blew it, sending the signal they'd been waiting for.

People began getting to their feet and gathering up their things, and when the chief lifted an arm into the air, swung it South, and started walking, they followed. There was no need to look back. Naaki Chava was already gone.

Wesley Two Bears trip to the river was uneventful, but upon arrival he found two large water birds feeding in the shallows where he usually tossed out his line, so he moved a short distance downstream. He had just thrown his line into the water when he heard what sounded like an explosion.

Startled, he turned toward the city as the big birds took flight. They were in a panic to be airborne and he was focused on the people he could see who were running, and he didn't see the birds flying toward him until it was too late.

The largest bird flew into the side of his head as it took to the air; knocking him off his feet. There was an intense pain and a loud snap as his hip gave way. He fell only inches from the water, unable to move and in terrible pain.

He shouted for help, but there were so many people screaming and yelling that they did not hear him. When the ground began to shake, it threw the water up into his face. He tried to crawl away, but every time he would move, he would faint from the pain, only to be awakened by the water sloshing in his face.

The last time he passed out, the water kept splashing, and his face was underwater and so he drowned.

After the shaking stopped, the water returned to its normal place. Smoke was blowing in Wesley Two Bears' face as he lay near the river's edge, his fishing pole crumpled beneath him.

His fishing trip was over.

****

Little Mouse was halfway up the mountain looking for fever root when the loud boom sounded. Startled by the noise, her first thought was that this was it. The mountain was going to die and she was on it. But then the top did not come off and there was no fire shooting into the air. Before she had time to rejoice, the ground began to shake, and she dropped to her belly and grabbed hold of the earth, begging and screaming at it to be still.

But the earth did not heed her cry and kept shaking and toppling trees, rolling rocks, sending all the birds in flight and every animal in the jungle into a race to get away. When the tree beside her cracked at the roots and began to fall, she knew she should have been running. But by the time the thought went through her head, the tree was down and she had been knocked unconscious by one of the limbs.

It was the smell of smoke that woke her, which made her panic. She didn't know where she was or what had happened, but she didn't want to burn up. She pushed and shoved at the out-flung limbs until she made her way out from under the tree, then dragged herself up to a standing position.

Her head was bleeding, her right knee and left arm were throbbing, and the smoke was so thick it made her gag. She stumbled and staggered on her way downhill. All she wanted to do was get back to Naaki Chava. Someone would help her there.

But after only a few minutes of walking she emerged into a clearing and looked down into the valley, expecting to see the city below, but it was gone. All of it! Gone! Reduced to piles of burning rubble!

"No," she said and started walking. "Noo!" she shouted as she lengthened her stride. "No, no, no!" she screamed as she began to run.

But it changed nothing. No matter how fast she ran, it was all too late. Her city was in ashes. The people were gone, and there wasn't a living soul in sight. She forgot about her injuries. She was immune to all the pain. She just ran and ran and ran until she reached the first pile of smoking embers, then stopped, heart pounding and choking on smoke.

"Hello? I am Little Mouse! I am here! I am here."

Smoke drifted between her line of vision and the city, and when it cleared, she looked up, straight toward the palace. She could still see the shape of it and her heart thumped once in thanksgiving.

That was where they'd gone! Everyone must be up at the palace! Yes! That was it! The city caught fire, so they ran, and they are safe with Cayetano and Singing Bird.

It didn't register that scenario would have been impossible. The city has been too large for all the people to fit into the palace, even if it had been built for the chief of Naaki Chava. She needed that fantasy to get her through the city, and when the wind blew burning embers into her hair and on her clothes, she put them out with her hands and kept moving.

She didn't know until she reached the palace that one of her sandals was missing and the other nearly burned through on her foot. She reached down and pulled it off, then tossed it aside without care. They would find her another pair. They would put medicine on her burns.

Blind to all the debris lying in the doorway, she walked around it and stepped into the first hall.

"Hello. I am Little Mouse. I have been hurt. Will someone help?"

A bird suddenly flew out of a doorway down the hall and came toward her, aiming for the light. She dropped to her knees as it sailed over her. She was shaking now so hard she could not stand. Shock was setting in.

"This is me! I am Little Mouse! Someone come help me! Help me!"

The words echoed. A wind whistled a warning as it moved through the palace.

She rocked back on her heels and began pulling at her hair.

"This is Little Mouse! I am here! I am here!"

A monkey dropped down from an opening in the ceiling and stared at her for a moment before scampering away.

She looked up, saw the clear blue sky where it shouldn't have been, and then saw the palace for what it was. Fresh blood was running down her face now; but not from the cut on her head. It was from the places where she'd pulled out her hair, and in that moment, her reality shifted.

"Little Mouse helped you," she mumbled as she staggered to her feet. "Little Mouse always came when you called, but you did not wait for her."

She looked around, trying to orient herself within the palace, then stumbled down the hall toward the place where they made the food. She was hungry and she was thirsty. And this would be home.

Chapter Fifteen

While Cayetano and Singing Bird led their people South, Tyhen and Yuma were looking for a safe path to continue their journey North.

They had been on the move for almost two hours, and as expected, the farther downriver they went, the less water there was in the riverbed. When they finally came to a place where the water was gone, they stopped to survey the sight. There was nothing left to see but dead fish, a few water snakes still writhing in the mud and a couple of stranded turtles. It was the absence of crocodiles that made it even more appealing.

Tyhen had dropped back a couple of paces earlier to talk with Nona, who was now sporting two black eyes from the blow across her nose, so Yuma began checking out the site on his own. He saw what appeared to be a good place to cross and went closer to check it out. The drop-off wasn't steep, but there was no way to tell how deep the mud was but to walk through it.

Both of the Nantay brothers, along with some of the elders, came running when they saw him start down the slope.

"What do you think?" Montford asked.

Yuma pointed. "I don't see any crocs anywhere. Can't tell if there are any sinkholes until we walk it."

All of a sudden Tyhen was behind him, then grabbing his arm. "You can't cross here. Get back."

Yuma turned around. "Why not?"

"Something is going to happen. We can't cross this. There isn't time."

Yuma frowned. "But we have to cross sometime or we'll wind up back where we started."

She held firm. "We can't cross here."

Johnston nodded. "Then we won't," he said. "I'll tell the others to keep walking."

"And stay away from the edge. Tell them not to get too close to the edge," she added.

Yuma's frown deepened. "What did you see?"

"A wall of water."

He shuddered. "You mean—"

Before he could finish what he'd started to say, the ground began to shake. It wasn't the first time they'd felt tremors since the big quake had ended, but it was the biggest one by far.

A few people began to weep and threw up their hands, beseeching the Old Ones to spare them once more.

"Get away from the riverbank!" Tyhen yelled, and people responded without question.

The ground shook more, and the people dropped to their knees and threw themselves on the ground. There was nowhere to go but down, and they were too weary to run.

The aftershock continued to rumble like an angry old woman who'd been disturbed from her sleep. By the time the tremor stopped, nerves were frazzled and tempers were short.

"We want to leave this place!" a woman cried. "Why can't we cross?"

Once the complaint had been made, another followed.

"I'm not afraid!" a young man cried.

Tyhen turned around and saw it was Nona's husband who was speaking.

"You can't cross here!" she shouted. "Stop yelling and listen! It's already coming!"

The New Ones listened. At first they heard nothing, and then when they did, they didn't recognize the sound.

"What is that?" Yuma asked as the whistling sound grew louder and louder until it had turned into a rush like the sound of an oncoming wind.

"I think the second quake sealed up the hole in the riverbed above us. I think the whirlpool is gone," she said.

They were all looking upstream when a wall of water appeared; rolling so fast it was out of its banks. People began screaming and running back into the jungle to keep from being swept into the flood.

Yuma grabbed Tyhen's hand, but he didn't need to urge her. She was already moving.

After the first wave passed, the water quickly found its level. It was still moving at breakneck speed, but now contained back where it belonged. The people stared in disbelief, well aware she had just saved their lives again.

Nona was one of the first to come looking for Tyhen, and she was dragging her husband with her. As soon as they saw her, Nona headed for her with intent, her husband still in tow.

"My husband has something he wishes to say."

When the young man ducked his head and looked

away, Nona gave his arm a sharp tug. "You had plenty to say a few minutes ago. Say it now or you will be the one cooking our meals on this trip."

The young man sighed. "I am sorry I questioned you, Tyhen. I am sorry I doubted you. I am a fool."

Tyhen bit her lip to keep from smiling. "I doubt you are a fool and you are forgiven. This is a frightening time for all of us."

He nodded quickly and then grabbed his wife and walked away.

Tyhen sighed, and then in a rare moment, put her arms around Yuma's neck and hid her face against his shoulder.

Yuma could feel the tension in her body. Her muscles were trembling almost as much as the ground on which they stood. He cupped the back of her head with one hand and stroked the place between her shoulder blades with the other. They were all dirty and sweating. His belly was growling with hunger, so he imagined hers was, too, and yet she never complained. Once she'd asked him to help make her tough, but he didn't think she could be any tougher. She was barely into her sixteenth year, but she was handling this burden like a warrior.

"I, too, need to apologize for questioning your advice. I am sorry. Will you forgive me?" he whispered.

"There is no need. I do not want an apology from you. You are my mate, my equal. We think and say what we feel to each other without care that it might offend."

He sighed, then wrapped her up in his arms and gave her a gentle squeeze.

"I hear."

She leaned back in his arms to look at his face.

"We need to find a place for early camp. Everyone is tired and hurt and hungry. Tomorrow we will find a place to cross. Today needs to come to an end."

"Agreed," he said, then dropped his pack, dug out a slightly bruised papaya and a very bruised banana. "You choose. I will eat the other."

She took the papaya, then slipped the knife from her belt and quickly peeled away the skin before cutting it in half. The juice was sweet and sticky, running down her arms and mixing with the dried mud and blood.

"Half for you," she said and then took a big bite of her own.

He peeled the banana and broke it in half, then traded fruit.

"And half for you."

She took it with a smile.

"Together we are one," she said.

"Together," Yuma said and ate his half of the small banana in two bites. "So when we find a place to camp, I want to wash from my head to my toes."

"We can't bathe in the river," she said. "Crocodiles."

"We can't go to the water, but we can bring the water to us," he said and patted his pack to remind her of the small bucket he carried in his pack.

"I will wash you if you will wash me," she offered.

His eyes widened. "In front of everybody?"

She frowned. "Being naked is nothing here. I said wash. That is all."

"Thank you for reminding me," he said and then grinned.

When she realized he'd been teasing, she actually laughed, then sighed. After all that had happened, she'd been thinking she would never laugh again.

"Are you okay to leave?" he asked.

"Yes. We should go."

"Since you are the Windwalker's daughter and have a very loud voice, I leave it to you to let everyone know."

She punched him on the arm.

He grinned.

She wasted no time as she turned to face them and raised her voice to be heard.

"Today has been hard. We are sad, we are hurt, and we are tired, but we need to go so we can make camp before dark."

They stood as one without question, eyeing the tall young woman with the mud-streaked clothing and blood dried on her face and then began to gather their things.

She bent down to pick up her pack when someone shouted out her name. Then another followed, and then another, and another, until they were chanting her name in unison.

When she turned to face them, they were shouting her name and pumping their fists in the air.

Yuma's hand slid up her back and he gave her neck a soft squeeze. Her eyes filled with tears, but instead of crying, she thrust a fist into the air and shouted.

"For peace!"

"For peace!" they echoed.

"For the people!"

"For the people!" they echoed.

She slung her pack over her shoulder.

Yuma threaded his fingers through her hand.

She tightened her grip as they walked away.

****

After six hours on the trail away from Naaki Chava, Cayetano and Singing Bird made camp where they stopped, urging the people to stay as close together as possible. The need to protect themselves from the deadly pythons and jungle cats was always there, so he set his warriors as guards around the perimeter of the camp with orders to change shifts every four hours. It would give all of them some rest time and should keep the people relatively safe.

After a brief meal of fruit and a small piece each of the baked flatbread she had packed, Cayetano unrolled their sleeping mats. The twins unrolled theirs as well. When they all lay down, Cayetano was on one side of Singing Bird and the twins were on the other side, making sure that whatever might land in their midst would have to go through all of them to get to her.

But she didn't just matter to her family. She was beloved by the people. She'd worked beside them in the fields, laughed with them, cried with them, and for the last sixteen years had given a part of every day to teaching them what they needed to know to change their lives. She was the heartbeat of what was left of Naaki Chava.

And so they slept body to body, dreaming again of the earth shaking and the city burning, and the people they'd known who had never come out.

The sun was already beginning to set when Tyhen and the New Ones finally found a place to set up camp. The first thing they did was refill their water jugs, and then they began gathering water to get clean. They had never been as dirty or as miserable in their life as they were right now. And as hungry and thirsty as they were, they wanted to be clean worse.

One after another people began to shed their clothes where they stood and then wash away the grime on their bodies and hope their weariness went with it.

Now that they had stopped for the night, they had time to think about the deaths. As the water ran down their faces, tears ran with it. The stories of their survival began to emerge as they described seeing people swept away right beside them, of the blood on their own clothes and bodies not belonging to them, and of the look of horror on the victims' faces as they realized what was happening.

Story after story emerged as the dirt came off and the skin came clean. They weren't just cleansing their bodies. They were cleansing their souls of the horror they'd seen.

Tyhen listened for a while as she waited for Yuma to return with their water, but then she shut it out. When Yuma suddenly appeared out of the darkness with a bucket of water and their water jugs both refilled, she breathed a quiet sigh of relief.

She stood up and let her shift fall down around her ankles. It was so dirty she didn't want to think about ever putting it on again, but she no longer had the luxury. Once they were through bathing, she would wash their clothing and lay it out to dry on top of their tent as they slept.

As weary as Yuma was, when he caught sight of her willowy body, the naked skin shining like a gilded statue in the firelight, it made his chest hurt. She was so beautiful—so brave—and she was his to love.

As she reached down to dip a rag into the water, Yuma took it from her.

"Here, my little warrior, let me," he said softly.

She didn't argue. She was almost too weary to stand. She had already tied her long hair away from her face and neck, so when the water first touched her skin, the sensation was so welcome she went limp, like she'd been holding her breath all day long.

Yuma saw the tension roll away with the dirt. When he began washing her belly, then down her long, slender legs, she had to brace her hands on his shoulders to keep from falling.

"I feel weak," she whispered.

"You aren't sick. You are exhausted," he said. "Just relax, I'm almost through."

He dipped the rag into the water one last time.

"Lift your foot, little dove," he said softly, and when she did, he washed it thoroughly, even between the toes, then washed her other foot and sat her down on the sleeping mat to dry off.

"I'm going to get clean water for my bath," he said and hurried off.

Her eyes were heavy, and as she waited for his return, her body began to sway, falling almost asleep and then jerking when she felt her chin dip toward her chest. She looked beyond the tent tops into the dark, watching for Yuma's return. The last thing she remembered seeing was a piece of yellow moon hanging just above the mountain's peak, and then she was out.

By the time Yuma came back Tyhen was on her side, her legs curled up toward her chest and sound asleep.

He washed quickly, and with the help of a nearby friend, got his back washed, then rinsed out their clothing as best he could, before tossing out the water. They hadn't eaten any food, but exhaustion was stronger than an empty belly and there was always tomorrow to fill it up.

He spread their clothing on top of the tent to dry and then managed to get her awake enough to crawl inside it. Before he went in, he set about building a smudge fire. The mosquitoes were swarming, drawn to the site by so many bodies. But burning smudge fires in the midst of the tiny tents and stoking them with certain green leaves harvested from the jungle helped ward them off.

And just to make sure they weren't kept awake by them in the night, Yuma crumpled up a medicine leaf to release its oils, then rubbed it all over their clean skin, even the bottoms of their feet. He didn't know what the leaves were actually called, but they left a slight peppery scent on the skin when crushed that he knew the mosquitoes did not like.

As soon as he finished, he tossed the last of the greenery on the fire, satisfied as he watched the smoke thicken, then crawled into the tent beside her and pulled her close against his chest. With the weight of her breasts against the backs of his hands, he took a deep, weary breath and closed his eyes.

****

Tyhen was dreaming. In the dream she was in the jungle with her mother. She could see her and all the others sleeping so close together that their bodies were touching.

The twins were sleeping side by side and Cayetano was holding her mother close against his chest. She could see the rise and fall of her mother's breasts and the frown on Cayetano's forehead. He never really rested, not even in sleep.

She saw the warriors standing guard and the piece of moon above them, heard the squall of a jaguar somewhere off in the distance, and felt a warrior's heartbeat jump at the sudden sound.

She moved silently among the weary travelers, seeing bodies with fresh wounds and new burns, hearing people snoring and others moaning softly in pain. She walked through clouds of insects feeding off the blood of people too weary to swat them away, and felt their sadness and despair.

The urge to wake her mother was so strong that it was physical pain, but she did not follow the thought because she knew they would not see her. Still, she could not bring herself to leave them in such a miserable existence without doing what she could.

She turned toward the moon and began to chant. As she did, a soft wind rose, stirring through the area and disturbing the insect swarms to the point that they swiftly disappeared. It wasn't much, but it was a small comfort she could add to their rest.

Despite the urge to linger, her spirit began pulling away. Still, the desire to look back was too strong to ignore. When she did, she saw the twins sitting up on their sleeping mats, their gazes fixed in her direction. She lifted her hand in greeting, and to her joy, they waved back. Moments later she was gone.

She woke up in Yuma's arms. When she smelled the smoke from the smudge fires, she remembered where she was and closed her eyes again, this time following the dream time to another sleeping fire, and an entirely different breed of travelers.

She could tell by the dark energy within this camp that they were bad men, and the amount of weapons that they carried and the number of scars on their bodies attested to the brutality of their lives. She sensed that they were outcasts, banned from different tribes for evils done, and she walked carefully among them in case there was a dark shaman who could see and track her.

The last thing she wanted was to call attention to her presence, but instinct warned her that the more she knew about these men, the safer her people would be. These men were raiders who killed for pleasure, stole for greed, and raped and then killed the women they took once they were done with them.

These men also knew nothing about the prophecy or the strangers who would threaten their future existence, and would not have cared if they had. They had no allegiance to anyone but themselves, and their numbers were large.

She looked around at the area in which they slept, but it was unlike anything she'd ever seen. It was not jungle growth, and there was only dirt beneath her feet. Their smoldering fires did not smell of wood smoke, but she didn't recognize the scent of what was burning. The half-moon hung in a sky so vast the stars looked close enough to touch, and the mountain range below it was unfamiliar.

Still at the edge of their camp, she heard one man grunt, then roll over and get up. When he began to walk through the sleeping men toward where she was standing, she froze. He paused to relieve himself and was almost through when he suddenly looked in her direction as if sensing he was being watched.

It was all the warning she needed that she'd been there too long, and when she left the camp, she didn't look back. She didn't want him to see her face.

****

The man was Yaluk, leader of the band of outcasts. He had not seen Tyhen's spirit, but he'd felt it, and then he'd caught a glimpse of something with the shape of a woman's body, but tall, very tall, before it disappeared.

Always wary of witchcraft, he went back to his bed with an uneasy feeling. He had no problem killing, but the world of the dead made him uneasy mostly because he'd sent so many there. He needed a potion, a talisman for his protection, and made the decision that he should visit his sister. She was the only member of the family that would still talk to him, and she lived with her man in the tribe to which he used to belong. It was nearby. She could get a talisman for him from the medicine man. The medicine man didn't have to know the talisman was for him.

When he woke the next morning, it was still on his mind. The men had plenty of food and drink from their last raid and he was fairly certain one of the women they'd taken was still alive. They would have plenty to occupy their time while he was gone, and after a few orders to his second in command, he headed out of camp at a trot.

It took almost two hours for him to reach the location, and the farther he walked, the angrier he became at the thought of being cursed. By the time he topped the rise above the home of his sister, he was in a terrible mood.

The settlement, which was along a river called Rio Yaqui, which was where the Hiaki, also called Yaqui, lived. And the fact that he had been exiled from the place where he'd been born, ate at him daily. But because he wanted a favor from his sister, he could not start trouble.

He watched the coming and goings down in the village until it began to get hot. He was tired and hungry and it was time to make his move. He began circling the area until he came to an arroyo that led to the back of his sister's home, jumped down in it, and followed it toward her house.

He could smell corn and squash cooking even before he reached the dugout. It had been a long time since he'd had anything but meat they'd hunted or stolen. He hid behind the dugout, waiting until people in the area had moved on and he could no longer hear voices. When he was certain all was clear, he circled the dugout and slipped in so quiet that Nelli never heard him enter.

Yaluk came up behind her, clapped a hand over her mouth to keep her from screaming, and then turned her around.

When the little woman saw who it was, she swung

the stick she'd been using to stir her stew and hit him on the side of the shoulder.

"Yaluk! Crazy man! Why are you here? You know you do not belong!"

He would have never tolerated being struck by a woman and let them live, but Nelli was his little sister and he needed a favor.

"I am sorry I frightened you," he said. "I just needed to make sure you would not cry out."

Nelli glared. She was small, even by their standards, and married life had turned her body to fat. Sweat was running out of her hair and between her heavy breasts. But the stew she'd been cooking outside was done, and she wanted to get in the shade, so she'd brought it inside to keep the camp dogs out of it. She was already angry with her husband for giving her a beating last night because her blood was flowing and he could not lie with her. Now her disgraced brother had come sneaking into her home and made everything worse.

"You do not belong here," she said. "You need to leave before someone sees you."

"I will leave soon, I promise, but I need something first."

"I have nothing," Nelli said.

"I want nothing from you, but I need you to do something for me."

She frowned. "What?"

"Is Cualli still medicine man?"

She nodded.

"Go to him and get a talisman for me against witchcraft."

She gasped. "What have you done?"

"Nothing, I swear. But there is a presence about me I do not like and I want to protect myself."

She was still in shock. "I cannot go to the medicine man. Everyone will know and then they will want to know why. My husband will find out and beat me again."

Yaluk frowned. "I will kill him for you."

Nelli shrieked and then clasped her hands over her mouth. "You do not kill my man! Who would take care of me... you? You are an outcast from your own people."

"Then I will not kill him. Stop shouting," he said.

Now Nelli was afraid to turn him down for fear he *would* do exactly that. "I will do as you ask, but he will need payment."

Yaluk nodded and pulled a gilded bowl from his pack and handed it over.

Nelli squawked again. "I cannot give him this. He will know the talisman is not for me."

Yaluk frowned. "Then what?"

She pointed to the ring on his little finger with the red gem.

Yaluk wanted to object. He'd fought the man in hand to hand combat who'd been wearing this and considered it a well-earned trophy. But he wanted free of the spirit-witch worse and ripped it off his finger.

"Here. Take it, but hurry back."

She glared and then pointed at the stew. "Do not eat all of my stew or my husband will beat me."

Yaluk glared. "You let him beat you, but you don't want him killed. You are a stupid woman, I think."

"If you were a woman, you would understand," she argued and waved the stick at him again. "I mean it. You do not eat my stew."

Yaluk threw up his hands in pretend defeat and smiled.

She curled her fingers around the ring and scurried out.

The moment she was gone, Yaluk picked up a shell and scooped a generous serving from the stew pot and proceeded to eat it, savoring the fresh taste of cooked vegetables.

While Yaluk was sneaking her food, Nelli was scurrying through the village. So much for not calling attention to herself, she thought. By the time she got to Cualli's dwelling, she was in a panic.

When he approached her, she burst into tears and then grabbed his hand and slapped the ring into his palm.

"I am sorry to intrude, but I have a need. This came from one of the strangers many years ago who gave it to my father. Now my father is dead and I want to trade it for a talisman against witchcraft. Will you help?"

Cualli frowned. "Who in this village is practicing witchcraft? I will put a stop to it at once."

"No, no, not here, not here. I cannot say more."

Cualli fingered the ring thoughtfully and then tried it on several fingers before he found one it would fit. That seemed to sway his decision.

"I have such a talisman. You may have it."

Nelli's relief was great, but her name meant truth, and she'd just voiced the biggest lie of her life. She wanted to faint.

"Thank you, oh great Cualli, thank you."

"Wait here," he said and walked into an adjoining room, only to come out a few moments later with a small leather bag tied with a strip of braided corn silks and three tiny black feathers at the knot.

"What's inside?" Nelli asked, as he put it in her hands.

"Look and you will die," he said.

She gasped, clutched it against her breasts, and scurried out as quickly as she'd come in.

Chapter Sixteen

It was most unfortunate for Nelli's husband that he chose to come back into their dugout while Yaluk was eating their stew.

Yaluk didn't know he was there until he heard a quick grunt. He spun around, the shell full of stew still in his hand.

"Who are you? What have you done with my wife?" the man shouted.

Yaluk dropped the shell, and before the man could move, shoved his knife into his belly, then stabbed him in the chest.

The man was still in his death throes when Nelli came into the dugout. Yaluk grabbed her again, once more slapping his hand across her mouth.

"I am sorry. He gave me no choice. Did you get it? Did you get the talisman?"

Her eyes were wild as she struggled to get free, and when he asked for the talisman, she threw it on the dirt floor at his feet.

He frowned. "You are a good sister. But your name has cursed you. You would never have been able to tell two lies."

Still holding her from behind, he thrust the knife into her chest over and over until she bled out in his arms. Then he dropped her where she stood, wiped the blood from his hands and arms with some of their bedding, and took the talisman as he left.

He paused outside their doorway, pulled a small branch off of a nearby bush and began wiping out his tracks all the way down into the arroyo, and then all the way back to the ridge above the settlement.

Only once did he look back, and when he was satisfied there was no cry of discovery, he returned to his camp.

****

When Tyhen woke again, she could see the beginnings of daylight about to push away the night. She stretched and rolled over, only to realize Yuma was already awake. She saw the want on his face and without a word, rolled back onto her side, making way for him to take her from behind. With little movement and his very skilled hand between her legs, Yuma quickly brought her to a climax.

The release not only filled her heart, but healed a walk-weary soul. It was a good reminder there was still joy to be had.

While she was still riding the ripples of pleasure that he'd given her, she felt him shudder, then bury his face against the nape of her neck to keep from crying out. There was, after all, a courtesy to be followed in making love in a crowd.

When the last aftershock of lovemaking had passed, he whispered softly against her ear.

"You are my heart and the breath that I take."

She sighed, replete. "Thank you, my Yuma. You know how much I love and trust you. I could not do this without you at my side."

"I promise you won't have to," he said and gave her a quick hug.

"I need to get up," she said.

"I will go with you and stand watch."

She scooted carefully from the tent. When she saw her shift draped across it all clean and dry, she slipped it on with a smile.

"Thank you."

"You are welcome," he said, then glanced around the area as he quickly fastened his loincloth. People were already stirring. Some, like them, were heading into the jungle to seek a few moments of privacy while others squatted where they were to relieve their bladders and thought nothing of it.

Tyhen was barefoot, but when they came back to their camp, she went straight to her pack and dug out the moccasins that Wesley Two Bears had given her.

"They will be better protection," she said when she caught Yuma watching.

He was already wearing moccasins that he'd made months earlier. They laced up past his calves with fringe all the way down the back. He'd made them in honor of the fancy dancers he remembered from the powwows of his childhood. He had always been fascinated by how the fringe danced with them as they moved. He'd made them especially for the walk, telling himself he was simply dressing to return to his roots. Now it would appear that he would most likely wear these out before he ever caught sight of his native land.

Tyhen saw Shirley Nantay approaching and waved.

"A little something to start your day," Shirley said and handed them each a piece of warm bread. "I don't have a lot of the ground corn left, but we need to eat it up before it gets wet in a river, or I lose it running from yet another hunk of some mountain."

"Thank you so much," Tyhen said as she took the bread in her hands. "I hope that we have run from our last landslide, but I will not promise anything about not getting wet."

Shirley laughed. "As long as we're alive to face the next day, I will not complain. Here, Yuma, this one is for you."

He took the bread and kissed her cheek. "Thank you, Shirley."

"No. Thank *you,* both of you. I will see you later."

She hurried away, leaving them to enjoy their treat.

Later, as they began to pack up their tent for the journey ahead, Montford Nantay came running back, out of breath and wet up to his thighs.

"I think I found a safe place to cross," he said. "It's only a couple of miles downstream. The riverbed narrows drastically, leaving only a short crossing in water, and it's not deep. I walked all the way across and back to make sure."

"You make a good scout," Yuma said.

Montford shrugged off the compliment. "We still need to stand watch on both sides. There could be a crocodile in the water at any time."

Tyhen shuddered and said nothing, remembering Yuma's near-death experience with one because of her.

"So we go now," Yuma said. "The faster we get everybody to the other side of this river, the better I will feel."

Soon the New Ones were on the march with Montford Nantay in the lead. As they strung out, walking in twos and threes all along the riverbank, their numbers covered more than a mile. But there was a bounce in their step that hadn't been there last night. This was a new day and they were ready to move on.

At first people were talking, and then as the reality of another day on foot dawned, they saved their breath. When they reached the crossing, they cheered.

Montford, Johnston, and Shirley locked hands and started across to show the others the path to take. There would be no wandering up or downstream in a hurry to get more across. Just three at a time and three behind, keeping a steady line moving through the cold, running water.

A few of the younger men armed themselves and crossed next so they could stand watch for crocodiles at the crossing, while another group armed in the same manner stayed behind for the same purpose.

Yuma, Tyhen, and an older man crossed next.

Tyhen flinched as she stepped in. The water was swift and cold, flowing immediately over the tops of her moccasins and up to her thighs. But they kept their footing and quickly got across. When they reached the other side, the first thing Tyhen did was take off her moccasins and dump out the water before putting them back on. They would dry on her feet and it wouldn't matter.

Once the people saw what was expected of them, they quickly organized and moved down the slope, stepping into the water without hesitation.

But now that they were finally crossing, the urge to get to the other side caused some to panic, and the rush to get in and out made them careless. More than once they were cautioned by guards to slow down.

More than half of the people had already crossed when a man and wife stepped into the water with their young son between them. The boy was twelve, but small for his age, and when he suddenly slipped and went under, the mother panicked, lost her grip, and began screaming. Before disaster could strike, the father yanked the boy back up and then glared at his wife.

"I know you were scared, but the scream did not help. Next time, don't turn loose," he said loudly.

Shaken, she could only nod.

Tyhen frowned, thinking his words were harsh. She understood a mother's fear.

But Yuma had seen Tyhen's expression of disapproval and leaned forward, speaking softly in her ear.

"His words reflect the greater fear. He doesn't want to lose either of them and yet it could have happened in a heartbeat."

And just like that, she understood that the father's fears had made his words too loud, and that he'd said them out of love, desperate to make them understand this was not an ordinary walk. Yesterday life had ended for many of them. He didn't want his family to be next.

She glanced up at Yuma. The sunlight was behind him, making his skin appear to glow, but she could still see his dark eyes searching her face, always watching, making sure there was no misunderstanding.

She nodded and held out her hand. He pulled her up then stole a quick kiss that made her smile. But the smile quickly ended when she looked back to the west. The sky was getting dark. Rain was coming, which would make the water deeper and swifter, which would make crossing dangerous; maybe too dangerous. The last thing they needed was to become separated.

She pointed behind him.

"Rain comes. They have to hurry."

"Don't move," he said quickly and headed toward the river at a lope. As soon as he reached the shore, he shouted to the people on the other side.

"Rain is coming. The water will become too deep to cross. Move faster."

All of a sudden the crossing took on a whole other meaning. Being separated would become a nightmare. And to make matters worse, a guard had just spied their first crocodile coming downstream.

"Crocodile!" he shouted, pointing toward the long, knobby snout barely visible above the water.

The ones who'd been about to step into the water ran back up onto the bank, while the others still in the water began to run, stumbling, some falling, all of them in unspoken panic to get to the other side.

The men with spears ran quickly upstream in an effort to kill it before it reached the crossing, and when they did, the crocodile submerged. Now that they could no longer see it, they had no way to know where it was. Was it swimming downstream or waiting beneath for the next person to cross?

Yuma was on the shore with his spear, scanning the swiftly moving water for signs.

"He'll have to surface somewhere. Watch for it," he yelled.

The people were now split in half, each bordering one side of the river as the thunderstorm came closer. One minute passed into another and then another and finally the croc came up, forced to surface to breathe.

The moment it appeared, the men began their attack, but they could not throw a spear hard enough from that distance to penetrate the leather-hard hide. One after the other, the spears struck and then bounced off the crocodile's back and began floating downriver.

One of the guards jumped into the crossing and caught the spears before they could float away while the men were left with using bows and arrows. But the metal-tipped arrows would not pierce the hide either, and a faint rumble of thunder increased the seriousness of the situation.

Tyhen knew what needed to be done. Windwalker had given her gifts for a reason. Just because she hadn't used them, didn't mean they wouldn't work.

She began hearing drumbeats as she slipped through the crowd, and when she grabbed a spear lying on top of someone's pack, the drums grew louder. She ran out of the crowd and was gone before Yuma even knew she was missing. By the time everyone finally saw her, they knew what she was about to do.

She was little more than a brown flash of arms and legs, running upriver toward the massive croc with a spear in her hands. Her long hair was flying out behind her, her gaze fixed on the croc's location with sure intent.

Yuma's heart nearly stopped. Even as he began running after her, he knew he was going to be too late to stop whatever she was about to do.

The drums were so loud when she left the ground that she didn't hear the people screaming.

No one could jump that high or that far, but she was doing it. She had just made a leap that took her high into the air, soaring twenty yards across the river, clutching the spear with both hands. When she began to come down, she raised the spear as high as it would go, and when her toes touched water, plunged the spear straight through the crocodile's head, killing it instantly.

They both went under, and seconds later, Tyhen bobbed up as the croc's body went down. She began swimming toward shore and was almost there when suddenly Yuma was beside her and pulling her out of the water.

He dragged her up on shore and then threw his arms around her without speaking.

She held him because he needed to know she was still breathing.

"I am all right. It had to be done," she said.

He grabbed a fistful of her hair and then touched his forehead to hers, too moved to speak.

She took his face in her hands, making him focus on her face.

"Yuma... make them finish the crossing. The blood in the water could bring others."

He gave her a last frantic look, thrust his spear into her hands and ran back.

The crossing resumed, but Tyhen stayed upstream watching just in case.

The people were crossing now in great haste, piling into the water without hesitation, and moving three by three with only a foot of space between them. If one slipped, there were several close enough to pick them up.

It began to rain just as the last ones were to cross. These were the people too injured to walk, the ones they'd been carrying on the travois. At that point, a dozen strong men waded back across to get them. With three men on one side and three on the other, they picked up a travois with an injured traveler still strapped on it and quickly carried him across while the other six carried another one right behind them. They repeated the trip until all nine people had been carried to safety.

Only then did the last guards make the crossing.

At that point, the sky unloaded. Tyhen started back, but the rain was so heavy she could barely make out the people awaiting her arrival.

"It is only rain," Tyhen shouted. "We were dirty, and now we will be clean. It is good."

They followed her into the jungle and once they stepped into the heavy growth of trees and vines, they were somewhat sheltered from the downpour by the heavy canopy above. After that they moved as one, their heads down to avoid rain in their faces, following the person ahead of them without looking up.

They were still walking when the rain stopped, and when the sun came out, and the insects followed. They pulled the flat, oily leaves from medicine bushes as they passed by them, crumpled the leaves up in their hands and then wiped them over their bodies. The insects were still there, but they didn't bite; and the march continued.

When the sun was at its zenith, Yuma called a halt, giving people the opportunity to relieve themselves and have a chance to get some food or medicine from their packs.

Tyhen was peeling the last piece of fruit, and Yuma had taken off his moccasins to treat a blister when somewhere within the jungle, someone screamed. Everyone could tell by the panic in the sound something was terribly wrong, but with so many people scattered throughout the area, there was no way to see who was screaming or why.

Yuma's first instinct was to protect Tyhen. He leapt to his feet and shoved her back against a tree, shielding her with his body and his knife.

Tyhen's flash of insight was swift and vivid. A big snake had one of the men in a death grip and the woman couldn't get him free. She could see men running with knives and spears, but the snake was huge and the man was dying in front of them.

Then she saw Montford Nantay running up with a knife in his hand, and even before he reached the snake, she sent him a message.

Montford, put your knife in the head!

Montford never questioned the voice that he heard or where it came from as he raised the knife and rammed it straight into the boa's head so deep it was decapitated from the body.

The death throes kept the boa's muscles in constricting spasms, but with less and less power. Finally, the men pulled the victim free and carried him away.

Montford's hands were shaking and covered in blood as he stared down at the snake, trying to come to terms with what just happened. He'd heard the voice. He even recognized the voice. But he didn't understand how she'd made that happen.

He took a deep, shuddering breath and began cleaning the knife and his hands with some wet leaves, then went to look for Tyhen.

****

The moment the screaming began, Yuma pulled Warrior's Heart and backed Tyhen against a tree. Yuma was still in a protective crouch in front of Tyhen as the shouts and screaming reached an ear-shattering pitch, when it stopped as suddenly as it began.

"What was that?" he asked as he sheathed his knife and turned around.

Not only was Tyhen mute to the question, but her eyes had lost focus and she had that faraway look on her face that meant visions. He stepped in front of her and put his hands on her shoulders. As he did, she blinked, and he knew she saw him.

"What happened?"

"A man was being crushed by a boa. Some men saved him."

"That's good. Do you know who it was?"

"No. I couldn't see his face."

"I'm going to go see," Yuma said. "Do you want to come?"

"I think I will wait here," she said and sat down to finish her fruit.

"Don't go wandering off without me," he cautioned.

"I won't. I promise," she said.

He quickly put on his moccasins and then caught a drip of juice on her chin with the tip of his finger and licked it off.

"Sweet, but not as sweet as you," he said softly.

"I love you very much," she said and put a piece of the fruit between his lips.

He took it between his teeth, and then in moment of playfulness, growled and snapped at her fingers like he was going to bite them as well.

She squealed and jumped.

He was still laughing as he walked away.

Tyhen shook her head, then got up and began to look for water. Always when it rained, certain bushes that had cup-shaped leaves were an available water source.

She quickly found one of bushes, drank from the leaves until her thirst was slaked and then used the water from another to wash the fruit juice from her face and hands. She was drying her hands on her shift when Montford Nantay appeared, and he wasted no time with why he'd come.

"I heard you," he said.

"Good. You saved his life."

"No. *You* saved him, little Dove. I don't know how you made that happen, but thank you. The man you saved is married to our sister, Lola. His name is Aaron."

Her eyes widened in surprise. "I didn't know you had other family that came with you to Naaki Chava. Why didn't I know this?"

Montford shrugged. "Aaron doesn't like us so much."

She frowned. "He should now."

Montford chuckled. "Yes, you are right. He should now," he said and then put his hand on the top of her head.

"You are a blessing, Tyhen. Thank you."

She shrugged. "You are welcome and no one needs to know this."

"Know what?" he said and walked away.

By the time Yuma returned, Tyhen had their things packed and was sitting beneath the tree where he'd left her, dozing in a small patch of sunlight that had found its way through the canopy.

He dropped down beside her and then woke her with a kiss. "Are you all right?"

She nodded. "I didn't mean to fall asleep."

"It was good for you," he said, and then added, "I found out what happened. A boa constrictor had a man caught in its coils. Montford saved him and it turned out to be Aaron, the man who is married to his sister."

"Is he going to be all right?" she asked.

"Yes. Nothing broken, but they wrapped his ribs for support. He will be very sore for several days."

"Good news," she said.

"Yes, good news," Yuma said and began gathering up their things as the walk resumed.

They had been on the move for almost an hour when they felt another aftershock that made everyone nervous.

"It is not a quake. It is nothing but a complaint," Tyhen shouted.

But it was a vivid reminder of what they'd endured. Within moments everyone became nervous and uneasy again until a woman in the march began talking to the people around her in French, and when someone responded, she would not answer them unless they used the same language.

It soon became a game that moved up and down the long line of marchers as the day progressed. French soon gave way to Spanish, then to English, and then to different dialects from their own native tribes.

Singing Bird would have been happy knowing the time she'd given to educating the people was a success, but it would be up to the New Ones to continue this tradition and teach the indigenous tribes. Once those tribes understood the power they had by reading and writing in different languages and understanding numbers, they would stand strong against all invaders and their empty promises.

It was nearing sundown when they reached the foothills of another mountain. One moment they were slogging through vines as thick as their wrists and then they were spilling out of the jungle into a clearing and coming face to face with the dark mouth of a massive cave.

Chapter Seventeen

Even the New Ones, who'd had access to many such destination places in the world before Firewalker, had not seen a cave this large. They crossed the clearing in a rush to see.

Tyhen stopped in front of it and closed her eyes. She could smell and hear fresh running water and knew, even though it felt older than time, that there were no animals living inside.

"We stop here," Tyhen shouted. "Here we will rest and heal. Here we can replenish our food stores and gather more medicines for the days ahead."

Little by little, the people ventured inside, some more daring than others as they quickly fashioned torches and carried them farther into the depths to explore. The fact that there were no bats was received with great relief. They weren't harmful, but nasty, and would have most likely fouled the water and the cave if was one of their roosts.

Once Tyhen was convinced the people would come to no harm, she let them explore and sat down just outside the cave on a large, moss-covered rock before easing the pack from her back. Her shoulders ached from the weight, and her knee was skinned and burning from a fall she'd taken on wet leaves earlier in the day. But considering what they had endured since sunrise, she could not complain.

Once Yuma noticed she was down, he took his water jug and went to find fresh water. The sound of the waterfall inside the cave was what they had called "white noise" in the time before Firewalker. It spilled down the cave wall into a large pool below, which then flowed on through an underground channel. It was plentiful and ever-flowing.

The moment Yuma dipped his water jug into the pool, he gasped. He hadn't felt water like this since before Firewalker. And when he took the first drink, it was so cold it made his head hurt. He looked up and laughed.

Johnston Nantay was on the other side of the pool doing the same task and lifted a jug to him in a toast. "Don't need ice cubes in this," he yelled.

Yuma gave him a thumbs-up as he filled his water jug and hurried back outside. He wanted Tyhen to taste this while it was still cold.

She had not moved from the rock and there was a gathering crowd around her. Someone had given her a piece of coconut, and she was eating as they talked. She looked happy, almost at peace. It was a good thing for him to see as he hurried toward her.

Tyhen felt his presence and looked over her shoulder to confirm the thought, then smiled.

His head was up, his shoulders back, and she could see the movement of every muscle in his body as came toward her. His forehead was streaked with tiny scratches and there was a thin cut on his cheek, but he would never have mentioned it. He had been raised as one of Cayetano's warriors, and as a man, he was afraid of nothing except losing her.

"Fresh water," he said softly as he offered her the jug.

She took a big drink, and then stopped in surprise. "This is good but strange. It hurts my teeth."

He smiled. "This is cold."

Her eyes widened. "Like cold and frozen?"

"Yes. Like cold and frozen."

She looked into the water jug in disbelief, thinking surely water like this must look different, too.

He smiled. Her innocence was childlike, but with a wisdom older than time. She could perform unbelievable, superhuman feats and yet was mesmerized by something as simple as cold water.

"You have quite an audience," he whispered as he sat down on the rock beside her.

"They saw what I did to the crocodile, but they don't know how it happened. They are curious."

"What did you tell them?"

She shrugged. "Not so much."

"They are the New Ones. They would understand the truth," he said softly.

She thought about her secret and then realized it no longer mattered who knew and who did not. They were forever separated from the founders of Naaki Chava and would never be with Singing Bird or Cayetano again. Maybe he was right. Maybe truth was the answer.

And as she was thinking it, she heard Adam and Evan's voices in her head.

Truth is always the answer, little sister. We saw you in our camp. We hope to see you again.

A brief pain of longing for what had been shot through her, but she soon let it go. It had no place in this world.

She took another drink of the water, but this time didn't swallow it all at once, and it didn't cause pain.

"I like this cold," she said.

He smiled and with the tip of his finger lifted a stray piece of her hair from her eyelash.

The gesture was one he often did without thinking, but she felt the love and intent. He wanted to make love with her. Tonight they would find their place to make that happen.

Then she felt fingers rubbing the leather on her moccasins and looked down to see a little girl standing at her feet. She had large brown eyes and a wide mouth curled upward in a smile, and as were many of the smaller children on the march, completely naked.

Tyhen stared. The girl looked familiar.

"What is your name, little one?"

"Patsy Two Bears."

"You are from Wesley Two Bears' family?"

"Grandfather," she said and then ducked her head.

Tyhen was wearing moccasins that had belonged to this little girl's grandmother and wondered if she knew it, too.

"You wear Gee-Gee's moccasins," Patsy whispered.

"Yes, your grandfather gave them to me. I am proud to wear them."

"Grandfather didn't come with us," Patsy said.

Her words were matter-of-fact, but there were tears in her eyes.

"Yuma, lift her into my lap," Tyhen said.

"Okay with you?" he asked.

The little girl raised her arms, so he picked her up and sat her in Tyhen's lap.

The moment Tyhen touched her, she saw Wesley Two Bears death. The shock was sudden and painful, and it was all she could do not to weep. She busied herself with settling the child into a comfortable position until her emotions were under control.

Silence ensued as the people watched the child settle into Tyhen's embrace.

"So, your grandfather didn't come with you. I know you miss him. My mother didn't come with me, either, and I am sad."

Patsy's eyes widened. "Why not?"

"Because she had to go with Chief Cayetano. They took your grandfather and the others to a safe new place to live."

"Will they like it?" the little girl asked.

"I hope so. Will you like your new home when you find it?" Tyhen asked.

She hesitated, then searched the crowd until she saw the smile on her mother's face and then nodded.

Tyhen gave her a quick hug. "Good for you," she said, then looked out across the crowd. "Patsy Two Bears had questions and came and asked for answers, and I gave them. You have questions but you have not asked."

They glanced anxiously at each other, a little guilty that they'd been thinking how to question what they'd seen.

She let that sink in as she kept talking.

"I understand your surprise, some would even say shock at what you saw me do. If it was not for what has happened in Naaki Chava, I would never have spoken this truth because I honor Singing Bird and Cayetano as more than my parents. Like all of you, he was my chief, and Singing Bird was a special woman, marked by the Old Ones. I held them in highest respect and still do. But we are on this long and dangerous journey together, and there should be no secrets. Ask what you will. I will tell you what I know."

Now it seemed intrusive to push their little Dove into revealing things that might be personal to her, and so no one spoke.

Yuma sensed their hesitation and embarrassment and because he knew this needed to come out, he slid off the rock and moved around to face her.

"If it pleases you, my Dove, I will ask the first question."

Tyhen pointed at him. "See this? It takes someone with the courage and daring of an eagle to speak first."

Everyone laughed. They already likened Yuma's daring to the large birds that flew above the clouds, and it seemed fitting that such a bird as an eagle would become the protector for a little dove.

"So, great eagle, ask me a question."

"How did you leap so far and so high, and then come down with such force to kill the crocodile?"

This was no more than she'd expected. Getting right to the heart of a situation was Yuma's way.

"I could do that because of powers given to me by my father before he died."

Everyone gasped. Some began to cry as others called out.

"Cayetano is dead? Is the great Cayetano dead? Did he die when Naaki Chava burned?"

Tyhen settled Patsy Two Bears a little closer to her heart. "Cayetano is alive and well," she said loudly.

"But you said—"

"I said my father gave me my powers before he died. Cayetano is not my father. I was already in my mother's belly when you began the Last Walk to escape

Firewalker. I saw people begging for water and then running from the white people who wanted to be saved. I saw Layla Birdsong's grandfather, my great-grandfather, die from the gunshot to his head. I saw the portal open and all of you running with your burned skin and bleeding lips. I saw canyons crumbling and bursting into flames. I saw people dying and saw those who were still alive running toward the Old Ones who held the portal open."

Yuma took a breath, willing himself not to cry because he knew what was coming.

"I also know of an act of great courage. When the world was about to end, Layla Birdsong ran back into it after one who had been left behind, a little boy who would not quit, who refused to die."

She put a hand on Yuma's shoulder. "It was this one, a brave young boy who saved my life even before I was born, a brave man who still protects me today, putting my life above the safety of his own. He is part of the prophecy that guides us all, as am I. I am the Windwalker's daughter, and he died in my arms, giving me his powers to make sure this quest does not fail."

There was an audible gasp from everyone around her as the realization of what she said sank in. They took a single step toward her, pulled to her truth like a magnet.

They'd watched her grow up and had never known, never imagined she was not Cayetano's flesh and blood. She'd kept the secret. Singing Bird had kept the secret. They wondered if Cayetano knew. And the moment they thought it, Tyhen spoke.

"Cayetano knew. He knew and did not care because he was also part of the prophecy. It does not matter how he was involved, but you can be certain he knew everything there was to know and helped all of us make it happen. And now we are here."

Patsy Two Bears had been listening quietly, but most of what had been said meant nothing to her because she had never lived before Firewalker. She didn't understand anything but Naaki Chava. She leaned back in Tyhen's arms and looked up.

"Will people still die where we are going?"

"No one lives forever," Tyhen said softly.

"I have one more question," Yuma asked.

Tyhen met his gaze and not only knew the words before they came out of his mouth, but she knew why he was asking.

"Ask me," Tyhen said.

Yuma's heart was pounding. He was afraid he would not be man enough to hear the answer. "You once told me that a Windwalker never dies, yet you said your father died in your arms. Was what you told me untrue?"

Tyhen felt the fear in his words as physically as she felt her heartbeat. No wonder he was so anxious about letting her out of his sight. He was afraid that she would die through some fault of his own.

"Help me," she said as she handed him the child.

When he put her down, the little girl scampered away, a little excited that she'd been so close to their leader, but happier to be back in her mother's arms.

Tyhen stared straight into his eyes, her gaze as steady as her voice. "It is true that Windwalkers cannot die... unless they give away their power. So your real question is will I ever die?"

He watched her chin tremble and thought she was

biting her lip to keep from crying when she surprised him with a smile.

"I will die one day when I give my powers to our child."

Yuma forgot about the people all around them. He was still reeling from the thought of giving her a baby when the rest of what she'd said finally sunk in.

"You mean, there will always be a Windwalker to lead our people—not just now, but in the centuries to come?"

"So the prophecy was told to me, and so it will be."

Yuma was speechless. He'd grown up thinking he knew exactly how his part would play out, and now he was struggling to find a foothold in what she'd said.

Tyhen knew he was in shock. She looked up at the people around her who seemed to be in varying stages of the same situation.

"Does anyone else have a question that needs an answer?"

A voice came from the crowd. "Tyhen, if you are a Windwalker's daughter, does that mean you are a god?"

She laughed, and the joy in her voice rang out across the crowd, making them laugh along with her. When they finally quieted, she shook her head.

"No, I am not a god. I am like any woman among you. I have my strengths, and I have my weaknesses, but like any woman among you, I have put myself at risk for those I love, which is what I am doing for you."

The cheer that went up was so loud it made the birds in the trees take flight and sent the monkeys in the canopy to climbing higher to get away from the noise.

She stood up on the rock, a tall young woman with the regal being of a queen and let out a war cry.

Yuma caught her as she jumped down into his arms.

The New Ones answered back with a cry that echoed from one side of the valley to the other.

Yuma's dark eyes mirrored his emotion as he held her firm within his grasp. "It is good. No more secrets to keep."

"No more secrets," she said, even as she thought about the enemy she'd seen they had yet to face.

All will be revealed in its time.

She blinked. That sounded like Evan! Were the twins completely tuned in to everything that was going on? What did they know that she didn't?

We don't know anything more than you know and we are not tuned in to everything going on. It's not our fault you send out such strong signals.

She sighed. And that was Adam, always making sure to lay the blame at someone else's feet.

It's because we're never wrong.

She laughed and Yuma thought she was laughing with him. She'd tell him about the twins later. As for the other, they'd heard enough for one day.

Once they went inside, Tyhen prowled the layout of the cave for almost an hour before she found a site she liked and set up their bed on the far side of a large boulder with a wall at their back. It was as private as she could devise for some much needed love-making later.

Once she was through, she began moving throughout the cave, making sure people had what they needed. Yuma was working with several of the younger men, helping the injured ones set up their sleeping tents and bringing fresh water to their fires, while a few of the best hunters left to scavenge for food.

For the first time since they'd left Naaki Chava, there was a sense of celebration. They had endured great hardships very early, but instead of breaking their spirits, it had pulled them closer together.

As sundown put the day to bed, they gathered in little groups around their fires to share food and trade their near-death experiences. Later, after their bellies were full and reality had reared its ugly head, they began speaking the names of those they'd lost and said a prayer for their souls. That sapped the last of the good feelings as they made their way to bed.

After a while, all was quiet. A few guards stood watch at the front, while the rest slept secure inside it. When it began to rain during the night, it only lulled them into a deeper sleep.

****

Tyhen and Yuma had fallen asleep early, but once everyone else had finally given up and gone to bed, they had roused, then turned to each other to make slow, sweet love.

Tyhen had been the first to wake, and her need for him was already stirring the air inside the cave. She couldn't let it get out of hand, but she also couldn't control it. She put a hand on the side of his face, watching as his eyes flew open.

"What is wrong?" he whispered and then saw her hair floating out around her like a halo.

Without another word, he rolled her onto her back and slid inside her. The wind stopped turning, and the few who noticed it attributed it to the rain outside.

Tyhen arched her back as she rose to meet his thrusts. Having him inside her was like holding fire. He made her hot. He made her hurt. He made her burn. Watching the changing expressions on his face as their bodies danced was a joy all on its own. She liked knowing she had the power to give him such pleasure.

Cayetano was so caught up in the feel of being inside her that he didn't notice her intense regard. His focus was to hang onto his own sanity until he brought her pleasure to a peak, and so the rain came down as they came undone.

The shift from feeling good to climax came between one breath and the next. Tyhen was looking at the shape of Yuma's mouth and remembering what it felt like on the nipple of her breast when she suddenly shattered. She closed her eyes to ride it out, letting wave after wave of the intensity roll through her until she was left weak and shaking beneath him.

Then she rode it all over again when Yuma let go and gave in to the explosion of pleasure that swept through him. When it was over, he collapsed on top of her in a shaking heap, too exhausted to speak.

Time passed. The guards at the entrance changed shifts. The rain ended. The sounds of the jungle came back to life as daylight hovered in the East.

She was still wrapped within Yuma's embrace when the ground beneath them shook so hard it threw her out of his arms. He reached out and grabbed her to keep her from rolling away.

"It's happening. Get up!" she cried as she jumped to her feet. She grabbed her shift and pulled it over her head as she ran, with Yuma right behind her.

People were on their feet, some shouting, others already crying.

"We are safe! We are safe!" she yelled as she ran toward the entrance to the cave. "It's not here. It's Naaki Chava. The mountain is dying."

****

They weren't the only ones awakened by the noise.

Little Mouse had made a shelter inside the palace rubble and when the ground began to shake, it rolled her off of her sleeping mat and across the floor before she managed to get to her feet.

She ran to the window, saw the horror of what had begun, and turned and ran. She ran out the back of the palace into the jungle as the burning rocks began to fall all around her. Twice she fell, and each time she got up, she left a piece of her burning clothing behind.

She wanted to scream, but that would have taken too much breath. Everywhere she looked, fire was falling. She paused once to look back and saw a running river of fire coming down the mountain and into the rubble of what was once Naaki Chava. She could not outrun that. Where to go? What to do?

And then she noticed that the fire was running with the flow of the land, which was toward the river, so instead of running away from the mountain, she would take a long way around and run toward it to get to the other side. Fire was still falling from the sky and everything was burning, but the river of fire was going the other way.

She didn't call for help. She didn't tell the fire god that she was Little Mouse, and that she was here running away from his might. She just kept slapping at the fire falling in her hair and ran as she'd never run before.

Even though the cave where the New Ones stopped was far below the tops of the tallest trees, they could see a bright red glow in the southern sky.

There were no words for what Yuma was feeling. They'd come into that place in fire. Now that the city had burned, it was being buried in more fire. Would the cleansing of the past never end?

Tyhen slipped her fingers through his as people crowded around them, some talking, others, like him, too shocked by what they knew was happening to speak.

"Oh no! Look! Look!" someone cried.

Suddenly the sky was awash in burning debris as the volcano began spewing burning rock and molten lava straight up into the air. The ground was shaking beneath their feet and there was a growing tower of smoke and fire silhouetted against the burgeoning dawn.

She thought of her mother and Cayetano. Did they get the others far enough away before this happened or were they once again running from a world on fire?

Adam! Evan! Talk to me. What is happening where you are?

"*We are running! I can't find Evan. Can you see him? Help me, help me, help me!*"

"No, no, no," Tyhen moaned and then dropped to her knees and closed her eyes.

Yuma grabbed her, thinking she was going to faint, then realized something else was going on.

"What is it? What's happening?"

"The others are in trouble. They didn't get far enough away."

Yuma groaned. "Can they still make it?"

"Wait. I need to help."

She had never spirit walked except when her body was asleep and didn't know if this would work, but she was about to find out. She grabbed Yuma's forearms, fixing him with a look that nearly stopped his heart.

"Hold me. Don't move me. And have faith I will be back."

Before he could question what she meant, he watched her take a deep breath and close her eyes. A heartbeat later, she fell into Yuma's outstretched arms. It appeared she had fainted, when in reality, her spirit left her body and was already gone.

He sat down on the ground with her, holding her firmly in his grasp. He didn't know what was happening, but she told him to hold her, and they would have to kill him before he'd ever let her go.

****

She used her connection to her mother to find them, and she did easily because their tie was strong. One second she was in Yuma's arms and the next she was with the others and shocked by what she saw. The New Ones who had been too old to go with her, were now running again for their lives along with the ones who had been born in Naaki Chava. The jungle was on fire behind them, and the burning rock was falling all around them. It was like running from Firewalker all over again.

Adam. I am here.

"Find him for me. Please! He wasn't beside me when the volcano blew. We started running. I thought he

was with us but then I couldn't feel him. I know now that he's not."

My mother and Cayetano?

"Right in front of me, leading us to safety. Hurry."

Yes, I will hurry.

She was hovering above ground as she looked behind her. There was nothing but smoke. She heard a high-pitched whine and looked up just as another burning rock flew over her head. Even though she knew she could not be harmed, it took everything she had to stay put.

Evan, Evan, talk to me, my brother. Where have you gone?

****

Evan woke, saw the sleeping camp around him and felt pressure on his bladder. He got up with the intent to relieve himself, which he did without incident, and was on his way back when the mountain blew. He turned around just as the first wave of burning rock spewed into the air. Then the ground rolled beneath his feet and he fell forward, hitting his head against a tree and knew no more.

He came to in a world on fire. There was blood in his eyes, smoke in his face, and no thought in his head but an inborn sense of self-preservation that made him run. But he was running the wrong way. While everyone else was running South, Evan Prince was running North into hell.

****

Tyhen knew that if he wasn't with the others and that if he was still alive and able to move, he had to be running like the rest of them, trying to get away. She closed her eyes and said his name again and again, but he didn't answer.

She went up higher to cover more ground, moving like smoke with the speed of light, scanning what was below. Just when she began to fear the search would end badly, she saw him, running in an all-out sprint, but in the wrong direction. She dropped down in front of him and held out her hands.

Stop, Evan! It's me, Tyhen.

He ran right through her.

Chapter Eighteen

Shocked, she spun around and flew past Evan again and tried to stop him, and again he ran past. That was when she saw the blood on his face and the gash in his head. She groaned. It was the head wound. He had forgotten how to hear. He didn't know how to see her anymore. What to do, what to do?

And then it hit her. She was the Windwalker's daughter. Even in spirit, she was stronger than man and equal to weather. She put her arms up into the air and made the wind come, and then made it spin around her. Faster and faster it spun until it was alive on its own, sucking smoke and fire into the funnel as it took her up into the treetops and then flew above the smoke until it dropped down on Evan Prince. It sucked him up into the vortex in mid-step. He screamed, but it was only from fear. He could thank her later.

****

Adam was running with both his pack and Evan's on his back and a four-year-old girl in his arms, so sick at heart he could barely breathe. Her mother was in front of him carrying her baby. They'd left the father a good half mile behind, crushed beneath a burning rock.

Adam saw it happen, heard the mother screaming

and stopped long enough to grab the little girl who'd fallen out of her father's arms. The mother didn't even see him. She just kept screaming.

He slapped her. Pointed at the baby in her arms and screamed.

"Run, woman, run!"

Still reeling from the blow, she turned and ran.

He was right behind her.

****

Cayetano and Singing Bird were running hand in hand. He wouldn't let her go, and she wasn't about to stop. She couldn't believe this was happening to her again and very angry with the Old Ones. They could have changed this outcome. They *should* have changed this outcome.

Her feet were burning and sparks were falling in her hair. More than once Cayetano gave her head a quick thump with the flat of his hand and she knew he was putting out fires. She could hear people screaming all around her. They were death screams. She'd heard them before. She wanted to scream, too, but was afraid if she did, she'd never stop.

She didn't know where the twins were or if there would be enough people left alive after this to even make a new city, and right now she couldn't let herself care. As long as Cayetano was beside her, she would bear what came to pass.

Cayetano felt like he'd lost his mind. This had to be a nightmare and when he woke up it would be gone. But the screams were too loud, the fire was too hot, and the falling sparks on his arms and legs were causing too much pain to be a dream.

The ground was moving beneath them with such force that it was difficult to keep his balance. Twice he had stumbled and gone to his knees, and both times Singing Bird had been the one who pulled him up. He didn't know her like this. She'd fallen back into the woman who'd run from Firewalker. It was yet another thing to fear. If they lived through this, which woman would stay?

After a time, Singing Bird became aware that they were now ahead of the fire rather than caught in its midst. With that realization came another, that no fiery rocks had come this far. She wanted to look behind her, to see if they were actually outrunning the danger, but was afraid to slow down. Her chest was burning, her sides aching, and her muscles were in spasms.

Finally, she began slowing down from sheer exhaustion and was about to take a chance and look back when she caught a glimpse of movement to her right. Then she saw what it was, and when it sailed over their heads and kept going, she stumbled and fell to her knees.

"What was that?" Cayetano shouted as he jerked her upright.

She leaped forward again without answering, couldn't bring herself to say the words that would break his heart. But the last time she'd seen anything remotely like it was when the Windwalker had rescued her from her attackers on the streets of New Orleans. Now she couldn't slow down. She had to know if she'd been seeing things or if another miracle was about to occur.

****

Adam Prince was still a hundred yards behind and still running with the little family that he'd saved, but with joy in his heart. He had never cried in his life, and up to this moment, he had been convinced he was incapable of emotion. But he was crying now and with his heart in his throat. Tyhen had just sent him a message.

I found him.

Despite the mortal danger they were still in, his heart was so full of joy he believed he could run forever.

****

Tyhen stopped the wind when she saw the ocean. She lowered her arms and dropped to the beach, then caught Evan before he fell. He was unconscious, which was just as well. She knelt beside him and heard his heart thump, although his skin was pale.

When he began to moan, she stood and moved straight into his line of vision. His eyes opened.

Evan, it's Tyhen, can you hear me?

She watched his eyes widen as he began to look around in confusion.

Look at ME. See ME.

He crawled backward.

"Where are you? Who's talking?"

She sighed. The blow to his head had played havoc with his psychic self.

It's Tyhen. Adam is coming. Cayetano and Singing Bird are coming. You are safe.

"Adam! Where's Adam," he mumbled, then stood up too fast, staggered forward, and fell back down on his hands and knees.

He's coming, my brother. Just wait."

"Brother? I am your brother?"

Tyhen saw movement up in the trees beyond the shore and stood up as Cayetano and Singing Bird appeared, with hundreds of others close behind them. They ran all the way to the water and then fell into it in exhaustion, grateful for the cool wet relief on their scorched skin and aching bodies.

Singing Bird ran straight to Evan and fell to her knees.

"My son, my son! You've been hurt."

The ache in Tyhen's chest grew with each moment she waited. She was this close to her mother and Singing Bird did not know that she was there.

Mother, I am here.

Singing Bird didn't react.

Tyhen sighed. There was too much dark energy from the sadness for her to hear.

Evan blinked, then reached for Singing Bird's hand.

"You are my mother?"

Singing Bird looked at Cayetano with tears running down her face.

"He doesn't remember us. It is the injury on his head. When he is well, it will come back. It has to."

Cayetano got a cloth wet in the ocean and then carried it back to her. Singing Bird began to clean the wound with gentle strokes, but she hadn't forgotten what she'd seen, and the only explanation for Evan being here ahead of them, was that he'd been carried within the wind, the same way she'd been taken off the New Orleans streets.

"Do you remember what happened?" she asked.

He shook his head.

"Do you know who I am?"

He blinked. "Mother?"

She sighed. She'd put that thought in his head when she'd called him son.

"Do you know your name?"

He frowned. "Someone called me Evan. She said I was her brother."

Singing Bird rocked back on her heels and scanned the beach. Cayetano was doing the same.

Tyhen's heart skipped a beat.

Look at me, Mother. I am here. I am here.

"She wants you to look at her. She keeps saying, look at me, Mother. I am here," Evan said.

Singing Bird stood up.

"Tyhen?"

Tyhen wrapped her arms around her mother's shoulders, and as she did, Singing Bird jumped, and then sighed and closed her eyes.

"I feel you, daughter. I cannot see you and I cannot hear you, but I know you're here."

Tyhen turned and put her arms around Cayetano.

He jumped like he'd just been burned. He felt of his chest, and his arms, and then looked at Singing Bird in disbelief.

"This is my daughter that I feel? How is this so?"

And in that moment, Tyhen felt Adam before she saw him coming, then when he ran out of the trees, she called his name.

Adam, we are at the shore. Straight in front of you.

He stopped. Even though the beach was filling up with more and more survivors, the moment they set foot on the sand, Adam had seen the light that was Tyhen.

I hear you. I see you.

He turned to the young mother who'd run with him. She was staring at the ocean with a blank expression.

"I am sorry that your man is dead," he said gently as he put the little girl down beside her.

The woman blinked as she shifted focus.

"Thank you for carrying my daughter. Thank you for saving us."

He nodded, touched her shoulder lightly, and then pointed toward the water.

"I have to see to my brother," he said and started running.

Evan is hurt. He can hear me, but he can't see me. He doesn't know who I am and I don't think he knows who anyone else is, either. Be patient. His memory will return.

Shocked, Adam stumbled.

"Where did you find him?"

Running toward the fire.

Adam groaned.

"I will never be able to thank you enough."

Tell my mother and Cayetano that they are loved and not forgotten. Tell her that I see them in my dreams.

"Yes, I will. I will."

And just like that, she disappeared.

By the time Adam reached his family, he was shaking. Exhaustion and shock had set in.

He threw his arms around Singing Bird and Cayetano without saying a word, and then dropped to the sand beside his brother.

Evan blinked.

Adam reached out and took his hand.

"Evan."

Evan shuddered.

"You hurt your head, but you're going to be okay," he said.

Tears began to roll down Evan's face. "I couldn't find you," Evan whispered.

Adam pulled him into his arms. "You were running the wrong way."

Singing Bird couldn't wait another second to ask what her heart already told her was the truth.

"Was that whirlwind I saw my daughter? Was that Tyhen?"

Adam nodded.

"She knew about the volcano. She sent me a message asking if we were alive. I told her yes, but that Evan was lost. I asked her to help me and she came."

Cayetano's grunt was pure shock. "That thing I saw was my daughter? How is that possible?"

"No. Your daughter made it. She was in it, and so was Evan. That's how she saved him," Singing Bird said.

Cayetano shook his head. "I do not think such a thing is possible."

"It wasn't her physical body that was here," Adam said. "It was her spirit."

Again, he shook his head. "No. I do not believe."

Singing Bird lifted her chin and met the fear in his gaze. "It was her and it is possible because that is how the Windwalker saved me in the other world before Firewalker. Now that Adam is here to tend to Evan, we have much to do. Your people are suffering. We need to see how to help."

Then she looked down and saw that his sandals

had burned off his feet. He had been running barefoot and didn't even know it. She pointed.

"It is a good thing I made the moccasins. I'll unpack them later."

He glanced at his feet and grunted.

She knew it wasn't the end of it between them, but she took his hand anyway and led him away.

****

The New Ones had gathered around Yuma, afraid to move, afraid that the Dove would fly away before she had time to save them. Someone had begun a chant, singing to the Old Ones for healing mercy. They didn't understand what was wrong with her other than she lay in Yuma's arms as if she were dead.

Yuma was anxious, but he had faith. He just wanted her back. Waiting like this without knowing what was happening was the worst kind of torture.

Almost an hour had passed, and during that time, Yuma had not moved so much as a hair on her head. He was looking up to see if the volcano was still erupting when he felt a jolt, like someone had jostled her. He saw the color and life coming back into Tyhen's face, and when she opened her eyes, he held his breath.

They looked at each other for a long, silent moment and then she sat up in his arms.

"Evan is hurt but safe. Adam is alive and so are Singing Bird and Cayetano. The jungle was on fire around them. Many people died. I saw the ocean. I am thirsty. Could I have the water that is cold?"

The singing stopped. Someone let out a whoop of

celebration that she was back, while the others heard her words and spread the story.

"I will bring the water," a young boy offered and ran into the cave.

Yuma just held her, feeling her heartbeat against his own. "You flew a long way today, my little Dove. I am grateful you have returned without your feathers being singed."

"I saw something today that I think you call a miracle."

"What?" he asked.

"The twins were crying. Maybe the shell around their hearts has finally broken."

"That is a miracle and I hope you are right," he said.

The young boy came back with the water and handed it to Yuma. "For Tyhen," he said shyly.

"Thank you," she said and drank thirstily as Yuma held it to her lips until she'd had enough. "This cold is good," she said, as she caught a drip on the edge of her lip.

Yuma nodded. "Yes, this cold is good."

****

There was equal turmoil at the Hiaki compound on the Rio Yaqui, but it had nothing to do with the ongoing volcanic eruption hundreds of miles away. The bodies of Nelli and her husband had been found the day before.

Cualli, the medicine man, immediately blamed the unnamed witch who Nelli claimed had cursed her and was going from house to house on a witch hunt of his own, even though Nelli said the witch was not here.

The Hiaki were not only afraid of the medicine man and his accusations, now they were afraid that the witch who'd cursed and killed Nelli and her husband would come after them. They began hanging charms to ward off evil spirits and making their own little sacrifices to the gods for protection.

Cualli hadn't had this much business since the year the river got sick and all the fish died. So when he began having visions of a young woman coming to save the people from invaders, he took it as a sign that she would rid their ranks of witches as well. The sign of her coming would be a white dove, and she was to be welcomed and her warnings heeded.

When he shared this news with the Hiaki, there was much relief and an easing of the tension among them. After that, the watch was on for the sighting of a white bird. Many sightings were seen at first but Cualli rejected them all, saying his vision said the sign was a white dove, not the white water birds with long legs that fed in the shallows along the river's edge.

Once their finds continued to be rejected, the excitement of the search soon paled. After all, Nelli and her husband had already gone on their journey to the Great Spirit and no one else had been troubled by a witch. So they forgot about looking for white birds, and for that matter, forgot about looking for a young woman with a message to save their people because their people were just fine.

But once the story had been told, the news continued to spread from one family in another tribe to another and another until, as fate would have it, the story came back to Yaluk.

****

It was after dark before Yaluk's men came back into camp this day, and one of the few times he had stayed behind instead going on the raid. So the fact that they were not only late, but appeared to come in empty-handed hit him the wrong way.

"Where is the meat? I wanted meat and women."

"We brought meat."

Yaluk set up. "Show me!"

"Yoji! Give Yaluk the meat."

A man came out of the shadows and laid a half-dozen fish at his feet.

Yaluk sniffed, and then hit both men across the face with the flat of his hand. "They are bad. These would make me sick! Do you want me to be sick?"

"No Yaluk, no. But it was all to be had. There has been a bad thing happen in the south. A great mountain threw fire into the air and many people died. The animals have all run away. The fish in the water there are dead. The city below the waterfall is no more. The city they called Naaki Chava is no more. The city to the east of Naaki Chava is no more. They are gone, all gone."

There was a knot in Yaluk's belly that had nothing to do with being hungry. He'd killed his sister for what turned out to be no reason. He hadn't seen that witch in his dreams anymore and now a mountain threw fire and all those cities died. Even Naaki Chava! He'd heard of that city. He couldn't believe it was gone.

"So there were no women to bring," he said.

"We found one, Yaluk. She has been burned some. Most of her hair is gone, but she still walks."

He frowned. He didn't want to be with someone nasty. He wouldn't bed a woman who had no hair or skin.

"Bring her in. I would see her," Yaluk said.

The man named Yoji ran out of the dug-out and then came back moments later dragging a small, dirty woman with no hair or clothes. It was obvious by the oozing places on her body that her burns were painful, but she said nothing. She didn't beg for mercy. She didn't cry out in pain. It made Yaluk nervous. His women always cried and begged. It was what made his man part get hard. He slid a hand over it but it was as uninterested as he was. The woman did nothing for him.

"Woman! What is your name?"

She didn't react to the shout. She just kept staring into space.

Yaluk stood up and walked toward her, but the closer he got, the worse she smelled. He was used to dirt. None of them in his camp smelled good, but the woman smelled like she was already dead.

He jabbed a finger into her breast. She didn't even flinch.

"Woman! What is your name?"

Maybe it was the tone of his voice or maybe it was the hard jab to her breast, but her gaze began to focus, and then she looked around at the men one by one, as if surprised by where she was now.

Yaluk slapped her.

"You answer Yaluk when he talks to you. What is your name?"

A thin trickle of blood ran out of her nose and down her lip, but she didn't bother to wipe it away.

"Little Mouse."

He laughed. "That is a stupid name. Where are you from, the city of rats?"

"I am from Naaki Chava."

He was surprised that she was here. "That city is very far away. How did you get here? What did you do? Do you have a disease? Did you lay with many men? Is that why you smell rotten?"

The questions seemed to insult her. She took a step away from him, as if it was now he who smelled the worst.

"I did not lay with men. I am a healer. I gather... gathered herbs and roots to make medicine for Cayetano and for his family. I made medicine for the Dove called Tyhen, the woman who was born to save our people."

"Did they all die? Are you the only one still living?"

She didn't say anything for quite a while, and then finally shook her head. "No, they left before the mountain died."

He sneered, "If you were so important, then why did they go away and leave you behind?"

An expression of great sadness washed over her as if she had asked herself that question at least a thousand times without getting a satisfactory answer.

"I was in the jungle when the earth shook. I fell and hurt my head. I woke, saw my city burned and all people gone. I stayed because I had nowhere else to go. And then the mountain died and I ran. I was still running when your men found me."

Yaluk wanted to make fun of her, but he didn't have the stomach for standing so close to her anymore. "They said that city is dead. Why didn't you die with it?"

Her eyes rolled back in her head and they thought she was going to faint, and then she blinked and fixed him with a hard, dark stare. "I have been trying to die every day. It has not happened yet."

Yaluk shuddered. That was what he sensed. She wasn't hurt all that bad. She wasn't bleeding. She was just done with this world, dying from the inside out.

He would not lay with her but he was curious. "Who is this dove? How can some bird woman save our people? Why do our people even need saving?"

Little Mouse glared. "You do not need to know. She is magic. She is pure. You are not the kind of people she came to save."

The moment she said magic, Yaluk's heart skipped a beat. Could it be? Was that the woman who had come into his camp? He had not seen her face, but he was sure he'd seen her shape as she turned to walk away, and there was one aspect of her appearance that would set her apart from any other women. Would this dead woman walking say it? He had to ask.

"What does this magic woman look like? Is she fat? Is she old? Is she ugly like you?"

Little Mouse reacted exactly as he hoped. Anger often made people say the truth. "She is young and beautiful with long dark hair and legs that run as fast as the wind. And she is strong. She knocked down a whole crowd of people with only her voice."

A chill ran through him. He didn't like the thought of a woman that powerful being a spirit in his camp.

"What is this? How does that happen?"

Little Mouse shrugged. "She stands taller than the men of Naaki Chava and she has magic. Beyond that, I do not know."

Yaluk tried not to panic. The spirit woman that he'd seen had been very tall. Why had she been in his camp? Then another thought occurred to him. Did his men just happen to find this Little Mouse in the jungle, who just happened to know the woman with magic, or was she part of a trap set by the witch to weaken him in some way?

He fingered the talisman Nellie got for him just in case she was a witch, too. "Take her away," Yaluk said. "I killed my sister for this talisman to keep witches away, and I will not lay with her. She is friends with a witch and she is diseased."

Usually the men took turns with the women they brought back after Yaluk was done with them, but if he didn't want her, they didn't either.

"What should we do with her?" Yoji asked.

Yaluk's eyes narrowed. He thought about having her killed, but that would be doing her a favor because she was trying to die. Suddenly, a thin smile spread across his face.

"Let her go," he said.

The men were stunned.

"Let her go? But—"

"Do you want to lay with her?" Yaluk asked.

They shook their heads.

"Do you want to kill a healer who is friends with a witch?"

And that's when they got it.

"No, no, we do not," they said.

"Then let her go. Get her out of my sight."

Yoji grabbed Little Mouse by the arm and dragged her out of the dugout, then circled the camp just to make sure none of the other men saw her.

Little Mouse went without argument. She'd already given up her spirit. She was just waiting for her body to die. When they got to the edge of camp, Yoji turned her loose.

"Go," he said and waved her away, but she didn't move.

"Go now. Yaluk has set you free."

Still she didn't move, and the man was at a loss as what to do. In a way, she was like all of them, homeless and unwanted, and in a rare moment of pity, he handed her his water pouch and a piece of dried fish from his hunting pack.

"Go, Little Mouse. If you are a healer, you can find another place to belong."

Her expression shifted, startled by the kindness. "Go where?"

He pointed. "Rio Yaqui is that way. To the North, now go."

This time she moved, and he stood and watched her stumbling shuffle until she disappeared into the darkness. When it dawned on him that he was in the dark alone, he turned and ran all the way back as if a witch was at his heels.

Chapter Nineteen

It was relatively quiet inside the cave considering the number of people crowded in it. Johnston Nantay had remarked to his brother that it felt as big inside this cave as it did inside the Superdome the year they'd gone to watch the Super Bowl. Montford started to laugh and then couldn't bring himself to do it. That life and world were so far away it made him sad to remember it.

Nobody knew exactly what had happened when Tyhen fell asleep in Yuma's arms, but she had awakened with very sad and daunting news for them all. The elders who'd stayed because it seemed the safer path to take had been forced, once more, to run from fire.

On the other side of the cave, Tyhen lay sleepless and staring into the dark. The constant rush of the waterfall covered up the loudest sleep sounds, like people snoring or children crying out in their sleep. The scent of smoke was constant from dwindling fires but not intrusive. The open mouth of the cave was a natural vent.

She was worried about Evan and sick at heart about the old people who surely had not survived that fiery race. And, she was concerned as to where she and the New Ones went from here. All of this felt off balance. They'd been on their walk for many days now and all they'd done was get themselves in trouble and watch people die. It wasn't how she'd expected it to begin.

Yuma was curled up against Tyhen, his arm around her waist. He could tell by the way she was breathing that she wasn't asleep, but after everything she'd told him, he was just as sleepless. Knowing Wesley Two Bears was dead broke his heart and he knew she felt the same. When she'd taken off her moccasins tonight, he'd seen the tears on her cheeks. She was like a dam, holding back too much pressure. She needed to let it all go.

So he blew on the back of her neck.

She rolled over, then put her arms around his neck and buried her face beneath his chin. "So many died," she whispered.

He closed his eyes. "I know."

"It felt like running from Firewalker again, didn't it?" she said.

"Yes."

"Are you sad, my Yuma? Is your heart breaking like mine?"

He held her closer. "Yes, I'm sad. Is this the time, little Dove?"

She shuddered. "Yes."

He laid his cheek against the crown of her head as the first tears rolled out from under his lids.

"Then we will cry."

****

Singing Bird was on the hunt for Little Mouse, while

still trying to come to terms with the fact that her daughter seemed to have acquired her father's powers. Evan needed treatment for his wounds and she didn't have everything in her medicines that he needed, so every group of people that she came to, she would stop and ask.

"Have you seen Little Mouse? Has anyone seen Little Mouse?"

And they would reply the same in varying degrees.

"No, Singing Bird. We have not seen her."

"We have not seen her at all."

"I saw her the day before the fire."

"I have not seen her since my foot was cut back in Naaki Chava," and the answers went on and on.

By the time Singing Bird reached the far end of the beach and realized there was no one left to ask, her heart was in her throat.

Either she died when the city caught fire or died when they were running. They would never have left her behind. She was heartsick when she began to retrace her steps, and by the time she got back to the twins and Cayetano, she was sobbing.

Cayetano was immediately upset. "What has happened? Why do you cry?"

She pointed to Evan's head and then couldn't catch her breath enough to speak.

Adam felt the pain and knew. "She can't find Little Mouse. She's asked everyone and no one's seen her."

Cayetano turned to his warriors. Nearly all had survived the fire and were gathered around them.

"Go! Ask everyone here. Don't miss a single one. Find out if anyone has seen Little Mouse, the healer!"

They didn't hesitate as they ran off to do his bidding.

Singing Bird collapsed at Evan's feet and then absently patted his knee as she tried to pull herself together.

"I have some ointment. It won't be as good as Little Mouse would have, but it will make it quit bleeding, and I have something for you to drink that will help you rest."

Evan was still trying to come to terms with the missing parts of his memory and was upset that she was crying.

"Don't cry. It doesn't hurt so much," he said, trying to make her feel better as she dug the ointment from her pack.

She was making a monumental effort to hide her distress. Many people had died and she knew it. It's just that Little Mouse and Acat had been the first people she could remember talking to when she woke up in Naaki Chava, and now this horror was mixed up with that sadness. It was too much to think about. She wiped the tears from her face and stood up.

"As soon as that medicine dries, I will come back and put bandages on your head. For now, you rest. I have to wash this sadness from my body," she said and headed for the ocean.

"Wait," Cayetano said. "You do not go alone."

Adam sat with his arm around his brother, watching them go.

Instead of taking off her clothes when they reached the ocean, she just waded into the surf. Everything on her was filthy. It was the easiest way to get clean.

Cayetano was more hesitant. The fact that he could not see the end of the water was frightening to him, but he could not let his wife be more daring, and so he stepped into the lapping waves like he was going to war.

It normal circumstances, it was something the twins would have laughed about, but none of this was a laughing matter.

Adam nervously eyed the cut on his brother's head. It needed stitches, but there was no way to make that happen here. And then he remembered something he'd seen Little Mouse do for a boy in Naaki Chava. He knew what he needed, just not how to get them.

"Evan?"

Evan blinked slowly. "What?"

"I need to go find something for your head. Will you promise to stay right here until I get back?"

Evan nodded, then rolled over on the mat and closed his eyes, too miserable to move.

Adam hailed one of the chief's warriors as he stood. "Watch him for me. Whatever you do, don't let him leave. I won't be long."

The warrior nodded, and Adam took off through the crowd at a jog. He was looking for some of the New Ones, especially the older women who liked to work beads. He'd seen them decorating their ceremonial clothing with quills and beads made from bone. If anyone had what he needed, it would be them.

It didn't take long to find them. Once they'd outrun the fire and reached the ocean, they'd chosen to gather in families. He knew who to look for and soon spied them sitting knee to knee in a small close-knit circle.

"Lucy... Alice... it is good to see your faces. I had no hopes when this race began that any of us would survive," he said.

The two women each shared a frightening moment then asked about Evan.

"Evan was hurt. He has a very deep cut on his head and I am looking for something to close it. Did either of you bring your beadwork with you? I ask because I need porcupine quills and I know that you use to decorate your ceremonial robes."

The two women began digging through their packs.

Adam dropped to his knees beside them, his hands shaking as he waited.

"Here!" Alice cried as she pulled out a small packet and unwrapped it in her lap.

At the same time, Lucy found hers and did the same.

"You are welcome to take what you need," she said.

The quills were not of equal length or size. Adam picked up a couple of the smaller ones thinking they would tear the flesh less when he pushed them into Evan's skin. He tested the points and the length, trying to guess how many he should take to close the gash and then how many extra in case some of them broke.

"Would you let us help you?" Lucy offered.

"You mean you would come and help me close the cut?'

They looked at each other then back at him.

"We sew beads on clothing. We can sew two pieces of skin together as well."

The notion of using porcupine quills to hold the flesh together was no longer an issue.

"And you have tools to make this happen?" he asked.

They held up small, thin needles made from the bones of tiny birds, and then spools of fine thread they had woven from the cotton grown in the Naaki Chava fields.

"This is wonderful!" he said. "Yes, yes, you can help me."

They gathered their things and followed him to where Evan was sleeping.

The women knelt beside Evan, one at his head, the other at his right side, as Adam moved to the left to wake him up.

"Evan! Wake up, my brother."

Evan opened his eyes. "Am I dead?"

"No. But your head is cut open and these good women are going to help me sew it shut."

Evan blinked. "Will it hurt?"

Adam nodded.

Evan sighed. "I already hurt all over. It cannot be that much worse."

The women pointed.

"There is sand in the cut. It needs to be washed clean."

Adam quickly ran to the water's edge filled a cup with water.

Singing Bird saw him and came out of the water.

"What are you doing? Evan can't drink that."

"No, no, not to drink. I found two women who will close the cut on Evan's head. They want to wash the sand away first."

"That's a wonderful idea," Singing Bird said. "I'll be right there."

Adam hurried back and began to work.

Evan winced as Adam diligently cleaned the wound, then looked up at Alice and Lucy.

"It is clean again. When you finish, I will put on more of Singing Bird's medicine. She'll be here shortly. I told her what we were doing."

Evan looked at the women.

One was older with much gray in her hair and the other was younger, but had a crippled foot. He could not imagine how they had survived that race through the fire, yet they had. They must be brave. He could be no less.

The older one patted his arm.

"My name is Lucy," she said. "This is Alice. We will be as gentle and as quick as we can."

"My name is Evan. I will not move. I will not cry."

Adam did a double-take. Bravery was not part of Evan's personality, or at least it hadn't been before. So it would seem they were both changing. First had come the emotions, something of which they had never previously succumbed, and now bravery? Would miracles never cease?

Adam grabbed his brother's hand.

"Just look at me, brother. This time tomorrow it will only be a memory."

"One of my first," Evan muttered. "I seem to have forgotten most of everything else."

Adam blinked. Dry wit *and* bravery? That blow on the head had turned his brother into a stranger.

Singing Bird came back as they were about to begin, still feeling guilty for losing her composure. She was soaking wet and dripping sea water, but she was her old self again. She dropped to her knees at Evan's feet.

"My sweet, brave son. This will be over before you know it."

Believing she would have to help hold him down, she clasped Evan's ankles, then nodded at the women as they began.

Their fingers were quick, their stitches sure. They didn't linger with the pressure, or make an apology every time their needles went into Evan's flesh.

His face lost all color, but he never flinched. By the time they were halfway done, he was shaking. His jaw was clenched and there were tiny streams of blood coming from the places where the needles had pierced his flesh, but he had not uttered a sound.

Adam felt every shaft of pain that Evan suffered and it was all he could do to stay quiet. His admiration for his brother's strength of spirit had undergone a huge change.

Singing Bird was still gripping Evan's ankles, but no longer because she thought he would move. She was keeping track of his pulse. It was rapid but steady, and stronger than she expected.

"They are almost through," she said as the women took their last two stitches, then pulled the thread through the flesh, tied the last knot, and then cut it with their teeth.

"It is done," Lucy said.

"You were very brave," Alice added.

Evan took a deep, shaky breath. "Thank you. When I am well, I will help you build your new homes."

They smiled and giggled, imagining one of Cayetano's shamans building a house, then gathered up their things and left.

"You were so strong, my brother. I am proud of you," Adam said.

Singing Bird rocked back on her heels and then stared at Adam. There was blood coming from his head in the same places as where the needles had pierced his brother's flesh.

"Adam! You are bleeding, too!"

He touched his forehead, frowning as his fingers came away covered in blood.

"I will wash it off," he said and headed back to the ocean with the piece of cloth.

Cayetano passed Adam on the way back. When he sat down beside Singing Bird, he pointed toward the water.

"What happened to his head?"

She pointed at Evan, who had finally passed out from exhaustion and pain.

"Every time they pushed a needle into Evan's head, his brother bled with him."

Cayetano's eyes widened. "This can happen?"

Singing Bird shrugged. "They are twins. Like us, they are whole only when they're together. And they have much power."

Cayetano felt of Evan's cheek. "He will have a fever."

She nodded. "I have something for that. Usually I would build a fire to make the drink warm before I gave it to him, but I have had enough of fires for one day. He can drink it without water."

Cayetano hesitated. He had news for Singing Bird that she was not going to like, but it had to be said.

"My warriors came back with news of Little Mouse. They found Acat on the other side of the beach. She said Little Mouse told her the night before that she was going up the mountain the next morning to get fever root so she would have extra to take with her when we left. She doesn't think she was back when the fires began. And, she never saw her when the people gathered at the temple. Either she died in the fire, or she wasn't back from her gathering. She doesn't think she ever left Naaki Chava."

Singing Bird moaned and then began to rock back and forth on her knees.

"No, no, no, no. That did not happen. We did not leave Little Mouse behind. Tell me we did not leave Little Mouse behind."

"I can only tell you that many people have lost their lives this day, as they did in Naaki Chava, and none of it was of our doing. What happened has already happened. Everything is gone."

She shook her head. "This will haunt me to the day I die."

They stayed on the beach for several hours, resting, and gathering strength for another march. There was no way to gather extra food for the days ahead or any animals to hunt because what was around them had burned or run away. And staying on the beach was impossible because the tide would come in and then there would not be enough space.

Cayetano eyed the sun, gauging the time between daylight and darkness and finally made the decision to get moving. He sent his warriors up and down the beach alerting the people to pack up what belongings they had left. As soon as they did, they were on their feet and waiting.

Singing Bird had given Evan a strong dose of medicine that lessened the pain of his wounds, and when Cayetano gave the signal, with his brother's help, he was able to walk out on his own.

****

Little Mouse wasn't afraid of the dark anymore. In fact,

she wasn't afraid of anything because she'd been trying so hard to die without success that a part of her hoped for an animal attack to hasten the process. But as fate would have it, that was not to be the case. And, now that the man called Yoji had given her water and a piece of dried fish when they kicked her out of camp, the sustenance had given her strength to keep moving.

Yoji had pointed her to the North, so she looked up to the sky, searching for what the shamans called the Guiding Star and used it as her touchstone.

Moonlight shed an eerie blue-white glow on the landscape as she trudged northward. She had never been in a place where she could see so far ahead or so high. There were trees and bushes here, but not like in the jungle. These trees did not grow standing thick against each other, and she could see sky through them from afar.

The ground was rough and sometimes rocky beneath her bare feet, and more than once she stumbled into a strange plant that had thorns. She had never seen cactus, but soon learned that once they stuck into her skin, they wouldn't come out. The first time it happened she tried to pull it out with her fingers. Instead, it broke, leaving the hooked barb still in her leg. The next time it happened she didn't touch it. She needed daylight to see what she was doing.

Once, she heard an animal howl, and then another, and then another joined in. She'd never heard animals hunting together before. She thought about being nervous and then reminded herself that if she were attacked by more than one, it would take far less time to die.

Once she stumbled and fell facedown on the rocky

ground. When she came to, her nose was bleeding, her lips were split and bleeding as well, and she thought she'd loosened a tooth. This made her frown. If she wasn't going to die, she needed her teeth. As she got up, she realized the water had leaked out of the bag Yoji gave her. She left the bag behind as she walked on.

Before long, she began to see a change in the sky toward the East. Another day was about to be born and she was still breathing. She didn't know what to make of that, but it had to mean something. She should have died many times in the past few days and had not. There must be something left for her to do.

Now the sky was turning a most beautiful color, pale like the pink orchids growing in the jungle back in Naaki Chava with streaks of blue like the long-tailed parrots that set on the roofs. There were tears in her eyes as she thought it because the orchids were gone and the long-tailed parrots had surely flown away. She thought about crying, but it was a waste of effort. It changed nothing.

When she finally topped the rise and looked down into the valley below, she couldn't believe what she was seeing.

There were dwellings scattered out along the banks of a river like Naaki Chava had looked in the beginning. Only the places where these people lived were dug partway down into the ground, and their roofs were mounds of dirt with grass on top, and there was no palace.

People were moving about between the dirt mounds, building cook fires, getting water from the river and carrying it to water the growing crops.

So, maybe she had found the place Yoji called Rio

Yaqui. She sincerely hoped they were kinder than the ones who'd captured her. Either she went down there to her fate or sat here until the sun baked her brain and she breathed no more. And, since she was too thirsty to sit and wait for the sun to get hot, she took a deep breath and then started down the hill.

****

A woman called Meecha was rekindling her cooking fire for the day. She dug through banked coals until she found some glowing embers and covered them with a few leaves of dry sage, partly because they caught fire easily, and also because she liked the smell it made when it burned. Then she added smaller twigs, then larger and larger until it was alive once more. Once the fire was hot, she hung her cooking pot over it. It was full of new beans from the field and enough water to make them cook. She was thinking to add some turtle meat when she heard a dog begin to bark. She looked and saw someone coming into their village, someone who seemed sick, or maybe crazy, because they were staggering as they walked.

She watched, remembering that Nelli and her husband had died from a witch's curse and as of yet no witch had been found. Then she remembered there was also a woman who had been marked by the Old Ones to save their people from strangers who had yet to come, but this was not a woman. Meecha couldn't see breasts and there was no hair on his head.

Then the closer the stranger came, the more certain she was that she'd been wrong. There were breasts, very small, but they were there, and she was definitely either sick or crazy, because she was talking to herself.

Meecha turned and ran toward the medicine man's dwelling, calling his name loudly as she went, which sent more dogs to barking.

"Cualli! Cualli!"

Other people heard her cry and came out to look, and they, too, saw the tiny woman staggering into camp, and like Meecha, were afraid to approach her.

Cualli heard his name being called and hurried outside.

Meecha was pointing and talking so fast he could barely understand what she was saying, and then he heard the word, witch, and then crazy, and started running.

****

Little Mouse saw people coming to meet her. They were moving very fast and shouting and she didn't understand all of what was being said. She had no idea what a sight she presented, hair both burned away and pulled from her scalp, seeping burns and untended wounds on her hands and feet, covered in gray ash from running through so many fires, and so tiny and thin she could have easily blown away.

Then a man came pushing his way through the gathering crowd and she heard the word medicine man, and thinking he was something like her shamans, she fell to her knees. Either they would offer her up as some sacrifice or they would save her. It was out of her hands.

"Who comes into our village?"

"I am Little Mouse," she said.

Cualli recognized the similarity in their languages. She was from the South, from the land of the jaguar and the jungles.

"Are you a witch?" he asked.

She frowned as if the question had been an insult and thumped a fist against her chest.

"No! I am a healer. I am sad and I am trying to die."

The people heard and they were sad with her. That was a terrible way to feel.

"Why are you sad?" Cualli asked.

"Naaki Chava is no more. The mountain threw burning rocks and a river of fire into my city and I did not die. Then a band of bad men caught me and still I did not die. They took me back to their leader, a man called Yaluk. I thought he would kill me, but after talking to me, he didn't want me and again I did not die. Then another called Yoji gave me water and told me to walk this way to find people, and now I am here."

The moment she mentioned Yaluk's name, the people began to talk. She didn't know what that meant, but they obviously knew him.

"You know Yaluk?" Cualli asked.

Little Mouse shrugged. "It was his men who caught me. They are bad. They hurt me and did not give me food or drink. Yaluk is bad, too. He said aloud the bad things he had done."

Cualli frowned. He didn't want to be thought of as no better than Yaluk and sent one of the women to bring water to her while he heard more of her story.

"This Yaluk is bad. He used to live here but we sent him away for hurting and stealing," Cualli said.

Little Mouse was dizzy. She wanted to lie down and

sleep and never wake up, but these people still talked and so she stayed awake because it was polite.

"Yaluk sent me away, but since they were not going to kill me, I was glad to go. He said he killed his sister."

Again, the talking started, only louder.

Cualli held up his hand and the talking stopped. "Yaluk said he killed his sister?"

The woman who'd gone for water returned and gave Little Mouse a bowl so full it was sloshing over.

She emptied it in one breath then handed it back to her with a very polite nod of thanks.

Cualli repeated the question. "Yaluk told you he killed his sister?"

"Yes. She got a talisman for him against witches and then he killed her. I think this is a bad man who hurts the person who has helped him."

Cualli threw his hands up in the air. Now he believed her, because the talisman he had given to Nelli was nowhere in her house when the bodies had been found.

"We will help you," Cualli said. "You can live here. We have no healer. You can live in Nelli's home. She has no use for it anymore."

Little Mouse blinked. Just like that, her quest to die had ended with a blessing and an offer of a home? She was too tired and hungry to turn it down.

"I will live here, then. But I have nothing and I would like to be clean."

"All that will be given to you," Cualli announced, then added. "Meecha, the Old Ones chose you to see this one coming, so you will help her."

Meecha nodded, while trying not to be daunted by the horrendous task ahead. The little woman was dirty and sick, and her wounds were infected, *and* she had no clothes. This day was not the day she had expected when she woke. Still, she was better off than this Little Mouse, and it might be good to be friends with a healer.

"Come with me," Meecha said.

Little Mouse sighed. "I have walked too far. I cannot walk more."

A man named Chiiwi stepped out of the crowd. He'd been listening to this little woman who had no hair and felt admiration for what she had endured.

"I will carry her to the river," he said and picked her up and took off walking without waiting for Meecha.

Little Mouse looked at his face as they walked. He was short like the people of Naaki Chava, like her. And he smelled clean, unlike her.

"I will smell better when I have washed," she said.

He laughed.

When she saw he had all of his teeth and they were white, she decided to like him.

Chapter Twenty

One Week Later:

Recuperation time was over.

The New Ones were getting ready to leave the cave. Stores of food had been replenished, new water containers had been made and refilled. Clothes were washed and medicines replenished. They had smoked meat, dried fruits, and all but one of the nine people who'd come into the cave on travois were up and walking, with the other one not far behind.

Like most of the New Ones, Yuma was anxious to get moving. Tyhen had been quiet for the past three days to the point that he had begun to fear there was yet another big disaster awaiting she had yet to disclose. When they slept at night, she clung to him like a burr, and when they made love, it was with desperation.

Finally, on this last morning as they were waking up, instead of making love when she turned to face him, he cupped her face, kissed her lips and then took her hands.

"Talk to me, and don't tell me nothing is wrong."

She exhaled slowly, almost reluctantly, like she'd been waiting for permission to tell what she knew.

"I keep dreaming the same dream. We are walking

our path and it takes us into a place that is very high on both sides of us, but they are not mountains."

"That is called a mesa... like a small mountain with the top cut off. Are they flat on top?"

She nodded.

"Yes, a mesa," Yuma affirmed. "And the place below the mesas is called a canyon. Remember Firewalker. We ran through canyons."

Her eyes widened. "Yes, like that! I had forgotten. Are we going to be back where Firewalker began so soon?"

"No, I would guess we will be crossing into what used to be called Mexico, if we aren't already there. The land is very different there than it was back in Naaki Chava."

"In my dream, we are approaching this canyon, and there are bad men up on the mesas but we cannot see them. Half on one side, half on the other. They will roll big rocks down upon us and throw spears. I will have to leave you to fight them. You cannot be with me. You will have to stay with the others."

He frowned.

"Now that you have told us, we can be on the lookout for such places, and we can send guards ahead to make sure we do not get trapped."

She nodded. "It is a good plan. What bothers most is that these men know who we are and still want us dead. Windwalker told me that word had gone out to all the people of all the tribes that we were coming. He said we would be welcomed. I worry that if this is going to happen, then I must have done something wrong. Why else would they want to kill us?"

Yuma shook his head. "You are wise in many ways,

my little whirlwind, but you are a child in many others. There will always be bad people who don't want to give up their power. And if there is a tribe without a shaman to receive the message, they will not know what your presence means. There are many reasons why bad men kill, not the least of which is pure greed."

"We have no treasures."

He rubbed a thumb across the back of her hand as he carefully chose his next words.

"But we do. We have women, many women, and in a place where there are many men, women are always a prize."

She shuddered as what he meant sunk in. "Then we have to make sure not to fall into the hands of these bad men. When we start into that canyon, I will change their plans."

Yuma frowned. "How?"

"Strong winds blow people down. Stronger winds can blow people away."

He nodded. "That is good. So now that we have a plan of our own, no more sad faces?"

She smiled. "No more sad faces."

"Everyone is ready to leave today," he reminded her.

"So am I. It was beginning to feel like we were hiding. I don't like that feeling."

"But I do like how it feels when I kiss you good morning," he said softly.

She leaned forward and closed her eyes.

Yuma's heart skipped a beat as he cupped the back of her head and pulled her to him. Such a beautiful face. Such a strong, loving spirit. He was a blessed man. And so he kissed her.

Tyhen straightened up with a smile.

"Good morning, my Yuma."

"Good morning, my love."

About an hour later, the cave was empty, the clearing void of human voices. They were once again on the march, happier, healthier, and better prepared for what lay ahead.

****

Singing Bird had lost her spark. Ever since she accepted her part in the demise of Little Mouse, it seemed to be the final loss she could not put aside.

She tended to the people as was her duty and kept the twins in food and care, making sure Evan's head continued to heal. But at night when she lay in Cayetano's arms, she felt empty. All she could do was hope that when they reached their destination, the work of rebuilding would be what she needed to fill the void in her heart.

Adam and Evan sensed her emotional absence far stronger than Cayetano. His days were full of duty and concerns and he had to put his personal happiness aside to get it done.

They'd walked a very long way since the fire and when possible, they stayed close to the coastline. At times, it made finding food for everyone easier. All they had to do was go fishing.

As for Cayetano, he had already seen two of the landmarks from the map he had put to memory and believed they were near their final destination.

When he reached a small rise in the landscape, he walked up on it and turned around for a better view of the people behind him.

His warriors were in place, moving with the marchers, but along the perimeters as guards.

The people who'd been injured during the run from the fire in the sky were nearly healed, while the others had adapted a slower pace to accommodate their elders. They'd lost far too many people to be careless with the ones they had left.

The twins stayed close to Singing Bird at all times, which gave Cayetano the freedom to do what he had to do, and they had surprised him. Their skin had turned darker from the constant exposure to the sun, and they were far leaner and more muscled than they'd ever been in their lives. They had become hardened veterans of this march and unless someone looked close, they could not tell them from the others.

But it was Evan who had changed the most, and not just in physical appearance. He'd begun carrying a weapon and moved with a loose, easy stride like the warriors, always watching the tree line along the coast to make sure there was no danger.

Cayetano searched the moving crowd behind him until he saw the twins with Singing Bird between them and was satisfied.

He was about to jump down when he noticed Adam react in a sudden and very anxious manner, and as he did, Evan took a fighting grip on his spear.

He turned and looked all around but saw nothing out of the ordinary, then told himself he had been concerned for no reason when Adam suddenly grabbed Singing Bird by the arm and pushed her behind him, as Evan started running toward the front of the line.

Cayetano could tell by the expression on Evan's face that something was terribly wrong. He leaped down from the rock and ran to meet him, his own weapon gripped tightly in his hand.

The moment Evan saw him coming, he increased his speed.

"What is wrong?" Cayetano asked as Evan slid to a stop.

"Warriors are coming. We think a whole tribe. They are wearing face paint and carrying weapons. The chief who leads them is called Teya. He has many scars on his face and belly from the claws of a jaguar."

Cayetano groaned. He had warriors. He could fight. But he was in a quandary as to what to do with all the others.

"Will we fight? Are they coming for women?"

"Adam doesn't think so, and I am not so sure. We think they are here because they have heard about the Dove."

"But she is not with us," Cayetano said.

"No, but her mother is," Evan said. "Adam thinks it will be enough."

"Where are they?" Cayetano asked.

Evan took a deep breath and then pointed over Cayetano's shoulder.

"Behind you."

Cayetano spun around, then grunted like he'd been belly-punched. He'd fought in many battles, but he'd never been this outnumbered. There had to be hundreds. His numbers were larger, but he did not have nearly this many warriors. If these people wanted, they could kill everyone here and he would never be able to stop them. It was his worst nightmare come to life.

They were coming up the beach at a trot, the black

feathers in their headdresses bobbing as they ran and the vivid colors of paint on their bodies gave them a frightening appearance.

He took a deep breath and started toward them, and when he did, Evan was right at his side, the spear clutched tightly in his hand.

"Your people have stopped. Your warriors come," Evan said.

Cayetano heard, but he kept moving forward. He wasn't waiting for them to catch up. When they were within a dozen yards from each other, Chief Teya suddenly stopped moving and held up his hand, signaling for his warriors to stop, too.

Cayetano held up his hand and his warriors froze.

One long look passed between the two chiefs and then Teya suddenly dropped his spear and went down on his knees, threw his arms up and his upper body forward and prostrated himself before them. Behind him, his warriors immediately did the same.

Cayetano gasped. "What is happening?"

Evan tapped him on the arm. "Singing Bird comes."

****

Singing Bird was in a panic. The moment the twins told her there was an army of warriors intending to intercept them, she knew this would be the day they died.

"Are you certain?" Singing Bird asked as Evan headed toward Cayetano to give him the news.

Adam nodded. "Yes, Singing Bird. I can see them in my head. The leader is called Teya."

She groaned and glanced around at the people behind her, then looked up ahead and saw nothing.

"Are there many?"

"Hundreds."

Her chin came up. "Then today we die."

"No, no, I do not think so. I think they come because of the Dove."

"But she is not here!" Singing Bird said. "What will happen when they find out she is not with us?"

Adam hesitated. "I think they already know this. But they have been given the story. They know the prophecy and they know you are a part of it. You are Singing Bird, the woman who gave birth to the Dove. You will be just as honored as the child you bore."

"You think they mean us no harm?"

"I know they don't," he said.

"Then what should I do?"

He smiled. "Remember the day you first went to greet the people of Naaki Chava after you had healed? Remember how you walked from the palace down into the city without the guards ahead of you?"

Her eyes widened. "Show no fear."

"Yes."

And at that moment, the tribe of warriors ran into view. There were far too many for them to fight and they had a frightening countenance. All she could do was pray Adam was right.

She shoved her fingers through her hair in a gesture of defiance and led with her chin as she took her first step toward Cayetano. There was a knot in her belly but purpose in her stride. The warriors looked fierce. She wanted to turn and run, but instead kept walking toward them with Adam at her heels.

When she was only a few yards away from Cayetano, she locked gazes with their leader, and the moment he saw her, he dropped to his knees and threw himself facedown in the sand. When the others followed, the knot in her belly relaxed. Adam was right. It was going to be okay.

She saw the shock on Cayetano's face when he turned around, then she smiled and the panic receded from his eyes.

"My Chief," she said softly as she slid her hand along his arm.

"They honor you," he said. "Accept it."

She stepped forward, still holding his hand.

"Teya, we are honored you have come to greet us."

The chief rocked back on his heels and when Singing Bird smiled, he stood. His warriors shifted into the same mode and stood behind him.

"Are you Singing Bird? Are you the mother of the Dove?"

"Yes, I am Singing Bird and this man is Cayetano. He is my husband and our chief."

Teya thrust his hand into the air and let out a single cry that his warriors echoed.

Singing Bird's heart leapt. She could only hope that Tyhen's first reception would be as welcomed.

Teya took a step forward, acknowledging Cayetano and then waved his arm toward all the people Cayetano was leading. "Our city is many sleeps from here, but we would ask to be allowed to walk with you as we return. My warriors are great hunters. When you make camp, we will feed your people as ourselves."

Cayetano eyed the other chief closely. He didn't want to be taken in by false friendship and put his people in danger.

"We will build our new city near the water just a few sleeps from here," Cayetano said, making sure the man knew they were not just passing through.

Singing Bird gave Cayetano a startled look. She hadn't known they were so close. Yet, she reminded herself, she hadn't been aware of much of anything but her own sadness.

Teya frowned. "My people used to live near the water," and gestured toward the ocean beside them. "But strangers came. They took our silver and our gold, left their babies in our women's bellies and did not come back. We moved farther away from the water to hide from them."

Singing Bird's eyes flashed in anger and Teya saw it.

"We know of this, and I tell you they will come back, each time taking more and caring less about what you think, and they will still find you and take your belongings and your women, and no matter how many times you run away, their numbers will increase and the day will come when there will be no place left to hide. That is why we *will* live near the water—to stop their thievery before it can begin."

Teya stared, his lips parted in shock. "This is what our shaman predicted."

"And he was right."

"How do we fight such people?" he asked.

Singing Bird thumped her chest with a fist. "We will conquer them with wisdom and power. Walk with us and I will tell you how."

And so they walked with Teya's warriors leading the way while others were sent ahead to hunt and set up camp.

It was only a short time before sunset when they arrived, led by the scent of wood-smoke and cooking meat. Cayetano's people began to set up their camps and wash their bodies in the surf, while others began refilling water bags and bottles from a nearby spring.

Teya's men had deer, wild pig, and many birds cooking on the fires, and banana leaves spread out on the ground covered with coconuts and fruit.

He had walked every step beside Singing Bird, riveted by the story of Firewalker and what their people had endured to make the change. As they finally sat down at their fire to eat, Teya's focus shifted from Singing Bird to her man.

"Cayetano, I would ask, as one chief to another, how will you battle these people who will come? How can we stop them?"

"Singing Bird says they cannot be stopped."

Teya frowned. "Then there is nothing to be done?"

"We do not kill them to stop them," Cayetano offered. "But as a people, if we stand as one, keeping our tribes as we wish, but united as a people, then when the strangers come again, they will be greeted, but with caution. There will be many among them who will wish to live here for their own personal gain, and that is when our power as a united nation matters most. We can grant them the right to make their home here if we wish, but they have to understand from the start, that the land is already claimed. That it is not free for the taking, and that we will not be moved from the places that are our homes."

Teya's eyes widened as understanding grew. "The strangers can live within it, but they cannot claim our world because it is already taken."

Singing Bird sighed. She'd been saying the same thing a dozen ways as they had walked, but Teya had not grasped the full scope of how it would work until now. Sometimes a man-to-man talk made everything better.

"Yes," Cayetano said. "Now we eat. I am hungry and my ears are tired of hearing words."

Teya grunted in assent.

Singing Bird blinked. Now they were saying she talked too much? She glanced over and Adam and Evan, who were grinning. She frowned at them, struggling not to laugh as she reached for some food. She hadn't been hungry in days, but now everything felt different. She'd had her first taste of success and it was good.

****

Three days later:

Teya and his warriors parted company the day before, but their trip together had cemented what would become a life-long bond between the two chiefs. By the time he and his warriors returned to their city, the story would be told and retold a thousand times, and it would set Singing Bird's place into their history.

Cayetano guessed they would reach their destination today, and when he had seen the last landmark a short while ago, he began moving the people faster. He knew they were trail-weary and heartsick, but so was he, and in the end it would all be worth it.

And it was.

When he found himself walking out of the jungle onto the broad white sands bordering the water of the vast ocean before them, he knew they were home.

He threw his hands up into the air and let out a cry of jubilation that was heard all the way back to the last people in line.

They started laughing and crying as they ran forward, because they knew what it meant. This was where new roots would go down, and the next time a ship full of strangers came to their land, they would be waiting with a whole new set of rules.

Singing Bird saw Cayetano's joy and smiled. She felt nothing but relief. They had come home. Now all they had to do was build it.

Mother, it's me. I felt your joy.

Singing Bird's heartbeat kicked so hard against her chest that it caused her pain. She grabbed her chest as her vision blurred.

"Tyhen! My daughter! I hear your voice. We have arrived at the place where we will build our new city."

I can see it through your eyes. Yuma sends you a message.

Singing Bird began to laugh through tears. Hearing from both her children at once was a joy she thought was lost to her forever.

"I listen. What does he wish to say?"

He says Adam and Evan have a new map Cayetano needs to see. He says they have given a new name to what was once called North America and South America. Do you understand?

Singing Bird was entranced that she could communicate so perfectly. It was like talking by telephone in the world before Firewalker.

"Yes, I understand."

And he says to tell you one thing more. If you have not already named the new city, that you should call it Boomerang. He said you would know what that means.

Singing Bird gasped as her throat tightened with even more unshed tears.

"Yes, yes, I know what that means. It was an object that when thrown, no matter how far or how high it went, always found its way home. I love it. I will tell Cayetano that his first son has already named our new city, but I have a question, my daughter? Why have you not talked to me before?"

We have had troubles, but they are mostly over now. I have felt your sadness, but your heart was so heavy you could not hear my voice. What happened that made you turn your heart away?

Singing Bird hated to say the words aloud again because they hurt her tongue as deeply as they hurt her heart.

"We lost Little Mouse. I think we left her behind."

What? No! Oh Mother, no! How did this happen?

"We are not certain. Acat said she was in the jungle gathering roots for the trip the day the earth shook. We don't know if she never came out of the jungle or if she had already come back into Naaki Chava and died in the fire, or if we just left her behind. It was an accident if we did. We waited and waited for people to gather before we finally left."

And that is why you cry.

"Yes, that is why I cry."

I am sorry. My heart had been sad, too. Wesley Two Bears died the day the earth shook and Naaki Chava burned. I saw the vision.

Singing Bird glanced back toward the ocean and the people dancing about on the broad stretch of white sand.

"That is done. We cannot hold onto that which we could not control."

I know. I'm learning.

"I love you, my sweet child. Come and see me in your dreams."

You have to be listening for the sound of my voice.

"I will listen."

Go now and tell Cayetano he has a city named Boomerang to build. I love-

And just like that, the voice was gone.

Singing Bird sighed, then wiped the tears from her eyes and went to look for Cayetano to give him the news.

****

Little Mouse was clean. She had food in her belly, medicine on her wounds, and for the first time in many days, clothing on her body. There was nothing she could do about her hair. Either it would grow back or it would not.

Meecha was ready to take her to her new home and had bluntly explained why it was vacant.

Little Mouse thought about living in a house where people had died and then decided they would not mind since they had Yaluk in common. Just because she had survived Yaluk and they had not had nothing to do with her.

Meecha led the way up out of her home and into the sunlight.

Since Little Mouse was no longer facing death by dehydration and starvation, when the sun hit her face, she took the greeting as positive.

"Are you strong enough to walk now?" Meecha asked. "It isn't far."

"I can walk," Little Mouse said.

They started across the compound in silence, but soon Meecha began to talk.

"Chiiwi has no woman," she offered.

Little Mouse frowned. The man carried her to the river when she was weak, not offered to lay with her. She did not like Meecha's curiosity. Still, she was new and she thought it best to know all she could so she would do nothing wrong.

"What is wrong with him?" she asked.

Meecha frowned. "He just never chose a woman."

Little Mouse shrugged. "Maybe he does not want a woman. Maybe he would lay with men. It is the same only different."

Meecha sighed. "No, not that. We call them two people and he is not one of them."

"Then it is his business," Little Mouse said. "Am I allowed to tend to the dead woman's garden and call it mine?"

"Yes, yes, Cualli said all that was hers is now yours." Then she eyed Little Mouse closer. "But her clothes will not fit you. She was very fat."

"I can fix," Little Mouse said.

Meecha tried to think of something else to say, but they had arrived.

"Here is your new home. If you have need of anything, you must just ask. We always share. When you are well, people will call on you for healing."

Suddenly, Little Mouse looked anxious. "I have no ointments or herbs to heal with, and what if the things I know do not grow in this place?"

Meecha thought about it and then smiled. "Chiiwi knows. He can help you."

Little Mouse shrugged. She didn't care who showed her as long as she could resume what was her passion and her trade.

Then a thought occurred. "Who did you use as a healer before me?"

Meecha shrugged. "We didn't have a healer, but sometimes Chiiwi knew what worked."

Little Mouse felt bad, like she was stepping into shoes that were already filled. "Then he was your healer."

"No. He is our best fisherman. He makes nets and hooks and knows where the best places are to hunt and fish."

The news lightened Little Mouse's heart. "Then I will ask him to show me... when I am well."

Meecha nodded. "It is good." She glanced toward the doorway to the dugout. "Do you want me to go in with you?"

"No. It is best I go in alone," Little Mouse said.

Happy that her duties were over, Meecha made a hasty retreat as Little Mouse opened the door, shoving it wide to let in the light, and then walked down the steps into the room.

There were dark places in the dirt floor at the foot of the steps. She thought it was blood. But the rest of the place appeared as if someone had just stepped away. The pots and dishes were sitting on a shelf. Dried herbs hung from the ceiling above a table with two stools. A bucket had been made from a short piece of a hollowed-out log and had rope for a handle meant for carrying water from the river, she guessed. The bed of skins and furs on the floor at the back of the room was large, made to accommodate two people. It would be the best bed Little Mouse had ever had.

She reached down and touched the dark earth, and then straightened.

"I am Little Mouse. Thank you for this home."

Chapter Twenty-One

Like everyone else in the region, Yaluk now knew the story of the medicine woman with great powers who was supposed to change history. He also had heard she walked with many people and that they were coming through his land. But he wasn't concerned with the future. He just wanted more power with as little effort as possible.

He sent eight of his best men out to scout the area. He wanted to know how many people there were with her and which direction they were moving. If the medicine woman was as powerful as he'd heard, then she would likely have great wealth to go with it, and that was his goal.

He'd been waiting for hours now for his men to report back, but so far without success. Frustrated and more than a little bored, he gathered up twenty more of his warriors and left camp. If he found them lazing about without the answers he'd sent them to get, he would gut them where they stood.

****

Tyhen's relief in knowing her parents had reached their new location was dampened by the news of Little Mouse. The little healer had been so much a part of her life in Naaki Chava that it hurt to think of what must have happened to her. And like her mother, the thought that she might have been left behind was horrifying. Little Mouse would have been so afraid on her own when the mountain died, and there was no way she would have escaped it.

And so she walked with that heartache added to all the others, barely aware of the hot sun on her face or the sweat running down her back. Heat was a constant where she'd grown up.

But when a child stumbled and fell a few yards ahead of her and she saw how red his face was and how dry and dusty his feet and legs were, it made her realize that while it was still hot, it had not rained on them in days.

She was thinking about finding a place to stop for a rest when the mother scooped up the little boy and settled him on her hip without missing a step. As she did, the child tucked his head beneath his mother's chin without a whimper. The sight of such acceptance touched her heart. Even the children seemed to know this march was unavoidable. She had witnessed tears, but they were few and far between.

However, seeing this little boy fall made her think of Yuma. He hadn't been much older than this one when they'd run from Firewalker, and he'd been on his own. A rush of emotion swept through her at the thought. He'd been so young, but so very, very brave.

She looked up to see where Yuma was at and remembered he'd told her earlier that he was going to walk ahead with the Nantay brothers, but she didn't see them anymore, and at first she thought nothing of it.

The people had just begun a climb up a long slope of land, and since she didn't see him ahead of her, she turned to look behind, didn't see him there either, and then her gaze locked on the view of where they'd been.

The geography behind her looked like someone had drawn a line on the earth announcing, here is where things will grow, and here is where they will not. There were still trees and many strange bushes, but she did not think this land on which they were walking would grow food, and there was no water in sight. She turned again to the people in front of her, and even though she had stretched to her tallest, she could not see Yuma anywhere.

She was on the verge of being concerned when she caught movement on the horizon just ahead. She stopped to watch, letting others pass by her, and all of a sudden three men appeared.

It was Yuma and the Nantays and they were running! Johnston and Yuma were on either side of Montford, and each had an arm around his waist to keep him on his feet. Then she saw the blood on the front of his chest and saw what no one else could see, eight armed men in pursuit only a short distance behind them and gaining ground. She leaped forward, barely aware that the New Ones were already arming themselves as she flew past.

****

Yuma and the Nantays were scouting ahead for landmarks to match the maps that they had. Because of the geographical region of the country through which they were now moving, their lives would depend on where they could access water, and how far they could go without it.

"Look there!" Montford said. He was smiling as he pointed off into the distance at a small cloud of dust. "That is something in a herd. I haven't seen animals make a dust cloud like that since before Firewalker."

Johnston nodded, but he was more interested in the terrain. It was getting rougher. He thought about all of the people behind them still walking barefoot.

"We need to get back and call for a rest so people can get their feet covered. These rocks are going to be too sharp for bare feet."

Yuma was listening, but his gaze was focused on a dip in the land off to their left. Twice now he thought he'd caught a glimpse of movement and was hesitant about going any farther until he knew what that was.

"What do you see?" Johnston asked.

Yuma pointed. "See that shadow in the land just ahead? It looks flat, but if you look closer, there is a slight dip to the surface. There's something down in it."

Montford looked.

Johnston stared. "I see what you mean. Something... no, someone is belly-crawling. See that faint poof of dust rising. Good eye, Yuma."

The hair rose on the back of Yuma's neck. He was thinking about what Tyhen had said about the bad men she'd seen in her dreams when a head popped up.

"There!" Yuma yelled.

The Nantays immediately notched arrows into their bows, ready to shoot if the target presented. And it did.

When the armed warriors sprang to their feet and came toward them on the run, both Nantays and Yuma launched their arrows, but only one man went down.

The others were too many and coming too fast to stop and shoot again.

"Run!" Johnston shouted, and as they turned, an arrow hit the back of Montford's shoulder and pierced the front of his chest, as well. He stumbled, his face wreathed in pain as Johnston grabbed him from one side and Yuma from the other.

"Move your feet," Johnston yelled, and Montford came to enough to follow directions.

"We've got you, Montford, just hold on to us," Yuma yelled. Then they began to run, carrying him between them.

It took a few seconds for them to get their footsteps in sync and then they took off. There was no way to know how many more warriors might be around, but the need to warn the others was paramount. If they could just get back over the hill before the warriors caught up, they'd be safe by numbers alone, but the little men were coming up fast and weren't wasting breath doing it. It was a silent race to the death and Yuma wasn't ready to die.

Dust rose ankle high as they ran over sharp rocks, dodging thorny cactus and dragging Montford between them as they kept their gaze focused on the high ground ahead.

When they finally topped the rise, their biggest relief was seeing the New Ones strung out all over the land before them.

Then Yuma saw Tyhen coming through the crowd, running in that long, fluid stride that made her look like she was moving on wheels. The expression on her face was set and he knew she was already aware of the danger.

When she drew even with him, their gazes locked. He got the message. Go take care of Montford. She'd take care of this.

The moment the three men were safely behind her, Tyhen channeled her anger and threw up her arms like she was tossing dirty water out of a bucket. The air rose with the motion of a tidal wave, gaining strength with forward motion until it was an impenetrable wall of mass and might, the perfect unseen weapon.

One second the eight warriors were coming over the rise and the next thing they knew, they were in the air and high above the ground, tumbling head over heels without anything thing to hold onto. The last thing they saw was a mass of people spread so far out on the ground below that they couldn't see an end. They were screaming and praying to the Old Ones, still trying to catch hold of each other when the wind suddenly died. And then so did they, dropping from a forty foot height onto the rocky ground below.

****

By the time Tyhen got back, women had gathered around the men and were digging medicine out of their packs. Johnston was in front of Montford, cutting the arrowhead from the end of the shaft, and Yuma was behind, ready to pull it out.

Yuma looked up. The grim expression on his face said it all. Before, all their danger had come from the earth and the elements. It was no longer the case.

"Is it bad?" she asked, as she dropped down on one knee beside Shirley Nantay.

"Bad enough," Shirley said.

Sweat was running down Montford's face and there was a muscle jerking at the side of his jaw.

"Get it out," he mumbled.

Johnston made one final cut in the shaft and the arrowhead fell into his brother's lap.

"It's off," Johnston said.

Before Montford had time to brace himself, Yuma grabbed the back of the arrow and pulled.

Montford moaned and fell forward into his brother's arms.

"I'm sorry," Yuma said as he tossed the arrow aside.

Shirley's expression was grim.

One of the women was carefully washing the blood from his shoulder, while Shirley was waiting to pour a healing powder into both entrance and exit wounds.

"What do you want me to do?" Tyhen asked.

Yuma looked up. "The ground is getting rough. No more bare feet. Spread the word."

She stood and turned. The expressions on the New Ones' faces were grim as she called out for all to hear.

"He will heal. The ground is bad. No more bare feet."

Once again, the people began digging through packs.

Yuma slid an arm around her waist as he came up behind her.

"The warriors were in hiding. They attacked us first."

She sighed. "We are in a new land. These people do not live the way we lived. Everything is strange. We must be careful not to waste what we have until we know where we can get more."

He lifted the hair from the back of her neck and kissed the spot right behind her ear that made her weak.

As he did, the wind circled around them in a soft, teasing manner.

Tyhen sighed as she turned in his arms.

"Be careful of starting something we cannot finish."

He groaned. "Yes. Thank you for the reminder."

She smiled. "So, do we know which way to go?"

"Toward water, wherever that is," Yuma said.

"I will see," she said, then walked a few steps away and closed her eyes.

At first all she could see was more land like this, then she looked farther and saw a river. She didn't know how far away it was, but she knew which direction to take.

"This way," she said, pointing north.

****

Yaluk was angry. They were almost an hour away from camp and still no sign of the scouts. After another half hour of walk, he stopped at a small watering hole in Chollo Pass that came from a natural spring up in the rocks. He then sent four of his men out in different directions to try and pick up a trail while the rest of them settled in to wait.

One man saw a covey of birds hiding beneath some brush and shooed them out. As they took flight, a half-dozen of the other warriors were ready with arrows and shot them down. A full belly always shifted the mood. Before long the birds were cooking over open fires.

The scent drew a pair of rangy coyotes who didn't

linger once they saw the men associated with the scent, and time moved slowly as they waited for the birds to cook and the scouts to return.

One of the guards Yaluk had stationed up on a ridge gave a whistle and then pointed.

Yaluk stood up and turned around. Even from here, he could see the dust cloud. Many people were on the move, but a long distance away. It reminded him of the time when he was young and his people had lost their water source. They had packed everybody up and moved and he had walked among the dust, choking and so thirsty he believed that he would die. But then they found the Rio Yaqui and settled. It had been a hard life, but there had been enough to be happy and live comfortably. Only Yaluk had never figured out how to be happy with what he had. He'd always wanted more.

By the size of the dust cloud, it had to be the witch woman and her people. He had many more warriors, but not with him. Now was not a wise time to attack.

Then he heard another whistle. The same guard was pointing in yet another direction. He turned to see one of his scouts returning. It was Yoji, the one he'd sent south.

A few minutes later, Yoji reached the spring and fell belly down onto the edge to drink and then got to his feet.

"Did you find them?" Yaluk asked.

"One dead with an arrow in his belly. I do not know this tribe," Yoji said, as he showed it to Yaluk.

"What about the others?" Yaluk asked.

"Found them a long distance away. All dead. No open wounds. No arrows in them. No spears, no knives had cut their bodies. Just broken.

Yaluk frowned as the other warriors began muttering to themselves.

"Did you see the witch?"

"No, but many people are coming from the South and they will not reach this place before dark."

Yaluk frowned. He didn't like knowing nine of his best trackers were dead. He liked it even less that they were dead without an obvious reason as to how that happened. It sounded like witchcraft to him.

He turned to the other warriors. "Bring the food with us and put out the fires. We go back to camp now."

Within a few minutes they had abandoned the spring, buried the offal from cleaning the birds, scattered the ashes, and brushed away their tracks.

****

The mood was somber as the New Ones made dry camp that night. Montford was feverish and in serious pain. Johnston feared the wound had an infection. Knowing one of their own was in peril made for uneasy sleep for everyone. Only the children were quiet, exhausted by the day's events.

Yuma and Tyhen had gone into their little tent early, but after a first sleep, they woke and made love with quiet passion. Having this physical bond was what kept Tyhen focused during the day. As long as she had Yuma to cool the fever in her blood and hold her when she slept, she could fight whatever lay in their way.

Still basking in the afterglow, Yuma lay spooned against her back with his hand cupped against her breast.

Tyhen could feel his joy. It was a heady thing to know she'd been loved by him since she'd taken her first breath, and even when she wouldn't admit it, knew she would love him forever.

Tell them to find a Yucca plant.

Tyhen jumped as if someone had just stuck a knife in her back, which put Yuma on alert.

"What's wrong?"

"Adam just sent me a message for Montford. I need to get up."

Yuma scooted out of the tent feet first and then helped her out.

Tyhen was scrambling, trying to pull the shift back over her head as Yuma fastened his loincloth.

"Poison snakes here. No bare feet," Yuma cautioned.

"Oh yes. I forgot."

A few moments later they were off. It was easy to find the Nantays' tents because they were the only ones up with a fire still burning.

Montford was lying face up on a sleeping mat, surrounded by some of the elders who were burning sage and saying healing prayers.

When Johnston saw them coming, he stood.

"He has a fever."

Tyhen grabbed his forearm. "Adam sent a message. I'm not sure what it meant, but he said find the Yucca plant."

Johnston turned around. "Who here knows the Yucca?"

One of the women sitting with Shirley stood up. "Luz Reya. She's Apache. She said today this place looks like where she was from."

"Do you know where she sleeps?" Shirley asked.

The woman nodded.

"Show me," Shirley said and took off through the camp behind her.

Tyhen could tell Johnston was scared and it showed on his face.

"I do not want to lose my brother," he said.

Tell them he will not die.

"Adam said to tell you he is not going to die," Tyhen said.

Johnston wiped a hand across his face, unashamed of his tears.

"Get a torch and take Yuma. I will show you where it grows."

Tyhen frowned. *Is it far?*

"Does it matter?"

There is not much moon. I asked to make sure I had a torch big enough not to burn out.

"Oh. Sorry. It is not far."

Tyhen rolled her eyes and turned to Yuma.

"We need a torch. Adam will show me where it grows."

Yuma took off to get greasewood they'd cut earlier. It burned bright and would make a good light.

"You two do not go alone," Johnston said. "After what happened today, we go nowhere in small numbers."

Tyhen wouldn't argue. She wasn't afraid of the dark, but she didn't know this land or the inhabitants.

By the time Yuma came back with a torch, Johnston had gathered up almost a dozen armed men, half of which were also carrying torches.

We're ready. Which way do we go?

"Do you see the big bear? Ursa Major?"

She looked up at the sky, searching for that specific gathering of stars.

Yes, I see the bear.

"Walk toward it. I am with you as you go."

Chapter Twenty-Two

They took off into the darkness with Yuma and Tyhen in the lead, walking in groups of three and four.

I can see you. You look very thin.

Montford is sick. Stop looking at my belly and look for this Yucca.

She heard a chuckle and then nothing.

Yuma walked beside her, but he'd given the torch to her to carry and stayed a couple of steps ahead. He didn't want to be night blinded by the torches if something came at them from out of the dark.

And it was a wise decision. They hadn't gone far from camp when he heard a sudden and deadly rattle.

"Stop! Don't anyone move!" he said as he grabbed Tyhen by the arm.

Everyone froze, and as they did, the warning rattle was easier to hear.

"What is that?" Tyhen asked.

"Rattlesnake," Yuma said, pointing just a few yards ahead of them.

Johnston ran up with his torch and held it low to the ground toward the snake. Instead of striking out, the heat from the fire sent it slithering off into the night.

"It wasn't very big," Tyhen said, mentally comparing it to the big jungle snakes she'd grown up seeing.

"It was big enough. One bite of his fangs and you die," Yuma muttered, then added. "Maybe not you, but we would."

She punched his arm.

He grinned, trying to lighten the mood, and it worked. As soon as the danger had passed, they moved on.

They'd walked almost a mile when Adam's voice was, once again, in her ear.

Just off to your left. Tall, spiny plant with long, thick leaves.

"He said just to our left," Tyhen said, pointing.

They hastened their steps, and within a few moments Yuma saw it. "I know this plant!" he said. "My grandmother had it growing in her garden back home. It didn't like Oklahoma weather, but she managed to keep it alive."

"Take the leaves, not the root, and take all you can carry. It has many uses, not the least of which is fighting fever and infections."

Thank you, Adam. I will tell Montford.

"You are welcome. We miss you, but tell Yuma that Boomerang is growing."

I will. Tell my mother... no, tell her nothing. It would only make her sad again.

"Safe travels, little sister."

And he was gone.

"We take the leaves," Tyhen said. "Take as many as we can carry. They have other uses."

They harvested them quickly then hurried back to find Shirley sitting with an older woman. Her hair was thick but short. She wore it parted in the middle and cut in a straight line across; about the length of her chin. She wore a shift similar to the others, but looser, and knee-high, lace-up moccasins

Johnston recognized her as a woman named Luz Reyas.

"Luz. You know this plant and how to use it for medicine?"

She nodded. "It has many uses but the Apache use it for fever and infections. Give it to me. This won't take long. Montford will be better by morning."

Tyhen knelt next to Montford and felt his forehead, as she did, he opened his eyes.

"Little Dove, you have come to flap your wings and cool my fever?"

She smiled. He was talking out of his head. "We brought medicine. You will feel better soon."

"Get some rest, my friend," Yuma said.

Johnston stopped them as they started to leave. "Thank you."

"You are most welcome," Tyhen said. "I am grateful for wiser people than me."

They knew she was talking about Adam.

"Yes, but he is there and you are here, and I am grateful for that, too," Johnston said.

Yuma laughed. "Agreed. Good night, my brother. Here's hoping we don't have to run any more foot races again soon."

Tyhen frowned. She had already come to the realization that the arrow that hit Montford could just as easily hit any one of the three. As sorry as she was about Montford, she was equally grateful it hadn't been Yuma.

Yuma held her hand as they walked back.

Tyhen looked up at the heavens again, absently

eyeing the Bear. She had known the stars long before her mother had taught her how to read. It was strange to think that sky was the same, no matter where you were when you looked up, then remembered she hadn't delivered Adam's message.

"Adam said to tell you Boomerang is growing."

Yuma grinned. "They really used the name I suggested to name the new city? I like that! You know, the countries we all came from will no longer be called North or South America, because those are the names white men gave them."

She frowned. "I don't care about the names. I just want what I'm supposed to do work."

"It will," he said, and as they reached their tent, he put out the torch and laid it near the banked coals of their fire.

They took off their moccasins, shed their clothes, and crawled back into the tent.

Tyhen curled up on her side.

Yuma curled up behind her.

He heard her sigh and closed his eyes. Tomorrow would come too soon.

****

Little Mouse's heart was healing. The burns on her body had begun to grow new skin and hair was beginning to sprout on her head like new grass.

She had cut down and re-sewn two of the dead woman's dresses to fit her body and even had a pair of moccasins for her feet. She ate two good meals a day, had all the fresh water she needed, and slept without dreaming, happy to wake to another day of calmness.

It had taken some time to go through the drying herbs hanging from the rafter as well as the crushed ones Nelli had stored in little pots. She didn't know their names, but she was learning how they tasted when added to food.

On the third day after her arrival, Chiiwi came calling. He brought her a big fish he'd caught in the river and some corn from his garden.

"This is for me?" Little Mouse asked.

Chiiwi nodded.

"What do I give you in return?" she asked.

"I asked for nothing," he said shortly and started to walk away when she stopped him.

"I have a question!"

He turned around. "Then ask."

"I am a healer, but I don't know your healing plants or where they grow. Meecha said you might show me."

He nodded. "I will show."

"When?"

He hid a quick smile. "When your feet are no longer sore."

She frowned. "I have not spoken of my feet."

"I am the one who took out the thorns. It takes longer than three sleeps to make them well."

She sniffed. "So when you know my feet are healed, will you come take me to the plants?"

"I will take."

"When?"

He laughed, and when he did she saw his white teeth once again. "For a Little Mouse, you make a very big noise. I will be back when it is time."

He walked away.

She took her wonderful fish outside and gutted it, then sliced half of it up to smoke and laid it on a flat rock near the hottest side of her fire, wrapped the other half in wet corn husks and put it in the coals to cook. She peeled back the husks on her new corn, cleaned away the silks and then pulled the green husks back up and laid them near the fire, as well.

She would have a fine meal today and the smoked meat for another meal tomorrow.

Afterward, she sat down and pulled off her moccasins then eyed her feet. Chiiwi was right. Her feet were not well. But they would be, and then she would go hunting for medicines with him. The idea of a trip with him made her heart skip just enough to accept that it was an interesting thought.

She did not smell bad anymore and one day she would have hair again, and Chiiwi had fine white teeth. He did not have a woman. She did not have a man, and her teeth were still in her mouth.

She sat down outside her dugout to watch the fire, making sure it kept an even heat to cook her fish, thinking about how far she had come from Naaki Chava and how hard she had tried to die. She was beginning to see why the Old Ones had not taken her with them. This was a different life, but it might become a better life. Only time would tell.

****

The new city of Boomerang:

Cayetano settled the city's new name as if it had been his idea. The Twins had urged him to lay this city out in a manner similar to Naaki Chava so that when strangers came, they would see it as more than a bunch of huts scattered about the jungle in which half-naked savages lived.

They began by clearing one long pathway and then people picking sites on either side of it where they wanted to build. As the huts went up, more paths were cleared; keeping them running either north and south, or east and west, intersecting when necessary to give it an orderly appearance.

The chief's new home would not be made of hand-hewn rock as had been in Naaki Chava because it was not readily available. But with the New Ones tools, they were able to saw down large trees and build substantial dwellings, the kind that would withstand strong winds and were far enough from the shore to be safe from the big waves that came with them.

They built the chief's residence in the shape of a long house and then built another one less grand for the warriors. The sound of construction was a constant, along with the concern of hunting and gathering enough food to keep everyone fed until they had the first harvest from the new crops being planted.

Singing Bird had some of their better craftsmen building looms for her weavers. One trader had already found their location, promising next time he came to bring back raw wool cut from their animals and to bring them some seeds of the cotton plant to start their own fields. Clothing would not last forever and going back to curing skins did not appeal to her. She had sacrificed a lot to take her people into a better future, not throw them back into living in caves.

The mountainous region was beautiful, but subject

to ocean winds they had not coped with inland, and so life was altogether a learning experience every day. But the day Adam and Evan came in with a gift for the long house, it stunned her.

Before Firewalker, they had never lived anywhere but on Bimini Island with Landan Prince, and yet they had devoured entire sets of encyclopedias, scanned the internet for constant sources of new learning, and above their psychic skills, she guessed their IQs were off the charts. She wouldn't have been wrong.

Singing Bird was inside the long house weaving mats for the floors when Adam and Evan walked in.

She looked up smiling while eyeing Evan's new scar and checking out Adam's attitude. They were smiling too, which told her all was well, and they were carrying something with them.

"What is this you carry?" she asked, eying what looked like a framed picture, which was something she hadn't since before Firewalker.

"It is a gift for your new home and it should be hanging in Cayetano's throne room. When strangers come to have an audience with him, they will see the scope of what the native people own and where they live."

Even before she saw it, she was impressed by the idea and quickly stood.

"Let me see."

They turned the frame around and quickly rendered her speechless.

It was a very detailed map done in colorful paints, showing what had once been the North and South American continent; from Canada all the way south through the United States, through Mexico, Middle

America, and all the way to South America. Everything about the shapes looked perfect, but the land masses were unbroken and unclaimed, save for the single name they'd put at the top.

One Nation.

They'd named the entire land mass One Nation, with First Nation being what had been North America, and Second Nation, being what had been South America. And the umbilical cord connecting the twin continents that made them one nation was what had been called Middle America; where Naaki Chava used to be.

"This is amazing," she said. "How did you come up with this name?"

"It was easy," Evan said. "The twin continents are like Adam and me. We are separate to look at, but the blood that ties us together makes us one, just like the land on this map. They appear as two separate places, but see the umbilical cord still connecting them? It makes them One Nation. North is First. South is Second. And there is Boomerang. And one day as you learn the locations of other cities, you will add them and see the nation of tribes as they are."

"Cayetano is going to be very proud of this."

Adam smiled. "Tyhen has seen our vision. She will make sure the New Ones also make copies of this same map. Tribal chiefs should know how vast the resources and people are to whom they belong."

"Thank you, my sons. Thank you very, very much."

"It was our pleasure," Evan said.

Adam nodded, and still they did not leave.

Something about the stillness with which they were watching her made her wary. "What is it you're not telling me?"

"Nothing bad. Tyhen and the New Ones are in what was once called Mexico. They are searching for water and adapting their way of life to the surroundings."

"Are they in danger?" she asked.

Evan sighed. "We agreed we would not lie to you. Yes, they are in some danger, but Tyhen is more than a worthy opponent. She is a fierce and dangerous person to have as an enemy, Singing Bird. She will keep them all safe."

Still suspicious, Singing Bird watched their faces closely.

"Her powers increased very drastically and all at once, it would seem."

"It would seem," they said.

"She has her father's powers, doesn't she?"

They looked at each other and then back at her and nodded.

"How did this happen?"

Adam hesitated. But mother and daughter would be forever separated and it seemed Singing Bird deserved, at the least, to know the truth.

"Tell her," Evan said. "Tyhen won't because she believes it would hurt her mother's heart."

Adam nodded. "Windwalker gave them to her in the temple at Naaki Chava. He's the one who told her when to leave."

Singing Bird turned pale. "But I thought he ceased to exist when the curse was broken."

"He stayed for her."

She moaned beneath her breath and didn't know it. "Where is he now?"

"He is no more. When he gave her his powers, he ceased to exist."

Singing Bird covered her face, but she wouldn't cry. When she lifted her head, her dark eyes were blazing. "I saw him in her like I'd never done before. I should have known."

"I tell you only so that you will know how safe she is. She cannot die, Singing Bird. Not until she gives away her powers to her child as he did to her. For as long as One Nation exists, there will always be a Windwalker's daughter to lead the people in it."

Singing Bird's eyes were shining with unshed tears, but the triumphant look on her face was dazzling.

"Then this has all been worth it!" she cried and turned and picked up the framed map. "Come help me find a place for this. We have a new world in the making. It needs to hang in a place of honor!"

****

This was the morning of the second day without fresh water and time was running out. Water containers were empty or nearly so. Food supplies were getting low and the heat of another day had set in for a long hot visit.

Today the New Ones who were taking the lead were Yaqui and Apache men, who like Luz Reyes, had once lived in this place. It was vastly different from their time, and yet somehow familiar. They were delighting in what could only be called forests of cacti, thickets of spiny plants double and sometimes triple the size of how they'd known them.

In the distance the marchers had seen wild pigs, some as large as small ponies, and big cats not unlike the jaguars from the jungles. With all these animals about there had to be water nearby as well. They would find it, and they would hunt food to sate their hunger. It was just a matter of time.

While many saw it as a vast, harsh land with its own brand of beauty, Tyhen hated it with a passion. For a woman born and raised in a lush green land with water at every turn, this was nothing short of her worst nightmare.

Yuma knew she was struggling to stay positive. It wasn't the heat that was pulling her down, it was the horizon. She'd grown up in a city with a jungle around her, and a mountain in front of her. She'd never been allowed to climb that mountain, and this horizon was too damn far. They needed one good thing to happen, like finding water before sundown.

****

Yaluk was elated. It had been a long while since they'd had the opportunity to take many prisoners with much wealth. Once his scouts had given him the direction the witch was on, he knew just where to launch his attack. They were heading straight through Cholla Pass, and once they spotted that small spring in the rocks about mid-way through, the distraction of finding water would serve to shift their focus from being on guard, to quenching their thirsts.

He'd stationed half his men on the East mesa and taken the other half onto the West mesa with him, giving them a clear view into the pass below.

It was all about finding the witch among her people and taking her down. He didn't know what she looked like. All he knew was that she was tall. People weren't tall in this land and especially women. She should be easy to pick out.

They'd been in place for almost two hours, watching the approaching dust trail when they got their first glimpse of the people.

Although he and his men were high above the pass, he was struck by their long arms and legs and the men's long easy stride. When he saw the leaders looking up as they entered the narrows, he flattened down even more, scooting backward so that his head would not be visible from below, and his men did the same.

Ten minutes later, Yaluk was in shock at the number of people still coming into the pass. And with no end in sight and many tall people, he had yet to pick out a woman who looked significant.

His men on the other mesa were waiting for his signal. He could start the avalanche of rocks he had at the ready and be done with it, but if the witch got away, this would only make things worse for him in the long run. He did not want to be a target for her magic.

And then he heard a man let out a loud whoop of delight and knew they people down below had finally found the water. He smiled.

****

Tyhen was uneasy. The moment they'd started into this pass the hair stood up on the back of her neck.

"Yuma!"

He turned. "I know. It's like your dream, isn't it?"

She nodded.

"What do you want us to do?" he asked.

She glanced up again and in that moment, knew she needed to be on the mesa, not looking at it from below.

"You keep them moving through. I'm going up," she said and saw disapproval in his eyes.

"And let you out of my sight? What if they hurt you?"

"Then they will be dead and I will heal."

Her anger stirred the air around him, lifting the hair from his neck and cooling the sweat on his brow and still he frowned.

"You don't make this easy. The day is bound to come when you meet something you cannot control."

"I cannot die."

"But I can die, and one day you are going to scare me to my grave."

She frowned. "You do not say that and we have a purpose. I know mine. Do you know yours?"

He threw his arms around her neck and kissed her hard and fast, uncaring who might be watching.

"Yes, I know my purpose," he said, and the minute he turned her loose, she ran back in the direction they'd come from and disappeared.

He headed toward the front of the line at a lope. They needed to know something was going to happen and he didn't have much time.

Precious minutes passed as he ran past the straggling line of weary walkers. He came around a bend in the pass just as he heard a yell of jubilation and was guessing someone had found water. At least he was hoping that was it because they were in serious need. However, finding water was going to stop progress through the pass, which would make them sitting ducks for an attack.

Chapter Twenty-Three

The moment Tyhen found a place to be alone she began to chant, feeling the power of the earth coming through her feet, up her body, and out of her hands. When it began to turn the air around her, her heart skipped a beat. The feeling was an anxious anticipation like just before she and Yuma became one. She hastened the chanting which turned the air faster and faster until she was standing in the midst of a wild, spinning vortex that took her up onto the mesa.

****

The men were poised for attack when they heard a roar. They turned, saw the spinning wind behind them, and panicked.

To Yaluk, it was frightening and unlike anything he had ever seen. It swept across the mesa like a ghost wind. Before they could run, it blew them off their feet and began dragging them across the rocky ground through rocks and cactus and leaving skin and blood behind.

They were screaming in pain, begging for the wind to stop, begging the Old Ones for mercy, but to no avail.

****

Tyhen already knew Yuma had done his part to get everyone to safety. When she saw the people running away from the water, she shifted the force of the wind and blew Yaluk and his men off the other side of the mesa, away from Cholla Pass.

Their screams ended abruptly when they hit the ground, but Tyhen's heart was hard. Better their screams than the screams of her people, she thought, as the funnel took her across the pass onto the East side of the mesa.

Having witnessed their friend's demise, those warriors were already in flight, but they didn't get far.

One by one, the spinning wind picked them up and took them high, then let them go, dropping them down onto the mesa below.

The New Ones below heard the screams, got brief flashes of the wind funnel, then a few minutes later it sailed down the length of the pass in an "all clear signal" and disappeared.

Yuma waved his arm. "It's safe. Back to the water," he yelled and began leading the New Ones back to the spring.

The pool of water was small and there were many people lined up to refill their water jugs, so it took a long time.

When Tyhen suddenly appeared in their midst, no one commented on her absence or what they'd seen. She was the Windwalker's daughter fulfilling her promise, and they showed their appreciation by quietly handing her a drink or a piece of food or offering her their seat in the shade.

Yuma had been watching for her and when he saw the look on her face, he knew she would remain silent for many hours now. It was how the violence affected her. He ached for a way to make it better, but as long as there were people willing to kill their own, she would not stop, and he could not spare her heart.

Tyhen had shut down. Not thinking about what happened was her way of getting past it. When they were ready to leave, Yuma searched her out at the spring and found her sitting quietly in a place of shade with her hands lying loosely in her lap, her gaze focused on a wet spot on the earth where someone had spilled water a short time earlier.

A large lizard was resting in the sun about ten feet above her head but no one noticed, or if they had, had simply let it be. Enough death had happened this day and no one had the stomach for killing a lizard that would not feed them all.

The sun was hot on the top of his head, but in that moment his body felt light, so vividly alive that if they had been alone, he would have taken her in his arms and loved her back to health. She was his heart—his mate—the other half of his soul, and when she hurt, he felt her pain.

He knew she sensed his approach because she suddenly raised her head and the look in her eyes made him hurt.

Save me. Love me.

He read the plea and took her hand.

She stood as he pulled her into his arms and then held her so close against him that they were bonded by the heat.

"You saved many lives. It is done. Hold onto my love, little dove. Let it go. Let it go."

He felt her shudder and then slowly slid her arms

around his waist. The longer they stood together, the tighter her hold became until she was shaking.

It was his reminder that this woman/child was not yet seventeen. In his world, before Firewalker, she would have been a long-legged girl on the brink of becoming a woman in lust with some equally lustful boy who would most likely break her heart.

Here, she was a warrior with the power of a god, battling daily for the people to whom she belonged. She had lost her innocence even before she was born, but she would never lose her man. He would cut his own throat and die bleeding to save her and she knew it.

He was her strength.

He heard her whisper his name.

"Yuma."

"I am here."

"Do we leave now?"

"Yes."

"Good. There are too many ghosts here. I am ready."

He frowned, and then pushed her back until her could see her face. "Remember what I told you? Why men like those raided and killed?"

She saw her own reflection from the sunlight in his eyes and shivered. "For women."

He nodded. "So if you had done nothing, which women among us would you have chosen to give away knowing the deaths they would suffer would be long and brutal?"

She blinked. "None."

He nodded and held out his hand. "Good answer. I have your pack. We go now."

She threaded her fingers through his, taking

strength from the firm grasp as they left the ghosts of Chollo Pass behind.

They walked north as she had ordained, and when the sun went down, they set up another camp. They were less than two miles from Rio Yaqui, unaware of how close they were to their destination.

Yuma put up their tent and laid down their sleeping mats, gave her a drink of water, then held the flap back for her to crawl in. She had refused food and he did not insist.

Later, Johnston came over to check on her and found Yuma sitting quietly at their fire watching a small grouse cook that he'd shot with his bow and arrow. They visited a few moments and then Johnston left, but not before leaving a piece of Shirley's bread for them to eat.

Luz Reyes brought a small pot of the mashed Yucca leaf and told him how to use it for soap to wash their hair.

Montford came a little later with some cactus blossoms and told him how to prepare and eat them.

And so it went until the people began bedding down for the night. They wanted to thank her for saving their lives but since she slept, they thanked Yuma instead.

When the last fire was banked and the coyotes began their nightly chorus of singing to the night sky, he took off his loincloth and took Warrior's Heart into the tent with him, laying it within easy reach.

Tyhen was curled up on her side, but he could see tears. She was crying in her sleep.

He scooted up behind her, put his arm across her waist and pulled her close.

She murmured something aloud, and he slid his arm beneath her neck, and then pillowing her head upon his shoulder, he quietly rocked her back to sleep.

****

Tyhen was dream-walking.

In the dream she was looking out across a land so vast it was like looking at the reflection of the sky, a place with no beginning and no end. No matter where she turned, the land was the same, seemingly flat with no trees or mountains, only knee-high grass waving in the wind.

And as she looked off into the distance, she saw many huge blackish-brown animals with mountainous humps on their shoulders and curved horns on their wooly heads.

Then something made them move, and when they did, they came toward her. They ran as one, sweeping ever so slightly in one direction, then rolling gently back in another, spilling down the slope toward where she stood until she could feel the vibration of their approach beneath her feet. She thought she should run, but there was nowhere to go, and so she stood in their path as they came toward her.

Their eyes rolled wildly like they could see her even though she was a wraith. The grunting and huffing of their collective breathing only added sound to their terrifying approach. The air around her was cold, but she could see heat waves rising from their backs, and when they were finally close enough to touch, she held out her arms and closed her eyes as they ran through her. And then she wept, knowing them as one living being knows another while the thunder of their hooves and heartbeats pulsed within her.

They ran and they ran until, finally, they were gone and she felt heavy and empty, like her ability to move had gone with them. Sad that they had passed, she looked to the direction from whence they'd come and this time she saw people. Like the animals, they came toward her, too, and she wondered if the animals had led them.

She heard an eagle cry and looked up. It was circling over her head without flying away. *Yuma*, she called, but it did not hear her.

And then more people were coming from another direction, spilling over the rise and moving toward her as if she was the only light in a dark land.

She began hearing voices and the thunder of many footsteps, and everywhere she looked, saw people coming toward her until she was surrounded on all sides and as far as the eye could see, and they did not sweep through her.

You can see me?

They knelt.

And her heart grew big and strong as she felt the love.

****

Yuma shook her awake.

As her eyes flew open, she grabbed for his hand.

"What is wrong?" she asked.

He cupped her cheek and brushed a kiss across her lips. "You were calling my name."

It was just turning light as she looked up at the

man leaning over her. His dark hair became a curtain around their faces, and for a moment she allowed herself to think what it would be like to be only *his* woman, and not belong to so many others.

"I was dreaming," she said, tracing the bottom of his lower lip with the tip of her finger. "I saw great beasts in many numbers and they ran through my spirit as I stood among them and I could feel their heartbeats. After they were gone, many people came, and I think these beasts led the people to me."

As always, he was fascinated by her abilities, not the least of which was her sight of things yet to come.

"The people have many names for those beasts. White man called them buffalo. They were the soul of the people of the plains. They fed us. Their hides clothes and sheltered us. Their bones became our weapons. They gave all they were to us and we thanked them."

She tugged on his hair, pulling him closer until he kissed her again. The wind shifted slightly inside their tiny tent.

"We cannot do this here," he said.

She groaned. "I know. It was just a thought."

"Do not lose it," he whispered. "One day we will have time to ourselves and great peace. Then we can stir the air into a whirlwind if we want."

"We will want," she said softly.

He smiled, ducked down until their foreheads were touching, and the rolled over onto his back.

"I hope there are no surprises for us today."

She closed her eyes, and as she did, saw a small village along a wide river. "I see people and I see water. It's very close."

He raised up on one elbow. "This is true?"

She nodded.

"The Nantays should know so we can get moving faster."

She stretched then rubbed the sleep from her eyes. "I will join you. Today is a good day."

"You were given many gifts last night while you slept," he said. "One you will enjoy came from Luz Reyes. She made some soap from the Yucca leaves for you to wash your hair."

Tyhen's eyes widened in delight. "Soap to clean my hair is a fine gift! Where did you put it?"

"All the gifts are outside beside your pack."

She scooted out of the tent with Yuma right behind her.

"I need to go," she said.

He looked around and then shrugged. "Pick a bush and close your eyes."

She laughed and strode off through camp to do just that.

****

It took almost an hour to get the people moving and another hour to walk two miles, but when they came over a ridge and saw the village and the river below, there was much rejoicing and a hastening of steps.

Tyhen was thinking about fresh water, getting wet all over and actually washing her hair, when she saw someone down in the village look up. She could tell he must be shouting because other people began appearing, coming out of the strange little houses buried partway into the ground. She saw them looking up at the ridge, and then there was much running about. She couldn't tell if they were excited or afraid but she knew there would be no trouble.

****

Little Mouse was at the river with Chiiwi. He'd been showing her where certain water plants grew that had roots for easing belly pain.

She was down on her knees in the mud, happily digging with both hands when she heard shouting.

Chiiwi climbed up the shore to look over the edge.

"Many people come."

Little Mouse rocked back on her heels, then quickly washed off the mud and ran all the way up the bank without stopping. Her heart was thumping so hard she did not hear Chiiwi calling her back. She had to see. Nobody here believed that she had known a great chief or been healer to his family, and when she mentioned one day that she knew the woman they called the Dove and had often tended to her, they had laughed. She did not mind that they laughed, but if this was Tyhen, they would laugh no more. She started walking back toward the village. She would wait and watch, but she had to know if it was her.

****

"I hope their shaman has seen the vision," Tyhen said.

Yuma nodded in understanding. No one wanted a repeat of yesterday, but then added for her understanding. "I think that in these tribes, the shaman is called a medicine man," he said.

"This is so?"

He nodded.

"Does that mean he is their healer?"

"It means the same as a shaman. Your people believe the shaman calls on the gods for his power, and we say our man is making strong medicine when he calls on the Old Ones. So he is called a medicine man for this reason."

"Do you have healers, too?"

"Yes, and often it *is* the medicine man, but sometimes it is not."

She thought about that, and then suddenly pointed up ahead. "We must be mindful of their crops and homes. We are many and they are few."

"I'll tell the Nantays," Yuma said and ran ahead to pass the word.

Tyhen was a little anxious. She wanted this meeting of a new tribe to be a good one and wondered if they would be able to understand each other's words.

By the time they reached the verge of the small village, every citizen was waiting to greet them.

It was obvious by the more elaborate clothing and the pipe that he cradled in his arms, that the short, stocky man with gray hair and crooked feet was their medicine man.

When the New Ones saw the kind of dwellings in the little village, some guessed they were Hiaki, or the Yaqui, as they became known or maybe Apache. They had once been in the same basic region.

They called Luz Reyes up to the front of the march because she spoke those languages and because she was so elated to be walking in this land of her ancestors, she had been crying ever since they came down off the ridge.

Then they reached the village, and when the leader spoke and it was apparent they could understand him, she stepped aside to let the medicine man speak.

"I am Cualli. We are the Hiaki. Does the Dove come with you?"

Cualli watched as the crowd began to part. A young man with long hair and an even longer spear came toward him. And just when he thought the man would speak, he stepped aside and Cualli saw her, a very young, very tall woman wearing clothing made of something other than the skins of animals. She wore moccasins on her feet like they did, but there were no feathers in her hair. He had never seen a woman who stood so high from the ground. And then she spoke and he felt her words on his heart and knew it was the Dove.

"Cualli, I am the woman you seek. I am called Tyhen. Do you know why we are here?"

Cualli's heart began to pound. He was standing in the presence of a woman with magic.

"I have had the vision," he said.

She smiled, and when she did, Cualli smiled back.

Tyhen pointed to the people with her.

"We are many, but would ask to clean ourselves in your river and fill our water bags."

"We would be honored," Cualli said.

"We will not harm your crops. We will not spoil your village, and we thank you."

"When you have rested, I would be honored if you and your elders would have food with us. I am sorry we do not have food for all."

Tyhen shook her head. "We feed ourselves. It is allowed for us to fish in your river?"

"The river belongs to no one. You may fish."

All of a sudden there was a large commotion behind Cualli, which made Yuma react. One moment he had been standing quietly to one side and the next he was in front of Tyhen, his spear held tightly in one hand to protect her.

Cualli blinked.

"Who is this man?" he asked, pointing at Yuma.

Tyhen smiled. "This is my man. His name is Yuma. He is the eagle who watches over the dove."

Cualli nodded, and then glanced over his shoulder, frowning as the commotion continued.

All of a sudden a little woman appeared, pushing through the Hiaki to let her pass.

Tyhen took one look at her face and leaped forward, scooped her up into her arms, and began to cry.

"Little Mouse! My Little Mouse! Singing Bird has been grieving for you for so long she became sick. We thought you were dead!"

Yuma saw her and let out a cry of delight, which echoed throughout the crowd behind him.

Little Mouse's heart swelled. The words were what she needed to hear. They did not forget her. They just got lost from each other.

Cualli stared. "You know this person?"

"Yes, yes," Tyhen cried as she put her down, then couldn't turn loose of her hand. "She was the best healer in Naaki Chava. She was Chief Cayatano's favorite. I have known her all my life."

Little Mouse lifted her chin, her eyes flashing, as if daring them to doubt her word again.

Chiiwi was at the edge of the crowd watching. His

heart was sad. She was someone important and they loved her. Surely she would go with them when they left.

Tyhen turned to the New Ones, and as she spoke, her voice carried all the way to the back of where they were standing.

"Go to the river. Do no harm to the crops, and if you wish to wash your bodies, remember to go downriver. We do not foul the water they drink."

As the people filed past in a quiet and orderly fashion, they nodded at Little Mouse or smiled to show their joy. But Cualli was shocked on an entirely different basis. He wanted to know how she could make her voice be heard in such a manner, and didn't hesitate to ask.

"How did you do that with your voice? Is it magic?" he asked.

Tyhen shook her head. "I am the Windwalker's daughter. The wind carries my voice when it needs to be heard. After we are clean, we will share your food."

Little Mouse heard that as a dismissal and took Tyhen by the hand. "Come little whirlwind. I will show you and your eagle the way."

Yuma smiled and winked, which made her giggle. He laughed with her, pretending he did not see her lack of hair and healing wounds.

"It is good to see you again, Little Mouse. Many people have mourned your death. It is good to know it did not happen."

Little Mouse could barely contain a strut as she swaggered through the crowd. Then she caught a glimpse of Chiiwi's face and stumbled.

Tyhen caught the look that passed between them

and raised her eyebrows at Yuma, who quickly hid a smile.

"Little Mouse, am I not to meet your friend?" she asked.

She ducked her head, smiling shyly as she beckoned for him to join them.

Tyhen eyed the little man curiously, sensing something was different about him, and then the moment their gazes met, she knew.

She smiled, and he smiled back.

"I am Chiiwi, friend of Little Mouse."

"I am Tyhen and this is Yuma. We are also her friends."

"I am showing them the way to the river," Little Mouse said.

Chiiwi pointed at all of the New Ones lining the shores in the act of washing themselves. "It is a very big river. They will see it."

Little Mouse frowned back at him. "They thought I was dead. I thought they did not want me. We have much to tell."

Chiiwi's eyes widened. He had not known her heart had that sadness.

And at that moment, Tyhen's heart broke. It was as she feared. Little Mouse thought they had not cared when they left her behind. She looked at Yuma as her eyes filled with tears.

He leaned forward, whispering near her ear. "Don't cry. You know how that hurts my heart."

Chiiwi patted Little Mouse's shoulder. It was as much of an apology as he could manage in front of strangers.

Then they reached the river and Chiiwi looked at

Little Mouse again. "I am a fisherman. I will catch fish for your friends," he said and hurried away.

"Is he your man?" Yuma asked.

Little Mouse frowned. "He is nobody's man. He will not take a woman, but nobody in the village knows why."

"I know," Tyhen said. "He is like the twins. He can hear what people think. So if they think bad things of him, he will not want them."

Little Mouse's mouth dropped as her eyes widened. Yuma laughed, leaned over, and whispered something in her ear that made her giggle and cover her face.

"Wait for me while I wash," Tyhen said. "When I am clean, we will talk. Is this a safe place to walk in?" she asked.

Little Mouse nodded, then sat down on a rock by the river and pulled her knees up beneath her chin, too overjoyed to say any more.

Tyhen dropped her pack, dug out the soap Luz Reyes had made for her and then took off her shift and walked into the river.

Yuma was right behind her.

"Hold out your hand," she said and gave him half of the soap she was holding.

Without another word, they walked out into the river until it was up to their waists, then began to wash, first their hair, then their bodies, then each other's backs. Then when they were clean, they retrieved their clothing and washed it as well.

As Tyhen was scrubbing her shift, she glanced back at the shore where Little Mouse was sitting and then back at Yuma.

"What did you whisper in Little Mouse's ear?"

He grinned. "I asked her if she'd been thinking good thoughts about Chiiwi. Since it made her giggle, I would say that she has."

Tyhen smiled. "I have to let my mother know we found Little Mouse. It will make her heart very happy."

"Do you think that Little Mouse will want to come with us?" he asked.

Tyhen shook her head. "She likes Chiiwi. She will stay here, and that is good. Everybody needs to belong to someone like I belong to you."

He took her face in his hands and kissed her soundly. "If I was not standing in water, I would puff out my chest and strut like the little roosters that used to be in Nantay's pen in Naaki Chava."

She giggled. The day was joyful. A lost friend had been found and they had water and good food to eat.

****

Singing Bird was cracking a coconut when she suddenly heard her daughter's voice.

Mother. I have news.

Singing Bird was already smiling as she laid down the machete and pushed her hair out of her eyes.

"Is it good news?"

Yes. We have reached a river called Rio Yaqui. Yuma says to tell you it is in a place you once called Mexico.

Singing Bird sat down on the steps leading into the long house, picturing where they would be.

"You have walked a very long way already. Is everyone well? Have you had trouble?"

Tyhen wasn't going to tell her about her battle with the outcasts. Ever.

373

We are well and had no trouble. But when we reached this river, we found someone who has been lost. Mother, we found Little Mouse!

Singing Bird leaped to her feet and started laughing and crying and then laughing again from the joy that filled her heart.

"I cannot believe this! What happened? How did we lose her? How did she come to be so far away?"

It was as you feared. She got left behind. She stayed in the palace until the day the mountain died. After that she ran away. Many days later she was captured by bad men and brought to this land. She is no longer captured and is happy in this village.

"My heart is so full of joy I can't stop smiling," Singing Bird said. "Will she go with you when you leave that place?"

No. There is a man who loves her. She will stay.

"Tell her I am sorry. Tell her I would never have left her behind had I known she was missing. Tell her for me."

I already did. She cries no more. I have to go. We send our love.

Singing Bird began clapping and dancing and then ran off to find Cayetano. It wasn't every day that someone came back from the dead.

Chapter Twenty-Four

The New Ones stayed two nights at the Rio Yaqui, washing clothes and catching fish and smoking most of it to take with them, while giving their weary feet a much needed rest.

Little Mouse was so elated to see the New Ones again that she spent most of her time within the camp, trading stories of their narrow escapes with her old friends.

Just before sundown on the first night of their encampment outside the Hiaki village, Little Mouse came looking for Yuma and Tyhen.

"You have not seen my home," she said.

"Then we will see it," Yuma said.

"You come now?" she asked.

Tyhen nodded. "We will come now."

Little Mouse pointed at their packs. "Bring those with you."

They did as she asked without question because Little Mouse always had a reason for everything she said and did.

When they reached the dugout, she led the way inside. They ducked their heads as they entered, but the room inside was high enough for them to stand upright.

"It belonged to a woman and her man who died and now it is mine," she said.

Tyhen was fascinated by the creativity of digging below ground to build a dwelling, and even more so by the roof over their heads. The dwelling was small, but it felt safe, like being wrapped in her mother's arms.

"It is very nice," Tyhen said.

Little Mouse gave Yuma a sly glance. "For the time that you are here on the Rio Yaqui, we will trade beds. You sleep here with Tyhen. I will sleep in your tent so I can visit more with friends I will soon lose again."

Yuma grinned, then picked Little Mouse up and swung her in a circle, which made her giggle madly before he put her down.

Tyhen's eyes widened. The luxury of privacy was something they had long since given up. "That would be a wonderful gift, and we thank you," she said.

"Good. Then I will go," she said and picked up a small pack and started up the steps.

"Wait. I will walk you back," Yuma said. "I need to tell Johnston where we are, just in case."

"I will wait here," Tyhen said.

Little Mouse pointed to a covered pot sitting on her table. "For you if you are hungry."

And with that she was gone with Yuma hurrying after her.

Tyhen turned and looked at the bed, which consisted of a large pile of skins and fur to soften the ground on which they lay. It was far from the comfortable bed she'd had in Cayetano's palace, but after all they had been enduring and the tiny tent and mats where they laid their heads, this place was more luxurious in her eyes than any palace.

"All for us. On this night there will be little sleeping," she said and clapped her hands.

****

Yuma ran all the way back to Little Mouse's dugout. Tyhen's name was on his lips as hurried inside, closing the door behind him.

Corn husks were floating in the air and beginning to move around the dugout in a circular motion. Leaves from some herb that she'd been drying were rattling where they hung and she was naked and lying on the bed of skins and furs.

He took a deep breath and then shed his clothes as he dropped into the bed beside her.

Tyhen ached deep in her belly for him to take her. She wanted to feel the power of his body and lose her mind. She parted her legs as she reached for his arm.

"Hurry, my Yuma."

He slid between her knees and then they were one. The corn husks floated down from the ceiling, coming to lie where they fell. The dry herbs no longer rattled, but their scents now filled the air. They made love in a room smelling of something peppery and of sweet sage, and when she came in a gut-wrenching moan, he let go and went with her.

And so it went for the next two nights. Working all day to refit their packs and making love at night among the skins and furs in a room filled with sweet sage.

For the rest of her life, the scent of sweet sage would be the trigger to make Tyhen ache for the joining.

****

On the morning of the third day, they were packed and

ready to leave when Cualli and the little Hiaki people came down to the river to see them off.

Little Mouse stood beside Chiiwi. The smile on Chiiwi's face was broad as Little Mouse waved her good-bye. Now that she knew what held Chiiwi back, she made sure to let her feelings show.

Tyhen waved and waved until her sight was blurred by the tears of a final good-bye. Then she caught Yuma watching her and it was his steady gaze that settled her heart. She shifted her pack to a more comfortable position and fell into step within the column.

Thanks to Cualli and several of the others from the village, the New Ones had several landmarks to add to the map that they'd made. They now knew where they were going, and they would follow this very river for a very long way to get there.

****

Once the New Ones left Rio Yaqui, it triggered what the people all over the nations had been looking for. When the dove came into their land, the birds began to appear.

Villages in all four directions began seeing white doves. They were showing up in the villages of the Chumash in the west, and in the villages of the Shoshone to the north. They were appearing to the Apache, and to the Comanche, to the Caddo, and the Crow.

Far to the north, the Blackfoot saw the white dove flying, and when it landed on the chief's dwelling for two days straight, they knew it was their sign.

The Sioux saw the dove and began to ready for the march.

The Cree and the Abanaki saw them. The Cherokee saw them. The Creek, the Shawnee, and the Crow saw the sign. Every tribe had been given the prophecy and they knew what had to be done.

Just like in the time before Firewalker, when the people had been shown Layla Birdsong's rescue by a Windwalker and began their mass exodus to Arizona, so now these people were on the move. The sign of the dove had been seen and heeded, triggering what would become the second gathering. This one would be even larger than before, and this time with tribes of people, who in the time of Firewalker, had even ceased to exist. But this time the people were not running away to save their lives. They were going to meet their future.

****

One month later:

The New Ones had followed the river until the river was no more. Then the path they took led them back up into the mountains, and the first day they woke up with a covering of white on the ground, Tyhen finally understood the frozen.

There was less than an inch of the pure white dusting of snow, but it covered everything in sight. The sky had cleared and the bright sun made staring at the landscape painful, and the absence of color and definition was disconcerting to Tyhen and the children who had never seen snow.

Even with the clothing the New Ones had provided

and the many hides they had tanned during their time in Naaki Chava to make clothing more fit for the cold, Tyhen couldn't get warm. She'd been born in the tropics and her blood was too thin, Shirley Nantay said.

The men stayed on the lookout for rabbits and foxes, for the big wolves and the bears. And when the opportunity presented, they took them down with their spears or with bows and arrows, thanking them for their sacrifice to keep the people fed and warm and they kept moving. Eventually, Yuma had enough white rabbit skins for her to make them both warm leggings, and Shirley showed her how to line the moccasins with rabbit fur so their feet would stay warm. And just when Tyhen was getting used to breathing cold air, they came down from the mountains into a less frigid temperature. They had been given a brief introduction of the winter that was to come, but for now they were back in lighter clothing.

One day not too long after the final descent, Tyhen saw a woman step out of the line with a young boy, and knew they were seeking a bush for privacy.

Something about the lay of the land and her inability to see what was behind the small line of trees made her hesitate to go on and so she stopped to watch and wait for them to come back.

Yuma was ahead of her a few yards, walking with Montford and didn't know that she was no longer in line.

She stepped up on a rock so that she could see above the people's heads, and in her mind, she also saw the big cat on a ledge above the mother and boy that they did not see. She sent a silent but urgent message to Yuma as she pulled her knife.

There is danger. Follow me!

She saw Yuma spin around and then lift his spear over his head so that she could see him. She pointed, then leaped off the rock and made a dash toward the trees where the mother had taken her son.

Yuma was only a few yards behind her and she knew he was closing fast because she could hear his heartbeat, but she couldn't wait because she could also feel the bloodlust of the cat ready to pounce.

Without a clear path to see where everyone was standing, she couldn't take a chance and use the wind without harming the mother and son, too, so it was going to come down to how far Yuma could throw his spear.

She saw the mother and son as she rounded the tree line at the same time she saw the cat. Its ears were flat, the long tail twitching, and even before she could shout a warning, it pounced.

She leapt forward, sailing over the mother's head and caught the cat in mid-flight. Her knife went into its back near the right front leg as they hit the ground at the same time. Tyhen lost the knife and her grip on the cat, and when it happened, the cat pounced and she was holding a hundred and fifty pounds of an angry animal with sharp teeth and long claws. And then it had her by the throat and everything went black.

Yuma rounded the trees less than five steps behind her, and when he saw her feet leave the ground, he lunged forward to try and stop her, missing her by inches.

The moment she landed on the cat, it rendered his spear useless. He couldn't throw it without hitting her. He was already running toward them with his knife in his hand, passing the woman and her son, who were running away.

The cat had Tyhen by the throat when Yuma reached them, and he had Warrior's Heart in his hand.

He drove the knife into the back of the big cat's neck just as the fangs sank into her throat. He was praying to the names of every god he'd ever heard of as he dragged the dead cat off of her body.

He dropped to his knees, saying her name as he began to assess her wounds, but she was covered in so much blood he couldn't tell what was hers and what belonged to the cat. There were scratches on her legs, on her arms, and a long deep scratch down the side of her cheek. But it was the bite marks on her neck gushing blood with every beat of her heart that scared him.

He picked her up in his arms, pressed his hand against the neck wounds, trying to stop the blood flow, rocking her back and forth in his arms and begging her not to die.

"No, Tyhen, no. You are my heart! You are my life! You cannot die! You said you cannot die. Please, please, hear my voice. Stop the blood. You have to stop the blood because I cannot."

Within seconds the place was teeming with armed men and weeping women. They took one look at her limp bloody body in Yuma's arms and began to wail. They thought she was dead. She looked dead. She wasn't moving, and it didn't look like she was even breathing.

****

Pain rolled through her in waves like the water that had lapped at the banks of Rio Yaqui. She knew the cat was gone because she'd felt the spirit leave its body.

Then she felt Yuma's hands and heard his voice. She tried to concentrate on the words but the pain was deep.

"Snap out of it, Tyhen! You kept me from burning to death. Now stop the blood leaking out of your body and do it now!"

Evan?

"Yes, it's me. Stop the blood. You can feel it leaving your body. It is that warmth you feel running down your skin. Stop it now."

So she did.

****

When the flow of blood began to stop, Yuma thought it was because it was all gone. But then the scratch on her cheek began to close, and then the ones on her belly, and then her legs, and then her arms.

Someone saw and shouted out to the others.

"The bleeding stopped. The scratches are going away. It is true! It is true! The Windwalker's daughter cannot die."

Yuma heard. He was witnessing the healing, but he needed to see her eyes. He needed to see her looking back at him. He was covered in her blood and his voice was shaking as he tried to wake her up.

"Please, my love, please. Open your eyes and see me."

So she did.

He took a quick breath. "Do you see me?"

"I see you," she whispered.

He gathered her up into his arms and then carried her out of the draw, and he continued to carry her in his arms until they found water in a swift-running creek.

While the New Ones were filling their water jugs and drinking their fill, he walked downstream with her and stripped her where she stood.

The cuts and scratches from the wounds were completely healed, but there would be scars. It made him think of the scars Laya Birdsong wore when she took them into the canyons to escape Firewalker.

"I will have bad dreams for the rest of my life," he said shortly as he helped her down into the water and began to wash away the dried blood. Even now, his hands still shook just thinking about what had happened.

"If I had waited, at least one of them would have died. There was no time to think," she said as she sluiced water onto her face.

"I know that in my head, but my heart is not happy about the decision," he muttered.

Her hair was wet and clinging to her face and neck as she wrapped her arms around his neck. Now he was as wet as she and he didn't care.

"I am sorry you were afraid, but I will never leave you. I swear on my mother's life I will never leave you."

He closed his eyes as their foreheads touched. Today had been too close to call.

****

And so they kept moving; one day much like the next and the next until one day the New Ones called a halt.

The elders gathered with the Nantays and with Yuma and Tyhen, and they studied the geography of their location against the maps that had been drawn, and then in the end, turned to Tyhen for the final verdict, but the result was all the same.

For the first time since the journey began, they would no longer be traveling due North. They were well into the land once called North America, and as close as the elders could guess, somewhere between what had been New Mexico and Arizona. They showed her their approximate location on the map.

"Where to from here?" Yuma asked.

Tyhen put her finger in the middle of the space.

"We go here. Into the heart is where we go."

The men looked at the map and then at each other.

"That's right about where Kansas used to be," Johnston said. "Why there?"

She hesitated then quickly closed her eyes, picturing it in her head before she answered.

"Because of the gathering."

"The gathering. What do you mean by that?" Johnston asked.

"Many tribes are on the move. They will be waiting for me there. That place has space and water for many people. It is where we have to be."

"Then that is where we go," Yuma said.

****

They moved on, stopping when they could to replenish their stores and making clothing for the time they called winter.

She didn't know yet what that meant, but if it was

colder than it had been on that mountain in the snow, she was not going to like it.

She remembered the vision she'd had back in Naaki Chava, where her feet and legs had been wrapped in furs and also cloaked in heavy fur. It was yet another thing to dread.

The march had taken on a life of its own. It became a thing that lived, powered by the feet and hearts of the people in it, and the mark they left on the land in their passing was like a slow-healing wound. There was grass beaten beneath so many feet that a blind man could have followed their path and dead trees gleaned from the woods to make their fires. Animals could not run fast or far enough to escape their arrows. And even though they longed for the fruits and vegetables readily available from the jungle, they were rarely hungry. With that many hunters, people were always fed.

Only once did they stop because of a death. One morning a man who had called himself Coyote Charlie did not wake up. When they went to check on him, they found his heart had stopped beating. He had been ailing for some time and talked about this moment with his friends and now he could walk no more.

At his request, they left his unburied body on the highest rise around them, so that he would have a shorter distance to travel on the road to the Great Spirit, and then they kept on walking because there was nothing else to do.

Life now was a kind of limbo like the time when a baby dwells in his mother's womb, growing bigger and stronger until the day of birth when it moves into a different realm. So it was with their lives as well. They were simply doing what they had to do to keep moving, growing leaner and stronger for that day when they would leave the protection of the Windwalker's daughter and do what was needed to make the change.

On this day when the sun had been slow to show its face and the wind had a bite as it breathed down their necks, they came over a rise and then stopped as if they'd run into a wall.

Slowly, the people began to fan out from behind, wanting to see what was holding everyone up, and they kept moving toward the front until they were three deep and stretched along the ridge for almost a mile.

Below was a sea of black moving as one across the slope of a hill and down into a valley and the thin ribbon of water that ran through it. They kept spilling across the land and with no end in sight.

Tyhen knew what they were because she'd seen them in her dreams. "I know this animal. It is the animal with many names," she said.

Yuma nodded, pleased that she had remembered. "Yes. Each tribe has a name for this animal, but the white man called them buffalo."

Tyhen was struck by the silence around her, and by the expressions on the New Ones' faces. Some were quietly weeping. Some had fallen to their knees. She leaned closer to Yuma, afraid her question would somehow be misconstrued as rude.

"Why do the people cry?" she whispered.

"It is our first sight of how the world used to be before the strangers destroyed the balance between earth, animal, and man. Our ancestors took this world as normal, and by the time the New Ones were born, this was no more."

"What should we do?" she asked.

"We wait until the animals have moved on. We do not want to get caught in their stampedes."

And so they stood on the ridge staring down into the valley below and watched the herd as it fed and watered, and the day grew colder and the wind blew harder and they took the clothes with fur out of their packs and put them on, and as the herd began to move, Tyhen began to hear drums.

At first they were faint, and very far away, but as they came down off the ridge into the valley, intending to camp by the water for the night, the drums seems louder.

Her heart skipped as a knot coiled low in her belly.

In this foreign place where nothing, not even the weather, stayed the same, she felt a sudden sense of the familiar.

"Yuma!"

He turned at the sound of her voice. "I am here."

"Do you hear them?"

He cocked his head. "Hear what, my love?"

"Drums. I hear drums."

His eyes narrowed. They must be getting near the place of gathering. "No, I don't hear them. What are they saying?"

She sighed, her gaze sweeping out across the vast plains of the land before them.

"They are calling me home."

The End